Never Ceese
By
Sue Dent

This book is a work of fiction. Names, characters, places or
incidents are a product of the author's imagination or
are used fictitiously. Any resemblance
to persons living or dead is completely coincidental.

Cover and book design by Suzanne Dent
Published by Journey Stone Creations, LLC
Edited by Arlene W. Robinson
with Terry Robinson
Printed in China by Global PSD

Acknowledgements

My most deepest, sincerest, heartfelt gratitude to
Teresa Phillips,
a loyal and cherished friend who encouraged
when most
would have found it easier to discourage.

The same and more goes to my editor
Arlene W. Robinson,
who tried to help me understand the
importance of a tincture
of patience.
(I'm still having trouble with that.)
To have it edited or not to have it edited
—that is the question.
No question here.
Thanks, Arlene!

To my
daughter Amanda
and
son Reece.
Mom's off the computer if you want
to use it—well, at least for a while.

A vampire . . .

A werewolf . . .

Can two who were
wronged make it right?

one selfless act
—By their faith.

**Never
Ceese!**

PROLOGUE

She was finally alone, all alone. Merideth had taken all six children with him, and she wouldn't see them again until much later, after the church service Merideth was leading ended. The weathered, horse-drawn wagon had never looked so full, and for a brief moment, Julia wanted to go along, too. Holding back tears as they pulled away wasn't easy. Yet when she could no longer hear the wagon wheels creaking along, or the steady plod of their mare pulling it, she regrouped. They would be back soon enough, and until then, she should enjoy this free time. After all, Merideth had planned this time alone for her. Julia wouldn't spoil it by being sad.

She would work in the garden. No, she would *sit* in her garden, and absolutely no one would bother her. But first, she must tidy up. *Yes*, she thought. *I will tidy up, then relax.*

She started in the small kitchen, but only had to spend a little time there. Her two daughters had cleaned it before they left. She moved on. Instinctively, she kept looking for a child to come darting out, a daughter or a son, calling to her for one thing or another. She paused, fought back another tear. Even when they weren't there, they were. She went along, picked up a shirt and scolded the child who had left it, though the child was nowhere around to be affected by her words. This time Julia laughed, realized how ridiculous she sounded. *I've been a mother far too long!* But she wouldn't have it any other way.

Julia didn't look at all like someone's mother. After six children, she still looked very much like an older sister. She and Merideth married young and had gotten started early. She hadn't had time to think about growing old and, consequently, it didn't seem she had. Her face was smooth, not one line or blemish, and only seemed to attract more attention than when she was younger. Men took notice, but she wanted none but Meri. He doted on her, took care of her and loved her like no other could.

Meri was a fine catch in his own right: a man of God, strong and humble, captivating and caring. She smiled knowingly, then carried the shirt she had collected from the floor back to where it belonged, all while thinking of the one person she could never get enough of.

In the small room where the boys slept, she placed the shirt on the bed closest to the door. But just as she began turning around to leave, a shadow overtook hers, a much larger one.

"Who's there?" she said, rattled. "What do you want?" But she got no answer.

She turned slowly, and stifled her scream. The man was much too close, blocking her way out of the room.

She would go. She would run. He would never catch her. "If . . . If you're here to see Mer— my husband . . . he's just out back. I'll go and get him."

But he grabbed her arm tight when she tried to get by.

"Husband not here. Children not here. Julia all alone. Julia woman of Go—" He stopped, placed the palm of his free hand against his forehead, as though trying to force some unimaginable pain away. After a moment, he spoke again. "Want Julia and husband to leave."

Why was he talking like that? What was wrong with him and how did he know her name? The questions came to her at once. She didn't care about the answers though; she just wanted to leave. She pulled again. "Please, let me go."

But he didn't. Instead, he led her outside, took her into the woods that thickened just past the garden, and handed her off to another man whose grip was just as firm.

"No words," the first man said. "No kill."

A feeling of dread overcame her as she watched the first man leave, then turned to face the one who now held her. She'd seen his lustful smile before. When Meri couldn't accompany her on her errands in town, she got those looks sometimes. They always made her feel awkward, uneasy. But not terrified, as she was now.

The remainder of that time was a blur as Julia forced herself not to think about what the man was doing as he forced himself on her. Finally it was over, and he left.

Julia felt sick, rolled over onto her side and took deep breaths. A twig snapped behind her. She started, managed to get to her feet but froze in fear. *Why won't they just leave me alone?*

The first man was back, moved toward her cowering form and spoke. "Julia not forget this day. Julia never forget. Tell husband to go. Only evil will stand here."

What happened next, Julia was sure no one would ever believe. Right before her eyes, the man turned into a wolf. The wolf came at her, tore his claws at her right side.

She managed to get to a tree and hid behind it, certain the wolf would come after her and kill her. She waited, eyes screwed shut, but nothing happened. Long moments passed, and she finally opened her eyes to see that the wolf was once again the man.

"Leave," he grunted at her.

Holding her bleeding side with her hands, she pushed through the pain and ran—stumbling, falling to her knees more than once—but eventually making it back to the house. The door was still open, she noticed, and, with what energy she had left, she stumbled inside, bolted the door and collapsed. When she was able, she tore at her already-ripped blouse to make long strips. Using them as bandages, she dressed the wound.

As she worked, the room became steadily darker; the sun was setting, her family would be home soon. She did what she could to pull herself together for their sakes. They couldn't know. No one could know. No one could ever, ever know!

When her family returned, they found her sitting in the tiny parlor, sewing.

She fumbled through the next few days. When emotion overwhelmed her, she simply went to her room. One morning her oldest son questioned her. She told him it was nothing, but his face told her he didn't believe her. She knew he'd go to his father, but no longer cared.

✷ ✷ ✷

The garden was where Julia went often to seek solace, and she was there when Merideth found her that afternoon, sitting and staring vacantly at her favorite rosebush, the one he gave her on her birthday: the one she nurtured like her seventh child.

In May of 1785, Merideth answered the call of God to go to Llandyfan, Wales. He took Bibles, medicines, his wife and small son. To the Baptists, who had established themselves in this new territory, Merideth was a Godsend. To the evil that had taken root all around, he was an adversary. Merideth won many souls over. For him and his family, it was a new beginning, something they were looking forward to. But now, his dear wife was troubled, and that troubled him mightily.

"And what thought has you staring so intently?" Merideth asked, his kind voice offset by his worry.

Julia broke herself from her trance, shook her head. "Nothing, Meri." She tried but failed to smile.

Merideth took a few steps closer, sat on his heels next to where she'd settled on a small wooden bench, one he'd made for her so she could sit while tending to her roses. "Our oldest son has come to me with concerns about his mother. I have been far too busy, I should have seen. You haven't been yourself, and I do so miss that. What is troubling you?"

She wanted to tell him but her words caught in her throat. The memory of that horrid day was still too fresh. All at once she felt the man's hands on her again, could hear him breathing close to her ear, smell the earth as he pinned her to the ground. She stared at Merideth, tried to push the memories away, but they couldn't be stopped. Tears threatened.

Merideth, seeing this, attempted to pull her toward him with gentle hands. But all Julia could see was the man in the woods. "No," she said, and flung her hands in front of her.

His alarm grew. "Julia, please, I just— If I have done something, please tell me."

She was staring at the ground when she spoke. "It is not you, it is me. I . . . I have shamed you."

"Shamed me?" he sputtered. "What are you saying? You could *never* shame me."

She took a wavering breath. "Two days ago, there was a man. When you took the children with you. He-He came into the house while I was alone— I tried to run, Meri, but he grabbed me and took me to the woods . . . to where another man waited and—"

"Julia," Merideth said, his breath going out of him, and then again, "Julia."

He took her by her shoulders this time, and Julia froze. After a second, though, she realized this was Meri, *her* Meri, and not some terrible memory. Seconds later, she relaxed, allowed him to hold her close, drew from his strength.

"I can't believe you kept this from me," he said, his voice catching. "I can't believe you— that you didn't say something sooner. Right away."

"I . . . I didn't want to upset the children."

In awe, Merideth held her at arms' length. "The children? Julia, what about *you*? What did you think would happen if you kept this inside?"

"I also didn't want to lose you. I couldn't bear it."

"As if I would ever consider leaving you!"

A tiny wave of relief washed over her.

"You are my life, Julia. My world." He pulled her close again. "We'll get through this. God will help us."

"There's more, Meri," Julia said, pushing herself farther away on the bench. "The man . . . the first man, he-he came back after the other man had . . . had—"

Merideth put a finger to her lips before she could finish. "None of it matters."

"But it's not what you think." She wanted to get the words out before fear overwhelmed her. "The first man, he . . . he talked about your mission, about the work you do." The words rushed out now. "He said we should leave this place and never come back. Said there was no room for good here, that evil prevailed. He then said . . ." she took a deep breath, "if we didn't leave, he would come back for the children and—"

11

She couldn't finish, and he wouldn't make her. Neither did he hesitate to respond. "Then we shall move—as soon as possible. We will leave this place."

"But Meri, this is where you felt the Lord leading you! You have sacrificed so much, worked so hard—it would be like giving up." She was remembering the stir he'd caused when he started baptizing. Immersion in water wasn't something familiar to anyone in the area then.

"The Lord will understand," he said without compromise. "I must protect you . . . our children."

"But you have done so much good here. If only I could have gotten away—"

"Listen to me, Julia! This was not your fault. It was a terrible thing that happened to you, but we will get through it."

"But Meri . . . I fear . . . I fear I am with child. *His* child."

Meri's eyes widened, but held none of the censure Julia had dreaded. "You really believe you are with child?" he said, wiping a wayward tear from her face. "His child?"

She could only nod.

"But it has only been two days, how can you—? The midwife was certain you could bear no more. We have tried, and—"

At last, her eyes met his. "I know how it must sound, and I don't want to believe it either. But I've had six. I . . . I know how it feels. All six times, I felt like I do now."

A long pause later, Meri said, "Then we will have another child—another blessing."

The words sounded harsh to Julia. No, they sounded foolish. How could this child ever be a blessing? "Not like this, Meri," she said, more tears breaking free. "Not like this."

"It will be fine, Julia. You'll see. We will call it a miracle. The children will be overjoyed. No one will know the truth but us . . . and we will never tell."

"You could love this child?" she said, not believing.

"As if it were my own. I love you, Julia and if this child is yours, then it is mine and it always will be."

"Meri . . . there is one other thing." Because of the bizarre nature of what she was about to say, she didn't wait for him to ask.

"Before the man left— the first man, the one who led me into the woods, he . . . he turned into a wolf."

For the first time, she saw disbelief pass over his face—and something else.

"Perhaps you were just overwhelmed by what happened," he said. "Delirious. It-It must have been horrible."

Julia eased up her blouse, carefully removed the strips of cloth she kept over her wounds and revealed what was beneath. The marks were deep and still looked fresh. "He told me . . . before he changed . . . you might need proof."

Her tears returned, but Merideth could only stare glassy-eyed. He had seen marks such as these before. A young boy and two men from his last mission. All three had died after being attacked by a wolf. All three bore marks identical to the ones his wife was showing him now. And all three had given him a message before they breathed their last breath. They had told him to leave and never come back.

"Did he bite you?" he asked awkwardly. "When he was the wolf, I mean."

Julia shook her head. "No. Just left these scratches." She had a hard time figuring out why he asked something so odd. "Is there a reason why you need to know that? Would-Would it make matters worse?"

"Just different," Merideth said, and reached out to help her ease her shirt back down. "Now, let's go have those scratches looked at."

🐾 🐾 🐾

As he left with her, the two responsible looked on from behind thick bushes. One was a man, the other . . . not quite. He'd been cursed centuries ago, his soul held captive by his own evil. He had cursed many, and would therefore remain cursed forever.

"All right," the one beside him said. "I did what you asked. Yet I still don't understand why you couldn't have done it yourself." He gave the same leering smile that had so frightened Julia. "You might have enjoyed it. I rather did."

The man listening wasn't bothered by the comment. His curse lessened his desire to indulge in the act the other man referred to, even made it difficult. Even if he had been able to, there was no way for him to do what the other man had done. The act, yes, but his seed wouldn't yield any offspring. He had tried many times before without success.

"Just seems odd to me you wouldn't want her for yourself."

The man gave a distant nod, but said nothing. He had other ways of getting pleasure. Spreading his curse was one of those. But since this interfering minister had come to live in the town, pleasure was hard to come by. It wasn't easy to get close to people who forever had a prayer on their lips or a cross around their neck.

He had to get rid of the minister . . . make an example of him so others wouldn't feel inclined to take up his cause. This was his territory. He was here first, and the minister was in the way.

"So when do I get the money you promised?" his companion said. "I need to be on my way." He gave a furtive grin. "Or maybe I'll just visit Julia again."

He put a hand to the talkative man's throat and squeezed. "Julia with child. No touch Julia!"

"Why would you care?" the man croaked. "It's not your child, but mine."

The accusation was true, to a point. Yet the scratches he'd left for the minister to see were potent enough to affect the child. Perhaps it would develop keen hearing or an enhanced sense of smell. He'd heard of a similar attack, which yielded a boy-child who could pick up a scent as quick as any dog. When the child was old enough, weaned from its mother's breast, the attacker, the one who'd done the scratching, took the child from his parents. In the same way, Julia's child would be his child. When the time was right.

Gasping sounds brought his attention back to the one at the end of his arm, and he loosened his grip slightly.

"All right," the man sputtered. "I won't touch her. Just give me my money and I'll be on my way."

He might have screamed if he'd known what was coming, but

14

he was dead the second the canine-like fangs pierced the large vein in his neck. He never felt his mutilated body being dragged, then dropped near the spot where Julia's attack occurred.

꧁ ꧁ ꧁

The gravedigger stood knee-deep in what he'd already dug out and shoveled a little longer, his task not far from done. The man's remains lay, covered, a few feet away.

There were no mourners.

Merideth was there to read last rites at the request of another who'd had other obligations, and Julia had come along with him. She often did when she could arrange to be away from the children. And Merideth had said the one they were burying had no family, no friends anyone knew of, and this bothered her. Julia believed everyone deserved a proper burial, so she stood by the grave of someone she didn't know, face veiled and head bowed, to pay her respects.

The gravedigger worked a little longer, then climbed out, plunged his shovel into the fresh pile of dirt and stepped far back, wiping beads of sweat from his forehead. "Whenever you're ready, Minister."

Merideth nodded, clutched his Bible, and knelt beside the body. When the gravedigger bowed his head, Julia raised hers, and when Merideth lifted the shroud covering the man's face, as he typically did to begin the service, Julia gasped, "It's him!"

Stunned, Merideth looked back toward Julia, turned slightly to the gravedigger. When it was clear the man hadn't heard her, he turned back to Julia. "You're sure?" he whispered.

She brought a shaky hand to her mouth and nodded. Merideth got up and went to his wife, pulled her close, noting her rapid breathing.

"I'm taking you home," he said, lifting her up to carry her back to their horse-drawn wagon.

The gravedigger was paying attention now, and looked confused. "But what about your duty?" he called after them.

Merideth's words were hard. "You shall have to find the Devil himself to bury that one."

A week after, Merideth and his family loaded their possessions and moved on.

CHAPTER 1

The trees appeared as dark columns, solid forms surrounded by a translucent moonlit haze: a thin, white veil of mist moving, hovering. It was thickest over the waters of a nearby stream, but thinned out near the banks. The light from the full moon gave the mist an iridescent sheen, a life of its own. The apparition-like blanket kept the cooler night air away from the ground, a subtle change in temperature many life forms responded to. The wolf did as well, and moved purposefully to stay beneath it, basking in the heat the mist kept close to the ground. That warmth would make things more comfortable later, when it did what it knew it must.

While the mist moved, the wolf followed the trail of scents it had left three nights ago, and re-marked some spots as it went along, to keep intruders away, other wolves would take notice. It stopped in an area surrounded by trees, where the ground was flat and mossy, and stared ahead. Rocks of various shapes and sizes marked an old riverbed. Larger stone formations lay beyond, and the wolf looked for the tallest one. It saw a thick stand of pines and looked east. The outline was visible. It moved on but stepped carefully, all the while sniffing for scents and searching.

After the rocks, the ground became softer beneath its paws. The wolf noticed imprints it had made on previous visits. It continued along as the earth became more mud-like.

The landmark was just ahead, very close to the stream. The wolf went to it, walked along the trunk of a fallen tree, and climbed to the landmark's highest point. Soon the wolf was where it wanted to be, at the very top, and it raised its head up to bay, loud and long. The haunting sound carried and echoed before ending. The moon was full, its pull strong. The time was right.

Because the moon was in a phase to facilitate, things would move quickly. The transformation wouldn't take nearly as long as other times. One had to be strong and experienced to transform without this advantage. And sometimes it was still difficult. Experience had a lot to do with it; so did remembering. The wolf chose this evening because of the moon, because of its pull . . . and because it had been so long.

The moon's gravitational pull controlled the tides. During the full moon, there were rumors, that murders and other acts of violence rose. Hospitals recorded more births. Mental facilities filled their beds. One theory pointed to the amount of salt in blood as the culprit, inferring that blood was affected by the moon's gravitational pull the same way oceans were. Just as waves formed, blood was drawn up into the brain, creating what some called "lunar madness." But this was only one of many theories.

The wolf wasn't aware of any such theories or research, but it had altered its diet nonetheless, seeking out foods that would help manipulate the four main salts in its blood: sodium chloride, magnesium, calcium and potassium, instinctively trying to achieve balance. It ate things it wouldn't normally consider eating, drank large quantities of water. It knew what it had to do, and it knew what it had to eat to do it. And as the wolf stood now, bathed in moonlight, howling again, the moon took control.

The pain was dull at first, but soon became much harder to ignore. The wolf gave a keening whimper, walked in tight circles on the flat rock it had climbed upon. Every muscle ached, every bone shifted. Physically and mentally, things were changing.

These feelings weren't foreign to the wolf. It had experienced them before. But it had been a while. One more turn on the rock, and it found it could no longer walk or stand, so it laid down.

Shortly afterward, it had a thought. A different thought. A *human* thought. *Relax. Stay calm. Must not fight it!*

It wanted to, though. It wanted to leave.

Another wave of pain hit and it cried out louder, with more high-pitched whimpers before silence prevailed. The transformation picked up speed, and the wolf became less wolf-like. Its skin stretched to accommodate its new shape; fingers and toes replaced claws.

In the glowing mist beneath the full moon, the near-human form stirred. It no longer whimpered, but groaned. And instead of howling, it cried. When it became aware, it remembered the ground-fog, opened its eyes, and saw that the mist had risen. Since it no longer had guard hairs or a thick undercoat to protect it from the cold, it welcomed the warmth being under it provided.

When it regained full consciousness, the wolf could tell it was no longer a wolf. It heard a dull roar and looked up as a plane flew overhead, low. The stars were no longer visible. Dawn wasn't far away.

Her muscles ached, but there was a lull in activity. Taking advantage seemed the thing to do. Lying on her back, she studied one hand, the other. "One, three," she whispered, improperly enunciating, not really conscious of what she should sound like but trying nonetheless. She stared at individual fingers again. "*Aon, trí*—no!" She could speak, understood more than one language, knew what language was. It was just too difficult right now to make the words come out, or to think of words. Yipping and barking were all she'd known for so long.

Frustrated, she tried again, but nothing she uttered made any sense to her. She'd take inventory later, when things were clearer in her mind. After all, it wasn't like she needed to talk to get around. She could always rely on things more familiar to her: her sense of smell and hearing. Yet she realized that these things weren't as they used to be either. Before, the plane's drone she'd heard would have bothered her, would have had her howling. As it was now, she barely noticed it.

She had to struggle to pick up her own scent, and couldn't hear the wolves she'd left behind. She sat up, bothered by how different things were, and raised her head to howl. But her howl became a human cry that filled the woods around her.

The changes taking place now were subtle, and afterward, she had an entirely new perspective on what she had become, as well as what she had been. Now, she understood why she'd stayed the wolf for so long, knew it was the easiest way. At least, until now.

Having the curse was bad enough, especially when she didn't ask for it or want it to begin with. But as long as she didn't curse another, there was the possibility it could be lifted. She knew this because of what Joachim told her. Joachim had taught her much, but Joachim was no more. He had killed another, and his fate was set. She would never forget the tortured look on his face the day he met his demise.

She wouldn't die like that. She *would not* die like Joachim. She didn't want to live forever, knowing she would never see Heaven. Yet, this was her dilemma. While cursed, she couldn't acknowledge the one thing she knew could ensure her eternal salvation. Having the curse meant that she couldn't entertain such thoughts. Doing so might kill her, or at the very least, cause great pain. Joachim had warned her of that. Still, she had tried many times, and was making progress. And then, when the voice came, she knew it was time to act on her long-held wish.

Spreading the curse was a great temptation, an overwhelming one. In her weaker human form, she easily lost focus. As the wolf, she was generally not as tempted; she could hide in a pack and stay away from people. But she didn't want to hide forever. She wanted to end what Joachim and the voice in her head told her could be ended. But she had to be human to do it. Had to have access to knowledge a wolf found useless.

It was early morning now. The first light of day was making its presence known in the eastern sky. The way down from her high perch wasn't as tricky to negotiate as the way up; hands and feet were better at climbing than paws. But she was still so out of practice. She'd clench her hands into fists, then open them, trying to figure out what worked best. She was still moving much like a wolf, occasionally walking like one without thinking about it.

It finally sank in when she knelt at a small pond to drink, and her reflection showed what she had become. A hand went directly to her head, patted around to feel what she could now see. Her hair . . . yes, it was called "hair." She remembered. It was short

. . . blondish brown, and it was sticking out in nearly every direction. She tried to smooth it, but her effort did little good. Her solution—let it be. It did strike her to make it look more presentable, but since she wasn't sure what "presentable" was exactly, she didn't see the point in wasting time.

The next thing was her face. It was more round than long, and seemed more . . . *grown-up* than the last time she took human form. But she hadn't physically changed. She couldn't. She just felt more grown-up. She examined further her nose, her lips, decided she was satisfied, and put her hands down.

Finally, she saw her eyes. They weren't the soft green they were before she was cursed, but a greenish-gold, closer to the hue they were when she was the wolf. Now she remembered—that was an unusual color for a human, and many looked twice when she had taken human form before. She would have to be careful of that.

She swatted at the water, upset. But she wasn't angry about what others thought; she just missed being the wolf, and didn't appreciate being reminded of what she had left behind. Despite her anger, she leaned down to drink heartily, using her tongue to lap at what she had just swatted, enjoying the way the water tasted and felt.

A memory jolted her, and she stopped drinking. An image of a man holding a black, worn, leather-bound book. From it, he read with thoughtful consideration to those listening. His voice was his gift. He used it to capture attention. Gaelic and soothing, his words were anticipated like the spray of the ocean on a warm face. But the words dealt with scripture. She had to work hard not to be affected.

"*. . . and he brought down the people unto the water and the Lord said unto Gideon, every one that lappeth of the water with his tongue, as a dog lappeth, him shalt thou set by himself; likewise every one that boweth down upon his knees to drink . . .*"

The pain was great, but she bore up under it, desperate to remember.

The voice faded, but then there was more. "*. . . and the number of them that lapped, putting their hand to their mouth, were three hundred men: but all the rest of the people bowed down upon* *their knees to drink water. And the Lord said unto Gideon, by the three hundred men that lapped will I save you.*"

After the memory grayed-out completely, she went back to drinking, her head throbbing from fighting the curse. Now, however, she drank as the three hundred had, bringing a hand to her mouth instead of lapping. She didn't know why this was important, but it felt right, and she drank until she had her fill.

More than before, she noticed how good the water felt on her hands and arms, and the thought came to her to bathe. But she hadn't been in her human form long enough to appreciate the benefits of doing such a thing. The desire never took hold.

Something that did take hold, however, was hunger. Her stomach was growling and complaining. At once, she looked around for something to eat, went for a rabbit and seized it before it could scurry away. She might have been human, but the wolf was still very much a part of her. She tore at her meal with canine-like teeth. Afterward, she listened to the voice leading her. *"It's time,"* it kept saying. *"I can help you."*

Then she crept off, standing occasionally as she adjusted to walking upright again, and searching, always searching.

CHAPTER 2

The gothic castle was rumored to have hosted kings and noblemen in its time, and in the centuries since its construction, had been well-cared-for. With a little imagination and a good storyteller, one might believe King Arthur once stayed there with his Knights of the Round Table to discuss battle plans. Its stone turrets and cathedral windows, just visible now in the slanted morning sunlight, certainly gave substance to such scenarios, and the ancient forest around it, plus the trees in front, recalled the days of Robin Hood. Yet it would take more than a good storyteller to convince Peter Drummond. The sight of the castle angered him—for one person to ever have so much more than anyone else.

Nudging his small herd of goats along, Peter approached the large structure and scowled at its cold, foreboding walls. He'd heard the tales, and scoffed at the insinuations. It might look regal to some, but not him. Maybe they could imagine a member of royalty walking out, but he couldn't. To him, it was just a sinister-looking place whose residents never seemed to want to come out. Peter rarely saw anyone. Neither did any of the other neighbors who passed the castle regularly with their herds, looking for fresh pastures to graze in. He and the neighbors were wary of being accused of allowing their herd to graze on land that wasn't theirs. Still, it was tempting sometimes.

Peter continued to nudge his goats, tried to rush them along before he could be accused of anything he wasn't guilty of. Most of the neighbors didn't see anything wrong with letting one or two of their herd stray close to the pastures' borders, and sometimes farther. They would just round them up later and discreetly head them home.

The day came when there was less rounding-up to be done though. The day when a few goats wandered off, disappeared. At first, there was only a little concern. But it happened again . . . and again. Word went out, and fences went up. Not all could afford to be so prudent; some simply didn't have the funds to create barriers. Peter might have had the funds had he worked a little harder. But he was a slacker of sorts, a man with no real direction or fortitude. Instead, he brooded about what life had done to him.

The castle's present owners denied knowing of livestock showing up or disappearing on their property. Peter didn't believe that. And he was certain they were responsible, somehow, for his three missing goats, missing since yesterday. He had to be certain; the alternative was to admit he wasn't all that great a herdsman, and Peter Drummond would never admit to such a thing.

His face reddened, and his ham-sized fists clenched. It was time for a confrontation, and right now!

🐐 🐐 🐐

Richard entered the parlor from the adjoining kitchen and went to the early-18th-century armoire he'd had carefully rebuilt to house his computer—one of the many conveniences added in the last renovation—and pulled its doors open. He found the power switch, flicked it on, and went back to the kitchen. It would take a minute for the computer to come to life. Enough time for breakfast.

The blood was in a cup, but he wanted it warmed a bit. He'd use the microwave. He placed the cup in the microwave and set the timer for thirty seconds, just long enough for him to marvel at how well the appliance blended into its new environment. The microwave was part of the last renovation as well, along with the large-screen television mounted behind a sliding panel on a wall in the parlor.

Richard was big on wanting to keep things as they were, had turned down adding other things certain to make his life easier because they didn't fit the present decor. But more than that. He didn't like being reminded how things had changed over time. Except for him. He'd gone so far as to turn down the satellite system he'd wanted so badly after being told a pole would have to be erected in one of his favorite gardens for the dish to sit on. They told him they could make it blend in, but he didn't believe them.

He'd been walking the earth as a vampire for over two centuries now. He wasn't sure exactly how long, and didn't care. Who he was before meant nothing to him. What he could recall, and all he wanted to recall, was that he hated being cursed. He hated it so much that he'd changed his name several times, to help him forget who he was before. Presently, and for the past century, his name was Richard Bastóne.

He'd bought the castle in the spring of 1944, paid for it with cash and was never questioned. It was in dire need of repairs, and the bank was desperate to dump it. Richard couldn't have been happier.

Of all the things he'd added, the computers were by far the most used. The Internet provided more information than Richard ever had access to before, and quickly. Through online courses, Richard had learned three new languages in three months, more than he'd learned in over a century of living. Now armed with an e-mail account and a flair for the English language, he found it easy to get what he needed most: blood.

He took the cup from the microwave, carried it to the computer and sat it carefully beside the keyboard. Then he settled in his chair and started typing.

> *My dearest mother requires a transfusion. Her blood type is AB positive and she is in desperate need. Any assistance you could give would be welcome.*

He added information to legitimize his e-mail, asked to have the blood shipped directly to the castle. It had taken a little trial-and-error to figure out how to get the fastest and best results, but he'd learned a lot over time.

25

Blood type was important; AB positive marked his mother as a universal recipient. It gave him more sources to draw from. Being a doctor was important too. He wasn't one, but became one through online courses and a little finagling. Deliveries came about once a week, and he kept a good supply. He had lost a supplier though, and needed to find another. This was the reason for this latest e-mail.

Richard took a moment to go over what he'd just typed, made sure it sounded right and sent it. He then checked his e-mail. His inbox was empty. With nothing left to do, he finished what was in the cup, left the computer and headed down the hall. Mamá should have called him by now, but hadn't. He wondered why.

He called her Mamá, but her name was Penelope. The change was needed to explain the growing age difference between them. It hadn't mattered so much when they were both young, but over time, it became an . . . issue. Penelope was eighty-two, Richard still just twenty-four, his age when he became cursed. But Penelope didn't like the idea of him calling her Mamá. "It sounds too maternal," she'd told him. Yet when he'd said it, added his charming accent—Gaelic with a twist of British—'Mamá' sounded anything but maternal. She absolutely loved it then.

༺ ༺ ༺

Penelope Cromwell got up and hobbled the short distance from her bed to her wheelchair. She knew Richard wouldn't be happy, but she simply wouldn't wait for him this morning. She was too excited. Besides, she needed to send an e-mail—one she didn't want him to know about.

Once in her wheelchair, she moved over to her computer and reached for the keyboard. Richard had been such a dear to make everything so convenient for her. She logged on, typed the message and sent it, finishing up just before he appeared in the doorway. When he saw her, he sighed.

"You aren't going to make me regret giving you what you asked for, are you?"

She wheeled back over to her bed and parked. "I thought you'd be happy I was using the computer."

Her coy response didn't sway him. "You know what I'm talking about. You're supposed to call me when you're ready to get up. But I should feel fortunate you aren't on the floor." He tried to sound chiding, but his voice reflected his concern.

"And good morning to you too!"

Richard moved into the room, brought his tone down just a little. "Do I speak to hear myself talk? Haven't I asked you to wait for me? It's the only reason I stay up past dawn."

The French doors were open, and Richard altered his path toward her to avoid getting too close. It wasn't full daylight yet, but it would be very soon.

His voice became softer, but still stern. "Do you think I relish the idea of coming in here one morning to find you on the floor with a broken neck because you're too stubborn to wait for my help? Or at the very least, you could call for Marissa."

"Your words are never wasted on me," she said, smiling. "I never grow tired of listening to your voice." And she didn't. She worshipped it, cherished each syllable that came from those lips. It didn't matter that she was now an old woman and time had stopped for him. She still loved him, and he knew it, even as he felt powerless to change things between them. But if her plan worked, perhaps that would soon change.

Her response seemed to quell some of his ire, and gave her time to notice he'd lightened his hair a bit more. It used to be quite dark and much shorter. Presently, it was long enough to be pulled back and tied: a look he once told her might help him appear a bit radical, more rebellious, like any good son should. She opened her mouth to ask him about the change, but he spoke first.

"I'm glad you like hearing me talk, but listening and paying attention are two different things." He knelt beside her, made sure the wheelchair's handbrake was set.

"Oh, bother!" She waved a frail hand. "You've become such a prude in my old age."

Penelope's intent was to draw some of the sting out of his

words, and she was pleased when his lips formed a reluctant smile. "That's better," she said. "I was beginning to think the Richard I've grown to love was gone."

He moved to sit on the edge of her bed. "I just worry about you."

"Well, you shouldn't, and if you'll quit being such a mother hen, I'll fill you in on what happened yesterday morning."

He cocked his eyebrow. "Yesterday? And I'm only hearing of it now?"

"You'll just have to forgive me, Richard. You know my memory's not what it used to be. And it happened after you'd gone to your basement. And you left the castle so quickly after you got up last evening . . . I just didn't have time to think about it until now."

He glanced away, then back to her. "Yes, well . . . I woke up with quite an appetite. So what did I miss?"

"Peter Drummond came by. He had a message for you. Left it with Marissa."

"For me?" Both eyebrows arched. "And he left it with our maid?"

She nodded. "He's missing three goats. Claimed they wandered onto the property at some point during the night."

He folded his arms in front of him. "He always claims his goats wander over here, but he never bothers to put up a fence, now does he?"

"You know he can't afford to, Richard."

"I don't feel sorry for him. He'd have the money if he didn't squander it all on loose women and bad booze."

"You know he does this?" The question was rhetorical; he didn't usually speak so colorfully without proof.

"Let's just say our friend Peter doesn't try very hard to keep what he's doing—when he's doing it—a secret." He made a disgusted noise in his throat. "Pigs make less noise."

"Richard! You haven't been—"

"Eavesdropping? Perhaps. But not to the point of watching. I'd like to think I have more respect for myself."

Penelope brought a frail hand to her chest. "I would like to think so as well. But even listening— Well, it makes me wonder what *you* were up to."

He sighed. "I had gone to have a talk with him, but apparently I caught him at a . . . bad time. And as far as bad times go, he seems to have many of them."

Her eyes turned wary. "You've gone there more than once. Is it really wise for you to be so physically close to someone you have such little regard for?"

"I didn't go there hungry. I never do."

"Still, you should be more careful."

"*He's* the one who should be careful," he said, scowling. "But what of it? He should find other ways to spend his money."

"Being a goatherder is a tough way to make a living, Richard. And while I don't condone what you say he was doing, I wonder if it's up to us to judge him."

"I'm not judging him."

Now, the question she must ask. "Well, if you're not judging him then, are you . . . are you—?"

"Helping myself to his goats, Mamá? Do you really think I'd take three goats in one night?"

He hoped the interrogation would end with those words, and had it not been for her look of disappointment, it might have. "All right, all right! I took one, but two nights have passed since then. And no more since. He was probably drunk when he counted them last."

"Richard, I . . . I thought we agreed not to stir up any more trouble. One or three, it's still trouble."

Her disconcerting words had him hating himself, loathing the vampire's need for blood. "I cannot help what I am. I've warned him more than once. It isn't my responsibility. And you know that as soon as he comes to see me, I'll pay him for it. I always pay for them. Ask any of the neighbors."

She looked, not at him, but beyond the French doors. "Was it worth it?"

He might have lied to anyone else, but not her. "Yes," he said. The blood was warm and fresh, and remembering just how warm and fresh brought a smile to his lips. "It was worth it, every bleat-

29

ing drop." He gave her a second to absorb those words, then said, "And what exactly are *you* up to this morning? I haven't seen you rise so early in some time."

He hoped she would take the hint and move onto another topic. She didn't. Instead, she fixed him with hurt eyes. "Since when does rising early cause suspicion?"

Richard leaned toward her a bit, his blonde locks, yet to be bound up for the day, falling casually forward. "Since that someone is you."

"And what of it? How much trouble could I actually get into at my age?"

Mamá didn't bring age up much, and when she did, he always felt bad. "I'm sorry," he whispered, searching her face. "I didn't mean to . . ."

"Oh bother," she said with a complacent smile. "It isn't your fault you've stayed as young and attractive as you have. It's just—well, sometimes, you're just not easy to ignore . . . and I'm an old woman."

"Age means nothing to me. You know that!"

"And you are too kind," she said quickly, brought one of her hands to his face. "We've had our time together. And I'm fine with what we share. Really I am."

He took her other hand, squeezed it. "But I don't want my presence to make you feel—inadequate."

She smiled at him. "I'm old, Richard. I *am* inadequate, in some ways. And your presence isn't going to change what time has wrought. I'm just glad I have someone like you to look at every day, to talk to . . . to be with."

"The feeling's mutual," Richard said, showing as much emotion as his curse would allow without pain, knowing she understood his restrained reaction. She accepted his kiss to her hand.

"And now, tell me something. Just how long do you plan to let your hair grow? And I do believe you've dyed it some more—bleached it, I dare say! Are you trying to get someone's attention?"

It didn't work. "First you answer *my* question."

"What question?"

"The one you keep trying to avoid."

"Only for the sake of keeping peace." She saw his look and sighed. "She's coming, Richard. I called to her again and she's coming. And she's very close, I can tell."

He felt like a father grown tired of his impetuous child. "We're not back to that again, are we? After all these months, without you mentioning anything about it? I was so hoping we'd gotten past it."

"One cannot get past the truth. I suppose you could ignore it for a while, but you can *never* get past it."

What's that supposed to mean? he thought, feeling lost. It was such an odd thing to say. Had he missed something, misunderstood?

"I know you could remember if you wanted to, dear."

He sighed pitifully, looked away. As always, she wanted him to discuss the things in his life he couldn't remember—his past, everything he was before the curse. She called it "forced amnesia," and she never stopped trying to get him to recall what he swore he couldn't. As if he could. What an odd time to bring it up, though.

He moved off of the edge of the bed and back down to release the brake he'd set when he came in. "You know how I feel about your probing. Even if I could remember, I don't want to." He straightened, looked away. "I'm sure Marissa has breakfast waiting for you. I'll push you to the breakfast room."

He reached for the chair's handgrips, but Mamá wheeled out of his reach before he could react.

"I told you," she snapped at him, "she's coming. I won't be going anywhere." The quick turn toward the French doors caught Richard off-guard, and before he could move, she was out on the patio. He wanted to go after her, but the rising sun stopped him.

"So your guest," he called after her, to try to stall her, "this one who's coming. It's a she? You never mentioned that before."

She paused at the door. "Yes, Richard. Our guest is a she. You're not going to lie and tell me that matters to you, are you?"

He would if it meant he could get her back inside. "Does this 'she' have a name?"

31

"Perhaps I'll just wait and let her tell you."

"You mean when she gets here?"

Mamá's response was a tired "Yes, Richard," which he took personally. "I'm sorry, and excuse me for sounding trite, but if this person—"

"She," Mamá said.

"Yes, sorry. If this—*she* were indeed coming as you insist she is, shouldn't she be here by now? I mean, you've been saying this—she's been coming for nearly fifty years. Mamá . . . don't you see how this must look to anyone else?"

Mamá glared at him. "She's had a long way to travel, and I don't care what I sound like to anyone else. And you shouldn't care either!"

She isn't serious, Richard thought. *She can't be.* "So, in all this time, no mode of transportation has been developed to speed this visitor's progress along just a little?"

He was walking a thin line, he knew, and Mamá's searing look made him realize just how slim. He tried to recover. "I suppose I was a bit too trite," he said, wincing at his inability to catch himself from going too far.

"You're not being trite, Richard. You're being sarcastic, and I expect better from you." Still at the open door, she turned her attention back to the distant horizon.

"I'm just saying I have a hard time believing anyone's coming. I didn't mean to offend you. Please tell me you understand. Please, Mamá."

Not looking at him, she said, "I shall have to think about how I feel."

"Well, then," he said to her back, "I'll come to check on you shortly. I'll get your breakfast and bring it . . . and perhaps I'll bring some for your friend as well, should she arrive while I'm gone."

Mamá looked at him, and he saw the hurt in her eyes. "It's not a child's tea party, Richard. And I would appreciate you not speaking to me as though I were some senile, imbecilic old bat."

"Please don't be angry with me, Mamá. I'm trying to make sense of it all. Really I am!"

32

"I think you should go now."

He didn't want to leave, not with her acting so irrationally. But he could use the time to think. He needed to come up with some way to get her back inside before he headed to his basement. She'd had pneumonia just last month. She still needed her rest. Maybe Marissa had an idea about how to get her back in. He'd already stayed up longer than he felt comfortable doing.

Mamá turned her head and glared. "Why are you dawdling? I said go!"

"I . . . Yes, I'll go. I mean, I'm going. But I'm coming back. And when I come back, we'll talk."

Sparked by her look, he headed toward the door, grumbling. "Fifty years . . . a snail travels faster!"

CHAPTER 3

Careful not to be noticed, she removed the shirt from the crudely constructed clothesline a few yards behind a tiny cottage, then dashed back into the surrounding woods. She didn't want to have to explain her actions, and wasn't sure she could. She had managed a few words as she'd walked along, and even a few choice words for the shirt, as she struggled into it. Wearing and putting on clothes were two things she would have to get used to again.

It didn't help that the shirt was big and worn either, but at least it was clean, and long enough to cover what she now remembered needed to be covered. But the sleeves! They hung down past her hands and, since the sun was getting higher in the sky, she no longer needed their protection against the morning chill. Also, she didn't like the way she couldn't feel the breeze when it did come. So, with difficulty, she rolled the sleeves up.

Yet she was still hot, and might have taken the shirt off if not for something she remembered; being clothed was more important than being comfortable.

Someone had reminded her of this once, when she was very young, perhaps four. Someone she now remembered meant something to her. The image of her father presented itself from memory, wisps of blonde hair falling about dark, caring eyes as he knelt to speak with her, his kind and gentle voice convincing her to listen. His skin was bronze, and it wrinkled slightly when he smiled. She could almost smell the salt air, which he sometimes had the scent of because he liked to sail occasionally, when time allowed. She recalled him working with her, trying to help her get dressed again, understanding when others wouldn't have.

She had made him late for something, and yet, he hadn't been angry with her. In fact, he barely took his voice above a whisper when he told her how upset Mother would be if she learned her daughter didn't want to wear the new dress she'd worked so hard on. She remembered telling him how it "itched her so," and she'd rather go without clothes than to suffer with the dress on. But then she remembered her next thought: Mother had worked half the night on the dress. She remembered waking and seeing Mother still sewing.

She had put the dress back on then. Father's puzzled expression prompted her to explain her change of heart. "I would rather itch than to make Mother feel bad." Her mother always seemed so fragile to her, more so after she'd heard about the attack by the wolf, understood about the four deep scars she'd seen by accident.

Father's dark eyes sparkled as he explained to her the importance of being clothed, more so when he explained the significance of her decision.

"It is a virtue to put others first," he'd said, "especially at your age and especially when it is difficult to do so." She remembered him leaning forward to lightly kiss her forehead, and him telling her to never cease being Ceese.

She didn't know what he meant, just that whatever it was, it was important. And that finally, she remembered her name.

Tears stung her eyes now as she walked, moving in and out of the brush. Being clothed might be important, but so was staying off the main road. No one had to tell Ceese that. Those who followed the road might ask questions, ones she wasn't sure she had answers to, especially since she didn't really know where she was going in the first place. She might have been more upset if she wasn't certain things would become clearer soon.

The woods on either side of the road thinned out, and she was forced into the open. After a few miles, she came to a bend in the road. Perhaps the castle was there, beyond the turn she couldn't see around.

Yes! she thought. It was a *castle* she was headed to, and a *woman* she was supposed to meet. The woman was old now, and

35

her name was Penny. At least, Penny was what Ceese called the woman when the woman was much younger.

She got the feeling the name "Penny" was short for something. But at the moment, she wasn't certain what it was short for, or if it even mattered. What did matter was that Penny felt responsible for Ceese being what she was. Penny believed the wolf in the woods had cursed Ceese, thought she should have tried harder to talk Ceese out of going that day. But in reality, the wolf was Ceese. Ever since, Penny thought Ceese had disappeared because the wolf took her. That wasn't true either. Ceese had run to protect Penny.

Ceese walked and remembered this, just as she remembered her own name, Cecilia Collette Porter of Port Hampton, Wales, born the eighth of January 1802. She hated her name, so her friends called her "Ceese." Penny called her this, and Penny was her friend. And if memory served her correctly, Penny was her only friend near the end, before she had to run away.

Ceese had been roaming the woods for decades now, devastated by what nearly happened with Penny. The wolf could've killed Penny, *would've* killed her if Ceese had stayed any longer. She ran to protect Penny, and she'd been running ever since.

But she had more control now, and knew Penny would be safe. She also knew Penny could help her. In what way, she didn't know. But the wolf had trusted her instincts for a long time, and didn't doubt them now. Ceese pushed on.

❦   ❦   ❦

Unfortunately, all Richard could get from Marissa was a blank stare and, a hesitant "Why not just ask her to come back inside, m'lord?"

Richard had forgotten just how young Marissa was. She'd lived all her life in the castle with her parents, whom had served Mamá and Richard, and took their places when they passed away a few years back. Marissa was obedient but painfully timid, and not terribly intelligent. So he simply said, to her rather useless advice, "Yes," then picked up Mamá's tray and left her to her chores.

He returned to Mamá's room, breakfast tray in hand, and then set it down on the dresser. Mamá was still on the patio. The sun was higher in the sky, and Richard had to stand away from the French doors to avoid the effects. He should've been in his basement by now, far from the sunlight, but he wouldn't go until he knew Mamá was back inside.

"Have you not been out there long enough?" he called out. "I have your breakfast and besides, I think it's quite clear no one's coming." He shielded his eyes, trying to see if she was listening, but it was too bright to see her face. Her right hand did move though, to set the handbrake. And then, he thought he saw Mamá push herself up and stand!

"You're right, Richard," she said, taking a solid step forward, and then another. "No one is coming. She's here."

Without seeming to give it another thought, Mamá walked normally, without any hesitation, traipsing out onto the lawn as if she'd never been in a wheelchair at all.

Mamá," Richard called out, his mind racing, desperate to get her back inside.

Forcing himself to look past the sun's glare, he thought he saw a sliver of shade between where he stood and the direction in which Mamá had taken off. Perhaps he could just dart out and—

No shade was enough. Immediately, he went down. Even through his clothes, his skin felt as though it was on fire. He covered his face with his arms but there was no way to truly protect himself.

Marissa heard him cry out and responded, sprinting to Mamá's room and out through the French doors. "M'lord," she gasped, "you know you can't brave the sun."

She ran inside, jerked the cover from Mamá's bed and rushed back to put it over him, giving him temporary refuge.

After a moment, Richard was able to say, from beneath the thick spread, "Help me inside."

"I—I'm not supposed to," she said. "It's dangerous. My parents told me it might tempt you. . . . *You* told me—"

"I know what we told you! But I swear, I give you my word, this isn't a test."

Still she stood, frozen. He thought about hypnotizing her, but from such distance, and with so little strength, it was pointless to try.

He'd just about given up hope when he saw her move. She helped him to his feet, led him back through the French doors and to Mamá's bed, then backed quickly away.

Richard sat, shoulders slumped, still sheltered with the coverlet Marissa had thrown over him. "Thank you," he gasped. "Now, go and fetch Mamá. There is a stranger out there. It isn't safe for her."

Marissa looked toward the door. "A stranger?" No one ever came out here unless they were summoned. But who was she to need an explanation? "Yes, m'lord, at once."

❧ ❧ ❧

Penelope Cromwell was eighteen again, in her soul and in her spirit. "I knew you would come, Ceese," she said. "I called to you!"

Ceese didn't feel comfortable speaking yet, so she replied with her thoughts, as she had in the years she'd been the wolf. "I am not certain how long I can help you. And I think it would be best to get you back inside."

The instant she finished transmitting her thoughts, the older woman faltered, weaving on her frail legs. Ceese caught hold of her before she went down completely, took her up easily and cradled her in her arms.

Marissa saw this, ran to assist, but Ceese's menacing growl held her at bay.

"L-Lord Richard asked me to fetch M-Miss Penelope," she stuttered, vainly holding her arms out, as if this stranger were going to do exactly what she suggested. "I can take her now."

Being stern wasn't something Marissa was good at, and her words only drew another snarl from the stranger.

Marissa put her arms back down. "Or, I suppose you could carry her."

Ceese had already begun walking, brushing by Marissa as

38

though she weren't there. Marissa followed, then rushed ahead to push open the doors she'd shut on her way out.

When Marissa entered, Richard spoke from the dark corner where he'd taken refuge. "So where is she?" he asked. "Where's Mamá?"

Marissa wrung her hands uneasily, looked back over her shoulder. "I-I let *her* fetch Miss Penelope," she said, indicating with a nod the stranger now stepping into the room.

Richard gasped, "Mamá!" His beloved was being carried like a limp rag doll, and by someone he'd never seen before.

While Marissa shut the French doors and pulled the shades, he made a motion to take her. The result was a vicious snap from the stranger.

"I wouldn't, m'lord," Marissa suggested, a little too late. "I-I don't think it's safe."

Richard put his arms at his sides and regarded the stranger. "Yes, I would have to agree with you on that."

"I don't think she will hurt Miss Penelope, though," Marissa offered. "I . . . I believe she wants to help her."

Richard studied the odd stranger for a moment. "If it's all the same, I think I'd like to hear it from her."

"I don't think she can talk," Marissa said.

Richard kept his gaze on the stranger. "Can't, or won't?"

"She won't hurt her," Marissa repeated, sounding certain this time.

Richard fixed Marissa with a stare, to which she responded with the only explanation she could come up with: "I don't know how I know this, m'lord, I just do."

Richard turned his attention back to the menace. "I have no reason to trust you."

Marissa spoke again. "And she would like me to tell you she won't give you one. She says you have no choice but to trust her . . . m'lord."

Richard didn't turn to look at Marissa this time. "She is directing you to say these things?"

"She is, m'lord. And I would very much like to leave now before she directs me to say anything else."

Richard nodded. When Marissa dashed from the room, he crossed his arms in front of him, gave the strange girl a wary look. "Well, your mouthpiece is gone. How shall you communicate now?"

It was a question he would very much regret asking.

He dropped to his knees at once, his head gripped by intense pain. The pain was like the headaches he used to get eons ago, only much worse. He put his hands to his temples, as if somehow this would help. Then, for no reason at all, the pain stopped.

There were words then, something about not hurting Penny. Richard didn't catch it all, but he got the gist. It wasn't the girl's intention to hurt Mamá, although hurting *others* didn't seem to be a problem.

Richard stood slowly, decided to just watch. After all, she was taking care to be gentle, easing Mamá's form onto her bed and covering her, seeming to have done this with far more strength than a woman should have. There didn't seem to be a reason to worry though. Not until she got on the bed as well, curled up at the foot and made use of what little space remained. His guard shot up again, but so, it seemed, did hers. She watched Richard, and he watched her.

But Richard couldn't watch for long. A beam of sunlight was cutting a path across the room. He had forgotten to pull the drapes. He got up at once and did this. She continued to study him, he knew, because he could feel her staring. Curtains drawn, he settled back in his chair, and she seemed to lose interest.

It was at this point Richard realized something odd. *Fifty years?* he thought. *This girl is no more than seventeen or eighteen.* Either this wasn't the "she" Mamá was expecting, or Mamá had a lot of explaining to do.

Time passed, and Richard used it to study the stranger at the foot of the bed. She had a distinct odor; like dirt and earth. Like a dog left outside for some time. Like Xavier, his wolfhound.

Then the menace moved, bringing her right foot up behind her right ear as if to scratch, hesitating and, seconds later, following through with the act. Then, suddenly, she used a hand instead, looking frustrated and angry. At last, she replaced the hand with her foot, seeming pleased, and then settled back on the bed.

He was astonished at seeing someone bend in such a way. He'd never met anyone quite as limber. He thought he might ask about that later, *if* she turned out to be civil enough to talk to. Then he thought of the pain he'd felt when he'd so much as asked her to talk, and changed his mind.

The menace grew still, and Richard began to pay more attention to other things. Most important, the way she was dressed . . . or, depending on how one wanted to look at it, the way she was not dressed. A shirt was all she wore, and he knew she'd taken it from Peter the goatherder's clothesline: It smelled of goat and Peter, and didn't fit her at all. Not surprising, since Peter was three times her size. It was relatively clean, however. Or at least, cleaner than she was, and her being covered meant more to Richard than what she chose to cover herself with. Particularly when she scratched in that physically challenging way. Where were her own clothes, though? Richard thought about this as he examined her. She wasn't hard to look at. Lean but not too scrawny, an almost-boyish figure, but with subtle curves. She was young, too young for him should he ever be able to rise above the curse to be tempted with desire.

Her hair was short and long, coming to her shoulders at the longest, just below her eyes where it was shortest. It fell about her eyes at times, eyes Richard noticed when she had come in. They had a hard greenish-gold hue about them, a color he couldn't recall ever having seen before. Next to the way she scratched herself, they were the most unusual thing about her.

He would have observed longer, but the menace's eyes finally closed. When he found his own lids growing heavy, he went to the hall to summon Marissa. She brought him a pint bag of blood, which he took back to his chair and drank, piercing it with his fangs and drawing from it. The blood would help ease his exhaustion, and help regenerate the damaged parts of his skin. And for help with one other thing he didn't want to think about right now. Not long after, he slept.

CHAPTER 4

Richard became immediately aware, sitting up in his chair and moving forward. Mamá was awake. Her eyes were bright, her smile beaming.

"You are all right," he said, and took her hand in his. He was careful to keep his voice low, though. He didn't want to disturb the still-sleeping menace at the end of the bed.

"Well, of course I'm all right. What time is it, Richard?"

He had lost track, had to look at his watch. "It's four in the afternoon. You've been asleep nearly all day."

Her face showed alarm. "And you've stayed here the entire time? Shouldn't you be in the basement?"

His coffin was the only protection he had against the vampire bats that plagued him and others like him. His need for blood and the bats' need for blood coincided. He'd patterned the coffin after others he'd seen, so the blasted bats couldn't find him while he slept. He could always control how hungry he got if he were awake—and was able to feed before the bats got wind of his location. But when he slept, it was more difficult. And if he got hungry while he slept, they sought him out and fed on him. They weren't pleasant creatures, or easy to get rid of. Mamá knew how Richard felt about them.

But Richard didn't sleep outside his coffin often, and when he did, he just made sure he never went to sleep hungry. He also made sure he never slept so long that hunger became an issue. The coffin ranked low as far as comfort went. But comfortable or not, it beat waking up with hundreds of bats all over him.

He showed Mamá the empty bag of blood. "You forget who you're dealing with."

"Yes," she said, and smiled.

Richard then looked toward the end of the bed. "Besides, I couldn't leave you here with—that."

Her brow wrinkled. "Whatever are you talking about? It's her. The one I've been waiting for. I told you she would come!"

"That is the 'who' you've been expecting? The 'she'?"

"Well, of course it is!" She leaned in close. "Now, tell me what you think of her."

"And you want the truth?"

"Always."

So he began, slowly at first, then rushing the words out. "Well . . . you failed to mention she would have fleas and might need to be vaccinated. And you also failed to mention she bites and doesn't bathe. Other than *those few things*, I suppose I could tolerate her, if you forced me to. Please tell me you aren't going to force me to." He'd only speculated about the bathing, but her unkempt state told him so.

Mamá sat up straight and whispered harshly, "Richard, those are horrible things to say about someone!"

"But you asked for the truth, and I fear she does have fleas. I've seen her scratching . . . like a dog. And growling like a dog. And she did try to bite me—"

Mamá gave him a dismissive wave. "Well, of course she bites and growls! And I suppose she could have a flea or two, but you shouldn't hold that against her."

He threw his hands in the air. "Why *shouldn't* I hold that against her? And why don't these things seem to bother *you*?"

She glanced away. "Well, I guess there's no point in keeping it from you now."

He reached the end of his patience. "No, I don't suppose there is. And truly, I think it's past time you told me what in the blazes is going on."

She turned her eyes back to his. "Well, don't you wonder how she can look so young? She's been headed this way for fifty years."

"Do we have to play these games? Really Mamá—"

"She's a werewolf, you see, and—"

"What!" He fairly leaped from the chair, turned away, then turned back. "Okay, let's play the game. Only let's start over. Ask me again about her being so young. I'll answer differently, and then you can say anything else *except* what you just said."

"Now don't get hysterical, Richard. I would have told you sooner, but I did so want you to meet her first."

"Oh, and a fine meeting it was. She nearly took my hand off!" He paced a few steps, then came back, stopping to look at Mamá, who was now propped against her pillow. He noted the blush in her cheeks, her eyes that shone like a young girl's, but was so overwrought by what they were discussing, didn't think about the significance. "She cannot be a werewolf, Mamá. Please tell me she's not."

Instead, Mamá went into a story. She'd grown accustomed to telling Richard things he didn't want to hear in this manner. "We were in the woods one day, sitting where we always sat to talk. It was late afternoon. We shouldn't have been out there at all, but . . . we were. A couple of boys from school showed up, Harry and Thomas . . . yes, it was Harry and Thomas. They said there was a pack of wolves. Said the pack had killed a number of cattle in the past month. They dared us—"

"Mamá," he said abruptly, "I'm quite certain I don't have the patience for you dragging this out."

She sighed. "All right. The boys left, and she and I kept talking. We heard a noise, and we went to see what it might be."

It was as if Mamá were there again, he could tell. And he allowed her to stay there for now.

"Ceese ran forward, and then disappeared into the brush." She looked at him with terrified eyes. "It took her then . . . It took her. I thought it was Harold and Thomas. I had no idea— And then I ran to get help!"

"Ceese?" Richard repeated, as though he had heard nothing else. "What an odd name."

Mamá nodded. "It's short for Cecilia, Cecilia Collette Porter. What would *you* have us call her?"

"I . . . don't know. 'Cecilia,' perhaps. Maybe Collette. But, never *Ceese*."

"What a strong opinion!" Mamá replied, looking at him sideways, suspiciously. "And why in the world would you care what's she's called anyway?"

He shrugged. "It's just odd. And since when can I not have an opinion?"

This time, Mamá shrugged. "Well, odd or not, she was attacked by a—"

"Don't say it," Richard said again, pacing once more, thinking and disbelieving. So Mamá didn't say it, and continued her story instead. "I ran to town as fast as my feet could carry me. I went everywhere trying to find someone to help, but no one would believe me. And Ceese was gone!"

She was lost in her own world now, and Richard was certain he didn't want to hear any more. He stopped pacing, took her by the shoulders and said, "Please tell me you're making this up. There are no such things as werewolves. You can't possibly be serious!"

Her look told him everything he didn't want to hear, and then her words did. "I *am* serious, Richard. Ceese is a werewolf. And it's a bit hypocritical of you to infer there are no such things, seeing as how you're a vampire!"

He didn't want to listen, had already decided he wouldn't. But then he was grabbed from behind, and the very thing he wanted to deny existed slammed him up against a wall. He winced from the unexpected impact, then recovered, only to be confronted by canine-like fangs and . . . *those eyes*, staring him down.

He attempted to free himself from its clutches but was unable to. And then, as if driven by some unknown desire, it moved its mouth close to the large vein in his neck and started to transform further, the semblance of a snout forming.

Mamá cried, "Ceese, no!"

The transformation stopped.

"It's all right, Ceese! Let him go!"

The menace relaxed, and Richard, finding his opportunity, pushed it away and headed for the door. He was the lord of this castle, and he wouldn't live in fear of anyone or anything. He wanted this "Ceese," this werewolf, gone!

"Where are you going?" he heard Mamá call out behind him.

"To find a silver bullet," he said, "and a big gun."

"She's my guest, Richard!"

He reached for the doorknob, spoke without turning it. "Your friend or not, she cannot stay here. I will not welcome her. Any more than I would welcome anyone else who tried to kill me."

Mamá's answer surprised him: "If she isn't welcome, then I am not welcome. She and I will both leave."

He whirled around, stunned, and Mamá tried to explain. "If she goes, I have to go. *I* am the one who called her. *I* am the reason she came."

"But *why?*"

Mamá's eyes filled with tears. "Because . . . Because it's my fault Ceese is what she is. We would have never gone into the woods if I had just tried a little harder to stop . . . if I had just tried to stop her."

He felt bad for Mamá, but still couldn't bring himself to accept this . . . this *werewolf.* This menace!

He turned to look at the young woman, tried to find anything about her worth pitying.

And then she spoke.

"I would have gone to the woods by myself, Penny," she said, looking as though she were about to reveal something she'd rather not reveal. "I would have. And— I was not harmed, as you thought. I could not have been, because the wolf you saw— It did not attack me. It *was* me. I was already cursed. I was already what I am now."

She'd lied! Richard whipped his head around to see how Mamá was taking this. Surely she would banish this menace for its deceit. He was pleased to see how stunned she looked, and then to hear her judgmental tone

"But all this time, Ceese— all these *years,* you let me believe it was my fault. How could you lead me on? How could you?"

The girl's accent was different now, Richard noted. Initially, he'd thought it boorish. But now it was heavily accented, a bit Gaelic, and interesting. Most interesting, though, was that she had suddenly acquired a workable vocabulary. But why had she not spoken until now? He wanted to ask, but he also wanted to listen. Mamá was upset.

"All these years," Mamá said, on the verge of tears, "I have never been so wrought with guilt!"

Richard looked back to the menace, whose face had lost some of its haughtiness. Richard might have felt sorry for her, but it just wasn't in him. No vampire could feel deep emotion.

"If only I could have told you," Ceese said, her accent losing some of its thickness. "But I feared for your safety. The wolf wanted to kill you, Penny. And it would have if I had not run. I . . . I just did not think before allowing you to follow me into the woods that day. I am sorry. But I have control of it now."

Richard could no longer hold his tongue. "Control?"

Both women's heads jerked toward him.

"Control?" he repeated. "Is attacking someone for no reason what you call *control*? Because I have several other words for it!"

"You were going to harm Penny . . . I thought."

"And so you nearly take my head off!"

"I'm sorry."

"Yes, well you *should* be," Richard sputtered. "And lying to a friend . . . Mamá deserves better! She should banish you now for your deceit."

"Richard, stop that immediately!" Mamá said. "She was just doing what she thought was best."

And then came the words Richard was afraid he might hear: "As if I could be angry with *you*, dearest Ceese." She patted the bed beside her and made room. "Now, come and tell me what you've been up to all this time."

Ceese brightened at once. Without looking at Richard, she went to settle next to Mamá.

Richard couldn't believe it. This werewolf had deceived Mamá, had *lied* to her, yet Mamá still welcomed her. "Well, well, it can growl, lie and *connive*."

The lips curled again, but only normal teeth were revealed this time. "I do not lie," she said. "To lie is to sin."

"Yes, well, we can only hope you put as much stock in the

other eight Commandments." The comment referred to scripture, and he flinched a little at the sudden sharp pain that shot through his head. But he recovered quickly for the sake of what he was trying to do. He was setting her up. He had said "other eight Commandments," knowing full well he should have said "other nine." But Mamá was such a stickler when it came to religion. If the werewolf didn't catch his error, didn't respond appropriately, then perhaps Mamá would dismiss her as a heathen and have nothing more to do with her.

But Ceese was ready. "Nine," she said, with confidence, "other *nine*. And which one of those other *nine* would you be worried about me not adhering to?"

She had said "adhering," and it was the word she'd meant to use, but the pronunciation was off, and Richard rushed to correct her. "It's add-*here*-ing, not add-*herrrr*ing," he said, twirling his "r" as she had done. "And I'm not worried about you upholding any of them. You can break them all for what it's worth to me. I'm only concerned for Mamá's happiness and safety."

Resentment crossed Ceese's face. "I would never hurt Penny. That is why I stayed away as long as I did."

"Yes, well, perhaps you didn't stay away long enough. Perhaps you should go back to wherever it is you came from."

"Richard!" Mamá said. "Ceese is a guest here, and you will treat her as one."

"Fine," Richard replied, looking smug. "Shall I have Marissa fetch you a bowl of water, then, or perhaps a *bone*?"

Ceese narrowed her eyes. "Would you not rather she fetch you a keg of blood . . . or perhaps a goat or two?"

Mamá covered her eyes with a hand and shook her head. "Well, that's so much better."

Richard didn't pay attention to Mamá's sarcasm. He was more concerned with what he'd just heard from this werewolf. He had told her nothing of himself, and she was asleep when he drank the blood earlier. "What do you know of me?" he demanded.

"What is there to know?" Ceese replied. "You have the look. I have come across many like you in my search. You grow faint in the light. You have pale skin." She paused, turned her head slightly and pointed to an area on her face. "And there is dried blood there. Perhaps you should check yourself in a looking-glass after gorging."

She smiled curtly at this, knowing it would do him no good to look in a mirror, no good at all. And her smile galled him. Richard wasn't vain, but he did miss the convenience of gazing at his reflection. And he certainly didn't appreciate being reminded he couldn't. Furthermore, he didn't like being toyed with. He was sure there was nothing on his face, like she claimed. But he was bothered enough to use the back of one of his hands to wipe with.

Seeing that, Ceese smirked at him. "Do you still wonder how I know?"

Richard did, but he wasn't about to ask.

She told him anyway. "I found a dead goat not far from here. It had no blood."

Richard looked at Mamá, who looked back at him with worried eyes.

"What did you do with it?" Richard said.

Ceese shrugged. "Why would you care? It was dead and buried."

He fought the sudden urge to strike her. Should Peter the goatherder stumble across what she claimed to have discovered, he would have enough proof to have every neighbor on his side. He gave her a hard stare. "I ask you again, and for the final time. What did you do with the goat?"

Mamá looked at Ceese and nodded. "What did you do with it, dear?"

Ceese considered her answer carefully, then said, "I ate it. I . . . saw no need to waste it."

All at once, Richard's look changed from anger to disgust. "You ate it?"

She looked him up and down, sneered. "*You* drank its blood!"

"Not after it had been buried for a day!"

49

She looked uncertain. "Well, it *was* a little drier than the other two."

"Other two?" According to the message he'd left with Marissa, Peter was missing three goats. One the night before, taken by him, plus two that Richard hadn't taken. The conclusion was clear to Richard. "But . . . why? Why did you steal those goats?"

"Wolf," she said. And then, "Sometimes, it is what I am."

"Well," Mamá chimed in with forced brightness, "at least we know Peter wasn't lying."

As if that is some consolation, Richard thought. "So what did you do with the remains? Did you leave them where they could be found?"

"I'm sure Ceese took care of matters," Mamá responded, ever hopeful. "After all, she doesn't want to be hunted either, do you, Ceese?"

"I should rather die cursed than to tell him anything," Ceese spat out.

He opened his mouth to respond, but Mamá had heard enough. "Ceese," she cautioned, "Richard has a lot at stake here. Please be a dear and tell him what you did with the remains."

"I will tell *you*," she said, then turned to her friend and spoke low enough so Richard had to strain to hear. "There was nothing left to worry about."

"What of the pelt, the bones?" Richard questioned. "Surely you didn't eat those!"

She glared at him. "I cast them aside. Which should matter little to you. Now, all anyone will be looking for is a wolf, not a cold-hearted, blood-sucking, lifeless—"

"Ceese," Mamá cautioned.

"*You!*"

"Well, at least *I* bathe occasionally," he rebutted.

"And for all the good it does," Ceese replied curtly. "Still, you smell of death."

Mamá's mouth fell open. "The both of you, stop it this instant. I've heard enough."

The two grew quiet and sullen.

Mamá looked at Richard. "Go and tell Marissa to get dinner ready."

He muttered, "As if she could be hungry . . . she's already eaten two goats, or perhaps *three*. Oh, but what of it, she's a werewolf . . . and a guest."

And then, he turned around in a huff and left.

CHAPTER 5

Mamá wanted so much for the two to get along, though she didn't expect it. Richard wasn't one to accept anything new without a fight or an argument. And Ceese, well, she was much the same way. That definitely hadn't changed.

"I do not like him, Penny," Ceese muttered when the silence became too much for her, "nor do I trust him."

"Oh, bother," Penny said, settling back against her pillow. "You never did trust anyone. But I'm telling you, dear, you have to trust him. Richard can help you."

When Ceese didn't reply, Mamá said, "Now, tell me . . . what happened to your beautiful long hair? I used to envy it so. I remember a time when it was down nearly to your waist."

"The wolf made me cut it. It didn't like it the way I fashioned it when I knew you."

"Is that how it is?" the elderly woman asked, her voice sad. "Its influence is that strong?"

"I . . . try not to let it influence me," Ceese said at last. Then, more in charge. "I control it, it does not control me."

"I see," Mamá replied, watching Ceese's face.

Ceese's shoulders sank a little. "It is not easy though. It is strong. But you can help me end this, can you not, Penny? You said you could help me. I want to end this." She seemed so desperate to have an answer, to *hear* the answer.

"I think I know a way, but you and Richard are going to have to work together. You have to at least try."

Ceese's brow furrowed, a hard ridge forming above her eyes, and Mamá smiled. "Now *there's* an expression I haven't seen in some time . . . and you won't earn many points here with it. I know you think you know what's best, Ceese. But in this case, you're wrong. And I know you know this . . . despite what you'd like me to believe."

The ridge softened. "I will try to get along, but it will not be easy."

"Nothing worth fighting for ever is."

From where she sat on the edge of the bed, Ceese looked down at the floor. "I have heard those words before."

"Your father," Mamá guessed, and Ceese nodded.

When the two of them were younger, Mamá remembered Ceese talking endlessly of her family. She never understood why Ceese wouldn't take her to meet them. It made no sense. It did now though, considering what she'd just learned. If Ceese acquired the curse before she met her, then her family, the ones she'd talked about so much, had most assuredly all passed on. Nevertheless, Mamá struggled with Ceese's intentionally keeping information from her. Struggled with why Ceese hadn't let her know before: hadn't told her she was, in fact, the wolf they were running from.

"I wished you hadn't held the truth from me," she said, putting a hand on Ceese's arm. "I would have understood."

But when Mamá touched Ceese, something went through her, and she pulled her hand away at once. "I thought you came here because you wanted to break the curse," she said uncertainly. "Why do I question that now?"

"I came because you summoned me," Ceese murmured.

Mamá knew she was holding back, and thought she knew why. "Ceese, I won't help you hurt Richard. I won't. I did call to you, but it wasn't so you could harm him. Do you understand?"

Ceese was silent.

"If you have come for any other reason besides breaking the curse, I won't help you."

Green-gold eyes bored into Mamá's. "That is the only reason, I swear it!"

"Oh? Then why do I sense something else? And I don't have to tell you not to lie to me."

Ceese's eyes filled with tears of guilt. "I would never lie to you . . . again."

"Then tell me," Mamá pushed. "I love Richard, and I won't let anything happen to him."

"What . . . What if Richard is one of the two who cursed my brother?"

"That's impossible!"

"But what if—?"

"I'm telling you he isn't!"

Mamá had heard the story many times before; Ceese used to tell it often. Ceese's oldest brother had been bitten by two vampires, had left home afterward. Their grief-stricken father had withdrawn into himself. Nothing was ever the same. Though she believed the tale, Mamá never gave it much thought until now.

"And when did this witch hunt of yours begin anyway?" Mamá asked gently.

"I have never stopped looking. I never will."

Mamá thought back now, tried to recall everything Ceese had told her about her family. "Wasn't this brother who was bitten called Richard also?"

"You think the name means something?" Ceese scoffed. "I have met many vampires named Richard. Besides, many vampires change this about themselves, among other things. And suppose they did not change their names, and this one's name truly *was* Richard? I would still suspect him. But not because of what he calls himself. Vampires are cold and heartless, the lot of them."

Mamá's brows went up. "Oh, so you're an expert on the subject now."

A pause, then, "I have some knowledge."

"Well, I have lived with *this* Richard for quite some time, and I'm telling you, he is the last vampire you need to worry about."

Ceese turned to peer at her friend. "Why? What makes him different, Penny?"

"Like you, he doesn't go around cursing others. Otherwise, I might be cursed. We're very close."

Ceese sank back a little, looked like she might accept what

Mamá had said. "All right. If you say so, I will trust your words. But I still contend the only good vampire is a dead one."

Mamá nodded at her honesty. *That* was what she'd sensed from Ceese a moment ago, when their hands had touched. "Very well, then," she replied. Now reassured, she decided to try to steer the subject away from Richard. "So, when were you born anyway, Ceese? If you don't mind me asking. It all seems so fascinating."

"The eighth of January, eighteen hundred and two. In Port Hampton, Wales."

Mamá considered this. "I do believe Richard has a few years on you."

"He is older?"

"He shares so little with me about his past, but . . . yes, I believe so."

"So, when did you meet this vampire, this Richard? And why does he call you Mamá?"

Mamá smiled. "I didn't think I'd like being called such a thing, but the way he says it . . ." She caught Ceese's frown and moved the explanation along. "Besides, if our neighbors think I'm his mother, it saves questions." She paused again, but noticed Ceese waiting. "I met him quite a few years after I knew you. I was twenty-five. Like you, his family was very important to him. . . . At least I suspect they were. He has forced them from his memory. He remembers a little about his father every now and again, but nothing else. And I've searched all kinds of records and never found anything significant on the Bastóne family, except they were religious zealots in their own right. Were fairly serious about hangings for the appropriate offense."

"Bastóne?" Ceese repeated.

Mamá nodded. "Yes, Bastóne. Perhaps you're right. Maybe vampires do change their names frequently. But I must emphasize that Richard isn't like other vampires, and you need to trust him."

"I do not need to trust anyone—or anything, especially not a vampire." Her words weren't as vengeful this time.

Mamá gently turned Ceese's head to hers and looked into

those strange eyes. "I thought you said you had control, and yet I feel I'm talking to the wolf."

Ceese's face showed anguish. "It is still very strong. It lies to me, and I fight with it at every turn to remember what is right. And then I fight harder to *do* what is right. But it wants very much to make me forget. It wants so much for me to curse another."

Mamá gave an understanding nod and allowed her hands to fall into her lap. "How is it you came to be cursed in the first place? It just seems so bizarre to have two individuals from the same family . . . first your brother, and then you. I know there were more chances, more opportunities for such a coincidence back then. I've done so much research about it. But, still, it's hard to fathom."

"I went looking for the vampires who cursed my brother," Ceese said. "Twelve years after he was bitten, a day after Father died, I set out looking. I went to the same clearing, but the vampires had gone. A new evil had come in their place, and I was not . . . prepared for it."

"The wolf?"

Ceese nodded, and could no longer look at Mamá.

After a moment, Mamá patted her hand. "We *will* break this curse, Ceese. But you have to trust Richard. He can help you."

"All right," Ceese replied with a heavy sigh, giving in a bit.

Mamá smiled back. "Now, *that's* the Ceese I remember."

All at once, there was a thunderous pounding from down the hall. Mamá was surprised to see her friend's hands form claws, and those teeth returned. She had collected some wolfsbane before Ceese arrived, not really thinking she would need it, just erring on the side of caution. Now, she wondered if she should go get it. "Ceese," she said carefully, "it's just someone knocking."

Ceese seemed to calm. "It seems we have another visitor. Sorry."

Mamá glanced down. Her friend's hands were hands again, and she fought to hide her relief. But she had to ask. "Is being startled all it takes for you to become the wolf? A knock at the door? Something so trivial?"

Ceese nodded again, reached up to scratch an ear just now losing its pointed shape. "Once I get used to it," she said, "it will not be a problem. And yes, being startled will rouse the wolf, especially when it is so easy to transform."

Mamá didn't quite know as much about werewolves as she did about vampires. "So it's easy?"

"Yes. But if too much time goes by and one does not transform, it becomes much harder. Some forget how. To transform completely though, is always more difficult."

Another round of banging came, but this time, Ceese was a little more prepared. The teeth were all Mamá noticed, and they disappeared quickly. Yet the second round of banging had Mamá worried. They rarely had visitors at the castle, and this one didn't sound friendly.

CHAPTER 6

Peter Drummond huffed a bit as he stood in front of the large door that marked the castle's main entrance, staring at it as if wondering where to knock. He struck an area near the center several times with a solid fist, then again when no one responded.

Finally, Marissa pulled the door open slightly and peered out. With their new guest's arrival earlier, she was a little more cautious than she might have otherwise been.

"I would like to speak with the head of the household," Peter belted out, his voice echoing into the foyer beyond. Richard, standing in the parlor, heard the thick cockney accent and was repulsed. He motioned for Marissa to show the man in before he could assault his ears again.

She led him to the parlor, then left while Richard moved toward a meticulously uncluttered desk. His back to Peter, he took a seat in an expensive leather chair. He never asked his guest to sit, nor did he address him right away. Instead, he pulled out a rectangular bin, a hinged box capable of being locked. "I understand you lost three goats last night," Richard eventually said, using the key he'd found. "Sorry to hear."

But he had not really thought before he spoke.

"How did you know I lost three?" Peter threw out, as if ready to fight if he didn't like the answer.

Richard cringed, thankful his back was to the man. "Marissa told me," he said. He hoped the speed of the lie would keep the man from getting more suspicious.

"Marissa? The little tart who showed me in?"

"Yes," Richard replied. *Tart*, he thought. *Does he refer to all women in such a manner?*

"I don't remember tellin' her how many I lost . . . but I s'pose I could have."

"Yes, well," Richard said taking some money out of an envelope, "it doesn't really matt—"

When Richard turned back, he saw Peter toying with a delicate antique balancing piece that occupied the center of a long sofa table. The goatherder was swinging the arm of it around on its pivot, with a finger.

Money in hand, Richard rose from the chair and strode over to him. "If you would please not *play* with that." He picked the item up and out of Peter's reach. "It's very old and quite expensive."

Peter scowled. "It wasn't like I was gunna go and break it."

Richard's forced smile resembled a scowl. "Of course not. But I'll just put it over here for now, if it's all the same to you."

Richard moved the item to the desk, leafed through the cash he'd collected from the envelope in the bin, making certain Peter saw the large numbers on each bill. "As I was saying, I understand you're missing three goats. And since most farmers are on a very small profit margin these days . . . well, I'd like to do the neighborly thing and give you this so you can replace them."

Peter crossed his bulky arms in front of him and regarded Richard with a scrutinizing eye. Richard couldn't resist. "Do I have to meet your standards before you'll take my money?"

"Keep your blasted money. You can use it to get a haircut."

Richard considered hypnosis, but decided against it. This man might actually be too stupid for it to work. Some were. He decided to try persuasion instead. "Come now, Mr. Drummond. There's no need to get personal. You could put it toward building a fence. So you won't lose any more of your stock."

"There won't be no fences," Peter fired back.

The man's arrogance ate away at what little patience Richard had left. He'd slept most of the day in a chair, wrestled with a werewolf, and was now being forced to deal with an imbecile. "Well, then, what *do* you want, Mr. Drummond? I'm not a man who has a lot of time to stand around and talk."

Peter's eyes narrowed and a nasty smile formed on his lips. "I'd daresay you are a man at all."

Richard was set back on his heels by the goatherder's implication. Maybe the imbecile *had* found one of the goats this werewolf was supposed to have buried.

Then a pang hit him, a deep, *serious* pang, and Richard realized he was hungry. Suddenly the space between them seemed like inches. He hadn't had any blood in quite a while. He'd been headed to the kitchen to get some when Peter showed up. Now, with such a meal before him, he could barely think of anything else.

"Let me get this straight," he said, trying to stay on track. "You question whether I'm a man?"

"That's right," Peter replied.

"And why would you question that, Mr. Drummond?"

"Because I think you're a pansy. You wouldn't know a good day's work if it hit you on the head. You stay in this castle all the day long, just like your father, only to come out at night and steal our goats."

That's what he meant by pansy? Richard thought, then pulled himself back to the matter at hand. "Excuse me," he said, looking confused. "Did I hear you right? Did you say 'our goats'?"

"That's right, *our* goats. Me and my neighbors. Everyone around here's sick of it."

"You've talked to them about this?" Richard asked, trying hard not to let the man see him studying his neck. "To your neighbors, I mean?"

"I have."

"And when do you find the opportunity to talk to anyone, Mr. Drummond?" he said, keeping his voice level. "I wasn't aware you ever had a spare moment."

"I *find* the opportunity—" Peter cast him a cagey glance. "And what do *you* know about what I do with my time?"

"Well, I suppose it's nothing really. I just have a hard time catching up with you myself."

This seemed to surprise the goatherder. "You've tried?"

"Oh, yes," Richard offered. "On numerous occasions. But you've always been—" He stopped, as though searching for the perfect expression. "How shall I say it? Preoccupied." He was looking back at Peter's face now. The man's jowls were set hard, his puffy cheeks turning red.

"You got no business snooping around my place, no business whatsoever!" Peter jabbed a finger to Richard's chest. "*You're* the thief."

It was time to set this man straight . . . if he could manage to do so without the urge for his blood overtaking him. "I banged loudly on your door, Mr. Drummond. I hardly call paying someone a visit 'snooping.' And I'm certain you have no proof of anything being stolen. If you did, I daresay I'd consider thievery an admirable profession . . . in light of how you spend most of *your* time."

He then leaned very close to Peter's left ear. "People in glass houses, Mr. Drummond. If I'm not mistaken, paying for the company of a woman is still considered illegal."

But getting that close to him wasn't wise. Richard was losing control. Fangs pushed forward and down . . . and then shot back up when Mamá came on the scene, bursting into the room, waving something in the air and heading straight for him.

"Richard," she said, "is this what you were looking for earlier?"

He hadn't been looking for anything, least of all what she now held out to him. He was startled by the cross she held—almost as startled as he was at the sight of her walking in unassisted— No, *striding* in. He nearly stumbled over his own feet trying to avoid her as she approached.

"No, Mamá," he said abruptly. Then, more composed when she put the cross away. "I uh . . . found what I was looking for. Thank you."

"Good," she said, sounded less alarmed but still looked concerned. "Because I didn't want you to think you had lost it. I know how much it means to you."

Richard's smile in return was contemptuous. "Yes, well, thank you for thinking about me, but I'm quite sure I haven't lost it—I mean, hadn't lost it." Clarification was becoming a tricky business.

"Very well," she said, satisfied. She then turned to their visitor.

Peter wasn't a stranger to Mamá. In the past, when she could take walks, she often found him napping under a tree while his herd wandered aimlessly about. During those times, they shared a greeting, a word or two. Like Richard and most everyone else who met him, she'd rather not deal with him at all. But with a little effort, she was able to force a smile now.

"So, Peter, did Richard tell you the news?"

Peter gave Richard a quizzical look, then turned back to her. "No."

"Well, there is a wolf about." She glanced to Richard as if she couldn't believe he hadn't offered this information already. "Isn't there, Richard?"

"Ah, yes! A wolf," Richard said, nodding but looking as clueless as the goatherder.

Mamá nodded. "And this wolf has taken several goats and sheep in the last few weeks."

Peter's stare was suspicious. "Excuse me, ma'am, but there hasn't been a wolf in these parts for some time. I would know. And others, well . . . they would have been talking."

"Oh, but it's true." Mamá looked to Richard again for his help, but he was still at a loss as to why she was saying this. Mamá had to know they would hunt her friend if she continued with this line of deceit. They might go as far as to kill her.

On the other hand, what did he care? He smiled at Peter. "Yes, what Mamá just told you is true. This wolf has taken quite a few goats and sheep."

Mamá seemed impressed by his answer, and Richard spoke with more enthusiasm. "It's a horrible situation, just terrible," he continued. "And we should all get guns. Big guns. *Accurate* guns—and go after it."

"Richard!" Mamá said.

She no longer looked impressed. Shock was what Richard saw now, genuine shock. What had he done wrong this time? "I, ah . . . I mean we should all watch our flocks more closely. Perhaps just keep guns with us . . . you know, in case we see something."

Peter's face contorted as he listened to the drivel. "We?" he spit out. "*You* don't have a flock."

Richard looked chagrinned. "Of course I don't. But, if I did, I'd still keep a gun close."

Instead of looking shocked this time, Mamá just looked annoyed, and Richard scaled back a little more. "Albeit a small gun," he used hand measurements to illustrate, "perhaps a pistol."

Mamá would listen to no more. "Marissa," she called out, "would you please show Mr. Drummond to the door?"

Peter took the cash from Richard's hand at the last moment, then strode the few steps to where the parlor emptied into the foyer. "I can find my way," he said, looked back to Richard and pointed a finger. "You just better hope we find a wolf!"

Richard pointed back, "Oh, you have no idea how hopeful I am."

Peter was forgotten the second he left the parlor.

Richard ignored Mamá's piercing glare, went back instead to the cash bin he'd opened earlier and closed it. "Well, *that* went well."

"Don't talk to me as if you have no idea what you just did. Don't you dare!"

Without her wheelchair, Mamá was a formidable foe. And with a stiff form and upraised head, she moved toward him. "How could you? I came in here to help you, and you started talking about guns!"

"I'm sorry," Richard tried. "You caught me off-guard."

"I caught you about to curse Peter Drummond!" Ignoring his penitent look, she snapped, "How was it you allowed yourself to get so close to him? It was careless. And then you start going on about guns."

"I am what I am." It was a weak defense, he knew.

She took a moment to study him before she replied. "You are who you *want* to be. And when you decide to be someone I can tolerate, I should like to talk to you again."

She turned to leave, but stopped when he spoke to her back.

"What did you expect me to say? You know I don't like her. I thought for a moment, from the way you were talking, she had done something to turn you against her."

"You didn't think at all, Richard." Mamá said this with a little

63

more kindness. "You are smarter than that. I shouldn't have had to explain what I was trying to do with my little story."

He appreciated her giving him more credit, but it didn't change the way he felt. "I don't like her."

Still with her back to him, Mamá nodded a slow nod. "If the truth be known, Richard, right now, I'm having a hard time liking *you*. I shall expect better of you in the future." She began walking, and disappeared into the foyer.

"It's not like I told him to use a *silver* bullet," he grumbled. But of course, there was no one to hear his excuse, only him. He moved the balancing piece back to where it had been before Peter started toying with it, then left the room as well. He would make amends with Mamá later, after she calmed down. And perhaps then, he could find out why an eighty-two-year-old woman was suddenly able to walk like someone fifty years younger.

๏ ๏ ๏

When he heard Richard approach, Peter stepped quickly back into the room he'd wandered into by mistake, staying there until Richard passed him. He thought he could make his way out, but had made a wrong turn somewhere and ended up in a library, then a large bathroom, and eventually back to where he started. He missed most of the conversation between Mamá and Richard while he was wandering about, but caught Richard's comment about the silver bullet. He wasn't sure what it meant, but he did take note as he spotted the huge main door at last, and exited.

CHAPTER 7

Dinner was ready and Marissa was waiting to serve it. But she would need a very long stick, with something on the end to grab things with, Richard observed, to serve from where she stood, pressed against the wall, at least five feet away, holding a tray of something. He guessed rolls because that is what Mamá had asked her to bring in next.

"Perhaps you should just take the night off," he said, then thought, *For all the good you're doing.*

Usually, when Richard occasionally gave her the opportunity to turn in early, Marissa put up a fuss. But all she said tonight was "Yes, m'lord," put the tray on the sideboard, and raced from the room. He didn't have to guess why. By going to her room, at least she'd have a door for protection against their new guest—a guest who had taken to eating on the floor next to where Mamá sat, looking as if she might snap at anyone who came too close.

Mamá seemed pleased by Richard's gesture, and broke her silence to tell him so. "The poor dear needs a night off now and again."

"Yes, well, I feared she might start *launching* whatever it was she had on her tray as opposed to bringing the food over as she usually does." He should've stopped there, but didn't. "She might have very likely hit our *guest* on its hard head—excuse me, I meant to say, it might have hit *her* on the head."

There was a low growl from the floor. Mamá looked down. "Never you mind what he says, Ceese. He's just in a bit of snit. He'll get over it soon enough."

With a sigh, he left for the kitchen to get some blood. He shared only two meals with Mamá: dinner and breakfast. Yet he rarely ate. When he did eat, Marissa had to follow strict rules: The food had to be very underdone or raw. Marissa had placed a raw steak on his plate tonight, but she could have left a leg of lamb for him to feast on, and Richard wouldn't have touched it. He had no desire for anything other than blood.

Mamá's guest certainly had an appetite, though, a voracious one. When he returned to the dining room, it was hard to ignore the gnawing noises from the floor. He tried, though, taking his seat and drinking his blood as though nothing were bothering him. He remained silent while Mamá fed Ceese from the table, stopping occasionally to pat her on the head as though she were the castle pet. But Xavier, the true castle pet, wasn't afforded such privileges. The wolfhound was put out at mealtimes.

"Richard," Mamá said, looking away from what she was doing, "are you going to eat that?" She was pointing to the steak on a platter in front of him, raw and untouched.

When he shook his head, she took the plate and set it on the floor.

The noise began again, and he could keep quiet no longer. There was just something about listening to the sound of meat being ripped and torn from the bone . . . "I do so hope you plan on training her," he said. Then, to Mamá's disapproving stare, "I know it's petty of me. It's just I'm not used to it."

"She's hungry," Mamá told him. "I would think you could appreciate her appetite. You can be quite boorish when *you're* hungry."

His expression turned sheepish. "Yes, I suppose I can."

But then, for no reason he could think of, there was silence. And he saw Ceese getting up, holding her plate, and moving to the chair next to Mamá. She placed a napkin in her lap and began to eat in a more acceptable manner, using her fingers to pull meat from the bone instead of gnawing it with her teeth. Had he not been so suspicious, Richard might have been impressed.

Mamá didn't look suspicious, though, just delighted in the way Ceese had seemingly come around. To give an example, Mamá took up her glass, took a polite sip, then set her goblet back down, all while Ceese watched. Ceese took notice and reached for her own goblet. She put it to her lips just as Mamá had done, but reverted to doing things the way she was used to doing them. She began lapping like a dog, her tongue darting down and then back up . . . until she could no longer get to the liquid that was left. She sat still for a moment, goblet to her lips and head tilted forward, and eyed a large pitcher in the center of the table.

Richard didn't like her look and took the pitcher at once, before she could get any ideas.

Mamá was holding her tongue, he could tell. He knew she was torn between telling Ceese what to do and letting her figure it out on her own.

The stage was set, but the performance failed miserably. Ceese went for a large serving bowl instead, dumped it of its contents and filled it with what was left of her drink, and Mamá's drink as well. Immediately she began to lap noisily, cutting her eyes at Richard while she did, as though daring him to stop her.

"All right, that's enough of that," Mamá said quickly, before Ceese could give him any more ammunition to use against her.

Richard was disappointed. He was enjoying watching Ceese regress, took pleasure in her inability to adjust. He knew Mamá would have something to say about it later, but at the moment, he didn't care. He just smiled.

"Let's get you bathed, dear," Mamá continued, taking Ceese by the wrist—her hands weren't anything anybody would want to deal with at the moment—and tugged gently. Ceese went along, but voiced her objection. "But I do not want a bath, Penny!"

"Everyone in this castle takes a bath," Mamá said. "Regardless of how they feel about it."

Ceese's gloomy face encouraged Richard. Maybe the requirement of being clean would send her back to wherever it was she'd come from. Maybe she'd leave and never come back. He had all of these wonderful thoughts as Mamá and Ceese walked off.

But Ceese stopped when she and Mamá reached the door, and turned to face him. "It isn't I do not welcome being clean," she said. "The wolf does not like being immersed in water."

Mamá shot Richard a chastising look. "Well, of course you

don't mind being clean! Why would Richard think otherwise? Now come along."

She pulled at Ceese again. This time, Ceese followed without speaking.

Richard waited in Mamá's room an hour longer than he normally would have waited. When Mamá arrived, she seemed surprised to find him still there. He was stunned she didn't look angrier and he voiced his relief. "I thought you would come in here ranting, Mamá."

She settled next to him on the small settee, took one of his hands in hers and sighed. She didn't rant but she did lightly chastise. "That was a terrible thought you had earlier, Richard."

"Yes, but I did just think it. How did I know she could hear . . . ?" He looked stumped. "What did she *do*?"

"She can sense things, Richard."

"Well, then, I guess I shall be careful how I *feel* around her."

Mamá squeezed his hand gently. "She's going to need you, Richard. She doesn't recognize it yet, but she is definitely going to need you. Once she realizes that, she'll be easier to tolerate."

"Well, will she be easier to tolerate any time in this century? Because I'm a very busy—"

He stopped when Mamá looked at him again, her look telling him she thought he could do better. "I'm sorry, Mamá. I couldn't help myself."

"You could try a little harder," she replied. "To get along, I mean."

"But it's so much easier not to."

"Richard—"

He sighed. "All right, I'll try. But only because you want me to. Just know it won't be easy for me."

Mamá seemed to accept his words, so Richard settled back on the sofa. "I have to know . . . how is it you can walk now? And look at you—you look at least thirty years younger than you did before she came here. Has Ceese healed you?

Mamá gave him a guarded look. "She is a werewolf, Richard, not a miracle-worker."

"How, then? What manner of magic is at work here?"

"She . . . She just retained some of my youth, I suppose. I'm not certain how she did it, but I don't think she'll be able to keep whatever it is she's doing up for long. Each moment taxes her, and I won't allow her to continue if it causes her harm."

He looked at her, his surprise genuine. "Won't allow it? You're allowing it?"

"In a way, yes. Oh, she might think I can't prevent her from doing what she's doing, but I can. And the second I detect it's harming her to keep this up, I'll no longer allow it. I—"

The clamor came from down the hall, a great splashing of water and things falling to the floor. When Richard and Mamá rushed in, they found the great marble tub nearly empty of all its water; most of it had been splashed out. And more than a few towels had been ripped and shredded: towels Richard had spent a small fortune on.

Ceese stood next to the tub, dripping wet and shivering, all while trying unsuccessfully to pull one of the tattered towels around her soaked form. And there were short, stiff hairs all around the tub, just like there were when Xavier got his bath.

"The wolf does not like water," Ceese said, speaking to Mamá, avoiding Richard's gaze.

Mamá broke into laughter at the sight and reached for the robe she had brought in earlier. "Undoubtedly!"

Richard saw no humor in the situation. Some of his best towels were now better suited for rags. Maybe Ceese thought her explanation was good enough, but he didn't. He grabbed up one of the towel remnants and held it up to Mamá. "I take it *the wolf* doesn't care much for fine linens either."

"Richard, they were just cotton towels," Mamá said. "They can easily be replaced."

"Exactly! So why would *a wolf* want to destroy them? My guess is a wolf wouldn't want to—but a disrespectful guest might."

Ceese looked at the floor. "The wolf was not interested in the towels," she muttered.

"Aha!" he yelled. "So, you confess. It wasn't the wolf. It was you!"

She was still looking down when she turned her head to the side to speak, her brow furrowed. "The wolf smelled sheep."

Richard couldn't figure it out . . . until he saw it, shredded, mutilated, and mixed in with all the other fabric remnants. "No," he moaned, and took up the largest swatch of cloth he could find. The ad had read: *Wrap yourself in the glorious luxury of lambswool!*" . . . used words like *exhilaratingly soft* and *hand-woven in Italy.* . . .

He looked at Mamá. "Tell me it isn't true. Oh please, tell me that my five-hundred-dollar bathrobe hasn't just been shredded because it smelled like a lamb!"

Mamá glanced at Ceese, but didn't see remorse—or any intention of apologizing. "Ceese didn't mean to do it," she assured Richard. Then, "Tell him, Ceese."

"The . . . The bathrobe was made from lambswool. The wolf smelled it." She punctuated her remark with a shrug.

There has to be more to it, Richard thought. *She couldn't have so little control.* A more worrisome thought came then: *And if she doesn't have any more control than this over the wolf, then . . . ?*

"Most cloth is a blend of other fabrics," Ceese said, pulling him away from his thought. "There is not enough of an animal's scent to tempt the wolf."

"Scent?" Richard blared. "The only scent this bathrobe *had,*" he waved the swatch for her to see, "was of detergent and fabric softener. Face it, you just have no regard! Tell her, Mamá." He wanted Mamá to join in, didn't understand when she wouldn't. And then, he saw her pale face, and forgot about the bathrobe.

"Are you feeling all right, Mamá?"

"Please, Richard. Do not wave what you're waving around." She cut her eyes to Ceese, standing very near her. "I don't think it's a wise thing to do—considering."

She then indicated, with a nod, where he should be looking.

He followed her eyes and saw what he'd been too upset to notice before: the canine-like teeth, the claws, the snout forming. Quickly, he tucked the swatch into his pocket, and Ceese struggled to recover.

"I told you," Ceese said after a moment, "the wolf can smell it."

Richard found himself muttering, "First I have to watch how I feel and now, I have to watch what I wear?"

His comment wasn't directed at her but Ceese responded anyway, cocking her brow as she had seen him do. "I would, if I were you."

A frustrated, rattled Richard left the room. Ceese watched him go, then turned to face a disappointed Mamá.

"I am sorry, Penny," she said. "But he made me feel responsible, and I was not responsible. The wolf did it."

As gently as she could, Mamá replied, "He believes you have more control, Ceese . . . and so do I."

Ceese removed the robe Mamá had given her, pulled a blouse on instead. Mamá had found it in the attic, along with some other things she thought might fit Ceese.

"He puts too much stock in things that do not matter," Ceese told her as she stepped into the slacks next.

"They were his things, Ceese. It's not your place to destroy them, any more than it's your place to decide whether they're important or not."

The slacks had a zipper and a snap. Ceese worked with the zipper until she mastered it, but didn't seem to want to bother with the snap. So Mamá secured it for her, assuming Ceese didn't understand how it worked since she'd been a wolf for so long.

"Well, I might try harder to please him," Ceese said, plopping down on the room's cushioned bench, "*if* he were not so hard to please. But he reminds me of . . . another Richard."

"Your oldest brother," Mamá guessed, and Ceese nodded.

"One could never please him either."

"Are you really trying to please him? This Richard, I mean?"

Ceese crossed her arms, looked hurt. "You see, Penny?" she pouted. "My brother would do what *this* Richard is doing—turn anyone he wanted against me."

Mamá settled beside Ceese on the bench. "Richard could never turn me against you, dear!"

But Ceese's mind seemed to be somewhere else now. "I miss him so," she said sounding gloomy.

"I'm sure you miss all of your brothers and sisters—your family."

"But Richard was different."

"Because he was cursed?"

Ceese nodded, her eyes filling with confused tears before Mamá could ask any other questions.

"Sometimes I want to be angry at him, but I cannot bring myself to. He is all I have left in this world, besides you."

Mamá paused, then said, "How can you know he still exists? Many vampires are hunted and killed."

"Because I sense he does," Ceese replied, adding nothing else.

"Very well, then," Mamá said, knowing Ceese was capable of sensing many things. "But perhaps you should stop comparing this Richard to him."

A haughty sniffle. "How can I when he acts so much like him?"

"I don't know, Ceese. But you are going to have to try."

"I was six when it happened," Ceese began without any prompting. "I remember everything. Richard did not hate me, but he always had Father angry with me over one thing or another."

"He never got you in trouble with your mother?" Mamá was fishing now, had never heard Ceese talk nearly as much about her other parent, and was curious. "Or did being in trouble with your mother just not bother you as much?"

"There were seven of us children. Mother did not have a lot of time to worry about—" Ceese stopped talking, seemed to think of something else. "Mother was attacked by a wolf when she was carrying me in her womb. They told me this when I saw the scars on her side one day and asked. Father said it truly affected her, and not to take it too hard if Mother could not bring herself to show me as much attention as she did the others."

Mamá was stunned. "A wolf. Now, *there's* some irony."

"Yes, well, it is what happened, and it affected her greatly."

Mamá noted her friend's hurt look. "Oh, Ceese, I'm sure your mother loved you just as much—"

"No, she did not," Ceese said quickly, brushing stands of wet hair from her face. "She did love me. Yet, Father loved me more."

Mamá nodded, decided not to push further. "And this brother. Richard. He would always have your father angry at you?"

Ceese nodded. "Yes, and then, when he ran away, after he was cursed . . . Father was never the same. I always thought things would be different if Richard left, but I never wanted . . ."

"Of course you didn't," Mamá said. "Surely you don't blame yourself for what happened to him." And then she had another thought. "And I know your father wouldn't blame you."

"Father never knew what happened to Richard," Ceese continued. "He just thought Richard took off, his beloved Richard, he just left. How could he not blame me?"

"How could your father not have known, Ceese?" Mamá asked, puzzled. "Being a vampire isn't something one can easily hide."

Ceese looked at the floor. "Richard ran off before Father could know."

Still, it didn't make sense. "Well, then, how did *you* know?"

"I followed him when the vampire came . . . I saw everything."

Mamá couldn't believe what she was hearing. "How is it no one tried to stop you, if you were only six? Did no one keep an eye on you?"

Ceese sighed, looked away. "Mother had taken Sophie and Raewyn with her to assist in delivering a baby. Father had gone for the day to help set up a new mission. Richard was the oldest, and was left in charge as usual. When the knock came, I was still awake. While the stranger at the door waited for Richard to get his coat, I saw his fangs. I didn't know what I was looking at . . . then. But I knew I must warn Richard. There was evil in those eyes, Penny. I could sense it."

Ceese stopped for a moment and Mamá waited, desperate to know more but afraid to push.

"Richard put Brendan in charge," Ceese continued at last. "And it was Brendan who saw me start out the back door. But when he tried to stop me, I threatened to tell Father I had seen him with the parson's daughter. Brendan left me alone, and I left the house."

"So you followed your brother."

Ceese nodded. "I was very quiet. They never heard me. The vampire led Richard down a path, telling him he needed Richard to read last rites to someone who had passed on. They stopped in a clearing. The second vampire was hiding behind some trees. Richard tried to fight them—"

Mamá could see the terrified six-year-old behind the brave façade. "It's all right," she told her, and pulled her close and held her. "You were only six years old. What could you have done?"

After a moment, Ceese pulled away from Mamá. "I did stop them from killing Richard. I prayed."

Mamá noticed she'd talked of praying with such little effort, such little resistance. Wondered how she could do such a thing. After all, praying, in the context she had spoken of it, was to infer something holy. She decided to ask later though, because the story was far too interesting to interrupt.

"When I noticed they had heard me," Ceese continued, "I walked out into the clearing, praying, and the vampires hissed and spat. And so I prayed louder and they fled. I went to Richard and saw on his neck where they'd bitten him—where his birthmark is, the very one he shared with Mother and I." She showed Mamá the butterfly-shaped freckle just below the nape of her neck. "There. Richard was not aware when I got to him, and so I pulled him close and just held onto him. I didn't want him to die."

Tears threatened to come again, but this time Ceese remained in control. "After a while, he woke up. But he was like *them* by then, and he showed his fangs. I started praying again, and he was able to . . . force the vampire back. He picked me up and carried me home. Told me to keep praying so he might not be tempted, but to do so quietly so he would not be compelled to leave me.

"Everyone was asleep when we returned, and he placed me by the fireplace and covered me with his coat. Made me swear never to tell anyone."

"It must have been horrible for you to see such a thing," Mamá muttered. And it no longer surprised her why Ceese felt the way she did about avenging her brother.

"Sometimes I still dream about it—nightmares." The eyes with the odd coloration hardened. "I will find the ones who did this to Richard."

Mamá sighed. "Well, right now, you just need to try harder to get along with *this* Richard. You can look for those who cursed *your* Richard later."

Ceese gave a weak nod. "Yes, well, I am glad you feel so certain I can do this—get along, I mean. I trust no vampire, or man."

"You trusted your father," Mamá said.

"Father was different. And besides, he is gone now."

There was a bitter edge to her words Mamá couldn't ignore. "I don't think your father would want you to be angry about his passing."

"I am not angry. Not anymore. I am just not very good at letting go. That is not something I do very well." Tears formed in her eyes again, but again, they held tight.

"Not being able to let go is a problem many people have," Mamá said, her heart sinking. Richard also wasn't one to let go of things, and she worried what would become of him once her time came.

Ceese sensed what Mamá was thinking and turned to face her. "You cannot leave, Penny. I will not let you."

Mamá smiled softly. "You overestimate your ability, dear. You can't keep me here if it's my time. You know that."

"Yes, but I do not want you to go."

"You and Richard can help each other. You must promise me you'll try."

"I will try," Ceese replied. "But only because it is important to you."

Mamá reached for the blow dryer to use on Ceese's wet hair, but thought better of it. After all, if a knock at the door could cause her to transform. . . "Here, lean down," she said, and began rubbing it with a towel instead.

While Mamá worked, she looked once more at the birthmark Ceese had shown her a moment ago, considering its meaning.

"Father used to tell me it was from an angel's kiss," Ceese said. "Mother had one as well."

"Well, I know those types of marks are hereditary," Mamá replied, startled that Ceese had caught her looking. "And now don't you look nice!"

Ceese didn't comment, and Mamá knew why. She was thinking about her family again. To distract her, Mamá said, "Richard usually spends some time on his computer each night before heading out to hunt. Perhaps if you hurry, you can catch him."

"Why would I want to do that?" But then, Ceese remembered. "Oh, yes," she said, her voice full of dismay. "Getting along. How could I forget?"

CHAPTER 8

The parlor doors were closed but not locked. She opened one side and peered in. Just as Mamá had said, Richard was at the computer. She went in, closed the door behind her, and tried hard to not look as though she had something against what he was, who he was, or that he was. She browsed around the room, giving him the opportunity to speak first, but when he didn't, she came up behind him and stared over his shoulder.

"What is that?" she asked, pointing at the glowing screen in front of him with interest.

Usually, Richard loved talking about his toys. But not right now, and not to the person standing behind him, distracting him from his work. He didn't understand Ceese, and surely didn't like her. Besides, he was too busy to answer questions right now. He was responding to an e-mail regarding a shipment of blood, one that looked like it might not be coming.

"What is that?" he snapped. "What is what?"

"That." Ceese drilled a finger at the interesting square box with all its colors, pictures and words.

"A monitor," Richard said, pushing the arm she'd brought in front of him aside.

"Well, then, what about *that*?" she said, indicating what his fingers were pecking.

"A keyboard . . . and, before you ask, those are speakers. That is a printer and that is a mouse." He pointed at each one and then sank back against his chair.

All at once a fist came down, and plastic flew in every direction.

In shock and disbelief, he stood, almost knocking Ceese off

her feet. "Why, in the name of—why did you do that?" As he spoke, he scrambled to try to retrieve every piece of the mouse, as if by some miracle it could be reassembled.

"You said it was a mouse," Ceese explained, looking confused. "I eat mice. They're tasty."

Mamá might have had patience with her but he certainly didn't. "It was the mouse for the computer—the computer's mouse!"

"The computer eats mice?" She peered at the computer. "But how? It has no mouth."

"No, you use the mouse to communicate with the—" He stopped, looked as flustered as someone explaining physics to a four-year-old.

"I'm not a four-year-old," Ceese moped.

"And stop reading my mind," Richard threatened, "or I shall take measures to block you. And you know I can do that."

"Fine," Ceese said. "But I do not know why you are so upset about what I did. It wasn't a *real* mouse. You said so yourself!"

"Well, it certainly isn't one now! And how am I supposed to work without it? How am I supposed to send my e-mails?"

"Why don't you just *tell* this contraption what you want it to do?"

"Do you think I'd be standing here doing nothing if talking to it was a poss—?"

But there *was* a microphone, and he had trained the system to respond to his voice—he'd forgotten about this option until now. With an occasional heavy sigh meant to induce guilt in her, he went over the procedure in his mind, used the keyboard to initiate the process and began speaking. In no time, his e-mail was sent.

"You're welcome," Ceese said when it was clear Richard was finished.

Richard whirled around in his chair. "You want my thanks? You destroyed my mouse!"

"I thought you said it was the computer's mouse," she snipped. "And anyway, I only destroyed it because you said it was a mouse. But it was not a mouse at all, now was it?"

"It *was* a mouse," Richard hammered on, "but you bloody well put an end to that now, didn't you?"

"Well, you don't have to get so bloody upset," Ceese countered, mimicking him. And then she seemed to lose steam.

"What?" Richard said, looking up at her after she grew quiet. "Have you run out of ideas on how to irritate me?"

Her look was brazen. "I shall never run out of those ideas. But for Penny's sake, I will try not to entertain such thoughts."

"Oh, I see. This was Mamá's idea!" He then had an idea of his own. "What do you say we pretend to get along? For Penny's sake. You know, when she's around. And then, when she isn't around, we don't have to pretend. It would make life easier."

Her stare wasn't to be reckoned with, and neither were her words. "You are what you are because you do what you do."

"True," Richard confessed, "but what of it? Is it a deal or isn't it?"

"I promised Penny I would try to be nice to you."

"Yes, but then you destroyed my mouse."

Ceese's eyes became dangerously narrow. "It is not my fault you do not call things what they are."

"And it isn't my fault you assume you know everything. It *was* a mouse!" He stopped himself, sighed. "It doesn't matter. I'll just get another one."

He shut the computer down, went for an ornate gold case he kept in a shirt pocket, and shook out a cigarette.

"How is it your hair looks as though it has been kissed by the sun when it is impossible for you or those like you to tolerate its rays?"

"I dye it," he said.

"Dye it?"

"Yes. Color it."

"Why?"

Richard stopped what he was doing and cocked a brow at her. "What difference does it make?"

"Exactly," Ceese replied. "What difference would it make? It is only hair. So why not keep it a more favorable color, so you don't appear so . . . pale?"

He resented her remark, she could tell, and while it wasn't her intention, she couldn't help but be pleased. But then he gave her a look, as if to say, *"Who are you to critique?"* And then he backed the look up with words. "Perhaps you shouldn't be so critical of other people. After all, *you* showed up in Peter the goatherder's rags."

"Perhaps you would rather I had shown up wearing nothing at all?"

"I would rather you hadn't shown up at all. But, here you are." He held out the cigarette case. "Care for a smoke?"

She didn't respond, and he didn't push. "Suit yourself," he said, and reached for the elaborate lighter he'd purchased while he and Mamá were on vacation. The souvenir, with its gulls and sailboats etched on it, brought back fond memories and helped calm him.

He prepared to light the cigarette.

"I wouldn't," Ceese said.

He glared at her. "Oh, so you don't condone smoking either. Well, I don't need a lecture about it from you. I can't die, so I hardly see the point of giving up the habit . . . or listening to you go on about it." An idea came to him. "It's very relaxing. Are you sure you don't want to try it?"

Ceese just stared.

"It isn't like it's going to hurt you," he added.

"I don't fear being hurt by it, but I—"

"Well, I can't force you," he replied, placed the cigarette between his lips, flicked the lighter's spur with his thumb.

The flame sparked, then shot up, and the wolf took charge. The lighter was forcefully batted away, sent flying across the room. Ceese then took Richard up, threw him to the floor and pinned him there, holding his arms over his head and getting very close to the vein she'd gotten so close to in her earlier attack. Only Mamá wasn't there to stop her this time.

"I am really growing tired of this," Richard said, trying to move but not being able to.

She was suddenly distracted. The lighter, still lit, had landed on one of his precious Italian rugs. As they both stared, it burst into flames.

Her distraction made her weaken her hold for an instant, and he took advantage, throwing her off. She hit the wall hard, and Richard ran to save what was now burning.

He stomped around and managed to put the flames out before it was ruined, then turned back to her. She was standing, but using the wall for support and holding her head.

"Have you no respect for other people's things?" Richard spat at her. But then he saw her pained expression, the way she was holding her head—had he hurt her? Did he really care?

For Mamá's sake, he had to care. "I'm sorry," he said, approaching slowly, ignoring that she began to look more menacing than hurt. "Please, let me help you. I-I just overreacted."

He took a few steps more, and saw anguish now, far more than before.

Ceese slid further down the wall. The wolf was getting jealous, and she was weak from the struggle, losing control. "Don't come any closer," she warned.

"Just let me help you. I feel badly."

"You-You don't understand. The wolf will kill you."

"Balderdash," Richard countered. "Let the wolf try!"

It was the last time he would throw out such a challenge. Perhaps the wolf couldn't kill him, but it could certainly inflict great pain. He found this out, as many others had, when she transformed before his very eyes and lunged at him. A claw tore through his right shoulder and raked his back just as he turned. And then the wolf was on him.

He was forced to his knees by the weight of it, but somehow managed to reach behind and grab the animal by the scruff of its neck. With great effort, he pulled it off and threw it back a few feet, giving him just enough time to scramble across the room. Without hesitation he pulled the two great doors leading into the hall open and then, just as quickly, pulled them shut behind him.

Breathing heavy and holding on for all he was worth, he waited. The doors shook when something hit hard, but otherwise held. Without shifting his weight on the doors, he took firm hold of both doorknobs, expecting them to start turning.

Then, he remembered. *Wolves don't have hands. They can't open doors.*

At the instant he had this epiphany, Marissa came around the corner. She turned white at the sight of her lord's back and shoulder. And then the massive parlor doors shook again, and she shrieked.

Richard responded by turning abruptly to face her, still pressing his shoulder against the door. He hadn't wanted her to see his back, hadn't wanted to explain.

"I-I have prepared our guest a room," the timid maid said, sounding as uncertain as she looked.

Richard brought his arms in front of him now, tried not let his pain show. But the scratches were deep, and hurt like hell. "Yes, well, I'll tell her if I see her."

"Shall I . . . Shall I get something for your back?"

"No. It's nothing, really."

But Marissa was still struggling with what she'd seen, Richard could tell. The poor maid's mind was working overtime.

"Has Xavier gone mad?" she finally spit out.

"No," Richard said at once. He didn't particularly like the dog, but he knew he'd have to condone putting the animal down for such an attack. Even so, he couldn't tell her Ceese was responsible. She might tell Mamá . . . *and I'm already in enough trouble with her over this blasted werewolf.*

He didn't care for hypnotizing humans, because it always made him feel like he was intruding. Now, it was his only option. "Marissa," he said. "You will not remember any of this."

"But your back—the scratches—"

"None of it," he said, and he saw her face finally slacken.

When convinced the hypnosis had worked, he said, "Now, why don't you turn in for the evening?"

"Yes, m'lord," she said. "Ah . . . Miss Penelope thought I should show our guest to her quarters."

Things had quieted in the room behind the doors. Perhaps Ceese was human again. But what if she weren't? "Perhaps we should just let our guest pass the evening in the parlor," Richard said. "She seems to have taken a liking to its—spaciousness."

Another blow to the door, and Marissa had little trouble agreeing. "Yes, m'lord," she said, then curtsied and ran.

ð ð ð

After she returned to human form, Ceese pulled herself to a standing position. Richard was gone, so he must have gotten away before the wolf killed him. She wasn't sure how she felt about this. If he were gone, he wouldn't be in the way. On the other hand . . .

She pushed up, saw the computer, the remnants of the mouse, and had an idea.

CHAPTER 9

Breakfast the next morning had Richard at his wit's end. Mamá had come on her own accord, still walking as though she'd never been in a wheelchair. Ceese, however, was nowhere to be seen. He regretted not being able to feel better about her absence, but as in all the good murder mysteries he'd ever wasted his time on, her not being there made him look guilty. And he knew he couldn't come up with a good enough lie if pressed.

But Ceese ended the suspense by showing up moments later, and actually took a seat at the table. This didn't lighten his mood, though. Ceese would make him look bad, he just knew it. And so he sat and waited for the inevitable: to disappoint Mamá once again.

"Good morning, Ceese, did you sleep well?" Mamá began. "I went to the room I had Marissa prepare for you, but you weren't there. Did you and Richard stay up late talking? He has such exciting stories. You know, he actually was hit by a train once."

Richard tried not to look concerned about what Ceese might say. But if Mamá learned the truth—that her guest had spent the evening in the parlor as a wolf because he had angered her to the point of transforming—she would be devastated.

"I didn't sleep at all," Ceese announced, seeming glum at first, then brightening. "I stayed up all the night—and toyed with that contraption Richard calls a computer. He was kind enough to show it to me and, I must say, it is quite the fascination with all of its little pieces and parts. Did you know it actually has its own mouse? Or at least, Richard likes to call it a mouse. Although it really isn't one."

If only she would read my mind right now, he thought.

Mamá's delight was instantaneous. "Did you hear that, Richard? Ceese has already learned how to work the computer."

"Yes," he replied, tight-lipped. "I heard."

Ceese looked at him. "I do so hope I didn't harm it. I know how important it is to you. But after you . . . left, I just couldn't resist. I had to tinker with it."

"She tinkered with it, Richard," Mamá repeated. "That's wonderful that she's showing such interest in modern things, isn't it?"

But Richard knew what Ceese was capable of, and he couldn't help but wonder what further damage she'd done. Besides, she was being far too flippant.

"Oh," Ceese continued, "and I particularly like the little voice which speaks every now and again, saying 'You've got mail—'"

Richard's head shot up and he pushed his chair back almost hard enough to make it topple over. "What?" *My shipments.* "If you . . . I will—"

Words failed him, and he ran for the parlor. Once there, he threw open the doors and went to the computer. But it was on and working fine. In fact, the mouse had been cleverly, if crudely, reconstructed with what appeared to be clear tape. He moved it about to test it, and it actually worked.

He heard a noise from over his shoulder, saw that Ceese and Mamá had come in behind him. He held the mouse up, shook it about. "How?" he said, shaking it some more, showing it to them, "how did you do this? How did you ever get it all back together? It must've taken you all night."

"I always take care of what I am responsible for destroying . . . or burning," she added, with a small glance at the once-fine Italian rug. He followed her gaze. It was half the original size. She had cut away the scorched area. Yet it was in relatively good shape, considering.

He was speechless, but Mamá wasn't. In spite of Ceese's attempts to make things right, the room was still in shambles.

She looked at Richard. "Is this your idea of getting along?"

85

"The wolf did it," Ceese confessed, her head hanging low.

Richard jumped in. "It isn't her fault. I angered her. She couldn't help herself."

He said it because he thought coming to Ceese's defense might soothe the anger he saw on Mamá's face—might make her forget what she was looking at.

But the disappointment remained on her face. And now, Ceese was furious, too.

"Is that what you think?" she said, those strange eyes blazing. "That I cannot help myself? That anger can transform me? That *you* can transform me? You might have angered the wolf, but *I* let it out. I control it! Only I! And I will take care of any damage I caused!

Richard did a quick scan of the rest of the carnage. Tables were broken, lamps shattered, chair cushions ripped and torn. And then he studied the computer's mouse. "I'm quite certain I don't have that much tape."

Ceese narrowed her eyes again, as she'd done the night before, drawing firm words from Mamá: "There will be no more disagreements! I won't have the two of you tearing the castle apart . . . not while I'm around to stop it." Mamá looked at Richard. "Getting along, indeed. Just look at this mess."

"You're right," Richard said, fully chastised. "I'll find Marissa and—"

"No." Mamá drew a deep breath. "It's just a room. And it does seem you two have made some progress. Just leave it for now. It will be fine."

Something wasn't right about her words, the way she was acting. "No," Richard insisted, "I'll take care of it, before I go to my basement I'll—"

Mamá took hold of his arm this time. "It's all right, Richard. Besides, I need to talk to you . . . before you turn in. I'll be in my room." She then turned and left. This time, her steps were shorter, less certain than before.

Richard turned to Ceese. "You know something, don't you?"

"I know many somethings," she said. "I know Penny wants to

talk to you and not me. Perhaps she wants to run you out, for all the trouble you are."

Her conceit wore through his good intentions. "You were the one who destroyed the parlor," he snapped, "not me. You said it yourself."

Ceese gave him a self-satisfied look. "I think you should go talk to Penny now . . . before you get yourself into more trouble."

With a sneer, he left.

CHAPTER 10

What does this werewolf know about anything, anyway? Richard thought as he entered and saw Mamá sitting on the edge of her bed. She looked more than just tired now. She looked weary, as if she'd been walking for a long time, not just the fifty or so steps to her room.

She patted the spot beside her. "Richard, sit down."

He settled next to her, his thoughts going in several different directions. What was she going to say? Was she going to run him out, like Ceese had inferred a moment ago? Or would *she* leave because he couldn't get along with her werewolf friend? From Mamá's tone, her look—either option was possible.

"Perhaps I've waited to long to say this."

Yes, came Richard's horrified thought. *She's going to banish me from the castle . . . all because of* — "I'm sorry," he sputtered. "I-I should have been more accepting, I should have— been nicer. Just don't push me away. Please, I couldn't bear it."

On top of looking tired, Mamá now looked confused as she took one of his hands in hers. "Dear, dear Richard. It isn't you. Where would you get such an idea?"

"I just thought— With the way I've been acting—"

"It's me, Richard. I'm sick."

His head jerked up. "Well, then, we'll call a doctor. We'll call Ceese." He actually started to get up, but she gently pulled him back down by the hand she was holding.

"Ceese can't help me."

The words hit him hard, as hard as the slashes Ceese's wolf-form had given him the night before. "What are you saying? Of course she can help you. She has already!" With his free hand, he motioned toward her wheelchair, now folded and tucked into a nook, then back at her. "Look at you. You're walking. You're as healthy as I've ever seen you—"

"Richard, I said Ceese can't help me, and I meant it. I have cancer."

Another slash, this one lower, deeper. He was a doctor— of sorts. At least, his online degrees said so. He knew about cancer, knew one could die from it. Still didn't accept it. "I don't believe you," he whispered. "You're just joking." Yes, it was a joke. A very bad one too. *She's lying. She has to be. And now, she'll tell me why.*

"It's not a joke, Richard, and Ceese can't help me with it."

"Why not? She's very accommodating when it comes to you."

Mamá reached up and stroked his cheek. "Richard, I need you to accept this and . . . I need you to promise me something."

"No," he said, turning away. "I won't listen, and I won't promise anything. You're not dying, so I won't humor you." He was angry, hurt, confused—emotions he thought had been killed forever by the curse. They were faint, but there.

After a few seconds he realized Mamá hadn't rebutted his words, so he turned back to face her. Her eyes held tears.

"Don't make this harder than it is, Richard," she said in a desperate whisper. "I've put off telling you to try and make it easier."

"Easier? You're the only one in this world who understands me, and you . . ." He couldn't finish.

"You've got Ceese now."

"What? . . . You didn't . . . you haven't . . . you brought her here for *me*?"

"Not exactly, but . . . in a way."

Another gray area. He hated gray areas. "Either you brought her here for me or you didn't. Which is it?"

"You have to take care of her when I'm gone."

"Oh, well, now I *know* you're joking. No sane person would suggest I could do what you're—"

But that was exactly what she was asking. "Why would you put this on me? You tell me you're dying, and then you ask me to look after this werewolf. This menace! Why? She can take care of herself. And besides, she can't stand me. She tried to kill me last night."

Mamá sighed. "Oh, Richard . . . she can't kill you any more than you can kill her. You know that."

He wanted to tell her about the scratches on his shoulder and back, wanted to tell her they hadn't healed as they should have. He wanted to tell her, but he didn't. Besides, he'd never been attacked by a werewolf before. Perhaps wounds such as those just healed slower. Still, though, he wanted Mamá to understand that he couldn't possibly do what she was asking.

"I . . . I would be lying if I said I wanted to care for her. I don't. But let's say I accepted the responsibility. It wouldn't matter. She doesn't want to be with me. She said it herself last night. Said the wolf hates me."

"But the wolf isn't her," Mamá said, "any more than the vampire is you. She has separated herself from it, just as you separated yourself from what *you've* been cursed with. She seeks only what you seek: to be free. To be in control of her destiny."

He knew what she meant. He had control, to a degree. But as far as wanting to control his future . . . become human again. Perhaps at one time he wanted this, but no more. "It's more about what *you* want," he said.

"You know that isn't the truth, Richard. But I understand if you can't bring yourself to say it."

She was right. He couldn't say it, or think it, or feel it. Not anymore, not the way he could before he was cursed. "Don't burden me with her, Mamá," he begged. "Please. Don't force me to make a commitment I can't keep. I wouldn't be able to live with the guilt when . . . you're gone."

He felt her hand on his arm. "She found me before breakfast and told me how she destroyed your computer's mouse last night . . . because you told her a mouse is what it was. Don't you see? There's too much out there she doesn't understand. Someone must help her. I would do it myself, but I . . . I don't have that much time left. You must!"

"How . . . much time do you have left?" His words felt as heavy as weights, his mood as dark as the darkest night.

"A month, perhaps a bit more."

Richard laid his head into his hands, ignoring the pain from the scratches on his back. He wasn't supposed to be able to feel the way he was feeling now. And then, in an instant, he didn't anymore.

He sat up. "I won't be her teacher. I won't!"

Mamá sighed. "I'm not asking you to be her teacher, or her guardian. Just help her get used to this world. It's so strange to her. And then, help her do what she came to do. . . . help her free herself from her curse. I know you can."

"No, I can't!" Richard shouted, fighting defiant tears . . . tears his curse would not allow to fall. "It didn't work for me. Or did you forget? *You* were the only one it helped, and you're the only one who knows why!"

Tears welled up in Mamá's own eyes at the bitterness in his words.

"I'm sorry," he said, "It's just I don't want to go through it again. You have to understand."

"It will work for you this time, Richard. I'm certain of it."

But he didn't want to talk about it anymore. "When did you learn of this cancer? It-It just seems so unbelievable."

"When we went to the coast," she said. "I went to see a doctor, a specialist, while you were sleeping."

Richard remembered the lighter from last night in the parlor, the one Ceese had batted away. He had purchased it at a small shop that stayed open late, had stayed in an accommodating cave during the day while Mamá supposedly visited with friends.

Richard's look changed. When he spoke again, it was a whisper. "Let me help you. You know I can. You can stay with me forever, just like we planned before—"

"No," she said at once. "It isn't what I want now."

"Why not?" he asked, determined to change her mind. "We could be together always. We had such dreams. Why do you want to give all that up?"

"No! I love *you*, Richard. I have always loved *you*. But this is what *I* want now. Please, try to understand. Your time will come.

Besides, I'm old. You can't make me younger. I'd be a burden to you, forever."

"You will never be a burden to me." He was feeling again . . . and this time, he held onto it as long as he could.

"I can't," she said, shaking her head. "I just can't."

He stiffened beside her. "What you say makes no sense. I should take you right here, right now!"

He grabbed her hand. She pulled it away. "I wouldn't allow it, Richard."

"You think you could stop me?" His eyes began to change, as she had seen them do many times before.

"Vampire!" she called out. "Don't think I'm unprepared. I have my cross and my garlic with me."

The vampire succumbed to the threat, but it took Richard more than a moment to pull himself together. "I . . . I cannot tell you how I will miss you."

Reassured now that Richard was in control, she said, "Think of it this way. I am going on to wait for you, in a place where we will one day meet again."

He barely got his eyebrow up before she added, "You will join me one day. You'll see."

"Mamá, in case you've forgotten, I'm cursed. And I can barely speak of the place where I know you're headed without—" The pain stopped him, and he grasped his temples.

"Heaven," she said for him. "The place is called Heaven."

"Yes," he managed, looking grim. "I know. But please don't say it again or I'll undoubtedly suffer for the rest of the day. And I need to rest. I should already be in the basement."

"Oh, bother," she told him. "I know you're strong. Now, recite John 3:16 for me."

"Mamá, please—"

"It will do your soul good."

She said this as if he had one, or at least, one he could call his own. But she had just told him she was dying, refused to accept staying with him. Why should he do anything like this? But then, he knew why. Because this was Mamá, and she was dying and he would do almost anything for her.

Mamá saw the hard time he was having, but wouldn't back down. "Richard, your father was a minister, was he not? A good man. A man you wanted to be like. And if not for the curse, you would have been. If not for me, do it for him."

With much reluctance, he conceded, drawing deep and fighting what he'd been cursed with. Not knowing the internal struggle he faced each time he recited, one would have thought he was cursing.

"For *God*," he spat out with disgust. "So loved the world," he continued spewing, looking at her sideways with a hate-filled glare. "That he gave his only begotten Son—" He grabbed his head now, with both hands. "*Pleeease*, I cannot—"

"Yes you can, Richard," Mamá prodded. "Finish it. Don't let the vampire win."

And so he dug deeper. His brow furrowed, his fist clenched. "That whosoever believeth in *Him* . . ." He was agonizing now, every muscle in his body tensing as he pushed on, for her sake. "Shall not *perish*—" He'd said "perish" very loud, as he always did, to help relieve some of the pressure of reciting. "— but have everlasting life."

He slumped over on the bed, away from her, still holding his head.

"And not on earth, Richard, but in Heaven."

"Yes," he moaned. "But please don't speak of— that place again, or my head will explode."

She ignored his complaining. "And you believe, don't you, Richard?"

"*Yesss*," he eventually hissed, despite the agonizing pressure not to say anything—and knowing it was a lie.

He looked at Mamá with the most extreme hatred when he said it too, but she just smiled.

"I knew you did believe it. And I believe your father would be proud."

She was delusional if she thought the part about his father would help. It never helped him. He remembered so little about the man. But he pretended to find comfort in the statement, again, for her sake.

She patted his hand, then leaned to take something from her bedside table: an envelope holding a wallet-sized picture and a note. Richard tried to look at the photo when she handed it to him. The ordeal of reciting always left his vision blurred, his head aching. Once he was able to focus, he studied the picture. The young woman in the photo had Mamá's eyes: warm, caring, determined and blue, And her hair was auburn, as Mamá's used to be. Her clothing was modern, but she resembled Mamá so much . . . and the resemblance reminded Richard of what he didn't want to remember about himself: who he was, and where he came from. He forced the memory away, hating who he could never be again.

Occasionally, in his mind's eye, he could see his father. But those occasions were so rare, he now questioned the accuracy of those memories. And accuracy was important, because he didn't want to look anything like his father, a man he'd once strongly resembled before the surgeries: a lift here, a tuck there. He wanted to distance himself from anything and everything he knew before the curse.

"No," he said aloud, to get the thoughts out of his mind.

"No, what?" Mamá asked.

"I meant . . ." He tried to deflect having to tell her what he'd really been thinking about, and pointed at the photograph. "No ring on her finger? I'm surprised she's not married." He forced a smile. "It's not hard to tell who she's related to."

"You really think so?" Mamá said, looking over his shoulder and smiling.

"She looks like you."

"You mean, like I *used* to look," she said.

"It's more than that. I mean, she *seems* to be like you."

"It's a picture, Richard. How can you tell anything like—?"

"Her eyes. They're caring, sensitive, passionate . . . just like yours."

"Well, it's good you have such strong feelings," Mamá said, "because I want you and Ceese to go see her. I told the woman I'm her grandmother."

Richard looked suspicious. "But you can't be. Perhaps her great-great, great—"

She laughed. "All right, you can stop there. But to avoid all those *greats*, I thought it simpler just to say she's my granddaughter. You see, we *are* related. I found this out when I was researching my family on the Internet. I was hoping to find out how my daughter's children—"

Richard was stunned. "You had children? You were married?"

She glanced away. "For a few years. A short time before I met you, a year after Ceese disappeared. I loved George very much, and grieved horribly when he died—"

"*George?*"

She nodded. "Yes. And what is with you and names lately? First Ceese, now George."

"I'm sorry. You just caught me off-guard. Married? I just assumed you would have told me something like this before now."

"Yes, well, George is why I could never be with you. It just wouldn't have been right—even if . . . even if you could have."

Richard gave an understanding nod, then asked, "And your child? What of her? What did you learn in your researching?"

A sad smile crossed Mamá's face. "She did all right."

"And you want me to remember *my* family," he said with a sad shake of his head. "Look what learning about your own family is doing to you."

"Well, it isn't all gloom. About a year ago, right after you gave me the computer as a gift, I found Cassie. It was the strangest luck. She was adopted, you see. She only had a little information on her mother, but it was enough for me to be sure we're related." She gave him a small smile. "But of course I couldn't tell her who I really am. Let's just say she's also convinced I'm her grandmother."

"But you're not."

She shrugged. "But we *are* related. You said yourself, we look alike. And my research indicates it as well. I just haven't been able to nail down exactly how. Still, I was able to convince Cassie." She paused, then indicated the envelope that had held the photo. "I want you and Ceese to go see her. Everything you need is there in the letter. Her address, phone number—even her e-mail address, and I know you'll like that."

95

"Why should I go see her? Because you think you're related?" It still made no sense to him

Mamá's eyes brightened. "No, Richard. Not that at all. She believes! She's been researching vampires and werewolves. Seems she's always been interested in . . . 'the bizarre,' she calls it. She believes vampires and werewolves exist, and she wants to help them."

Richard sighed. "I don't know, Mamá. I'm growing weary of chasing after this belief of yours. And . . . if you weren't here, why would I want to continue?"

"But that should be the very reason why you *do* continue. So you can be with me again. And what if Cassie can discover a way . . . an *easier* way? And Ceese can help you if you let her." She patted his hand. "It's too bad you aren't able to remember more about your family. Ceese seems to draw such strength at times from what she remembers."

"I had a father," he told her, his face a blank. "And I struggle to remember anything about him. And for all the good remembering my family would do me now. They're all dead."

"Well, memories stand for something."

Richard gave a harsh laugh. "A waste of precious time."

"Well, I would hope you wouldn't forget *me*."

He looked up at her, regretted his words. "I will never forget you. Ever!"

Mamá squeezed his hand tighter. "Nor I you, Richard." Then all at once, she looked weary again. "I must rest now. We can talk more later. But I do have your promise, don't I? You'll find Cassie, and take Ceese with you when I'm gone?"

He allowed his head to fall forward once, then twice, kissed her hand lightly, then left to head for his basement, tired and now as depressed as he'd ever been in his long life.

※ ※ ※

Ceese saw him come out of Penny's room just in time to duck back around the corner, and waited to follow, keeping her distance.

The door Richard disappeared behind was near the kitchen, at the end of a long hallway.

She crossed her arms, thinking. There was nothing about his walk to suggest he was upset, but his gait didn't seem nearly as arrogant as before. Perhaps Mamá, as he called her, *had* banished him. But since he had forbidden her from sensing his thoughts, she would have to wait and watch to find out.

But if Penny *had* banished him, why wasn't he leaving?

Then she remembered the sun. Perhaps he was just waiting for nightfall.

"It is a wonder," she said quietly, shaking her head, ". . . a wonder Penny has tolerated you as long as she has."

She left then, needing to find a place to rest as well. Getting along with Richard was going to require a lot of energy, and she was tired after the long night and the morning that followed.

CHAPTER 11

It was dark, and the moon was up. Richard hadn't had any fresh blood in over twenty-four hours. He didn't need it to survive—the steady supply in his refrigerator assured that. But often, fresh blood was the only thing capable of satisfying his hunger. Otherwise he was overwhelmed by the urge to bite another, to curse another. Normal hunger pangs couldn't compare. That's why Peter Drummond had been a temptation to him.

He started in the pasture and made his way through the tall grasses. A couple of nights ago he'd taken down a deer, and hoped to find another tonight. He sniffed at the night air, started off, but then stumbled, landing on his hands and knees.

He turned while getting up, to see what the obstacle had been, discovered a goat. Why hadn't he smelled it? But it was dead, and any blood had long since soaked into the ground.

He checked to see if he could tell whose brand or mark was on it, and cursed. It belonged to Peter Drummond!

"Wonderful," Richard moaned, turning loose of the mutilated body and setting out to find the culprit—or rather, Ceese. She couldn't be so careless, not if she was going to stay for any length of time. *But I won't make a habit out of telling her these things,* he vowed. *She has to be more responsible.* At least for his sake, and maybe hers as well.

He followed a scent he picked up, headed for the woods. Not long after, he heard someone fire a gun, then a noise off to his left; a scurrying-about in the low brush up ahead near where the woods started. No voices followed, no footsteps either, so he approached with caution.

The wolf lay on its side, its breathing labored. Blood had

matted its guard hairs—the coarse hair covering the softer hair beneath—and the wound still poured blood from what appeared to be a bullet wound.

Richard struggled with the thoughts running through his mind. It was Ceese, it had to be. There were no other wolves around; Peter had been right when he said this. And the imbecile was probably the one who shot her. Likely, the goatherder had gotten a gun, as Richard suggested in the parlor. Or perhaps already had one. And now, Ceese was hurt, possibly dying.

Then Richard remembered something else. Hearing the front door open, then close the day Peter had come by and insisted he could show himself out. But the noises happened *after* he and Mamá finished their conversation in the parlor. Had he heard when Richard muttered about the importance of a silver bullet? If he had, and the bullet was silver, then death would follow.

What if she did die? How would he explain? If he told Mamá that Peter shot her, then Mamá would blame him for all the talk about guns. And if he said nothing, Mamá would surely suspect he'd had something to do with it. Her grief might take her away sooner. Begrudgingly, he decided to see if he could do anything for Ceese.

He drew nearer, and the wolf remained still. Maybe she was already dead. He put a hand out to examine the wound near its shoulder, but the wolf jerked its head up at once and snapped, catching and nipping the side of his hand.

"It wasn't my fault," he said drawing back. "I didn't know the fool would actually get a gun. Just let me just see if I can help."

He made another effort to get closer. He heard the low growl, saw the fangs bared, and became hostile himself. "Then die for all I care!"

"He can hardly help it," a voice from behind said. "He doesn't understand a word you are saying or what your intentions are."

Richard turned. Ceese was moving toward him, then past him to where the wolf lay. She settled next to it, rubbed its head, made noises it seemed to understand; it made noises back. Not once did it try to bite her.

"How touching," Richard sneered, forgetting his hand for the moment as it healed.

"His name is Long Tail," she said. "Well, not really. But I would have to turn into the wolf to tell you exactly what we call him."

"Long Tail works for me," Richard said quickly, getting the impression she just might do what she suggested if he didn't discourage her. And he didn't need any more scratches. "Is he dying?"

She measured him with her eyes. "Do you really care, or are you just hungry?"

"Does it matter?"

"I just like to know what I'm dealing with." She was speaking truthfully, he could tell. She knew much of her curse, but wanted to know more about his.

His smile was smug. "You're dealing with a vampire. One who is . . . well, hungry."

"So you don't care about Long Tail."

"Let me help clear things up. I'm hungry, but I'm also concerned, worried that you might not let me take him before he dies. And if you don't, the blood will not be nearly as—palatable. Do you understand what you're dealing with now? Are we all on board?"

"You don't mince words, do you?"

"Not when it comes to blood." Even as he spoke, he fought his bloodlust so he wouldn't bound right over to Long Tail and face Ceese's wrath.

As if he'd heard Richard's thoughts, Long Tail whimpered, and Ceese stroked his fur. "He might make it," she said. "He's strong. But it won't matter. The pack will kill him if he tries to return to them. He doesn't understand the . . . the hierarchy. He thinks only of himself. The others know this, and they will not welcome him back if he is injured."

"Nice bunch."

"*Pack*," Ceese corrected. "Nice pack. And it's survival of the fittest. The weak don't survive, only the strong."

"I think there's a song in there somewhere," Richard quipped. "But what of it? Does he know they'll kill him?"

Ceese nodded. "But he would rather die with the pack than to die alone. Wolves need each other." She bit her lip and looked away. "They cannot survive alone."

But you can, can't you? he thought, seeing a difference he'd not seen until now. *You can survive alone, hunt alone . . . cry alone?* Was there moisture in those eyes? She looked down before he could really tell, and he glanced down at his hand. The bite mark was just a scratch now. And, unlike the ones Ceese had given him the night before, this one had almost healed. He said, "All I know is, wolves are very aggressive."

"You should never approach any injured animal," Ceese said, as though everyone should know this.

"I . . . I thought it was you." He hoped she wouldn't push him to reveal his true motive.

"I would have reacted the same way Long Tail did, had it been me instead of him."

"Oh, well, there's gratitude for you," he said, continuing the smug-fest, "I'll try to keep that in mind the next time I try to save your life."

She nearly choked. "Save my life! You were just worried about what Penny would think if you didn't try."

He tried to avoid looking as though he'd been caught. "Nevertheless—"

"Nevertheless, nothing. *You* told Peter Drummond to get a gun."

He shrugged. "What of it? Many people deal with wolves that way."

"*Big* guns, *accurate* guns," Ceese recited, enunciating every word just as he had in the parlor with Peter.

"All right, fine. I said it! But Mamá was the one who let on about a wolf in the first place. And you were eavesdropping. Quite a nasty little habit."

"I just pay attention," she said, not at all liking the way he seemed to have turned the tables on her.

"Well, I'm sorry I'm not able to talk to animals the way you seem to be able to. I'm no Dr. Doolittle."

Ceese's face showed her confusion, and he told her a bit about

101

the man who claimed he could converse with other living creatures. "Or something along those lines." he added with a wave of his hand.

"No human can talk to animals," Ceese replied. "That's absurd."

"It's fiction. A story someone makes up to entertain."

Ceese considered this. "Like a lie?"

His sigh was pained. "No. A lie is when you make something up to deceive or hurt someone . . . or when you take the truth and change things around—" He struggled, couldn't come up with anything better. "All right," he finally said. "Yes, a story is the same thing as a lie."

He pointed to the wolf. "Anyway, what about Long Tail? He doesn't look well. Perhaps you could go back with him, to the pack. Perhaps you could convince the others to give him another chance."

The idea had come to him in an instant, and seemed right. While he might lose a meal, he might also get rid of a werewolf. Perhaps if she went back with Long Tail, she would decide to stay with the pack. If she did, he wouldn't have to worry about the responsibility Mamá was trying to force upon him.

Ceese looked off. "Zade wouldn't allow it."

The way she had spoken, she knew this person, and respected him. "Zade?"

"He leads the pack," she said. "Every challenge, he has won. He has led for many moons."

Richard detected something. But was it animosity, or affection? He couldn't tell. Curiosity ruled, though, so questions followed. "Do you fear him? Or do you want to lead, like he does?"

She just stared at him, and he wondered if he'd gone too far, wondered if she might transform right there in front of him.

"Zade is a wolf. I am not. I am not concerned with leading or helping to lead."

Her tone wasn't angry, and he decided to push. "But if he wasn't a wolf . . . or perhaps if you *were* one, and were to go back—"

Her look shut him down.

"Well, I don't suppose it matters," he said. "What about Long Tail? What should we do about him?"

"I think we should put Long Tail out of his misery. The pack is going to kill him anyway. He shouldn't have to suffer until then."

Richard tried not to appear too eager. "I could help out there."

Ceese nodded. "Just leave what's left for me."

The order took Richard aback. "You would eat your own kind?"

"The wolf isn't 'my kind.' I am what I am, and they are what they are."

And Zade is what he is, Richard thought, certain there was more to this Zade than what Ceese was telling him. And though he didn't verbalize his thought, Ceese stared hard.

"What?" Richard challenged her.

"Nothing."

She seemed to get the message, and Richard might have pursued the matter, but he was too hungry to care. He did question why she was leaving, though. After all, she had expressed an interest in eating as well.

She stopped walking but didn't turn around. "I'm going to warn the others. They'll send out scouts, try to find Long Tail. I don't want them to meet with the same fate."

"Why would you care? If you're not one of them, I mean."

Still without turning, she said, "Long Tail brought this on himself. The others didn't. I'll tell them Long Tail is gone, and there is danger for them here. I'll be back before the moon passes from here to here." She pointed at the night sky as she spoke.

"Ah, I don't suppose you could be more specific?" he said, not understanding.

The only thing she added was the word, "Soon" before moving into the darkness.

He heard howls as he gorged, some close, others not so close. And he surmised Ceese was doing just as she said she would. He was surprised he didn't hear more gunshots, but then decided

Peter must be asleep, or otherwise preoccupied . . . celebrating perhaps, because he thought he'd killed the wolf he believed was stalking his herd. Of course, if the goatherder were paying attention, the howling now would tell him otherwise.

❧ ❧ ❧

Ceese was gone for about an hour, but since Richard hadn't looked at his watch when she left, he had no real way to judge exactly. He did pay attention to what time it was when she returned, however. Once she got started, it took her less than ten minutes to finish off Long Tail.

She saw him checking his watch. "What is that? And why do you keep staring at it?"

Mamá was right, Richard thought in wonderment. *Ceese really doesn't know about modern life.* "It's a watch. It helps one keep track of time."

"Like a clock?"

Richard cocked a brow. "Yes, like a clock."

"Why not just use the stars, the moon?"

"Because I don't know how to judge time that way. Besides, it isn't possible to take the stars and the moon with you everywhere you go. And how would one tell time during the day?"

"Well, what of it? Is the passing of time really so important? There's day and there's night. When hunger comes, one eats. When one is tired, one sleeps. When one hurts, time eases the pain—sometimes." She looked confused for a moment, then noticed his interested stare. "It was what my mother said when my father died."

She turned away, as if to hide what it was she was feeling, or rather, not feeling. Ceese wasn't capable of the kind of emotions she knew before she was cursed. She could pull up hazy memories of them. But what it was like to love was one thing. Feeling love was another. From what she had learned about vampires, she knew Richard's curse worked along those lines as well. His response about not caring for Long Tail was evidence of that. Ceese felt bad about her mother's words when she remembered

104

them, but only because she couldn't feel worse about her father's death. *When there is no pain,* she thought, miserable, *what is there for time to ease?*

Richard couldn't hear her thoughts, but suspected what she was struggling with. He took a step toward her and spoke to her back. "It's no wonder we are what we are."

She whirled around to face him. "It's no wonder *you* are what *you* are! No wonder you would count yourself a casualty of your curse. Well, I'm *not* a casualty. Perhaps I can't presently feel love as I used to. But I can still *feel*."

"I'm sorry," he said, and rushed to change the subject. "Back to the watch. Would you like to understand how it works?"

Her response wasn't enthusiastic, but he would take what he could get. After all, she had managed dinner for the both of them. He owed her something.

They found a nearby tree and sat, leaning against it.

"So," he said after a moment, "you say you know what a clock is?"

She nodded. "We couldn't afford one of our own, but Father had a timepiece he kept in his pocket."

Richard nodded, then directed Ceese's attention to his watch. "These are called hands," he explained, and added quickly, "but that's just what they're called, not actually what they are. Like the mouse-that-wasn't."

She nodded, but didn't smile.

"The long hand moves with each minute, and the short one moves with each hour."

"And what are hours and minutes?" she said. "I cannot recall."

"Can you count?"

"Do you think me uneducated?" she snapped in reply.

"Don't be so defensive. Just count until I tell you not to."

She did as he asked, and when she got to sixty, he told her to stop. "There. Sixty seconds is one minute. And an hour is when you count to sixty, sixty times."

"How boring," Ceese mused. "And why would anyone want to waste their time?"

"Exactly," Richard said. "So we have watches."

"So you can watch them?"

"Well, yes, but only occasionally . . . when you need to know the time."

All at once, she jumped to her feet and pulled Richard up and along by a hand, led him into a clearing and pointed toward the brilliant night sky.

"Look there," she said. "The Big Dipper."

It was a clear night, and the stars were bright and numerous. He worked hard to find the Big Dipper but her pointing had helped. "Yes, I see it."

"Now look down—that star there." Again she was pointing.

"The North Star," Richard verified.

"Yes. Now, imagine a line from the North Star up through those two stars of the Big Dipper—the two just above the North Star. The North Star is the center. And the North Star, along with those other two stars, makes a pointer. Do you see?"

Richard nodded. "Yes, I see."

"But the pointer doesn't move in the direction of the hands on your watch. It moves the other way."

He was amazed! First by how much she'd learned from their talk, and second, by how much she already knew. "You learned this from a wolf?"

"As if a wolf can tell time," she said, amused. "No. My father showed me. . . . He fancied himself a sailor, but work kept him too busy to really . . ."

"What did he do? What kept him so busy?"

"He was—" The pain was sharp, but she pushed through it. "—a minister."

"You shouldn't do that," Richard said, not realizing he'd put his hand on her shoulder until she turned to stare at it.

"Does how I feel bother you?" she asked.

"No," he said, jerking his hand back and looking at it as if it had acted on its own accord. "I just thought you might fall. I-I didn't want to have to explain to Mamá how you might have hurt yourself . . ." It was borderline ridiculous as far as explanations went, so he just stopped. And how could he explain what

106

he didn't understand anyway—how he felt? "Back to this time thing. How do you tell time if there are clouds—if you use your father's method?"

"Does your watch always work?"

"No, but I usually just get a new battery or a new watch if it stops functioning."

"Then perhaps you should do one or the other. Your watch indicates it is sometime after three. The stars say it is much later."

Richard looked at his watch and realized she was right. He looked to the east; the sky wasn't as dark as it should have been. In an instant, he turned and took off, heading back to the place they'd just come from. There, he scavenged around until he found a good-sized limb.

"What are you doing?" Ceese asked, coming up behind him.

Richard talked as he stabbed at the ground. "I have to bury what's left of Long Tail."

"Why?"

"Because I've witnessed others being cursed by merely eating the meat of an animal a vampire has fed on. No animal I've ever taken has ever been found." He looked over at her. "Except for the one you did."

His scrutinizing look made her think. "But I don't feel any different, and I ate the meat."

"Yes, well, I'm fairly certain your soul has to be in good standing for the curse to take hold. And since our dilemma is just that . . ." He shrugged, then continued to dig.

"I want my soul back, Richard."

"And I suppose you could have it," Richard replied without thinking, "if you could but go to hell and get it."

He noticed the effect his words had, but not in time to take them back.

"I do so hate you!" she spat out, then darted off.

"Ceese," he called after her. "I didn't mean it the way it sounded."

But she was already gone.

He might have given chase, but he had to bury Long Tail. There wasn't much time left before daybreak. He returned to what he had to do, not noticing the presence just off to his left at first. When he finally realized he was being watched, he stopped to turn, hoping it might be Ceese returning. But then the figure stepped out of the shadows and directly in front of him.

This wasn't Ceese. He recognized the pants though. They were Peter Drummond's. But it wasn't Peter wearing them. And Peter would never be able to bulk up to this man's size. The pants were zipped but not snapped. *Just like Ceese wears hers,* he thought, *unless I tell her otherwise.*

"I dare say," he said, straightening slowly, "Peter Drummond will soon have to go around without clothes if this thievery continues."

The eyebrows were thick and dark; the eyes held the same golden hue of Ceese's, and hinted at the animal this man could become.

Richard followed the man's disgruntled gaze to the ground, and then it dawned on him.

"Oh, that's Long Tail," Richard said. "And you have a name?"

"Zade," he said, and looked back up at Richard.

"Zade," Richard repeated, keeping his voice casual. "Well, Zade, I haven't got much time to chat, though I wish I did. But, you see, the sun will be up soon. So, if you'll excuse me. . . ." He went back to pushing dirt around so it covered Long Tail completely, and considering what he had just learned. Zade was a werewolf, not just a wolf, and Ceese apparently didn't know it! Or if she did, she chose not to tell him.

Then he noticed, as he worked, the werewolf just standing there.

"You know, you could help," he threw out.

Zade instantly grabbed his stick and held tight. Richard tried to take it from him but couldn't.

"Get your own shovel," he said, but Zade remained silent.

Richard sighed. "I suppose you want something."

"Where go Ceese?" Zade asked, sounding very much the way Ceese sounded when she first showed up. And like Ceese, Richard saw this werewolf was anything but ignorant. There was knowledge in those eyes, though he didn't seem to have the ability to articulate it. Richard knew he needed to watch himself. But he also knew he needed to make a point, and quickly, since the sun had a schedule to keep.

"Well, Zade, it's clear English isn't your first language, so I'll try to put this in a way you can understand. I don't know 'Where go Ceese,' nor do I care."

Zade was quiet for a long moment, studying Richard, and went as far as to sniff at him at one point.

Richard took a step back. "That's quite enough of that."

Zade straightened, stared, and then made a noise. "Hmmph!"

"What do you mean, *hmmph*?" Richard grunted back.

"Say 'no care,'" Zade replied. "Say 'don't know where go Ceese.' Zade say do know, do care."

Richard regained control of his makeshift shovel and went back to covering Long Tail. As the last bit of dirt hit the grave, he muttered, "Do *not* care."

"Do, too," Zade replied, but when Richard turned back to him, he was gone.

"Do not!" he called out, and then he too left, grateful he had time to spare.

He found himself sprinting the last few yards back to the castle, then practically diving through the front doors, closing them at once behind him, frantic and yet relieved.

Zade was a werewolf . . . quite a revelation. And Ceese hadn't told him. There was definitely something there. He mulled it over as he headed to his coffin.

CHAPTER 12

Richard had a hard time catching up with Mamá, or with Ceese in the days following his discovery. When he did see the two, they were always together, often accompanied by Xavier, Richard's wolfhound. The dog hardly came to Richard anymore, and for the most part ignored his master. Richard might have been more bothered if he cared about the animal. But nurturing a pet, to Richard, was hardly worth the effort. Mamá was the one who insisted he have one, thinking it might help him appear less cold and distant to others. While he didn't mind being Xavier's alienation, he was upset about losing something else to this werewolf: first Mamá's attention, and now Xavier's.

To add insult to injury, Ceese broke her silence one afternoon to tell Richard the animal didn't like being called Xavier, or being domesticated. Richard had laughed at this. How could the dog know it was domesticated? Ceese informed him Xavier just didn't understand any other way. She also said she had taught Xavier the difference, and he'd learned quickly.

And there it was. Richard had lost his dog and Mamá, all in the same period of time.

And then, one bright morning, he had a reason to be cheerful. Or at least, not as dismal when Mamá asked Marissa to summon him to her room.

"What's this?" he said as he entered. "You and Ceese have run out of things to do?" He looked around, as if expecting Ceese to jump out, at any moment, to take Mamá away from him again.

Mamá's face held sympathy. "I'm sorry, Richard. Ceese and I have just had so much catching up to do. You understand, don't you?"

"And now you're finished?" Richard asked, moving to sit next to her on the bed. "Three days, and you're all caught up?" In spite of his flippant tone, he wanted to believe it was true. He missed being around her. "So long as you're happy," he said.

"I'd be happier if the two of you could get along."

"Well, then," he said. "You should be ecstatic. We haven't fought in three days."

"Richard, you two haven't *talked* in three days."

"Perhaps you've found the solution, then."

Mamá sighed deeply. "What happened the other night, when you and she went out? Ceese won't tell me. All I know is when I talked to her the next morning, she was . . . distant. And she had destroyed nearly every timepiece in the castle. I know you know something."

He shrugged. "I showed her how to tell time."

"So in turn, she destroys everything having to do with the subject? You had to have done something else . . . said something. I won't be angry," she added. "I just want to know."

She seemed so desperate for the truth, so he gave it to her, rushing it along so it might not sound as bad, finishing with, "She said she wanted her soul back, and I told her she could go to hell and get it."

"Richard!"

"I didn't mean it the way it came out, but she ran off before I could explain. And now she won't talk to me. Although she *did* pull herself from her busy schedule to tell me Xavier doesn't care a thing about me anymore."

"You weren't hurt by that! You care little about Xavier."

"He's *my* dog," he proclaimed, and jerked his head toward the French doors, where Xavier and Ceese were out romping on the lawn, passing by the doors often enough to make Richard suspect they were taunting him with their closeness.

"Richard," Mamá tried, "it's not your fault Xavier hasn't ever warmed up to you—"

"Yes, I know. It's the curse. But what of it? *She* doesn't seem to have the same difficulty I do. She's no different than I am, and yet she laughs, smiles, and look," he jerked his chin toward the window, "the damned dog is licking her hand. Xavier has never licked me. Not once."

"Do you envy her because she can do these things?" Mamá said, her voice soft.

He shook his head. "I don't envy her because of that. I *hate* her." He gave a bitter laugh. "That's one emotion I have full control of."

"Maybe she can help you."

He turned, his look softening. "You never give up, do you?"

"Not when it comes to you." Her smile was welcome.

"How are you feeling anyway?" he asked. "With the . . . cancer. You look tired."

She shrugged. "I have my days."

"You know, there's a lot being done for cancer these days. Perhaps you could—"

"Please. We've talked about this. I'm glad you're suggesting medical treatment as opposed to . . . well, cursing me. But you have to accept that I'm dying."

His expression sank. "You can't blame me for trying."

"No," she said, and reached out to smooth his already-smooth hair. "I don't suppose I can. Now, go to your basement. It's already midmorning."

With a nod, he kissed her hand lightly and left.

Mamá waited until he had gone to call for Marissa. The visit had taken everything out of her, and the pain was back, much worse than before. It was time to summon the doctor, for what little he could do.

❦ ❦ ❦

When Richard came up for dinner the following evening, the dining room was empty and dark. Nothing was as it should have been. A storm raged outside, and almost-constant lightning lit the room.

He called out for Marissa. When there was no response, he walked to the parlor, then through it when he found no one there. But the parlor was hardly the place to sit and chat anymore; couches sat without cushions, windows waited for new drapes.

By the time he reached the main hall, he was more concerned than ever. The castle's front rooms were deserted. Lightning flashed, dimming the lights momentarily. Thunder boomed, filling the expansive space around him with its echoes. He felt the sudden need to run and did so, heading down the hall to Mamá's room, where another bolt of lightning and thunderclap announced his appearance.

A startled Marissa stood to face him with a troubled stare. "I wanted to come after you," she said to his hostile look. "But you were in your basement. And I—"

He held up a hand to silence her, too rattled by his gut feeling to listen to her. Mamá was lying on the bed, not moving, not talking—just lying there with her eyes closed. Ceese was perched on the far side of the bed, holding one of Mamá's hands with both of hers. Her shoulders sagged, her head hung down.

"Mamá," he managed, rushing to the bed. She barely looked alive. Ignoring Ceese, he jerked his head toward Marissa, who now stood next to the door. "Is she—?"

"No, m'lord," Marissa said at once. "But the doctor said it wouldn't be long." Her countenance seemed to shrink, and she turned away rather than face his scowl.

Marissa turned back toward the bed a moment later, saw him looking at Ceese. "She's been with Miss Penelope ever since she collapsed this morning," she said. "She won't leave. I believe she's . . . helping her in some way."

Richard's head whipped around at hearing her compliant tone. Mamá was quite possibly dying, and unlike him, Marissa was capable of showing emotion. And all the timid maid could muster was a synopsis on what Ceese had been up to.

"How can you possibly know she's helping her?" he snapped. "Perhaps she's making Mamá worse."

"I . . . I suppose I don't know for certain," Marissa replied, shrinking back. "May-May I be excused, m'lord?"

Richard barked his agreement, then settled down next to Mamá and took her hand. She looked so frail, so ashen.

"You have no magic left?" he asked of Ceese, making sure she heard the blame in his voice.

"It isn't that," Ceese managed. "She won't let me help her. I'm trying. She just won't allow it."

Her words forced him to recall what Mamá had said, about her being able to control what Ceese was doing. And indeed, Ceese looked as though she was struggling, had been fighting for hours at some Herculean task.

"I . . . kept her here so you could bid her farewell."

He couldn't tell whether Ceese wanted him to thank her for this, or whether she just wanted him to know. He did know he didn't want Ceese around now. There was so much he wanted to tell Mamá. So much he wanted to say to her. "I should like to be alone with her."

"She is very weak. If I go, she goes."

He didn't push. Instead, he pressed the back of his hand against Mamá's forehead, the sides of her face, and tried to pretend he wasn't as concerned as he was. His spirits lifted when Mamá's eyes opened.

"Richard," she said, attempted a smile. "I'm so glad you're here. I . . . have to go now."

"But you said a month or two." His voice cracked.

"I know, and I'm sorry. I thought I could last longer. But my being here is hurting Ceese."

"She's strong," Richard threw out, as if he knew this for certain, even while Ceese looked more and more like someone fighting just to stay conscious.

"Richard," Mamá said, pulling him back to her. "I won't let what she's doing for me hurt her. I've already told you this. This isn't Ceese's fault. I don't want you holding her responsible once I'm gone. Do you understand?"

"I understand," he said, but didn't mean it. He did blame Ceese, and always would.

"You must stay together," Mamá begged. "Promise me you will. Go see Cassie. Together. Promise me."

He wouldn't lie. Not when these might be the last words his

friend might hear. "Mamá," he started, but she wouldn't let him finish.

"It's too important—" Her eyes lit up. "Richard, you do know, don't you? You don't want to remember, but you do."

"Know what, Mamá?"

"About Ceese!" She said this as if it were so obvious, which only made him more confused.

He shook his head. "I . . . I wish I did, but I don't know what you're talking about. Know what about Ceese?"

Mamá's smile faded a little, her weak lips barely able to make the upward curve. "It's just as well," she managed to squeeze his hand, "not knowing, I mean. All in good time."

"Mamá, please," he implored. "Why do you speak in riddles?"

"It's just . . . I don't want to force you to remember something you choose not to. And I can't bear to leave this earth with you thinking me a lunatic."

"I would never—"

"If I told you what I know is true, you would. I must go now, Richard. . . . Please help Ceese."

He squeezed her hand, prepared to explain, yet again, why he couldn't look after Ceese, but all at once, the hand went limp.

"Mamá?" he called out. "Mamá?" But there was no response.

He sat for a moment, tried to feel something—anything but hatred and blame. Mamá had tried so hard to help him do this, help him overcome his shortcomings. But no matter how hard he tried, hatred and blame, and now pain, was all he felt. And Mamá wasn't there to reassure him, so all he did was become angrier.

"She is gone," Ceese announced, and he bolted to his feet, marched around the bed, reached out and took Ceese by her shoulders, lifted her up.

"You bring her back," he demanded. "Do you understand me? You bring her back!"

Ceese was so weak, she could barely hold her head up. "I cannot."

Then she saw fangs and managed to gather enough strength

to grasp the cross hanging around her neck, the one Penny had kept in the desk beside her bed. Penny had given it to her the day before. Ceese held it out for him to see. "She said you might not be able to control the vampire."

He released Ceese at once, turned away from her, and found himself facing Mamá's lifeless form again. His frustration and hatred peaked, and he stormed out of the room.

Ceese had managed to remain standing after Richard turned her loose, but after he was gone, she fell in a heap, exhausted and unconscious.

◆ ◆ ◆

When she became aware, she had no idea how much time had passed, just that she could no longer hear thunder in the distance or detect lightning flashes in the darkened panes of the two windows she could see from where she lay. She tried to get up, to decide what to do next, but found she didn't have the energy to stand. Trying to keep Penny on the earth had taken much out of her.

Slowly, her strength began to return, and after a short time, Ceese realized she could push herself up with her hands, could move close enough to reach one of the four bedposts. She took hold of one and pulled herself up, slowly and with great effort. Everything seemed to spin for a second, but she closed her eyes and held tight, giving her head a chance to settle. Feet planted firmly now, she opened her eyes and focused, found herself looking at Penny, who at this point just looked like someone resting, at peace.

"Why?" Ceese whispered. "Why wouldn't you let me help you?"

After a moment she could look no longer look, and turned away, remembering her father's death. His sudden illness, the unusual way her mother acted. Claiming to fear his illness might spread, Mother hadn't allowed anyone in, neither did she allow anyone to view his body later. Epidemics were common during those times, cures in short supply. The reason was accepted by most

116

Despite this precaution, despite Mother's efforts to keep the family away, Ceese had seen her father, when the door had opened wider than it was usually allowed to open. He looked like Penny did now—so pale, so cold-looking.

Brendan and Raewyn, the two oldest siblings at home, made a plea for the sake of the other children, but nothing anyone said seemed to matter. And so her father was buried in an unknown location, had his coffin carried by strangers.

Ceese had come to terms with all that, just as she would somehow accept Penny's passing. Time would ease her pain; those had been her mother's words. And she remembered them now, though it didn't help much to do so. She couldn't grieve, because she couldn't truly love. But she recalled, just a bit, how it felt to love. Maybe those words couldn't help her right now, but they gave her hope. Perhaps one day, she might actually benefit from hearing those words once more; about time, about the easing of pain. For now, she could only imagine the grief, the absolute loss she should be feeling but couldn't. Perhaps she should be glad. Losing Penny might hurt worse than losing Father, because she could have kept Penny alive for at least another month, maybe longer if Penny had let her. But Penny wouldn't allow it and in the end, Penny's will won out.

Ceese looked once more at the body of her friend, then moved toward the door, wanting to get away from her failure to prevent Penny's death.

But then she saw, right next to Penny's door, a hand-painted portrait of her friend, posing in her favorite garden at the castle, the one they had romped in for an entire week. Her frustration grew. She ran to seek refuge in another room, ducking inside and pressing herself against one of its walls. She closed her eyes and tried not to feel angry about not feeling anything, about not being able to grieve.

She opened her eyes and things got worse. Without thinking, she had taken refuge in Penny's private dressing room. The memories were everywhere here; a mirror, a hairbrush on an oval tray, one she remembered Penny using only the day before. Ceese went to the table, picked up the brush, and threw it full force across the room. It struck a much larger mirror, shattered it into a multitude of sharp, reflective shards. Her anger had peaked; now, she felt a familiar, yet unwelcome feeling come over her. The wolf wanted out.

"No," she said, fighting against it. "Not here." She worried the wolf might take advantage, might find Penny's lifeless form and she pushed the thought from her head, didn't want to think about her dear friend being mauled and mutilated.

Ceese then sent the table the brush and oval tray had been sitting on crashing to the floor. The rest of its contents went with it. A bottle of perfume, a scent Penny wore every day, broke and filled the air. The fragrance overwhelmed Ceese. She grabbed an armful of clothes hanging nearby and tried to soak the fragrance up. But it didn't help, and so she just ran again, into the hall. She didn't know where else to go. The memories were everywhere.

Finally, she felt the wolf succumb. She backed up against the wall and slid to the floor. Tears finally came, angry, frustrated tears, and then she grew quiet. But silence didn't prevail. There were other noises in the castle, crashing sounds, and she got up and followed those to the parlor.

Just before she entered the room, the noises stopped. But pushing the large doors open was no easy task. Something blocked them, and whatever it was, it was big. She finally pushed enough to get her head into the opening, and realized it was a bulky chair. She pushed a little harder, and was finally able to squeeze through.

Once inside, she stood in awe. The chair wasn't the only thing out of place. Desks and couches had been thrown. Every wall not constructed of stone had gaping holes in it.

A familiar tapping got her attention. Richard was at his computer, typing away as if nothing at all was wrong.

She approached slowly and settled in the only other chair still in one piece. "There is no greater peace than knowing one will spend eternity with God," she recited from memory, causing Richard to turn at once, his eyes burning.

She had done it again! She had said something sacred. Her hands flew to her temples in anguish.

"Serves you right," Richard said, as she sat doubled-over, and went back to his computer. "Pretending you're something you're not, something you can never be."

When Ceese was able to speak, she said, "I'm sorry I said I hated you the other night. Penny told me you didn't mean what you said—about my soul. About where I had to go to reclaim it."

Richard gave her a hard, quick glance. "Did it make you feel better, hearing that? Because if it did, you might like to know I only told her that to pacify her."

When she didn't reply, he gave her a longer glance. She looked exhausted, and was wearing the same clothes she'd worn the day before. And then, he noticed her slacks. Again they weren't fastened—zipped, but not snapped.

"What is it with you werewolves anyway?" he said callously. "Don't any of you ever fasten your trousers?"

Embarrassed, she remedied the situation at once. "It isn't because we don't like to fasten our pants, it's just we—" She stopped.

"What?" Richard said. "Did I stutter?"

"You said werewolves."

Richard cocked a brow. "Well, I guess we don't have to ask whether you were paying attention now, do we?"

"You told Penny you knew nothing of werewolves. Said you'd never met one before."

"Yes, well, I do recall telling her something along those lines in a *private* conversation I had with her."

She ignored his snide words and asked, "And since then you have?"

"Perhaps."

Ceese began to put the pieces together. He must have met Zade. It was hard for her to hide her reaction to this revelation. Ever since she left the pack, she suspected Zade would come after her. She just never thought he would go to Richard.

"He could have killed you," she said, digging, knowing Richard wouldn't tell her he met Zade if he thought she wanted to know. And she did want to know.

119

"Fancy that," Richard replied. "He could have killed me, and yet, here I am."

"What did he say?"

"And why should I tell you? It was a *private* conversation. I think I'll keep what was said to myself."

The anger and frustration she'd felt before were back. The wolf was knocking on the door of her soul. She stood, picked up her chair and threw it. It tumbled into the corner of the room, landing on a pile of ruined drapes. "You don't know what you're doing!"

He gazed at her, eyes level. "I'll take my chances."

"You go right ahead, then. And I'll take my apology back. I do so hate you. And I always will."

He watched her scale the toppled furniture with ease, and then, she was gone, leaving the same way she'd come in.

Richard sat back and sighed, muttered, "That went well," and went back to his computer.

He might have felt worse about it, if he'd been able to feel anything in the first place. Yet what was the point of trying now? Mamá was gone. So he worked a little longer, shut down the computer, and went hunting. Close to dawn, he found a deer and fed on it. Afterward he headed back to his basement, to hide from the day, and from his duty. Mamá had wanted him to take care of Ceese, and he had possibly run her off. Mamá wouldn't be happy, but Mamá was now gone. Marissa would see to Mamá, would make sure she received a proper burial, and he would visit her grave later. He would then go on, living life as he had before Penelope Cromwell showed up. He didn't need her. He didn't need anyone. Most of all, he didn't need a werewolf who hated him as much as he hated her.

CHAPTER 13

The next night, the moon was full and high, and Richard couldn't help notice, without thinking about it, that he'd looked up to see what time it was by the stars. Until then, he hadn't thought anymore about Ceese, or what might have happened to her, or where she might have gone. And then he heard the howling of a wolf. It had to be Ceese, unless another member of her pack had come to look for her. Perhaps Zade. He knew this to be a possibility now.

But there was something familiar about this howl. He'd heard it the night Ceese had gone off to warn the others while he fed on Long Tail. It *was* her. And her howl was unnervingly close. Oddly, it grew louder as he neared the hollow where Mamá had asked to be buried. He entered the hollow, wary.

The ground was unconsecrated, per his instructions, and the wolf circling the marble headstone was larger than any he'd ever seen. Still, he didn't know if it was Ceese. The only time he'd seen her as a wolf, she was attacking him in the parlor. Then, he was too busy defending himself to get a good look. The scratches she'd left were still with him. They weren't as deep now, but neither were they gone. The memory of that night made staying back now seem the smartest thing to do.

Yet the more he watched the wolf, the more certain he was it was Ceese. It circled the grave, and whimpered and howled occasionally, and he couldn't help but shake his head in wonderment. To be able to go against the curse and do what she was doing—grieving. If she were, in fact, grieving. Either way, going against the curse or pretending, it was more than he could do. And if it were the latter, if she was pretending . . . well, no performer could have done a better job of convincing. Her pain seemed great, her sorrow deep. He was almost tempted to applaud. But, of course, he didn't want to draw attention.

She carried on for some time before beginning the transformation back, and Richard was mesmerized when it started. Limbs elongating, fur disappearing as she returned to human form. He had never seen anything like it—it was so different from his own transformation, so painful-looking. He suddenly had a new respect for her. A new understanding, too. She could have killed him when she attacked him before, yet she didn't.

Ceese was fully human now. Richard noticed her shivering in her nakedness, and looked around for the shirt and pants she'd had on the last time he saw her. But he saw nothing. She must have traveled from somewhere else.

With a resigned sigh, he removed his coat and went to put it over her. Ceese saw him and bolted into a nearby stand of trees.

For a moment, Richard pretended that he hadn't seen her scurry underneath the longer branches of one of them. He waited instead for her to calm, thinking she might let him help when the cold became unbearable for her.

It seemed to work. A few minutes later, when he called her name, she responded, then came out and allowed him to cover her. She didn't resist when he lifted her shivering body into his arms either, which he did at once, before she remembered just how much she hated him. Her eyes closed and her body went limp, and he was glad. At least he wouldn't have to explain, right away, why he felt compelled to take care of her, especially in light of the way he'd treated her the last time they were together. It would have been a difficult thing to do anyway, considering he didn't really understand himself. He just knew he couldn't leave her out here now, even though, a couple of days ago, he would have welcomed the opportunity.

She was such an easy burden to carry. The only problem was the cross she still wore. He'd noticed it when she was the wolf, had seen it glinting in the moonlight. When he picked her up, he made certain it hung away from him, watched carefully so it didn't come any closer to him than he could help as he carried her.

He wondered how she could wear it at all. He would never be able to rise above what he'd been cursed with, could never do something as daring or as dangerous. He wanted to ask her about it, but the question would have to wait until she woke up.

As though she had heard him, she stirred. He stopped for a moment, wondering what would happen next. Would she jump from his arms? Would she run off again, possibly fight him?

She did none of these things, just stared up at him. And Richard couldn't escape the feeling that he had experienced her look before, or something very much like it. He didn't know where the feeling came from.

Groggily, Ceese moved her head around and stared up into dark treetops. After a moment, she turned her face to his and said, "Richard?" When he shushed her and told her to rest, she said the oddest thing: "We must tell Father. He will know what to do. He will be able to help you."

After saying this, she rested, and he was certain she was dreaming.

The manor in sight, he plodded on, and moments later, they were at the front entrance. Lights were on, but only a few. Ceese stirred as he climbed the steps to the front doors, more aware but still weak; it seemed an effort for her to hold her head up, so she just let it rest against Richard instead.

"She is gone," she muttered. "She is truly gone."

"Yes. It's what she wanted, though. She's happy now." He didn't say these words for Ceese's benefit, yet realized he wouldn't be upset if she somehow drew comfort from them.

"It's what I want too," Ceese added as he moved on. "I want to be happy like she is."

He didn't know how to address what she'd said, wasn't sure he wanted to. He did know he didn't want to make her angry. So he kept his thoughts to himself, grateful she didn't push for a response.

He carried her to a room far down the hall from Mamá's. His idea was to place her on the bed there, and he had just managed to pull the covers back when Ceese sprang to life and grabbed onto his neck with renewed strength. Startled, he overcompensated and nearly tripped over his own feet backwards.

"What is it?" he sputtered.

"I don't want to lie there," Ceese replied, desperate. "Please don't put me there!"

"It's but a bed!"

"Yes, but people die there."

She's delusional, he thought. *She has to be.* "You're just tired," he said. "It will be fine." As he spoke, he attempted to lower her again, but she pulled herself up and wouldn't turn loose of his neck.

He had carried her nearly half a mile, and was desperate to go to his basement and rest. He had fed, so he wasn't worried about the damn vampire bats. But they were always on his mind and he wouldn't have to worry about them at all in his coffin—if he could just get to it. "Oh, come now," he said. "Not everyone dies in a bed." But then he realized most people actually did. "Well, at least, it isn't the fault of the bed itself."

"I don't want to be put there. Please!"

He looked around. "Where, then? The sun will be up soon, and you can't go to the basement with me."

"The floor."

With a sigh, he lowered her there.

"I'll get you a cover," he said, and moved to the large chest of drawers behind him, extracted a lightweight blanket, then shut the drawer he'd pulled it from and turned back to the bed. But Ceese wasn't where he'd left her.

He did a quick scan, wondered where she'd gotten off to. She could have gone out the door, he reasoned. But to do so, she would have had to walk past him. And why would she leave in the first place? She'd seemed calm after he'd put her down.

Then he caught a quick movement near the bed. He got on all fours to explore what he'd seen. In spite of himself, he fought a laugh. "What rationale would drive a person to hide underneath the very thing which scares them so?"

"Not many die here," Ceese replied.

"Yes, well, I suppose you have a point there." But what was the fuss all about anyway? He found the blanket he'd brought over with his hand, pushed it toward her. "Sleep well."

She spoke before he could get away. "Please stay until I fall asleep. I don't want to be alone."

All at once the feeling returned, the very one he'd had in the woods when she first awoke. And he was certain he'd heard her words before. But just like earlier, when he was carrying her, he rationalized that it was just a feeling.

"It won't be safe," he replied. It was the only thing he could come up with.

"But I have the cross Penny gave me," she said. "I'll keep it close."

"Yes, well, perhaps I was referring to *my* safety." The wolf was a force to be reckoned with, and he had wounds to prove it.

"Oh," she said, sensing his thoughts, forgetting his earlier warning not to. Then, "Please, Richard, just until I'm asleep."

"All right," he said, giving in. "But only until then."

And so he slid beneath the bed and instructed her to keep her back to his so he wouldn't be tempted. She did as he said and fell silent.

Richard listened to her soft breathing for about five minutes and decided, from the sound of things, he could probably leave without her knowing. Only now, he was tired himself. And while the floor wasn't at all comfortable, being next to Ceese was. He couldn't explain it, but just having her there felt right. He did think about the possibility of the bats finding him, but he had fed before he found her and he could get up later if need be and get more blood from the refrigerator—

"Nos da iwch," Ceese whispered.

It wasn't English, he knew, but it sounded strangely familiar. "Pardon?" he asked, and she repeated what she'd said.

He understood it the second time. It was Welsh, a language he must have studied at some point in the distant past. "Ah, yes . . . and good night to you too."

And as the sun broke over the horizon and warmed the day, the werewolf and the vampire slept.

CHAPTER 14

"Look," the well-dressed man said, scowling at the man and woman sitting across the conference table, "this college can't afford to turn down a 4.7 million dollar grant because we can't find the right person to run the program. And I'm absolutely convinced that my cousin is perfect for the position."

To paraphrase a certain politician, that depended on a person's definition of "perfect." And certainly, the pair glaring at him now had plenty of reason to question their advisor's definition, and his motives. What they didn't know was that Phillip Darden, head of Financial Affairs, was his cousin's sole support at the moment. They did know, however, that Phillip's cousin, Clayton Henderson, PhD, was in more than a little trouble. He'd been all over the news, local and national, his method of stem cell collection being the controversy. In fact, Clayton. Henderson had been fired from his last job for harvesting stem cells from unauthorized sources. The lab he was working for was federally funded. Such activity wasn't tolerated. Or legal. But the biggest problem came when he was caught the second time. After that, he had to go. And now, he was mooching off his dear cousin, who would do just about anything to get Henderson a job, and out on his own again.

"How do we know he won't pull the same crap here?" Probst Fair, eternal pessimist, spat out. "The biomedical engineering program's brand-new, and that would be all we need, a bunch of feds breathing down our necks because one of our professors is soliciting some young coed for her stem cells."

Mary Pemberton, who'd been on the board far longer than either of the two men could remember, gave a pious sniff. "Well, I can't say I appreciate Mr. Fair's wording." She paused, stared indignantly at her adversary, then continued. "Yet I have to agree. How *do* we know he won't do it again?"

Cousin Philip was ready. "Basically, because he won't have the chance. He'll be director in name only. And until we get the program off the ground, he'll just be teaching physiology. How controversial could *that* be? And," he added, giving them his oiliest smile, "you've heard the amount he's willing to work for. Just think what we could do with the difference between that and what we would have to pay someone . . . less in need than he is right now."

That reminder decided the matter. They made certain the new director signed the required confidentiality agreement, and forced him to meet with the full board and apologize for what he'd done at his former job. The agreement also stipulated that he not be personally involved in any research on stem cells again.

Clayton Henderson, being the kind of person he was, took this to mean he could do whatever he wanted to on his own time, and willingly signed the agreement.

❧ ❧ ❧

And because he despised the idea of teaching, and considered anyone with less than a master's degree an imbecile, his hapless students often felt his ire. Today's class was a good example.

Henderson stared at the clock on the wall. Everyone else seemed to have an acute interest in it, but he saw nothing about it to hold his attention. The others were looking as captives though, *his* captives, for the next thirty minutes at least. That was fine with him; that very morning, the dean told him that several students had filed formal complaints. Being able to torment the class would help take his mind off that.

He spoke in an intentionally flat, monotonous tone when he called on his first victim, a thin blonde on the second row who didn't look thrilled about being targeted. He'd looked at a piece of paper he'd taken from his desk and found her name.

"Ms. Thompson," he droned.

She pushed herself to the back of her seat and gave a sullen, "Yes."

He wondered if she'd been one of the ones to report him; she looked very much on edge. But, she would do to give his superiors what they'd asked for: student participation.

"When you signed up for this course, did you have a permanent address?"

She seemed uncertain about how to answer. "Yes?"

He looked up from the paper, glared at her. "This isn't *Jeopardy*. You don't have to answer in the form of a question." He squelched the round of snickers with a look that said, *You could be next*, and all snickering ceased. He then continued. "So, yes, you have a permanent address?"

She nodded this time, as if afraid of repeating her mistake.

"Good." He shoved the piece of paper at her. "Then would you write it here, in the appropriate spot? Apparently you have terribly upset the balance of things by not doing so, and the school is desperate to restore equilibrium."

She breathed a sigh of relief, took the paper and began writing. Meanwhile, Henderson went back to his lecture, loathing his Cousin Phillip for talking him into this, and himself for listening.

Ten minutes passed in his lecture, and he was reminded that it was time for more student participation. This time he zeroed in on a young man in the fourth row, one of the few who'd seemed to have taken the warnings about his class seriously.

"Mr. Kincaid," he said. This got everyone's attention; their professor rarely addressed anyone without looking at his roster. Those who found themselves nodding off were revived, and now sat on the edge of their seats.

Mr. Kincaid sprung to life too, and Henderson posed his question. "Define, if you would for the rest of the class, phospholipids."

Rodney Kincaid wasn't exactly known for his intellect. Not many could believe he'd survived this long in college except that he stayed jacked up on caffeine, popping NoDoz like candy. His look alone, with his radically dyed hair, dark black at the roots

128

and neon-blonde at the ends, suggested an urban calling, perhaps standing on a street corner somewhere, hanging out. It was extreme, even for a college in New York City.

"Phospholipids," Rodney repeated boldly. "That would be the major membrane lipid. You know, the one with one end charged and the other being nonpolar."

"And how does this relate to physiology?"

Confused silence prevailed as Rodney continued. "Thudichum concluded that phospholipids are 'the center, life, and chemical soul of all bioplasm'."

Henderson's smile was curt. "Perhaps we should all pay as much attention as Mr. Kincaid."

The bell rang, and dazed students filed out of the classroom, avoiding Henderson's gaze but giving Rodney amazed glances.

Rodney waited until the coast was clear before making his way down to where Henderson stood. "That was classic!" he said. "Did you see their faces?"

"I'm so happy I could accommodate. Now, what do you have for me?"

"It's always about you, isn't it?" Rodney said, grinning at the professor's hard glare. "Okay, okay, don't go clinical on me. Cassie's got a lab tonight. I'm gonna get on her computer and see what I can find for you, so just chill."

"I will *chill* when I have new information."

"Yeah, well, maybe tonight then. You can check your computer." Rodney turned to leave.

"Rodney," Henderson called out. "Your friend Josh. Tell him to stop by my house later."

Rodney turned back, suspicious. "*Josh* knows where you live?"

Henderson nodded. "And what's odd about that? *You* know where I live."

"Yeah, but you just met him the other night— and come to think of it," he scowled, as if remembering something disturbing, "Josh smelled like he'd been smoking pot after he came back from 'chatting it up' with you outside the club. And I know he didn't have money to get any for himself."

"Is there a question in there somewhere?" As he spoke, Henderson kept his face and voice neutral.

"It's just—well, Josh has a little bit of an addiction problem."

"Wouldn't Josh's addiction be *Josh's* problem?"

Rodney's reaction was immediate and defensive. "Maybe. But he's my friend, so I'm telling you, keep the drugs out of it."

Henderson sighed. "So, are you going to tell him to stop by, or do I have to call him?"

"I'll tell him. Just remember what I said."

"Yes, well, perhaps you should take a bit of your own advice and just— chill."

"*Oooh*," Rodney said, "trying to fit in, are you, Professor? Yeah, you might look good with a few body piercings."

Rodney started to walk off then, up the tiered lecture hall floor, speaking loud into the hall so the others couldn't help but hear. "Yeah— I don't know, Dr. Henderson. I'm pretty sure I aced your last test, but thanks for asking."

Clayton Henderson almost regretted arranging for Rodney to be in his class. Had only done so after learning he was Cassie Felts' roommate. But despite how the young man irritated him, it had worked out well. At least so far. And he needed Cassie enough that he was willing to tolerate Rodney.

Anyone who worked with stem cells knew that those harvested from living embryos were the most desirable: more flexible and versatile to work with. Henderson's collection method had gotten him fired. But now that he knew about Cassie Felts, there was a chance he could have even more interesting cells to work with. All it would take was time, and the right opportunity—one he hoped Rodney would eventually provide.

He remembered this as he returned to his office and dug through his files to find the one marked "Cassie." When he located it, buried at the bottom of the drawer, he smiled. He opened the file and scanned the contents. It held all the work the two of them had done so far. Henderson was interested in immortality, in living forever, and Rodney's roommate, Cassie, was interested as well, only in reverse order. She was convinced that supernatural beings existed. Vampires and werewolves in particular. Not only believed in them, but believed stem cell research might cure them of their curse. When she claimed to know a vampire and a werewolf, ones wanting their curse lifted, he knew he had to hire her as his graduate assistant.

She didn't offer this information right away, of course; it took time to get it out of the altruistic young woman. Mainly because she knew about the controversy surrounding him. Hell, *everyone* knew after the picketers spent a week with their signs, marching around the university. Finally, he was able to convince her, telling her the controversy surrounding him was a mistake, a set-up. That he'd been misjudged by the same kinds of people who would likely misjudge her, too, if they knew of her odd beliefs. And in a world where such things happened every day, she believed him.

Their meeting was fated. He was sure of that. He'd been late for something, and she'd been in a hurry to get somewhere. They collided. Books hit the ground, papers scattered, and an entire thesis on the possibility of vampire existence landed at his feet. She hurried to scoop it up, but he was quick to grab it before she could. He'd looked enthralled, dumbfounded, and swore he'd always been interested in the subject. But when he asked if he could read it she had grabbed it from him, telling him it was her personal research and would never be published.

He looked disheartened—which took no deception, because he was—and said, "I've done much research on the subject. I can show you but I . . . I don't really like to advertise it. Not many understand."

She still wouldn't show him her thesis, but did agree to meet him at the library later.

He'd guessed she was the gullible type, and he was right. He knew he had her when he told her he dreamed of finding a cure for those who claimed to be vampires, getting the idea from a movie he'd just seen and making his own performance riveting. She bought it, and eventually, she trusted him completely. They studied late at the library digging for information, scheduled meetings with people who claimed to be vampires and werewolves, and shared their thoughts on the matter. Cassie never doubted his intentions after that first day, and he took advantage.

Henderson's parents had died when he was young. After that, he moved in and out of foster homes, old enough to not be molded by whatever religious preference he was introduced to, and too cynical to care. Young Clayton put little stock in the afterlife, or in the words of those who tried to tell him he should. Living was just something you did until you died. Whatever happened next, well, it just didn't matter.

Yet he wasn't in any hurry to find out about that next stage. For most of his life, he'd searched for ways to live forever. And if what he'd recently learned from Rodney's snooping panned out, he was on his way.

CHAPTER 15

What are you doing?" Cassie snapped. "No way are you supposed to be using my computer—*no way*!" As she yelled, she yanked at the band holding back her auburn hair. It fell to her shoulders and her blue eyes flashed at Rodney, making her look like a female Mel Gibson in the movie *Braveheart*.

Rodney jumped up as if on fire, hit a few keys and then backed up, hands buried in his pockets, his belt the only thing keeping his jeans from sliding any further down.

"There's this . . . ah, computer virus going around," he said while she placed her books onto a table near the door, dropped her backpack beside it and headed over. "It screws with the system registry. I was just downloading this patch. I thought you might appreciate not losing all your *precious research*. If you don't believe me, check for yourself!"

"Don't think I won't," Cassie said, taking the computer mouse in hand and plopping into the seat Rodney had just vacated. The chair was still warm, very warm. She couldn't help but wonder how long he'd been sitting there.

"Besides, you left the thing on when you went to class."

"I . . . was in a hurry. And if I did leave it on, I didn't leave it on for your benefit. And you should have known that!"

She scrolled through the computer's history files while watching Rodney out of the corner of her eye. He had moved to the futon, which also served as his bed. The apartment wasn't large, and neither was the living-dining combo they were in. Even if she hadn't noticed him heading to the futon, she would have known where he was. The only other place to sit was the kitchen table.

Cassie felt him staring at her back as she clicked the mouse, and after a moment, he moved to stand behind her.

"So, are you convinced now?"

She clicked a few times, ended up at a website supporting free virus detection downloads and patches. "I just wish you'd have waited for me." She was still angry, but her relief made it come down a notch.

"Your hard disk might have been toast by then," he said, then headed for his backpack. He slung it over his shoulder and headed for the door. On the way, he passed by the stack of books Cassie had unloaded in her rush to the computer. "*The Wolf Within*," he muttered, "*A Werewolf's Bid for the Future*. Where do you find this stuff? Don't you have enough going on with those theories you have about vampires?"

Rodney was one of the few people who knew anything about her fascination with vampires and werewolves. She had told him so she wouldn't have to hide everything. But she hadn't told him everything, just that she was exploring the possibility of their existence. All he'd had to say was "Cool."

Cassie wasn't sorry she'd told him but, often, he wore her patience thin. "Vampires aren't a *theory*, Rodney, and don't you have somewhere else to be?"

"Yeah, I do. Got some computer lab work to finish."

He inhaled sharply, and Cassie turned around to face him.

"Oh, really? You'll have to do better. Or did you forget being ordered to stay away from the computer lab? It's only been a week since you crashed the entire system, you know."

"I, ah . . . I meant to say I'm going to the library to use *their* computers. But if it makes a difference, I *do* have to go to the computer lab later . . . to empty out trashcans. My punishment. You know, garbage in, garbage out. It'll probably be late before I get back."

He looked so pitiful now, her heart softened a bit. "I guess I don't have to ask you whether you have your key or not. I don't want to have to wake up and let you in. Again."

He'd jingled the key in the air so she could see it.

Her eyes darted back to the computer screen. "Wait a minute."

Rodney steadied himself, holding onto the doorknob, tried to stay cool. "Yeah, what is it?"

"Did you see any e-mails? I was expecting one, and I don't see any new ones here."

"Well, *duh*," Rodney threw out, "I was downloading a patch, not checking your e-mail."

Cassie absently nodded and Rodney went on.

After he left, Cassie leaned back in her chair, considered her busy week. She was beginning to feel like a professional student. No, she *was* a professional student, at least right now. After a year at a community college, she'd come to Templeton University. It seemed the best decision; she had no idea what she wanted to do with her life. A university, being larger, meant more choices. She quickly learned, however, that having more options only made things more confusing. And after she graduated with a degree in biology, she decided to stay on to get her master's. And maybe by then, she figured, she'd know what to do next.

But a year into her graduate studies, Templeton added the biomedical engineering program. And she desperately wanted in. Wanted to put some facts behind what she was doing. Her research so far was based on theories, supposition. If she could learn more, it would give her research substance, credibility—and access to what she needed to take it much further. For one thing, she was convinced there were differences between human blood and that of vampires and werewolves. With access to the right lab, and to a vampire or werewolf, or both, she could find those differences, no matter how small—and finally be able to know whether these creatures were what they claimed to be.

And what a nice boost to discover one of her professors, Clayton Henderson, the head of the BME program, was interested in the same thing. Oh, sure, she was suspicious at first. The professor's controversial background, his motive . . . what did he want with her? But he'd worked hard to win her over. And when he explained how he felt stem cell research might offer vampires and werewolves alike a cure . . . well, she was in. He'd also promised to let her in on what he'd learned so far too, *after* she was a little deeper into the program. For now, he'd gotten her a make-work position, a foot in the door to the real research she wanted to do someday.

She went along with his plan. After all, Dr. Henderson had been doing stem cells research for one of the largest research firms in the country. If he said she needed to learn more before he could share, than she would learn more.

❧ ❧ ❧

Dr. Henderson didn't answer his home or cell phone, so Rodney had to talk to the professor's voicemail: He'd forwarded the e-mail, as Henderson had asked, then deleted it from Cassie's computer.

After leaving the message, Rodney headed to the library. Maybe he'd make enough money doing what he was doing for the professor to get his own computer. It was an easy way to make money. Sure, old Henderson wasn't his favorite person. That was certain. And he was still uneasy about Henderson's sudden interest in Josh, who had enough problems. But, he didn't have to like Henderson to work for him.

The only thing he was bothered by was Cassie. He liked her, and didn't really want to snoop on her. And what if she found out? She'd be devastated. But then, he wouldn't have to worry if he was careful, and he planned to be careful. And as long as he was, Henderson's money would keep rolling in.

CHAPTER 16

Richard had been working with Ceese for the past week, helping her relearn the things she'd have to remember if she didn't want to stand out once they got to New York—a city Richard still wasn't certain Ceese was ready to take on. But during the time they spent under the bed, she'd talked him into it. He had no desire to leave the castle, but Ceese worried there'd be nothing left of it if he stayed. That argument was compelling. The castle reminded him too much of Mamá, and he wasn't dealing with the memories well. Each night since she passed on, he'd ransacked a new room, or revisited one he'd ransacked previously. The loss of his once-cherished possessions meant nothing to him. In those rages, which he had no control over, anything reminding him of Mamá was destroyed. So unpredictable were his tantrums, Marissa had taken to going to bed early and getting up very late. Perhaps the change of scenery would help, he decided. But he wouldn't go until Ceese was ready.

When Ceese entered the dining room, the only room still intact, he quietly pulled her chair out, and she took her seat. When she remembered to put her napkin in her lap, he was immensely pleased. Remarkably, she had dressed in a manner suggesting she cared what others might think. She'd worked on her hair as well. The cowlicks and uneven layers were still untamed, but one would be hard-pressed to say it looked unpresentable. He had to ask her to fasten her pants again, but decided not to chastise her. It never seemed to make a difference anyway.

Marissa served, but seemed nervous about it, still unconvinced despite Richard's words about how much their guest had changed.

"Just put the plate of food down in front of her," he said. "She won't try to bite you." He felt obligated to add, "Any more."

He noticed Ceese trying all sorts of looks in an effort to convince Marissa; her brow went up, then down, then furrowed. It was comical . . . until she belted out, her accent still quite Gaelic, "Oh, do hurry! I'm famished, and will most assuredly pass away in this very spot if you don't bring that food!"

Marissa only shifted her weight and looked uneasy.

Ceese turned to him for help, something she was doing a lot lately. "Tell her," she implored.

"Please, Marissa," Richard insisted. "I understand your reluctance, but it's fine. Really."

Marissa considered his words, but her face held the same fear it held when she was nearly crushed by a grandfather clock Richard had toppled during one of his tantrums. He hadn't known she was there, but neither had he checked. Now, she took a few cautious steps forward, placed the plate on the table in front of Ceese and immediately backed up, closing her eyes for a second and looking as though she were counting her blessings on her ten fingers and ten toes, grateful Ceese hadn't bitten off any of them. She then rushed off to the kitchen.

Ceese resisted the urge to dig in, but rather cut her piece of raw meat and chewed it properly, with her mouth shut.

Richard's brow went up. "Well, I must say, I *am* impressed."

This was truth. Until a few nights ago, she'd been eating under the table. And Marissa had great need to worry about her fingers and toes then; Ceese had taken a nip at her more than once. But things were different this evening. Adding to the experience, Ceese held up a polite finger to indicate she couldn't respond to Richard's remark until she finished chewing, then wiped her mouth with a napkin before speaking. "And so when do we leave for this place? This New York."

"As early as tomorrow if you continue like this."

Encouraged, Ceese decided to try her hand at small talk, another area where she seemed to come up short. Talking wasn't the problem; her instinctive choice of subject matter was. She wanted to talk of wolves, or things pertaining to her past. Both topics would put her under heavy scrutiny. Especially since her talk of wolves was in relation to her being one, and her past went further back than most would find plausible.

"Ceese, you're doing well tonight," Richard told her when he could bear it no longer. "But it would be better if you didn't discuss these things with others at all. Perhaps you can come up with other topics, and try them out on me."

She nodded, then said, "Will you be wrecking the castle tonight?"

Richard froze, decided she hadn't meant it the way she'd said it. "It's my way," he replied, hoping she would take the hint and move on.

But taking hints was another thing she didn't do well. "Well, your way could cost whomever it is we stay with in this New York a . . . a pretty penny."

"It's New York," he said suddenly, "not *this* New York. And you need to get it right." He stood, threw his napkin down, and headed out of the room.

Ceese sat quietly for a moment, then went after him. He had drilled her the day before on apologies and the proper way to do them. She didn't care if she'd upset him—couldn't care—but she'd learned how to apologize. And now, she knew she should.

꒰ ꒰ ꒰

She found him in the parlor, at his computer, and took a couple of tentative steps before stopping just inside the door. "Perhaps I'm not ready," she said. "This etiquette . . . it's far too complicated. It's much simpler when one is a wolf. When I was with the pack, I never had to wonder when to speak, or what to say, or how to say it. I . . . ah, it wasn't my intention to anger you."

"It isn't you," Richard said without looking at her. "You'll be fine."

Ceese scanned the room with her eyes. It was a disaster, and no repairs had been attempted lately. She did manage to find one item: a piece she recognized at once and went to, amazed she hadn't noticed it before. But it seemed to stand out now, being one of the few things in the room still in one complete piece.

"I haven't seen one of these in a long time." She screwed her face up as she examined it, then glanced up at him. "How old are you anyway?"

Richard ignored the question. "You have some knowledge about what you're looking at?"

She nodded, and her looked turned reflective. "In its time, it was used by moneychangers. To know the exact amount of precious metal a coin contained. Father collected them. It was a hobby of his. He had one very similar to this . . . just like it. But that was too long ago for me to remember exactly. I do remember how distraught Father was when one of his came up missing. . . . 'round about the time . . ."

Thinking, Ceese tinkered with it a little more. "Father never stopped trying to figure out who might have taken his."

"Like I said, they're very hard to come by."

Ceese turned back to him. "Well, anyway, I'm very sorry for what I said at the table. I didn't mean to upset you."

It took everything inside him, including the memory of his promise to Mamá, but he smiled. "What do you say we just call a truce?"

"I'd like that," Ceese answered, and held out her hand. "Let's shake on it."

Richard did, then went for a cigarette, and intentionally ignored Ceese as he lit it. On occasion, he still asked her to join him, and she declined each time.

"Why is it you never accept my offer?" he asked, and held up the cigarette.

She looked startled, as though his question were another test she desperately didn't want to fail. "Should I? Is it part of this etiquette?"

Richard shook his head. "No. I'd just like to understand. It isn't like smoking can affect you the way it affects others. You can't get cancer—" He stopped, let the memory of Mamá pass. "You can't die. So why not?"

"My father was a minister. I thought your father was a minister as well, and you yourself wanted to become one."

He bit back his first response: Mamá must have told her this, and he wasn't happy about Ceese knowing. "I hardly see your point," he finally said. "What my father did has nothing to do with the subject."

"Well, it might matter one day," Ceese offered, "if we're ever able to lift the curse. And then you'll be forever sorry you ever started that . . . that blasted habit."

Richard couldn't help laughing. "And what of it? One doesn't go to hell for smoking."

"Have you forgotten your body is the temple of the—?" she stopped, dealt with the pain of having a sacred thought, then continued. "The body is the temple of that which is holy."

"Well, *there's* an interesting way to approach the problem."

"Oh, so you think it's easy to say this? Well, if you think it's so easy, why don't you have a go at it? Try to say the same thing."

But he couldn't. Could barely think the word "holy," much less utter it. He looked at her with newfound respect. "How do you say such things with such ease?"

She shrugged. "Practice. And I started out with something easier. You can say 'unholy' without any trouble, can't you?"

He tried and did.

"So instead of saying 'that which is holy,' perhaps you can say something like 'that which isn't unholy' for a while. Before you know it, you'll be able to say 'holy' all by itself. And then you might actually be able to say God."

Richard looked on in disbelief; she appeared not to suffer at all. But then her expression began to change, slowly at first, then faster. Her face contorted, became a maze of lines. And her hands flew to her temples. "*Ahhhhhh*," she cried out.

"Are you all right?" he asked.

"That one hurt," she confessed. "I've still got a long way to go."

"Well, you've certainly put more effort into it than I ever have."

A more composed Ceese straightened then, her breathing still slightly labored. "I want to be free of it, Richard."

141

Her look was so desperate, but he refused to be the salve Mamá always was with her. "There's no guarantee anything Mamá told you will work," he said. "Mamá's head was full of dreams and hopes. Her experience was— There was never anything to substantiate her claims."

Ceese seemed stunned. "What of that? You don't believe her?"

"I don't believe anything I don't understand."

"Well, this is very interesting."

"How do you mean?" he asked, taking a long draw on the cigarette.

She took a deep breath before answering. "I'm certain you didn't understand vampires before you were afflicted with the curse. This would mean you didn't believe in their existence. Do you believe in them now, Richard? Does everything have to bite you on the neck before you believe?"

"Perhaps not," he admitted, then took hold of the computer's mouse, moved it around and clicked it a few times. A second later, he looked back up at her. "Well, we've got our plane tickets. We'll leave a week from tomorrow. And I hope you find what you're looking for then."

Ceese looked confused. "What's a plane, and why do we have to catch one?"

His sigh was deep, his concern still great. There was so much she needed to know, and he wasn't sure where to start. But then, he looked at the computer in front of him with new eyes.

"Come here," he said, and beckoned her with a wave.

As soon as she stood over his shoulder, he loaded Google.com, typed in "the history of aviation," and went from there.

CHAPTER 17

The next evening, they left the castle together. Richard headed for the woods, and Ceese took off through the pastures. Both needed fresh blood, and both knew where to get it.

The stiff breeze carried many scents, and Richard had no trouble picking up the tantalizing aroma of a buck. He stalked it for nearly half an hour, then readied to make his move. But just before he did, there was a gunshot. The buck bolted into the night.

Cursing, Richard considered which he should do: go after the buck, or go after what had frightened it. He chose the latter, because the deer was now too far away. It would take more darkness than he had left to find it.

The smell of gunpowder was strong. Richard followed the scent, and soon had the shooter in his sights. It was Peter Drummond, standing alone, holding the gun. When he saw Richard approach, he aimed the gun at him.

"I hit it," he blubbered as Richard came closer and disarmed the imbecile.

"Hit what?"

"The wolf! It was huge. Much bigger than the one the other night." He pointed to the ground, to a trail of blood leading back into the woods. "I wounded it. I've never seen such a wolf. It was going after my goats. But I got it."

From the goatherder's description, he'd definitely shot Ceese. Richard turned the gun on Peter. "You're certain you didn't kill it?"

Peter's hands flew up. "Yes. Yes, I'm sure! Do you see it lying around?"

Richard lowered the weapon, emptied it of its remaining shell and stared in awe at what he held.

"You're still using silver bullets?" he muttered in disbelief.

"Aye," Peter confirmed, more encouraged to talk now since his gun was empty and not aimed at his head. "There's a rumor it might be a werewolf, and the neighbors and I took up a collection to buy—"

Richard's response was to break the rifle over a knee before heading off into the woods, ignoring Peter's words concerning compensation for what he'd just destroyed.

ᴥ ᴥ ᴥ

Ceese had managed to transform back into her human form, had struggled into her clothes before being overwhelmed by the effects of the bullet lodged in her leg. Fortunately, the goatherder's aim was horrible. But the presence of silver in her body was taking its toll. She managed a few steps after dressing, then collapsed.

When Ceese came around, she saw Richard. He had eased her over onto her back, all while trying to get her to respond. He couldn't see the wound, but she knew he could smell the blood. "My leg," she moaned.

Richard ripped the fabric where she indicated and looked. "It's in deep," he said. "If I can get you back to the castle—"

"She shook her head. "No time. Take it."

He looked around, as if by some miracle he might find something other than a sharp stick or some otherwise useless item.

"*Fangs*," Ceese urged, clinging to consciousness. "Use them."

Richard sputtered, "Well, I hardly see how I can do that. Fangs . . . I'm not like you. I can't partially transform. It's all or nothing."

"Do it," she said gripping his arm. "I can help you control it—just, please . . ."

She could tell he had no idea what she was talking about, but he let the transformation begin.

It was easy since there was blood to encourage it, but it was also different with Ceese helping. She nodded at his look of surprise when he was able to stop at just the fangs, completely stop. Leaning down, he bit into her wound, manipulated the bullet until he had it, then sat back up.

When Richard leaned down to show her what he had, she grabbed at the cross around her neck, yanked at it until it came free, and pushed it hard against his chest, finding bare skin just above his shirt collar. Richard cried out, fell back, then stared at the charred impression on his skin in amazement.

"Well, you're bloody welcome," he said. "I save your life and you brand me!"

"Sorry—so sorry," Ceese managed before exhaustion took her over.

⁂ ⁂ ⁂

Just before she passed out, she saw Richard settle against a nearby tree. When she came around, he was still there. When he saw her eyes open, he said, "Such a quick recovery? I've taken silver bullets before, yet I've never been able to recover as fast."

Her reply was simple. "I think it was luck you found me when you did." She noticed his chest. The area still looked burned, although not as bad. "How are you?"

"Well, I'm certain I've felt better."

Her tone became less sympathetic. "I wasn't certain what you had in mind."

"And so you branded me?"

"Sorry," she tried again, and Richard gave in a little.

"I suppose I could let bygones be bygones. . . . What's done is done. But you should be more careful."

They sat quietly for a moment. Richard, however, had questions that wouldn't wait. "Why were you in the pastures, anyway? You had to know it wasn't safe. Peter Drummond's a menace, but he's not the only fool wandering around."

She glanced away. "I had no intention of lingering, I was just passing through."

"And something stopped you?"

145

"Something caught my eye," she confessed, "and I stopped to look."

It wasn't enough. He wanted more. "*What* caught your eye?"

Ceese looked back at him. "Your curse is strong, Richard. I had more trouble than I should've helping you hold the vampire back. I fear it's because your curse is . . . everlasting."

Richard chortled. "Whatever do you mean? The only way it can become everlasting is if I curse another and I'm certain I haven't."

But Ceese had been in the back pastures where Richard buried most of the goats he'd fed on. One of his more recent meals had been unearthed, cooked . . . and eaten. And the one who'd done the eating was dead.

She told Richard this. To his shocked reaction, she asked, "Didn't you say one could become cursed just by eating the meat from an animal you have fed on?"

"Yes, but *I'm* not affected. Only if I do the biting does this become an issue. I just don't like the idea of being responsible for cursing others."

Ceese considered this. "Did he die cursed, the one whom I found?" This seemed to trouble her greatly.

"Doubtful," Richard told her. "Most are too weak to handle the curse. I've known many who died because of this very thing. And if this young man was who I think he was—" He stopped, thought. "Tobias. Quite an unfortunate chap, both parents dead, homeless. Wasn't much bigger than a whisper last time he came to the castle begging for food. I'm fairly certain the curse never took hold."

He looked at Ceese. "What did you do with his body?"

"I buried it, along with what was left of the goat. Then I left to find you. But I found Peter instead and, well . . ." She pointed to her leg.

Richard nodded pensively. "I think it's time we headed back to the castle."

"But you haven't eaten, and neither have I. And I just saw a rabbit dart around behind that bush. You know there has to be more where it came from."

"You're in no condition to be hunting," he said, noting the wound still on her leg.

"No, but *you* are capable."

He gave a cautious smile. "Are you asking?"

She looked past him as if she saw something, heard something he didn't hear. "There'll be no need to ask for anything if you don't hurry . . . unless you can outrun a wolfhound."

He looked around and chortled loud this time. "Are you suggesting Xavier is on the hunt? That creature couldn't fetch a ball, much less a rabbit."

"Are you willing to bet a fat, juicy hare on what you think? And just for the record," Ceese added, "if there isn't a lot to go around, Xavier won't share."

The dog in question charged out of nowhere, bounded over Richard in hot pursuit and ran toward the bush. The rabbit flew out of the bush, and Xavier pursued it.

"I would hurry if I were you," Ceese added.

And Richard did, sprinting after the wolfhound seconds later.

"Blasted dog," she heard him shout. "Get away from my rabbit!"

CHAPTER 18

The following week passed quickly, and Ceese used the time to bring Marissa into her fold: something Richard wasn't at all sure about. And except for his nightly rages frightening her, he couldn't figure out the change in Marissa. In the past, he'd always been able to count on the young maid. Now she seemed always to be somewhere else. Presently, he couldn't find her to ask her where Ceese had gotten off to. Ceese had to know they needed to be at the airport soon. He'd reminded her several times already today. Annoyed, he continued his search.

Richard passed Xavier on his way through the parlor, and smiled. "Did you really think you had a chance at catching that rabbit?" he said. "I daresay I'm better at hunting than you any day."

The dog, as he knew it would, simply ignored him.

He checked a few more rooms. Then, at Marissa's room, he heard voices.

He knocked on the closed door. There was a scurrying about, then things got quiet.

Certain that Ceese was in there, Richard pushed his way in at once, but was chagrinned when he saw the startled maid whirl around to face him, then freeze like a statue. Ceese was nowhere in sight.

"Excuse me," he said. "I thought I heard you talking to someone. I don't suppose you know where Ceese has gotten off to?"

Marissa clasped her hands in front of her, but didn't reply.

"I just need to go over some things with her before we leave," he said, wondering at the maid's odd behavior, looking at her out of the corner of his eye as he walked around and randomly searched.

Then he saw movement under her bed. Marissa stifled a squeak when he headed there.

"I would have looked here first," he said staring at the dark-but-familiar form he found there, "but I thought you'd know better than to hide in the most obvious place."

"Perhaps that's why I did, then," Ceese replied.

He hunkered down to see her better. "And why are you hiding at all?"

"Perhaps I'm resting."

"You just admitted you were hiding," Richard said, exasperated. "Now, come on out."

"I won't."

"Excuse me?"

"She's frightened," Marissa blurted, then put a hand over her mouth.

Richard kept his eyes on Ceese. "Frightened? Of what?"

When Ceese didn't answer, Richard turned back to Marissa, who wouldn't answer, then back to Ceese, who had better.

"Flying," Marissa blurted once his back was to her, clearly torn, Richard noticed from her outburst, between being loyal to him and loyalty to her new friend. Then she ran from the room.

"A good *wolf* wouldn't have betrayed me," Ceese grumbled after Marissa.

"Yes, well, while Marissa is basically good, she's hardly a wolf. Now come along so we can talk about this problem you have."

"I don't have a problem," Ceese said as she moved out and stood, snapping her slacks just as Richard went to do it himself. "I just don't think I'll like flying. Especially not after you showed me what you showed me on the computer. Those two brothers—"

"The Wright brothers," Richard filled in.

"Yes. They didn't impress me much."

"Well, flying has come along way since their time. I showed you this as well. And this is what you told me you wanted, more than anything. Remember?"

Ceese looked down. "I just don't want to do the flying part . . . don't think I can."

Richard extended a hand. "Come with me."

Ceese backed away a bit. "Why?"

"It's seven p.m. Our flight's not scheduled until ten, and it will only take a half-hour to get to the airport. And before we go, there's something I'd like to show you in . . . Mamá's garden."

Ceese loved the gardens, but didn't seem sure about visiting the one Penny had favored over all the others. She followed Richard nonetheless, and when Richard stopped walking at the very middle of the garden, she stopped too.

A tall stucco wall surrounded them, covered with fragrant vines and flowers that blossomed only in the moonlight. She and Penny had come here often, but Ceese wasn't aware of any interest Richard had in this place.

Just as she was about to ask him about that, he turned his back to her and said, "I want you to put your arms around my neck from behind and close your eyes. I don't want you to open them until I tell you to . . . no matter what."

Ceese didn't move.

"What is it?" he asked, looking back over his shoulder.

"You want me to get on your back?"

"Yes, why? Are you scared? Afraid of a vampire—a big bad wolf such as yourself?"

It worked, and she moved in closer, but then stopped again.

"What is it now?" he said, impatient.

Ceese took the necklace with its cross, arranged it so the cross hung down her back. "I wouldn't want to be accused of *branding* you again."

Richard appreciated the gesture and told her so, then, "We don't have long before we have to leave, so please hurry."

"You promise not to bite me?"

"Not the least bit interested," he said. "Remember? I fed only an hour ago."

"Well . . . all right, then."

Once she was in position, Richard took hold of each of her legs. And with her on his back piggyback-style, he lifted off. Levitating wasn't something he did much any more, for fear some neighbor might see him, but he did miss it.

150

He felt Ceese tense when they became airborne, and said, "Keep your eyes closed."

She grabbed on tighter, and didn't lighten her hold until Richard was back on the ground.

"All right," Richard said, "you can open your eyes now."

Ceese did, and looked around, but didn't notice they were now on the other side of the back wall—a solid wall, six feet high. "I-I heard that vampires could do that," Ceese sputtered to him, "but never actually—"

She took a few steps away from the wall, looked around again, then stared at Richard long and hard. "You—You tricked me."

"I merely wanted to show you how silly your fear of flying was." Richard replied. "See? You went up and over that wall, and you're fine."

Ceese stood quiet for another moment, appeared to consider Richard's words. Finally, she spoke. "Can I have another go at it, this time with my eyes open?"

He went much higher than before, and Ceese reacted much like a child experiencing some great thing for the first time. "The lights," she gasped, very close to his ear, "they look like stars on the ground. And look, they're moving!"

"Automobiles," Richard told her. "You'll see more of them in New York City." A few vehicles had passed the castle, but she hadn't seemed interested in them.

"Oh, yes! I've heard," she said. "And they move without horses, don't they?"

Ceese said nothing else for the longest time. When she did speak again, she had a question for Richard: one she'd asked before, and he hadn't really answered. "Will you tell me now why you color your hair?"

Richard allowed them to move lower suddenly, eliciting a gasp from her. Then he said, "I'll answer your question *if* you answer one for me."

"I shall . . . consider it."

"All right. Why do I constantly have to remind you to fasten your pants?"

151

When she didn't reply, he asked, "Do you still want me to tell you why I dye my hair?"

"Not if it means I have to answer your question."

"Very well, then. Let's have no more talk about hair or pants. Is there anything else you'd like to know?"

"Well, it seems odd you didn't show me you can fly before tonight. Were you keeping it a secret?"

"It's more like levitating, and no, I wasn't keeping it a secret. I just don't need the neighbors talking." It wasn't a lie, but neither was it the truth. And before he could stop the thought, he remembered a night when levitating had actually worked against him. He forced the thought away and continued. "And sometimes it's an annoying ability. Like when you try to throw yourself from a high cliff with the intention of hitting the bottom. Instinct kicks in and . . . well, you can't."

"Why would you want to do something so painful?" Ceese asked. "Unless you were trying to—" And then, she understood. "It's a sin to kill one's self!"

"You don't mean it," Richard said, punctuating his cynical remark with a sigh.

Ceese left him alone after that.

ﻙ ﻙ ﻙ

They flew a little longer until Richard decided he needed to check the time, instinctively thought of his wristwatch, but decided not to give Ceese a scare by letting go of one of her legs. Instead, he looked at the stars in the sky. They didn't have much longer, so he turned to head back.

As they approached the woods again, hovered just below the treetops, Ceese pointed, jumped from his back, landed in a crouch and darted off into the darkness. Stunned by her action, Richard returned to the ground and followed, calling after her.

When he reached her, she was kneeling on the ground in front of Xavier's prone form. Ceese turned to look at Richard, angry. "He's dead, and I know who shot him," she told him, and held up the casing she'd found. It was silver.

Richard nodded, fixed Ceese with a hard stare. "I destroyed his gun after he shot you, but he must have another. Let's bury our friend, and then we'll go pay the goatherder a visit." He glanced at the sky once more. "But we have to hurry. We don't have much time."

"Neither does Peter Drummond," Ceese said, and started a hole in the soil where the ground was softer. Her face was unreadable.

Working together, the task took only minutes, and Richard couldn't stop thinking about what Ceese had just said. Once the last bit of dirt was placed over the grave, he asked, "Did you have something in mind for our friend, or were you just talking?"

She stood, sniffed at a passing breeze, tilted her head a little to one side and sniffed again. "I have something in mind. Take me north of here. I'll tell you as we go."

❦ ❦ ❦

Richard didn't bother knocking but rather barged into the small cabin, pushing the door with such force it banged against the wall before closing back again. Peter leaped from his bed, fumbled around for his trousers, and nearly fell trying to get into them. His companion for the evening was equally startled.

"Get out," Richard snarled at the woman, who'd taken a blanket from the bed to cover herself with. She wasted no time, rushed along without stopping to gather her clothes. The door slammed shut behind her.

"You got no right," Peter started as Richard began pulling things down from shelves, ransacking closets and cubbyholes. Things fell, other things broke.

"Where is it?" Richard said, pulling the last item out of the last closet. "Where did you hide it?"

"I-I don't know what you're talking about," was the stuttered reply.

Richard moved in close, prepared to make a threat, but then he saw what he'd been looking for. Reaching down and around Peter, he took the rifle sticking out from under the bed. It clicked as he readied it to be fired and turned toward Peter in one smooth motion. "If I pull the trigger, will I blow your head off? Or did you need *two* bullets to shoot a defenseless dog?"

"It-It was just a dog. I thought it was a wolf. I was protecting my property."

Richard took aim.

"I told you, I thought it was a wolf!"

"Yes, and I suppose you thought *I* was a wolf when you practically shot at me the other night too."

"Ah . . . uh. One can never be sure."

Richard noted the empty bottles everywhere, the smell of liquor in the room. "No, I don't suppose one can be, especially when one is heavily intoxicated."

"So shoot me," Peter threw out. "Go ahead. They'll know it was you, and they'll take you away."

Richard nodded and lowered the gun. "You have no idea how tempted I am— but I'm going to let you live. But only because I believe those coming next will do a better job of finishing you off."

"Finishing me off?" Peter said, recovering some of his brashness.

"For murdering Long Tail, and then Xavier."

"Who the blazes is Long Tail . . . and Xavier?"

"The wolf you took down the other night, and the dog you shot tonight. *My* dog." Suddenly, being noble felt right.

There was a howl in the distance and then another, and another. The cottage's door opened wide and Ceese entered. "Judgment day has come," she said to the terrified goatherder. "Long Tail and Xavier rest in peace. It remains to be seen if you will."

Peter watched as Richard broke his new gun, just as he'd done before. He continued to watch as Richard purposefully pulled his front door from its hinges, to give the approaching pack easier access.

"You can't leave me like this," Peter babbled when he realized what was happening. "I have no weapon, no way to protect myself!"

Richard gave him a harsh smile. "I'd run, then."

※ ※ ※

As he and Ceese lifted off to head back to the castle, he asked her, "Will they kill him?"

"Would it bother you if they did?"

"Not at all," he answered, landing just shy of the castle lawn and letting her down from his back. "But it does seem odd you would condone such an act."

It seemed to take the wind out of her sails. "He took lives. He deserves to die."

"Many individuals do, but you seem to be taking this personally."

"Long Tail was a brother to me."

"You said you weren't one of them. You even ate him."

"I know I'm not a wolf, but sometimes it's hard to forget. They were my family for so long. And what's wrong with wanting Peter Drummond dead? It isn't as if you, or I, are doing the killing."

"Oh, I can deal with it," Richard said, not really wanting to believe a part of him could actually condone murder. "However, I'm not so sure you can. I believe you're forcing yourself to deal with it to rationalize something you *want* to believe is right."

Curious eyes met his. "How do you know what I believe?"

"How can I not know? You make no effort to hide it."

She turned away, but he continued. "You say you aren't one of them, but you can't let them go. Why? What's holding you back? If what you say is true, and you are what you say you are, then you should be able to just leave them."

"It's . . . not that easy."

"Perhaps you should stay, then. Forget about trying to get your curse lifted. . . ." Then, he gave her his best punch. "Zade obviously understands you and cares about you."

He had her attention again. "He said that?"

"Not in so many words," Richard recalled, "but yes." He thought of the relationship he and Mamá had shared over the years, remembered how much it had meant to him. "Are you sure you don't want to stay with him? If he's like you, then—"

155

"He isn't like me," Ceese snapped. "He has cursed others." And then, much slower, "He cursed me."

So, she's afraid of him! It made perfect sense now, and intimidation was a powerful persuader. Richard wondered if she were going to be able to rise above it.

Until she said, "But I don't fear Zade. He's helped me in some ways too." She didn't elaborate.

Richard had to know, and he wanted her to tell him. "So what are you saying?"

"I want to go with you, Richard. I want to leave this place. I want to break this curse. Mamá said Cassie can help, and I believe her. We need to go to her."

He nodded. "Then we should be on our way."

CHAPTER 19

The taxi screeched to a stop in front of the airport. Rodney got out first, followed by Kyle, then seconds later by Josh, who couldn't seem to move fast enough. He still had hold of the door when the taxi sped away to get to the next potential customer. He was yanked off the curb he was trying for but recovered before being pulled down completely.

"Hey," he shouted after the driver.

Rodney, watching, shook his head. Under different circumstances, Josh might have said more, but his friend was suffering. The whole time in the taxi, Josh complained about his aching tongue, still recovering from the piercing incident a few days back. Infection set in and required a visit to the emergency room. Josh mostly ignored the antibiotics, but took the prescribed painkillers like candy. Josh wasn't exactly loopy, tonight, but seemed on edge. Rodney wondered if asking Josh along tonight had been such a good idea, after all.

Kyle didn't seem worried, though, just amused. "You really told off that cabdriver, man," he said with a smirk. "I especially liked the part where you said, 'Hey'."

Josh took offense, moved toward him, eyes blazing. Rodney waved at Josh to slow him down, then reached out and pulled Kyle aside. "What are you doing?" he hissed. "I don't need this."

"Sorry," Kyle said, putting up both hands and smoothing back his red hair. "But he's like a zombie, man. How many painkillers has he popped today anyway?" And then, "It was just too easy."

"Maybe, but maybe you should remember the last time you thought he couldn't react fast enough to hurt you. You nearly ended up in the emergency room."

"Yeah," Kyle said, grinning stupidly. "I almost had him then."

Rodney sighed and gave up. "And what's up with this jewelry?" He pointed to Kyle's nose chain. "I'm pretty sure I told you to tone it down for this."

Kyle had several earrings in both ears and a stud in his right brow. Rodney was fine with those. But the thin chain connecting Kyle's left earlobe to the left side of his nose was new, and would stand out in a witness's mind if things went wrong tonight.

"Fine," Kyle said, and unhooked and removed the chain. "Happy now?"

"Sure, yeah," Rodney told him. "Now you look like a punk who forgot his chain."

"Well, *he* has dreads," Kyle protested, pointing back to Josh. And, in fact, Josh did have dreads, and jeans sagging as low as he could wear them. "You're gonna say something to me when he looks like *that*?"

Kyle had a point. "Wait here," Rodney said, and walked back over to Josh, who was still scowling at Kyle. Rodney's only chance to avoid a fight was to separate them. He couldn't send Kyle away—Josh was obviously stoned, and that wouldn't work for the plan. So Josh had to go.

"Josh, I need you to do something for me," he said, wondering if Josh was hearing him. "Dr. Henderson rented a car for us. The place is right inside the airport. I need you to go down and get the keys. Just wait for us there. Can you do that?"

Josh nodded.

"Thanks, man. The car should be in my name. All you should need is this confirmation number." He handed a stub of paper over.

"Got it," Josh said, and sauntered off, offering a hand sign as he backed away, bringing his right hand; three fingers straight, two bent, some crossed, in front of him, and then reaching for his groin area with his other hand.

Rodney held out both hands and shrugged—he didn't get it—but apparently, Kyle did: He made a gesture of his own, with the middle finger of his right hand, which Rodney quickly batted down when he got close enough to do so. "Would you grow up? You're drawing attention."

"He started it," Kyle said, smirking as only Kyle could.

"Just come on," Rodney pleaded, waving Josh on his way. "Dr. Henderson will start wondering if we don't show on time, and I don't want to piss him off. There's too much money at stake."

⚡ ⚡ ⚡

They had taken the latest flight possible so they could make the entire flight at night. Yet Richard still decided to wear sunglasses, and had dressed to cover as much skin as he could. He'd also used a self-tanner to help darken his hands and face so he wouldn't draw unwanted attention by being so pale. But most of it just absorbed into his skin and made little difference.

Though she was almost as pale, Ceese didn't have to worry as much about her pallor. She had enough color not to be questioned. And she had spent a few days outside with Marissa, which had helped some.

Her unusual-colored eyes, however, were another matter, and Ceese absolutely refused to wear shades. Her long bangs helped hide some of the mystery of irises that were more gold than green, though, and Richard decided not to push the matter. He'd learned many her age wore odd contact lenses for self-expression, had seen some pictures in a magazine. She didn't look nearly as bizarre as some of those models. And he felt better after seeing how few people reacted at the airport. Most just seemed mildly curious, giving Ceese nothing more than a passing glance.

They switched flights once, and while Richard knew he would have to explain things to Ceese along the way, he never imagined it would be so difficult. She didn't understand motors, or anything electronic. They had to take the stairs in all instances because Ceese decided escalators were evil, as were elevators—and any other modern convenience she didn't understand. Richard tried to explain, but discovered it took less time to just agree with her and take the stairs.

But then there were all the strange new sounds around her.

159

Loud ones especially unnerved her. Richard had already felt a claw form in one of the hands he was holding when an infant just behind them cried out. He got her to stuff her ears with cotton to avoid any other such reaction.

These things seemed to work, until they discovered they'd be late for their connecting flight if they didn't take the airport's internal subway system. No amount of explaining how much time it would save them helped; Ceese removed the cotton from her ears and balked when the subway car's doors hissed opened in front of her.

"Evil?" Richard guessed.

"The devil himself," she confirmed when an automated voice repeated brief safety directions in several different languages. "Do you not hear him?"

"We have to do this," Richard said. "If we don't, we'll miss our flight."

Meanwhile, the doors slid shut, the train pulled away and Richard sighed. He had all of five minutes to convince her before the next train arrived.

"Why can't we just walk?" she asked. "Why must we take this thing to where we have to go?"

"Oh, fiddlesticks," came a voice from behind her. Ida Mae was ninety years old, and was traveling with her granddaughter, Lindsey, who she handed her cane to before grabbing one of Ceese's arms for support. "Young woman, it's not as bad as it looks."

Richard tensed at the look Ceese gave the woman, but Ida Mae just patted her arm and said in a sappingly southern accent, "If an old woman like me can ride this thing, then you can too. It'll be fine. You'll see."

And like a miracle, Ceese allowed the woman to nudge her along, leading her into the next train.

Within minutes, they were at the appropriate concourse, and Ceese had made a new friend. Ida Mae stayed on the train, however; she and Lindsey, her favorite grandchild, were headed to baggage claim. But Richard noticed, right away, that when Ida Mae turned loose of Ceese, the woman was standing on her own, not holding onto anything. Never had he seen anyone look as amazed as the elderly woman did when Ceese waved at her and walked to where Richard stood.

"Where to now?" Ceese asked. But her nonchalance didn't play well with him.

"What did you do?" he asked, trying to keep his voice level.

"I'm certain I don't know what you're talking about."

"You did something to Ida Mae," he said pointing back to where Ida Mae was standing just a moment before. "That woman . . . Ceese, what did you do?"

Ceese started walking. Richard followed, willing himself to be patient. "You need to tell me, Ceese. If you did something, you need to tell me."

Ceese stopped short and turned. "I did nothing. There was nothing to be done."

It seemed, for a moment, she would explain no further. But then she took a deep breath, closed her eyes and then opened them. "She didn't have this *arthritis* like the doctors said. She just thought she had it because the doctors told her this. Her joints were just stiff."

Richard's face contorted. "Ceese—stiff joints is, in fact, what arthritis is!"

"Oh."

"What did you do?"

If she were making a decision, it was a tough one. Richard could tell by the way she bit her lip, studied the floor. "There is a place in your mind," she said, "where one can go . . . to get relief from pain, if one but knows the way. All I did was to take her there. She helped me, so I helped her."

Now Richard's eyes closed, and he rubbed the bridge of his nose, hard. "You can't help people, Ceese." He stopped rubbing, looked at her. "If she talks to anyone about what happened, they'll try to find you. They'll want to know—" Someone passed by, too close. Richard waited. "—what you did, and how you did it. Do you understand?"

"She won't tell anyone," Ceese replied. "She promised."

He had to make her understand the danger she'd put herself in, and him if he chose to stick with her once they arrived in

161

New York. "Just don't do it again. I won't help you anymore if you do."

"All right," Ceese said, her voice hollow. "If it's important to you."

"It is. Oh, you have no idea how important it is."

❧ ❧ ❧

By the time Ida Mae and Lindsey reached the airport lobby, Ida Mae was practically jogging. Lindsey, struggling to keep up, was talking excitedly into her cell and telling whoever it was about the change in her grandmother. But then a surprisingly strong hand took the cell phone from her.

"No," Ida Mae said. "You mustn't tell."

Lindsey looked at her, unbelieving. "But why not?"

"Because I promised. You can't say anything."

Shaking her head, Lindsey returned to fighting to keep up with the newly spry Ida Mae, all while thinking she needed to work out more often.

❧ ❧ ❧

Ceese slept most of the way through the long flight, but Richard didn't. It was his time to be up. His altered biological clock wouldn't let him rest easily. So instead he sat, watched people walk past his aisle seat, and tried not to transform. But it was a struggle. He had gorged before they left. Yet there was *so much* of what he needed right there, within reach. At one point, when a stewardess leaned over him to ask if she could get him anything, he felt fangs emerge. But just before the urge overwhelmed him, Ceese roused, grabbed hold of his arm. Her thoughts became his.

If I can wait, you can wait.

He hadn't felt such restraint since the night Ceese helped him in the woods, the night he'd had to take the bullet from her leg. The fangs retracted.

"I'm sorry," the stewardess said to Ceese. "Did I wake you? I just stopped to see if he needed anything."

162

Richard cleared his throat. "No, we're fine."

The stewardess smiled but seemed a little disappointed. Ceese read her thoughts and found out why. The stewardess was hoping he and Ceese weren't romantically involved, and would try to get his phone number later. Or perhaps this handsome, charming man would ask for hers.

"He *said* we didn't need anything," Ceese snapped.

"Oh," the stewardess replied, composing herself. "Well, I'll be around if you do need anything." She then nodded and headed off.

"You didn't have to be so abrupt," Richard said. "You could have said what you needed to say without the tone. It wasn't her fault. I'm in need of blood."

Ceese looked at him, befuddled. "Meaning what?"

"When I'm in need, others are drawn to me."

"Preposterous!"

"No, it's true." He gave her a sly look. "Why? Did it make you jealous?"

"Jealous?" Her eyes widened, her mouth dropped open. "No, it made me sick! To have no more respect for one's self." Then her face fell. "Do you think she's attractive?"

Richard laughed. "You *are* jealous!"

"I certainly am not! I just don't believe your story—your saying she was *drawn* to you."

"All right, then I'll prove it." Richard took a quick look up and down the aisle. "Select someone. A complete stranger. Pick one, and call them over."

"Him," Ceese said, pointing at a male steward.

Just as Richard predicted, the steward didn't need much prodding; he practically stumbled in his rush to get back to where they were. There was a lilt to his speech, though, a drawing out of vowels, and his movements were more effeminate than masculine.

Richard eyed Ceese to see if she'd noticed this. Her quizzical look told him she had. But then her look changed; her brows set in confusion.

Ceese held her response, waited for the disappointed steward

163

to leave before exploding. "He prefers men over women. It's an abomination!"

"Yes, but what of it? I told you the lure was strong."

"I don't care what you say," Ceese said. "I think you can control what you do."

Richard shook his head. "The hungrier I get, the worse it gets." Just as he finished his statement, another flight attendant stopped by to ask if they needed anything.

Ceese fumed. "Oh, do leave us alone! We don't need anything. Why don't you go help someone else?"

Richard was alarmed at seeing Ceese get angry; he didn't want to deal with the wolf on an airplane thousands of feet above the earth. "We're fine," he said to the woman.

As soon as she left, he turned to Ceese. "You really should get a handle on your anger. And, yes, I can control the 'luring,' as you call it, to some degree. I'll put forth my best effort. But, please, work on controlling your emotions. I've never known anyone so temperamental."

Ceese groused, found her thin pillow with her head, and turned away from him.

Her brooding didn't hold out for long. "Why was he—the steward you lured over—why was he in a closet, Richard? And why does he choose men over women?"

There were at least forty-five minutes left in the flight, and Richard was certain he was going to need every one of them to explain.

CHAPTER 20

Rodney and Kyle stood where they were visible to anyone exiting the concourse. Both held crude signs made from scrap pieces of cardboard they'd found lying around. On each piece of cardboard, Rodney had written "Cassie Felts."

"What if vampires can't read?" Kyle asked.

"He sends her e-mails," Rodney replied. "How could he do that if he couldn't read?"

"Well, what if Cassie finds out you've been intercepting her e-mails and sending them to Dr. Henderson?"

Rodney glared at his friend. "How's she gonna find out? I covered my tracks."

"Oh, right," Kyle said, gearing up. "I forgot. You're the big computer expert. Tell me again. . . . Why won't they let you back in the computer lab? Oh, yeah, I remember now! You took down the entire system when you tried to install something you pirated off the Internet."

"I fixed that," Rodney said, not at all pleased by Kyle's bringing this up.

"Yeah, but not before they banned you from ever using the school's computers again."

Rodney sighed. "Look, Cassie's not gonna find out. So just relax."

Yet Rodney knew Kyle wouldn't relax. It wasn't his nature. And besides, Kyle was in almost as deep as he was now. "You better hope she *doesn't* find out," Kyle added, "because I don't want to get kicked out of school."

Rodney gave him a casual shrug. "I told you, man. Nobody's

gonna get kicked out of school. Dr. Henderson knows what he's doing."

⛧ ⛧ ⛧

Richard and Ceese disembarked without incident. Though it was clear some were still drawn to Richard, no one else asked if they could help them, so Ceese didn't have to react.

Richard saw the two young men first, saw the signs with Cassie's name, and was immediately suspicious. He had expected Cassie herself.

He pulled Ceese a little further along, then directed her to fall in behind him. But she wouldn't turn loose of his hand, and kept staring ahead at the two men. He still didn't like her, but had learned to respect her ability to sense things. His e-mail had been specific. Things were to happen exactly as he stated, or they wouldn't happen at all. And besides, it was now three o'clock in the morning; daylight wasn't far away. He wanted answers, and now.

"Ceese," he said, "if there's something I should know about those two, tell me."

When she didn't reply, he repeated her name, but she remained silent. He turned his head partway to look at her.

"It's nothing," she finally replied, then did as he had asked, falling in behind him, then stopping when he did.

As soon as they neared Rodney and Kyle, Richard asked, "Where's Cassie?"

Instead of answering, Kyle nudged Rodney in the ribs and muttered, "I told you it was them, dude. And check out those sunglasses—in the middle of the night."

"It's very rude to speak of someone when they're standing in front of you," Richard said to Kyle, then glared at Rodney. "And it's even ruder not to answer their question. Where's Cassie?"

Rodney had seen every e-mail Cassie sent Richard, and vice-versa, had gone out of his way to reread them before they left to refresh his memory. He lied with confidence. "Cassie couldn't come," he said easily. "She sent us to get you. We made signs. We rented a car."

166

"Why would she send you and not come herself?"

"Her car broke down at the last minute. She asked us if we could help her out. She said you might not believe me, but hoped you'd trust her."

Rodney's face was unreadable, so Richard looked to Kyle, who had the expression of someone watching a suspense-thriller. A box with popcorn wouldn't have looked out of place in his hands, its contents being eating slowly, one popped kernel at a time.

After a pause, Richard said, "Let's go, then."

Ceese responded at once to Richard's signal to follow, and walked with him while Rodney and Kyle led the way.

If Kyle was impressed by Rodney's ability to lie to someone who looked as though he could do great harm to both of them, it didn't show. And he had more questions for Rodney. "Dude," he said to Rodney, his lips barely moving, "I don't like this. There's something freaky about them. And get a load of the freaky chic. What's up with those eyes?"

"She's a werewolf," Rodney whispered.

"What?" Kyle stammered. "Why didn't you say something?"

"Because, *moron*, werewolves don't exist. Geez, do you believe in the Easter Bunny too?"

"Well, why did you say she was one if she isn't?"

"It's just what I read in one of the e-mails. But, just for the record, I don't believe she's a werewolf any more than I believe he's a vampire."

They rounded a corner and Kyle barked, too loud, "What else did the e-mail say?"

"Nothing else," Rodney answered as they approached the baggage carousel. He noticed sweat-beads on Kyle's forehead. "Quit looking so suspicious."

"Suspicious?" Kyle said, his eyes darting about, checking out anything and everything. "Oh, I'm sorry, do I look suspicious? Dude, those two aren't right. Do you understand what I'm saying? They're not right!"

"Fine," Rodney replied. "Let's just get through this, okay? We'll drop them off at Henderson's place, and we'll be done with them."

"No," Kyle said quickly, "we'll get our money first, and *then* we'll drop them off."

"Yes, now relax."

"I'll relax when I see the five hundred dollars—the five hundred dollars *each*, that is."

❧ ❧ ❧

Richard stood by Ceese and watched for their bags to come around. Clearly, Ceese was still trying to deal with all the loud, strange sounds around her. Back on the plane, Richard had tried, but she refused to put the cotton back in her ears. So before the anticipated blast of the horn signaling that the luggage carousel would start rotating, he put his hands over her ears so she wouldn't be startled.

Rodney glanced over at them when the horn sounded, trying to figure out why Richard had his hands over Ceese's ears when the rental car agent showed back up at the counter. At once she began going through her spiel about damages and insurance. Rodney listened but didn't listen—until Richard caught him staring. Then, he gave his attention back to the rental car agent.

The rental agent finally left, and Rodney turned to Josh. "Where is it?" he asked just before their conversation turned heated. Moments later, Ceese and Richard, bags in hand, walked up to Kyle who had purposefully separated himself from his friends for the moment.

Richard jerked his chin at Josh, then asked Kyle. "Is he someone I should know?" Richard glowered at Kyle, then Josh and Rodney in turn, as though waiting for an explanation.

Kyle said, "Uh . . . you mean Josh, dude?"

Richard was dressed all in black: tailored black slacks, black turtleneck and a long black coat he carried over an arm. He'd pulled his blonde hair back for the trip. Ceese stood next to him, intimidating in her own right.

"Yes, *dude*," Richard drawled at them, "Has Josh done something wrong?"

Kyle couldn't resist. "Dude, it's Josh. Everything he *does* is wrong. But then, I guess you wouldn't know that."

"No, I guess I wouldn't."

Kyle shrank back a little at the ice in Richard's voice. "I-I'm sure he'll be through yelling at him soon."

But Richard didn't have time, or patience. He walked over to them, Ceese following.

". . . because, I just talked to—" Rodney stopped short, noticed he was being listened to. "—*Cassie,* on my cell. And *she* said there'd be some money for us when we got the car. Said she arranged it that way."

"Dude," Josh replied, "there must be something wrong with *your* hearing. I already told you there wasn't any money. The woman didn't mention a thing about it."

"It's in his pocket," Ceese blurted out. "He's going to buy something called 'weed' with it later."

If her words hadn't caught their attention, her Gaelic accent would have. Josh seemed all at once nervous. "Hey," he said, "not so loud." He looked around, dug out what he said he didn't have. "I forgot about it, that's all. And she's wrong about what I was gonna do with it."

Kyle, standing next to Rodney, leaned and whispered, "She can read minds, man!"

"Right," Rodney whispered sardonically, "like she couldn't tell from looking at him."

Josh appeared to have recovered from Ceese's revelation, but it was clear how he felt about her divulging his intentions. It wasn't any of her business what he was going to do with the money. And nobody liked a rat.

"It *is* my business," Ceese told him, "if what you do affects Richard and me."

"Ceese," Richard warned. "Leave it alone."

"Yeah, cease that," Josh seconded, then added an unnecessary gender slur. He found himself on the floor, with Ceese easily pinning him down despite his being twice her size.

"I'm not *that*," she said, extremely close to his neck. "I'm not what you said!"

Richard knelt down and spoke into her ear, "This isn't helping us."

Her response was a low growl.

Rodney sighed. The last thing they needed right now was create a scene. "Josh, tell her you're sorry."

Josh, pinned to the floor, said, "What?"

Rodney's jaw clenched. "Apologize, dude. Tell her you're freakin' *sorry!*"

"Okay, okay, I'm freakin' *sorry*. Now get off me!"

Ceese only leaned in closer. Josh's eyes grew wide.

"Damn it, Josh!" Rodney yelled. "Say it like you mean it."

"All right," Josh shouted. "I'm sorry! I've never been sorrier! Just let me up—please. I'll never call you that again. It was wrong, and I'm sorry."

After another tense moment, Ceese gave in, or seemed to. She said something else, but it wasn't in a language the others would understand. Richard did, though. The word *blaidd* meant "wolf" in Gaelic. And remembering Ceese's true nature, he was suddenly very glad Josh had apologized.

"Perhaps we could move along now," he said, standing with Ceese.

But the two of New York's finest that sauntered up then felt differently. The call from the rental car agent, plus what they'd just seen, meant they weren't about to let anyone go anywhere yet.

"Is there a problem here?" one asked, and Richard went right to work, moving toward the two men, making eye contact. "Everything's fine here, officers. But thank you for asking."

"Things don't look fine," one said.

Richard clasped the man's shoulder. "I assure you, everything is fine."

The hypnosis worked. For a moment, the man just looked lost. Then, his expression changed to a more normal one. "Well, if you need anything else, just let us know."

The two moved on, and Richard walked back to where the others were.

"How'd you *do* that?" Kyle asked, dumbfounded. "They *never* let anyone go."

But Richard didn't feel like explaining. "I think, before something else happens, we should leave."

Josh, rubbing one of his shoulders, led the way.

CHAPTER 21

Just as Richard instructed her to do before he left, Marissa checked his e-mail. Sure enough, a new message was in his inbox. It was from someone named Cassie, who wanted to know if Richard and Ceese had changed their minds about coming to New York.

"Oh, dear," she whispered. What if this person never got their message?

Marissa noted the time of the message with alarm, and made a difficult decision. Richard had told her to check his e-mail, but not to send any. Yet this seemed like a terrible emergency.

She e-mailed Cassie back, told her Richard and Ceese had already left and they should have been there by now. To explain better, Marissa resent the first e-mail, containing Richard's confirmation of the time of their New York arrival.

As Marissa signed off, she heard the voice calling her from the dining room and rushed to respond. The stranger had arrived shortly after Richard and Ceese left, had taken charge. She briefly resisted him, hiding in her room, not smiling when he asked her for one thing or another. But his charm soon won her over, and she acceded to both his requests: he would stay here until Richard's return, and she was to tell no one of his visit.

※ ※ ※

Cassie couldn't believe her eyes. How had her e-mail not gotten to her? She'd gotten all the others. Or at least, she thought she had.

She looked at the e-mail she'd just received from Marissa

and gasped when she saw the date and time on the original—the e-mail she never received.

"Rodney," she breathed. The time and date were exactly when she remembered finding him at her computer. "He lied to me!" she whispered. But why? And why would he delete her e-mail?

She shrugged off her confusion, her anger . . . her questions. She had to get to the airport. Her visitors were surely standing there, wondering what had happened to her.

She got up, went to the spot where she always put her keys, but discovered them missing. She raced downstairs to see if perhaps she'd left them in the car, but they weren't there either. She used her cell phone to call a cab, and waited for it, hoping it would hurry.

❧ ❧ ❧

Josh started the car, then produced a CD from somewhere inside the large bomber jacket he wore like a second skin. *Headbangers Ball* was scrawled on the CD in black ink. He'd downloaded it yesterday, despite warnings from his well-to-do brother, who hadn't wanted Josh on his computer, didn't want him using his account to steal music off the file-sharing websites Josh visited regularly. But Josh did it anyway. He couldn't afford the CD, and his brother wouldn't give him the cash to buy it. Josh smiled smugly and cranked the volume up.

Ceese didn't react well. A claw dug into Richard's leg, he cried out, but absolutely nothing could be heard over the siren-like squeal of tortured guitars. Richard lunged over the backseat, ejected the disc. Both Josh and Rodney stared in wonder as the hand that had taken the CD then crushed it.

"If you have any more of these," Richard said, "you might think twice before playing them."

"Wha-What about the radio?" Josh sputtered.

"I'll destroy it, too." He let the pieces of the CD fall into the seat between them and sat back down. Ceese had calmed.

After taking a moment for his heart to quit thumping as hard,

Josh proceeded to drive. He'd been adamant about wanting to, and Rodney had reluctantly given in to avoid another scene.

He didn't pay much attention to where Josh was driving though. Instead, he concentrated on *how* he was driving. The first sign of swerving or radical maneuvering, and he'd put his foot down. But Josh did fine . . . until he made a drastic left turn into a part of the city Rodney wouldn't consider safe in the daytime, much less at this hour of the morning.

"Hey, man, this isn't the way there," Rodney began, but stopped when Josh took another hard turn into an alley.

Before any of them could react, Josh slammed the car into park, reached under his enormous bomber jacket and produced a handgun.

Stunned, Rodney backed up against the passenger-side door. This definitely wasn't in the plan. "Whoa . . . dude, Josh . . . man, what's up? And what are you doing carrying a piece? Put it away!"

"Just get out," Josh said.

"You're not gonna shoot me," Rodney told him, tried to sound certain.

"You're right." Josh aimed into the back seat. "But I'll shoot *them* if you don't get out. And the bullets . . . they're silver."

"Have you lost your mind?" Kyle said from the back seat. He'd drawn the shorter straw, and was sitting with Richard and Ceese. "You know, the one you claim to have every now and then?"

With shaking hands, Josh pulled the hammer back.

Rodney reacted, barked back at Kyle, "Would you shut up? You're not helping."

And then Rodney tried to think. Josh had said *silver* bullets. How would he know the significance of that? Rodney only knew because of Cassie's interest, and the few movies he'd seen about werewolves and vampires. But Josh's background was different; he didn't watch much television unless it was sports. So how did he know?

"Did Dr. Henderson put you up to this?" he guessed.

"Just get out," Josh repeated, turning the gun on Rodney again.

174

This wasn't like Josh, nothing like him, and Rodney's shock made him disregard his fear. "What's this about, dude? I don't get it."

Josh's face showed sudden rage, and he swung the gun back at Richard and Ceese. "Never mind what it's about! Just get out, or I'll shoot them right here! *I swear, man . . .*"

"Okay, okay," Rodney said, trying to force an easy tone. "Let's not get crazy." But things were already crazy, and it looked like they could get crazier if he didn't handle this right. "Just put that thing away. Just put it away, and we'll take these two on over to Dr. Henderson's. . . . You know, like we planned."

Rodney had been facing Josh, but was sitting so he could see the rearview mirror too. He glanced at it, and swallowed hard. He saw Kyle and Ceese, but not Richard. He looked harder. Richard's image wasn't reflected in the mirror, but his clothes were. Rodney assumed his RayBans would have been too, had Richard still had them on.

Josh's next words yanked his attention away from the mirror.

"*We're* not taking them to Henderson's. Things are different now. So get out."

Rodney nodded, pushed the button to unlock all the doors, then took his chance: He grabbed Josh's extended arm, forcing it up toward the roof of the car. "Go, now!" he shouted.

Richard, Ceese and Kyle wasted no time following his order.

Initially Richard was in the lead, but Ceese easily ran ahead, darting down the side alley and scaling a fence as if it wasn't there. Richard followed, but when he heard a gunshot, he took Ceese to the ground and covered her. Had he thought, he would have realized he'd overreacted. Josh and his silver bullets were too far away to reach them now.

"I think we're safe," Ceese gasped, then turned to see fangs heading toward her neck. "Richard, no!" she yelled.

But he wasn't listening. The vampire had control.

She rolled out from underneath, reached for the cross at her neck but discovered it missing. Eyes darting, she finally saw it lying on the ground, too far away for her to reach.

And then the vampire moved in front of it. She would have to go through him to get to the protection of the cross.

The wolf threatened to come out, but Ceese fought it back. Someone would surely die. "You get out of my way or—"

"Or what?" the vampire said, a grim smile on his face. He took a step closer.

"Or I'll," she struggled to think, then remembered, "or *God* as my witness, I'll summon the wolf."

She took a step toward him as she said God's name, affected by the utterance but holding in her anguish. It worked; he fell back a step and she darted past him, grabbed up the cross and forced it toward him. Within seconds, Richard became himself again, and Ceese dropped to the ground, holding her head.

"I-I'm sorry," he said, shoulders sagging, head hanging low. "It's just I'm in such desperate need."

Ceese took the hand he offered. "We must both show great restraint," she sympathized.

But before she could continue her admonishment, she saw something in the darkness, something scurrying on the ground. She went for it and came back with a large rodent.

"Hah," she exclaimed. "Now, *this* is a mouse." She eyed it hungrily, but held it out to Richard. "It isn't much, but at least it isn't me."

He took what she offered, pierced it with his fangs and drank. He then offered the drained carcass to her and watched as she devoured it.

"How do you *do* that?" he asked.

Her mouth gaped open. "I didn't question *your* method of feeding."

"No, not that," Richard said. "How do you forgive so easily? How do you bring yourself to feel such things? Forgiveness, compassion—you were practically my next meal, and yet you offered me food first. Is the curse of the werewolf not as strong as what I've been cursed with?"

"It's strong," she said carefully. "But so am I."

Richard shook his head. "There has to be more to it."

"Your faith, Richard. How strong is what you believed in before you became cursed?"

He looked away. "I . . . don't remember."

Ceese tore at what was left of the rat with her teeth, swallowed. "Penny said you couldn't."

"Let's not talk about her."

"Do you want to forget her, like you forgot your past?"

"I . . . I just don't want to talk about it. And we don't have time. That maniac could find us at any second."

"If you want to feel, then you will remember," Ceese replied, implacable. "Penny believed your faith was strong. And if there's any truth to what she believed, then it's in you to feel these things you say you can't. It's in you, Richard. It always has been."

And then, Richard ended it. "It isn't safe here. Things have taken a turn I didn't expect. We should go back to England. We'll hide from the day, and make arrangements to return to the castle tonight."

Ceese gasped. "No. We've come too far. No."

"In case you didn't hear, they were taking us to be handed over to some doctor of some sort, probably for research and who knows what else!"

Ceese shook her head. "Rodney will help us. He's looking for us now."

Richard sighed. "This *Rodney* is the reason we're in this mess." He rethought his plan to leave, made a decision. "We'll try to find Cassie on our own. I have her address."

"Rodney isn't a bad person," Ceese insisted. "He'll help us."

Another sigh, heavier than before. "I don't care. I don't trust, him, Ceese." But her look . . . she seemed so convinced. "But if you trust him, I guess I can try." Somehow he knew it wouldn't be the last time he'd give into her will.

※　※　※

Rodney checked Josh's gun after he wrestled it away, took the bullets out of the chamber and examined them under the rental car's dome light. As Josh had claimed, they were silver. He looked at Kyle, who had returned to the backseat but left the door open, just in case he had to run again.

When Kyle shook his head, indicating he had no idea what

any of it meant, Rodney looked at Josh. "You want to tell me what this is about?"

Josh looked like someone who'd just run a long race he had little training for. "It wasn't supposed to be loaded," he muttered. "I didn't know it was loaded."

Rodney was inclined to believe him. Josh did have problems, but he was only devious when it came to drugs. He wasn't a violent person either. And Rodney couldn't help but wonder, especially after what Ceese had said earlier about his buying weed . . .

"You're not using again, are you?"

He was referring to cocaine. Rodney knew he'd had trouble staying clean.

"Dr. Henderson gave me some," Josh confessed. "He told me if I brought Richard and Ceese to him, on my own . . ."

His voice drifted and he leaned his head against the drivers-side window, leaving Rodney to fill in the blanks. *Why Josh, of all people?* Rodney wondered. Cocaine wasn't cheap, and it was risky to get.

"Why?" Rodney asked. "What's Henderson's game, using you like this?"

But Josh was already sinking into withdrawal. "I don't know, dude! Don't you get it? He gave me coke. What do I care why?"

"How long?" Rodney said. "How long's he been giving it to you?"

"Since that night—at the club."

Rodney shook his head, suddenly hated himself for getting his friends involved.

"He said the gun was empty," Josh offered, sounding pitiful. "I swear. He said it wasn't loaded."

"But you knew about the bullets. Said they were silver."

"He told me to say that. Said it would scare you."

"He gave you coke?" Kyle asked.

Josh nodded, tears of fear forming in his eyes. "Yeah, man. But you can't tell him I told you, Rodney."

"I just don't get it," Rodney said. "He gives you drugs, a gun with silver bullets—"

178

"And you could'a killed us with it," Kyle added, doing a great job of sounding self-righteous.

"*You* were gonna take the extra money," Josh quickly said, scowling at Kyle.

"What money?" Rodney turned his gaze to Kyle, who squirmed under it and glared back at Josh.

"I think the operative word here is *was*," Kyle said. "But unlike *you*, I didn't take him up on his offer."

"Yeah," Josh replied, "but only because he wouldn't give you as much money as you asked for."

"Hey, that's not true—*I* thought our friendship was worth more than what he was offering."

Rodney sat quietly, and the other two fell silent.

Knowing his two friends had schemed behind his back was hard to take, but Rodney couldn't go there right now. "Just forget about it," he said.

"Forget about it?" Kyle erupted. "Just for the record, we *kidnapped* two people! That pretty much means we're *kidnappers*, and could be charged with *kidnapping*! And if that's not bad enough, now we're involved with a drug dealer! Man, I can't believe this! Why do I always let you talk me into things?"

Rodney shot him a look. "Nobody twisted your arm, okay? And besides, it's not like that. We didn't kidnap anybody."

"Only because they got away!"

"Nobody made them get in the car, okay! They came on their own. And nobody was going to make them stay at Dr. Henderson's place if they didn't want to. He told me so himself. He just wanted to talk to them."

"You don't know anything for sure," Kyle shot back. "He told Josh that gun wasn't loaded too!"

Rodney sighed. "Okay, I don't know that for sure. But I know I didn't kidnap them."

Kyle crossed his arms and looked disgusted. "Well, I hope you can convince the police when those two send them after us."

Josh grimaced. "I'm on probation, man. They'll put me away."

Rodney glanced at his friend, who looked and sounded as

desperate as Rodney had ever heard anyone sound. "They're not going to turn us in, Josh."

"Why wouldn't they?" Kyle asked. "Josh held them at gunpoint."

Josh's look turned even more dismal.

Rodney shook his head. "They won't, because they're exactly what those e-mails said they were. And they aren't about to go to the police."

"Now *you're* talking crazy," Kyle said. "There are no such things as vampires or werewolves. Or did you forget?"

So Rodney enlightened Kyle, and explained about how he hadn't seen Richard in the rearview mirror when he should have.

"It was dark," Kyle countered. "Things were crazy. How could you see anything?"

"I didn't have any trouble seeing *you.*"

Kyle shrugged. "Well, I guess it doesn't matter anyway. They're gone."

"Yeah, well, now I have to find them. So if you two don't *mind*, take this car back to the rental place."

Rodney dug into his pocket and came out with what was left of the professor's money. "This should cover any extra charges the rental place might try to tack on."

"You mean like payment for that hole in the roof from the bullet?" Kyle said as he took the wad.

Rodney looked up at the hole and scowled. "Yes, like payment for the hole in the roof. If they even notice." He got out and shut the passenger-side door behind him.

Kyle realized what Rodney was about to do, and lunged out of the open back door. "You're not seriously gonna go look for them?"

"Yeah," Rodney said, looking around. "I seriously am."

CHAPTER 22

Rodney listened for Cassie to pick up as he walked along with his cell phone pressed against his ear, hoping he didn't lose the signal before she could answer.

"Come on," he muttered. The alley he walked through now seemed almost darker than the night around him. The only thing he could make out was the trash cluttering the ground and a few skeletal-looking cats slinking in and out of it. He welcomed the glow from the phone.

Another few rings, and he heard her restrained hello. "Thank you," he said in relief.

But Cassie took the remark differently. She'd seen the Caller ID, knew it was Rodney. "What do you mean, thank *you*? Do you have any idea how angry I am right now? I just got an e-mail—an e-mail from someone who wanted to make sure I got their *first* e-mail. I saw what you deleted, Rodney."

"Look, I know you're angry, but I need you to listen for a minute—it's important—"

"Oh, I'm sure it's important to *you*. But right now, I have other concerns. Like where my two friends are. And I bet you know. So tell me. And be specific. Thanks to you taking my keys, I'll have to give a cabdriver directions."

Rodney had just stepped out of the alley onto an equally deserted side street. "I didn't exactly *take* your keys," he said.

"Rodney, I don't have time for this—"

"Yes, you do, Cassie—please. Look . . ." He paused at hearing a sound, then continued when it didn't happen again. "Just stay there. I'll bring your friends to you."

"They're with you?"

"Not exactly—but I'm gonna find them."

"What do you mean you're gonna find them?"

Rodney looked around the rundown neighborhood as he said this, hoping they might walk out of some alley and save him from the mess he'd gotten himself into. But that wouldn't happen, of course. He took a deep breath, dove in headfirst. "It just means I'm out looking for them. I told them to run when Josh pulled a gun on them."

Cassie's reaction had him holding the phone away from his ear for quite a few seconds.

"Josh didn't shoot anyone," he offered when she grew quiet. "He was told the gun was empty." And then Rodney told her about Dr. Henderson, and the deal he, Kyle and Josh had worked out with him. Told her the professor was going to pay them for taking the vampire and werewolf over to him first. And Josh, apparently, had worked out a little deal of his own with Henderson. It surprised him how much information he could squeeze into thirty seconds.

"Dr. Henderson?" Cassie said, confused. Then she smiled knowingly. He was trying to shift the blame. "Nice try, Rodney. But I'm not buying. Dr. Henderson would never go behind my back like that. Not everyone's like you."

"But that's just it," Rodney said quickly. "He *is* like me. No, worse than me. That e-mail . . . the one you said I deleted. I did delete it, right after I sent it to him. And all your other e-mails, the ones from Richard, the ones from your grandmother . . . you know, Grandma Penelope . . . I sent those to him too. He paid me to."

She was, for the moment, speechless.

"I'm sorry, Cassie," he said quickly. "I know you probably don't believe me, but I am. And I *am* out looking for them now. That's why I need you to stay there. What if they show up there and you're gone?"

It was a valid point. Richard did have her address. "Fine. But you better find them. And if I find out you're lying about this too—"

"I'm not! I swear. I wish I were." *Besides*, he thought, *who could make up this kind of stuff?* "Oh, your car keys? They're on top of the refrigerator."

She walked to the refrigerator, patted around where he said to look, and found them. "Okay," she said, "I have them, and I'll wait. But after you find them and bring them here. I want you to start packing."

Rodney might have been more bothered if Cassie didn't threaten to kick him out at least once a month. But she needed his half of the rent as much as he needed hers. Secure in that knowledge, he clicked off and kept searching.

❦ ❦ ❦

There were at least three of them, and Rodney felt a knot in the pit of his stomach when they surrounded him. No gang could have looked more organized. Their top-buttoned flannel shirts and ragged-heads completed the total picture of intimidation.

Rodney made a vain effort to dial his cell phone before the apparent leader took it away, looked at it and grinned. "You're gonna need 9-1-1 *after* we get through with you." He sounded and looked very Hispanic.

The speaker took a step closer, and his friends moved in beside him.

Rodney struggled to see if there were more of them, wondered if he might have a chance if he ran. But then he was hit hard in his midsection. His breath went out of him along with his escape plan. He couldn't run if he couldn't breathe. The second punch sealed it. He couldn't run if he couldn't walk either. He dropped to his knees, gasping.

"You got some money for us?" he heard another one ask, his accent similar to the delinquent who'd just hit him.

Rodney didn't have to answer; his pockets were already being rifled through.

"Some other gang took it," he managed to say.

A quick kick brought his silence. "There ain't no other gang around here," the one doing most of the talking informed him.

183

"Well, that's good to know," Rodney croaked before being pulled to his feet.

Rodney smelled liquor as the one holding him drew back an arm to hit him again. He prepared himself as best he could, closed his eyes and winced, but the impact never came.

"Let him go," a voice said . . . and amazingly, the punk preparing to hit Rodney did just that.

Rodney dropped like a rock back to the ground.

"You lookin' for trouble?" the punk threw out. "You wanna piece of us?"

"Oh, I'm sure he wants more than a piece," Rodney called out, grinning in spite of his pain. He'd just recognized the owner of the voice.

"No, no trouble," Richard said easily, and pointed at Rodney. "We just want him."

The "we," Rodney knew, meant Ceese was nearby.

"Well, you can have him," the punk said, "*after* we're done with him." His cronies had a good, quick laugh at that.

Richard smiled at them. "I'm quite sure I don't want to wait."

The punk chuckled. "Well, I'm *quite sure* you don't got no choice."

"I think you should reconsider," Richard replied, and took a step forward. Rodney forgot to breathe when he saw the fangs, and the gang's reaction.

"Hey, look," one of the punks said. "It's Dracula, man!"

The leader laughed, took a fearless step forward, and pulled out a knife that he opened with the flick of his wrist. "Oh yeah, well . . . bite me if you're fast enough!"

Ceese stepped out of the shadows then. "You *want* him to bite you?"

"Yeah, sure." The leader laughed again. "And you can bite me too!"

The kid's arrogance seemed to rise when he saw Ceese was a girl. Rodney wondered if he might make the same mistake Josh had made, call her something she'd rather not be called. But nothing like that came out of his mouth.

Ceese continued to look flustered. "You want to be bitten? I've never known anyone to *want* to be cursed."

Rodney couldn't help himself. "Yeah, well," he piped up, "welcome to New York."

There was another kick to his ribs, a cheap shot for his cheap shot. But the action only pushed Richard further along, and he let the transformation go to the next level. The gang's reactions weren't far behind.

"Geez, is he for real?" one said.

Somebody else commented. "I don't care if he is for real, hombre. I'm out of here. *Vamonos!*"

Within seconds, Rodney, Richard and Ceese were alone in the alley.

Rodney managed to stand, noticing that Richard looked much more human than he had just moments ago. It was a reassuring sight. But he also noticed something else: Richard didn't look happy.

"I have little use for betrayers," Richard said, giving him a hard stare.

"Yes, but *this* betrayer can get you to Cassie," Rodney reminded him. "In fact, I just talked to her on my cell phone and told her everything. I'm ready to take you to her."

"I've seen your kind before," Richard continued, moving closer. "You don't impress me. You lie to get what you want, and you see nothing wrong with it."

Rodney wanted to move backward, to run, but worried he might lose the vampire's respect, or worse. "Okay, you've nailed me," he said. "Normally, that's what I do. But this is different, okay? I'm gonna take you to Cassie."

Richard remained stone-faced.

"Look, I'm a nice guy." Rodney looked at Ceese for help. "Tell him I'm a nice guy. Tell him I'm not lying. You know about people, don't you? You knew about Josh. Tell him."

"He's telling the truth," Ceese said. "For what it's worth."

"There, see? Ceese says I'm a nice guy. And you have to believe her. . . . You two, you're like a team, right? Like Batman and uhhh . . . well, Ceese."

Richard was silent for so long, Rodney couldn't stand it. "Oh, come on," he said, imploring the vampire. "You have to believe her. I'm a nice guy. I didn't know any of this would happen—not like it did, anyway."

"You will take us to Cassie." Richard's reply was more like a directive, and Rodney nodded quickly.

"Sure, yes, whatever. But you have to get me to a phone. Those punks took mine, and we're a good ways from the apartment." Rodney looked around as he said this. "I'll just call Cassie and get her to come get us. I'd hail a taxi, but I'm pretty sure no respectable cabbie would come into this neighborhood. I'm not even sure the cops do."

He'd spoken out of concern, but neither Richard nor Ceese looked worried. "I guess you guys don't really need the police for protection, huh?"

Richard ignored his attempt at humor, said only, "We need to get to Cassie."

"Yeah, right. We could find the nearest subway—"

"NO!" Ceese's cry was louder than Richard's, but they both were shocked.

"Ceese doesn't like subways," Richard explained. "And as hungry as I am right now, I hardly think it wise to be surrounded by fresh bl—"

"Don't," Ceese said, as if his words could cause something bad to happen.

"No, don't," Rodney seconded. He'd already seen Richard with fangs once. He had no desire to see that again. And Richard had *the look*.

❧ ❧ ❧

They seemed to choose the darkest alleys, Rodney noticed, and he had to struggle to keep up. He fell over trashcans, ran into walls, and otherwise kept them from moving as quickly as they wanted him to move. And Richard's muttered comment to Ceese about daylight told Rodney why Richard was annoyed about his inability to keep up.

186

Finally, Ceese took Rodney by the hand to lead him, but he had to yank his hand away instantly.

"Okay, this is just too freaky," he said while rubbing his wrist and grimacing. "Are you wired or something?"

Richard glared at him, a question in his eyes.

Rodney held up his hand. "It hurt."

"Oh, sorry," Ceese said. "I forgot you're human. I'll try to make that more bearable." Had it not been dark, Rodney might have noticed she wasn't speaking to him through any conventional manner. And if he *had* noticed, he probably would have dismissed it as an illusion. But illusion or not, he wasn't about to take her hand again not before he could ask her why her touch shocked him. Richard was quick to speak as Rodney hesitated.

"If you don't take her hand," Richard said, and gave a mean smile, "I might be tempted to bite you."

Richard was very close to Rodney's ear when he said this. Too close, Rodney decided. He did as Richard asked. After a moment, the jolting sensation became a bearable throb, and his relief was immense.

As they went on, her touch became even easier to tolerate. Comfort, however, was no longer an issue. Richard's irritability was. Rodney had no desire to be bitten by him, so he just held tight and followed, going where he was tugged, surprised at how quickly he could move when he could barely see his own hand in front of his face. Ceese seemed to know exactly where to step, though. Rodney followed without question until he began to recognize landmarks himself: familiar sounds, smells.

"There," he said, pointing, "there's got to be a phone somewhere down this way."

Richard looked at Ceese, and they both looked at Rodney.

"I know what I'm talking about," Rodney said to their indecisiveness. "I grew up around here."

"You'd better be right," Richard snarled, and they followed him down the dark street.

CHAPTER 23

It was nowhere near dawn, and the street at the end of the alley was already waking up. There was foot traffic, and some storefronts were open despite the early hour. Rodney left to make his phone call, and Richard sank back against a cold brick wall. If things hadn't gone wrong, he would have had blood by now. Cassie Felts had assured him of that. Now, his need was beginning to wear on him.

Out of nowhere, a bat swooped down and settled on him. "No!" he said rashly, taking it up and slamming it against the wall.

The action got Ceese's attention. He quickly explained about the pesky creatures. "There'll be more if I don't get some blood soon," he added. "A lot more."

Ceese looked at the one on the ground. "I don't see how ten, or even twenty could really be such a big problem. It's so small. Its body is no bigger than my thumb."

"Ten or twenty," Richard snorted. "Ten or twenty would be a walk in the park. I'm talking hundreds . . . hundreds of biting, licking, worthless—" Before he could finish another swooped down, and he took care of it in the same manner. "I can't control it much longer, Ceese. I'm in desperate need of—"

"Don't say it," Ceese cautioned again.

"How can I not say it? I need blood and I need it now!"

"I can look for more rats," she offered. "Maybe I can find something bigger."

"I appreciate your efforts, but I need more than what a rat or two can give me." He peered up at her. "Aren't you hungry, too? You've had next to nothing since we left."

"I don't require much food, unless I need to transform completely. If I don't plan on doing that, then I can go for some time. Joachim used to say, like a camel."

"Another one of your werewolf friends?"

She nodded. "But he's gone now."

He saw no reason to ask or to prod further. Knowing as much as he knew about Zade was enough.

Desperate to help, Ceese moved to the very edge of the alley. There were so many signs, she decided to try her hand at reading, something she hadn't done much of in the past two centuries. There had to be something in this strange place helpful to Richard.

"What does b-a-n-k spell?" she asked.

"Bank," Richard told her, "but must we really have a reading lesson right now?"

"Does one put things in a bank—like they put things in a closet?"

Richard rubbed his temples hard. "Some other time. Please."

"But if one stores things in a bank, then perhaps you might like to know about this bank."

"And why would I want to know about this one?"

She looked back toward the street again. "Because, the sign I'm looking at now . . . I'm pretty sure it reads: 'Blood Bank.'"

Richard literally flew to her side. "You're unbelievable," he said. "Let's go make a withdrawal."

Rodney returned to the alley a few minutes after they'd left, having failed to do what he had set out to do, to suggest they move on. He was still working on a way to break the news to Richard when he discovered both he and Ceese were gone.

"No," he said, panic swelling his throat. "First I find them, then I lose them, then I find them, and . . . *awwww man*," he groaned. "Cassie's gonna *kill* me."

"Lookin' for those two that was over there?"

Rodney whirled around to see a wino, who pointed unsteadily toward where Richard and Ceese had been.

"Maybe," Rodney said carefully. "You seen 'em?"

"They went thata way."

Rodney looked, saw Richard first and then Ceese. He took off, dodging in and out of traffic to cross the busy street.

⅔ ⅔ ⅔

The blood bank wasn't open for business, hadn't been in some time. "Sorry guys," Rodney said once he got to where they stood. "According to that sign I just passed, it's on the other side of town now."

Richard pulled roughly at the burglar bars. "There's got to be something in there!"

"Doubtful," Rodney said. "The place is deserted. And if you pull those bars off, you might set off some kind of alarm. I wouldn't recommend it."

He said all this without considering how close Richard was standing to him—until he saw Richard staring at his neck. Unaware he was doing so, he pulled his jacket collar up high.

The sound of tires screeching made them all look toward the street. Rodney realized, after a second, it was his wino-informant who'd been hit. Apparently, he'd stumbled into the path of a delivery truck.

By the time a crowd finished gathering, the police showed up. Richard glanced at Ceese, who cringed at the noise of their sirens, but remained human. An ambulance came next. The medics got the homeless man off the street and onto a stretcher. Afterwards things returned to normal, as if nothing had happened.

"Where will they take him?" Ceese asked, never having seen an ambulance before.

"To the hospital," Rodney said.

"What will they do to him there?"

Rodney turned his head to face her. "You don't get around much, do you?"

Richard rolled his eyes. "She's been a wolf for two centuries, maybe more. She doesn't understand a lot of things."

Rodney's eyes widened. "Two hundred years? Whoa!"

Ceese glared at Richard. "I thought you said I couldn't talk about that."

190

"You can't. *I* can."

Ceese turned back to Rodney. "Will, they fix him at the hospital?"

Rodney nodded. "Yeah, they'll stitch him up, give him blood if he—"

Suddenly they were both looking at him.

"They'll give him blood, Richard," Ceese said. Her eyes never left Rodney's.

"Only if he needs it," Rodney said, feeling like he'd been left out of a joke. "They don't just go around handing it out."

"Richard needs it, or else the bats will come and feed—"

"Ceese," Richard said, "you can't talk about vampires either."

"You never told me that—"

"I'm telling you now. No talk of wolves or bats—" He looked around to make sure no one else was close enough to hear. "Or vampires."

"Fine," she said crossing her arms. "Rodney, that man was intoxicated. Would Richard need to be intoxicated?"

"Intoxicated?" Now Rodney was *sure* he'd been left out of the joke, or maybe was the butt of one.

Just then, he figured it out. "Oh, you mean to walk out in front of a car. No— I mean, yes. Who wouldn't need to be drunk to walk in front of a car?"

"So one *would* have to be intoxicated?"

"I . . . I'm not sure I understand what you're asking. . . . No, I don't suppose you'd *have* to be intoxicated to—"

Ceese moved before he could finish his sentence, taking hold of Richard and shoving him out into the traffic. Made clumsy by surprise, he managed to avoid one car and rolled over the hood of another, but landed directly in front of a Mercedes. The solid thud came next and Richard went down, his head smacking against the hood, then the ground.

Rodney raced out the moment it was safe to do so, with Ceese following, pushing through the crowd that had re-gathered.

"Richard," he called out. But the vampire was unconscious. Rodney saw something dark, put a hand on it, and came back with blood on his fingers. He looked over at Ceese.

191

"What'd you push him for?" His voice was a harsh whisper. "You could have killed him!"

"Richard can't die. At least, not like this. And besides, he needed blood."

"Well, right now, he's losing blood. And, *besides*," Rodney added, "there are other ways to go about getting it. Better ways."

"Well, you didn't say that," Ceese said, offended.

"Well, you didn't ask," Rodney mocked. "Besides, how was I supposed to know what goes on in your head?" And then he saw the driver of the Mercedes emerge and run wailing toward them.

"Is he all right?" the fastidiously attired woman asked, pinning an expensive-looking clutch under an arm as she talked. She was elderly, Rodney guessed in her seventies, and her overly sprayed white hair stayed in place despite the breeze that had her mink stole billowing around her. "I tried to stop," she sputtered, "but he was just *right there*."

Her looked turned to fright. "I don't need this on my record. They'll take my license. Can't we just say he fell? That I didn't hit him? Couldn't we say that?"

She flashed what looked like at least three hundred dollars out of her clutch. Now, she had Rodney's attention.

"Money?" he said, showing fake disgust. "You mowed down my brother and you want to give me money?"

"Here's everything I have on me—five hundred dollars."

She looked desperate. Rodney took advantage. "Fine," he said and pocketed the small fortune. "Just be more careful next time."

"Oh, I will!" the woman agreed, and moved back to wait for the police.

"You're almost too good at this lying," Ceese said, respect on her face.

"That means *so much*, coming from someone who just pushed their friend in front of a car." He might have said more, but the ambulance had just arrived.

"He's bleeding," one medic yelled, causing Ceese to call out, "He needs blood."

"Yeah?" the medic replied carefully, uncertain how to take the woman with the wild contact lenses. "If he needs blood, we'll get it for him. Do you know what his blood type is? You a relative?"

"He takes all types," Ceese replied.

Rodney intervened. "Uh, what she means is, he's a universal donor."

"Let's just get him to the hospital," the medic said, applying pressure to the small wound on Richard's head.

Ceese gave the man an eager nod. "Yes. That would be good. They have blood there."

The medic gave her a curious look but said nothing.

While the medics moved Richard to a stretcher, a police officer walked up. Rodney and Ceese stood.

"Does anyone know what happened here?" the officer asked, noting the way Ceese wouldn't look at him directly.

Rodney did his best to cover for her. "She's just a little upset right now," he offered. "Richard is our . . . brother."

"And your brother was hit by this car?"

"Yeah," Rodney confirmed. "He lost his balance coming off the curb and stumbled out into the street."

"That's not how it happened!" a voice called from the sidewalk. "The chick pushed him!"

Rodney could feel Ceese against his back now, and he felt like a fool. With all the people standing around, someone was bound to have seen what had happened—including him taking the woman's money.

"They was all three standing there talking, right? When that chick," the man pointed directly at Ceese, ". . . that one there, she pushed the blonde dude."

"Is that how it happened?" the officer asked Rodney.

Rodney stared over at the sidewalk while the officer scribbled something on a small pad, then turned back to the officer and said, "Sir, I'd bet five hundred dollars he didn't see what he's saying he saw." Then he added, to make sure the man heard, "But what would I be doing carrying around *five hundred dollars*?"

The now extremely motivated young man on the curb took

the hint. He had seen the money exchange, and from his look, couldn't believe his luck. His story changed at once.

"Naw, man, he's right. I didn't see nothin'! Must've been lookin' at somethin' else. I'm supposed ta wear glasses, but I can't afford 'em. So I didn't have none on. My mistake."

The officer scribbled something else down and then asked for Rodney's phone number. Rodney gave his parents' number, the one they had before they changed it several years back. He was pretty sure the officer wouldn't check anytime soon.

"Okay," the officer said. "I guess your story sticks for now. You're free to go."

Rodney waited until he was certain the officer wasn't paying attention, pulled Ceese along and begrudgingly handed the five hundred "easy come, easy go" bucks over to the wise guy. "I hope you sleep well tonight," he snapped as he saw his windfall disappear into the man's pocket.

The man grinned. "I know *I* will."

With a sigh of regret, Rodney led Ceese back to where the medics were working with Richard.

The medic searched Richard's neck, then his wrists, using his stethoscope. "I don't get a pulse, man. . . . Get the defibrillator!"

"Of course he doesn't have a pulse," Ceese said. "He's a va—"

Rodney put his hand over her mouth. "Vegetarian," he finished, hoping the two now looking at him were too concerned with Richard to really care how little sense he was making.

They ignored him anyway, began preparing the machine to do its work.

Rodney whispered again to Ceese. "You sure he can't die?"

"Yes, why?"

"Because they're fixing to shock the hell out of him."

When Rodney said this, Ceese reached out and put a hand on one of Richard's legs. No one was paying attention but Rodney. After a few seconds, the medic examining Richard said, "Hold up! I got a pulse."

Rodney turned to Ceese who responded to his quizzical stare. "He is breathing now, too."

Rodney looked at her, uneasy. "For how long?"

"Long enough."

❧ ❧ ❧

When convinced that he was stable enough to transport, they loaded Richard into the back of the ambulance. The medics allowed Ceese and Rodney to ride along. A few minutes into the trip, the ambulance swerved.

"Take it easy," the medic kneeling beside Richard yelled.

"Can't help it, man, there's bats everywhere. Hitting the windshield like bugs!"

Rodney looked at Ceese. Ceese shrugged. "Richard says I can't talk about it."

"It's just as well," Rodney replied. Deep down, he knew he didn't want to know.

CHAPTER 24

Cassie had no trouble finding the hospital after Rodney's call. Finding out exactly where the three of them were inside it was another matter. And then, gaining permission from the suspicious nurse was the third roadblock. That one took a lie: that she was Richard's sister.

The curtains were drawn and the room was dim. Cassie noticed Rodney stiffen when she walked in, but saw him relax when he saw it was her. Had he known her present mood, Cassie thought, he might not have relaxed.

"What happened?" she hissed at him. "Why didn't you tell me how badly he'd been hurt?"

"He's all right," Rodney assured her. "He can't die. At least, that's what Ceese says."

"Ceese is here?" Cassie said, looking around.

He jerked his thumb over his shoulder. "Yeah, she's my newly acquired shadow." Then, over his shoulder he said, "It's just Cassie, you can come out."

Ceese, shorter and slenderer than Rodney, moved out from where she'd been hiding behind him, eyes downcast.

"And oh," Rodney said to her, "Cassie wants to know why we're in a hospital. So, why don't you tell her, Ceese?"

"Richard needed blood," Ceese said, coming to stand next to Rodney, her accent and her eyes catching Cassie's attention at the same time.

"So you came to a hospital to get it?" Cassie was looking at Rodney when she asked this, not expecting Ceese to answer.

"There's more," Rodney said.

"I pushed Richard in front of a car," Ceese continued. "Rodney said he didn't need to be intoxicated."

"I think my exact words were you *would* have to be intoxicated to walk into traffic."

"Yes, but then you said you really didn't need to be."

"Yes, I *did* say that," Rodney pointed out, "but you didn't let me finish my sentence—"

"Okay," Cassie said, putting up a hand. "I don't think we're getting anywhere with this. You can tell me the rest later, when Richard's out of here. And we've got to do that as soon as we can." To Rodney's puzzled look, she explained, "Having Richard here is dangerous. What if someone comes in here with a mirror?"

"Rodney told them his religion forbade him to look at his own reflection," Ceese said. "He lies very well."

Cassie's eyes bored holes into Rodney. "How did you explain everything *else* odd about him? Things like, no heartbeat, no breathing—"

"Hey, it's okay. He has both of those—right now, anyway. Ceese did something."

Ceese nodded. "I . . . helped him."

Cassie was instantly suspicious. "How did you *help* him?"

"I gave him some breath and a heartbeat."

Cassie's voice remained level. "For how long?"

Rodney looked like a third-grader who knew the answer and desperately wanted to share it, raised his right hand up to complete the picture and said, "Oooh, pick me, pick me."

"Cut it out," Cassie said, tight-lipped. "How long's he going to appear human?"

"Long enough!" he said, and his tone turned sarcastic. "That's what Ceese told me when I asked. Ceese is *full* of useful information."

Cassie sighed. "Well, she'll have her hands full teaching *you*, won't she? So what are they saying about why Richard's still unconscious? How long has he been out?"

This time, Rodney's reply was subdued. "Ceese thinks he's unconscious because of his need for blood, but they won't give him any. They've ordered tests. . . . I couldn't think of any way to stop them."

Rodney looked crestfallen, but it wasn't in Cassie to make him feel better at the moment. "This isn't good," she said. "In fact, based on everything I've read, this is very bad. If they just tested his hemoglobin—they always do that right away—all it will show is anemia. . . . he hasn't had blood in a while. But if they did more tests, they'll start asking questions, and soon."

"Well, I'm sorry," Rodney snapped. "I guess I should have thought about all of that *before* Ceese decided to push him in front of a Mercedes!"

"Well, *you* should have been a little more responsible," Cassie replied. "Ceese didn't know any better."

"This isn't my fault," Rodney sputtered. "Ceese knew what would happen to Richard before she acted."

"Oh, right! She knew they'd bring him to a hospital and order all kinds of tests and—" Cassie stopped, noticed Ceese's creased forehead, her lost look. "Let's drop it. Right now, we need to get them out of here."

"There is no 'we'," Rodney said as he started walking past her to the room's door. "I'm finished here."

Cassie stopped him with a hand on his arm. "Oh, no, you don't. You're going to help fix things. Despite what you think, this is your fault."

"I already *have* fixed things," Rodney said curtly. "I found them. My job is done." He pulled away and this time, succeeded in pushing past her.

Cassie decided to let him go. Ceese, however, had words. "Please, Rodney, don't go. I . . . I need you."

Rodney paused, looked back. "You don't need me now. Cassie's here. She'll know what to do."

Cassie noticed Ceese's desperate look. "You can't leave her, Rodney. You got her into this. You have to help get her out."

There was a look on his face Cassie didn't understand; it was almost as if, suddenly, he wanted to stay.

"All right," he said. "But after I help you get them out of here, I'm gone."

Ceese perked up, and Cassie could have sworn there was a smile, though it was hard to tell. It might have been easier if those eyes didn't take the focus off almost every expression.

"Where am I?"

The voice was Richard's. Groaning, he raised his head from the bed, seeing Ceese first, then Rodney, and then a woman he didn't recognize.

"You're in a hospital," Cassie said, moving toward the bed. But then those eyes, those dark, alluring eyes, stopped her. His voice, his look, everything about him made her want to tell him whatever he asked. *That must be how he lures his victims,* she guessed. A noteworthy finding, but she couldn't turn her eyes away long enough to consider its implications.

"I feel like I've been hit by a train," he moaned, then gave a sour chuckle. "And I know, because that happened to me once." He looked at Cassie. "But what did happen?"

Cassie wasn't sure how to respond, but she didn't have to; Ceese was ready to fill him in. "It wasn't a train, Richard. I pushed you in front of a rapidly moving automobile. You have two broken ribs and ah—contusion. I heard the doctors and nurses talking."

Richard struggled to understand. "Thank you for filling in the blanks . . . I think."

"You're welcome," Ceese replied, beaming.

"I'm afraid there's more to it," Cassie said. "I don't know about your injuries, but Rodney said they did blood tests. We've got to get you out of here."

Richard looked around at several empty I.V. stands. They were giving him some clear fluid, but nothing more. But . . . I'm too weak to walk. I still need—"

Cassie's hand disappeared inside her tote bag. Seconds later, she retrieved a blood-filled pouch and handed it to him. "They were talking about vampire bats on the local news just before I left. I remembered what Grandmother told me about what happens if a vampire gets too hungry."

When he finished she handed him another, while Rodney stared in dismay, first at Richard and then at Cassie. "So when did you start packing blood?"

"About the time you started stealing my e-mails and kidnapping my friends."

Rodney's face contorted, and he simply watched while Richard pierced the second bag with his fangs. When Richard finished with his meal, she said, "I've got more at my place. Remember?"

Again that look. "Take me there."

His clothes were in the room's tiny closet, and Cassie got them for him, helping him into them but stopping when she saw the scratches revealed after his shirt caught on the bandages on his back. Richard caught her looking and said, "They're nothing to worry about," and continued to dress.

"The wolf doesn't like him," Ceese offered. "It wanted to kill him."

Rodney had seen too, and shook his head. "Man, you need to pick your friends a little better."

Richard's brow arched. "And my enemies."

"Hey, I made up for what I messed up."

"You haven't yet," Cassie informed him. "Now, go cause a distraction so we can get them out of here."

Rodney glanced at Richard. "It's daylight outside. Isn't he allergic?"

Cassie nodded. "Yes, but I parked in the garage. And I put blankets in the trunk so he can cover himself until we get back to the apartment. He'll be fine. Now go!"

"Where do I meet you?" Rodney said.

Cassie thought about lying to him, telling him another parking garage, another level. It would have been so easy. But she didn't know how or if Ceese would react. "Level three, near the elevator," she muttered.

Rodney hesitated, but then left.

ᘔ ᘔ ᘔ

Richard, Cassie and Ceese stayed by the door until they heard the clamor from down the hall, then slipped out of the room.

They took the stairs down one level, went through the basement, and headed for the elevators to the parking garage. They exited at level three, and Cassie directed them to her car, running while looking back to make sure they weren't being followed. Once at the car, Cassie opened the trunk and started pulling out the blankets for Richard to cover himself with. Richard climbed inside the trunk instead.

"I'll ride here," he told her. She didn't know if lack of air was an issue for him, but since he didn't seem concerned, she decided not to argue.

Ceese got in the backseat, and Cassie started the car. She then drove around to where they'd just come out and waited with the vehicle running. Once again Cassie thought about driving on, about leaving Rodney to fend for himself. It was tempting. They were in the car; the car was running. And Rodney had her madder at him than ever before. She could just drive.

But Ceese seemed to depend on him, and Cassie couldn't bring herself to disappoint her. Besides, Rodney had such a hurt reaction when Ceese begged him to stay, Cassie wondered if he weren't attracted to her as well, in some odd way. So, as much as she hated to admit it, she probably needed him.

As they waited, Ceese anxiously stared out the window, looking much like a pet waiting for its owner.

At least the wait was short. But Rodney didn't come out where Cassie had expected. Instead, he exited through some doors near the elevator. He'd apparently had to take the stairs. He was sprinting now, and it was clear why seconds later, when a horde of orderlies emerged from the elevator, giving chase.

"There he is," Ceese announced, but Cassie was already pulling around.

Rodney reached the car, and with one motion, yanked the back door open and jumped inside.

"Go!" he yelled as one orderly gained ground and lunged. Cassie floored it, the opened door slammed shut and Cassie prayed. She wouldn't be able to handle it if they followed her very far. She wasn't good at driving fast, or at the very least, driving in a panic. And the small group of young men in hospital garb didn't look happy.

She didn't relax until they were off hospital grounds, didn't slow until she was a good block away. That's when she found Rodney in the rearview mirror.

"Okay, I saw the posse chasing you. What did you do?"

"I, ah . . . caused a distraction, like you said."

"Yes, I understand, but what did you *do*?"

"Well, there was this cart full of dirty bedpans and . . . I knocked it over. Everything inside the bedpans went spilling out onto the floor, and . . . onto a couple of guys. I'm pretty sure they were with the ones chasing me."

"Okay, I don't have to hear any more," Cassie said, struggling not to be sick. In her Girl Scout days, she'd helped out one summer at a local hospital. She had little trouble filling in the blanks of Rodney's story.

"Well, you asked," he said, seeing her reaction.

"Yes, I know I did," she said through gritted teeth, hoping she could quell the nausea before it got the best of her. "Just don't say anything else . . . please."

"You spilled excrement onto the floor so we could get away?" Ceese said, looking as though he'd done some great thing.

"Yeah," Rodney replied, seeming surprised at how much her appreciation mattered. "I guess you could say I sort of pissed them off."

"Oh, that's good, Rodney," Cassie said. "You should share that with some of your friends. Oh, wait, do you have any?"

"Ha, ha," Rodney mocked. "I've got friends." *Double-crossing friends, but friends nonetheless.* "And, you know, the least you could do is thank me."

"*I* will thank you, Rodney," Ceese said.

Cassie's car was borderline midsize. Ceese was already close to Rodney. In a heartbeat, she was a good bit closer. And in an instant, her lips were on his.

The touch in the alley was nothing compared to what he felt now, and no matter how hard he tried to pull away, he couldn't. He wasn't sure he wanted to.

"Rodney," Cassie said, glancing in the rearview mirror, "I'd be careful if I were you."

At first, Rodney didn't seem to be listening. He paid a little more attention, however, when pain became an issue. There were teeth, sharp pointed teeth, and then, when he opened his eyes to try to make sense of what was happening, he saw why.

Ceese was transforming.

Rodney moved as far away as he could, as fast as he could, all while Ceese moved quickly to her side of the car, leaning down in the seat so her head was resting in her hands.

"Well, *that* was interesting," Rodney said, then looked at the blood he'd wiped from the corner of his mouth.

Ceese raised her head a little to look at him. "I'm sorry," she said, her eyes moist, her face anguished. "It's the wolf. It won't let me . . ." She closed her eyes tight as she fought with some unseen force. "It won't let me." And then she buried her head again.

What won't the wolf let her do? Cassie wondered. It was obviously something she wanted to do. And when she figured it out, it occurred to her that it was something Rodney might have wanted as well.

"I'm sorry, too," Rodney said, and moved over to put a calming hand out. But Ceese met it with a determined stare.

"No," she growled. "Don't . . ." Then, calmer, "Not now."

Rodney snatched his hand back.

The front seat suddenly looked very inviting, so up front was where Rodney headed. His action drew curious stares from other motorists in the lane beside them, and a loud protest from Cassie.

"Watch your feet!"

"So, did you ditch the vampire?" he asked once he'd settled into the front passenger seat.

"He opted to ride in the trunk," Cassie replied. "And now I wish *you* had! I'd appreciate a little warning before you go climbing around. I could've pulled over, you know."

"Sorry. But I had a situation back there. And what were you trying to tell me in the middle of all that anyway?"

Cassie didn't feel right talking about such things with Ceese listening from the backseat, so she kept her voice low. "It's the curse," she said. "Vampires, werewolves . . . their curse won't allow them to be . . . intimate. At least, not without serious repercussions. According to what my grandmother wrote, the pain is quite intense."

Rodney shook his head. "It was just a kiss."

"Maybe it meant more to her," Cassie said. She noticed how shaken he still looked. "Are you going to be okay?"

Rodney sighed. "Just for the record, I don't think I'll ever be okay again."

Cassie frowned at the glowing predawn sky, wondering if *she* would ever be the same either.

CHAPTER 25

They parked close to the apartment building's back entrance, waited until the coast was clear, and then opened the trunk. Richard covered as much of himself as he could with a blanket and, once inside the building, was none the worse for wear. Ceese took his hand and stayed close to him, glad to see him up and about again.

The apartment was on the fifth floor of a ten-floor complex, but they took the stairs instead of the elevator. After seeing Ceese's reluctance to get on the one at the hospital, Cassie was certain Ceese would put up a fight if they tried. But there was another reason: Fewer people took the stairs, and that might help them having to explain Richard's blanket, or Ceese's strange-colored eyes. The only person they encountered was a maintenance man who exited the stairwell one floor below them.

Rodney entered the apartment first, and immediately said, "Man, it's dark in here. What gives?" Then he noticed the spot over the futon, where the two windows were. Or, where they used to be. "Aluminum foil and duct tape," he said. "Good idea. A nice, yet eclectic touch."

Cassie's response was to shut the door, plunging them into total darkness.

"Hey," Rodney said, "you could at least wait until I find the—" His shin caught the corner of the coffee table. He cried out, grabbed his leg and fell back onto what he hoped was the futon. A few seconds later, Ceese located the lamp and turned it on.

"Hey, how'd you do that?" Rodney said.

Ceese shrugged. "It's the wolf. And I followed your screams."

He noticed her amused expression. "Oh, yes. Make fun of the guy who can't see in the dark."

Her expression fell. "I didn't mean to make you feel . . . I'm sorry if I . . . I'm sorry."

Rodney rolled up his pant leg, grimaced again. "Oh, no, it's okay. Have your little fun at my expense."

Ceese darted off, headed for the nearest open door, which led to Cassie's bedroom. Richard's look was smoldering, and Cassie stood nervously by, remembering her grandmother's warning about Richard's temper. She hoped she wouldn't need the cross she'd put in her pocket before leaving to meet them at the hospital.

"It isn't her fault she is what she is," he said to Rodney, "or that she doesn't understand how to react in certain situations."

"I'm sure Rodney didn't mean anything by it," Cassie said quickly. "He didn't mean to upset Ceese. Did you, Rodney?"

"No," a contrite Rodney replied. "It just came out wrong."

"Many things you say come out wrong," Richard grumbled. But then he let up a little. "I guess it's good she doesn't really care about how you feel."

This puzzled Rodney. "How do you know?"

Cassie started to answer, but Richard held up his hand. "Emotionally, she can't feel anything. She just likes to pretend she can every now and then."

"Oh, right," Rodney scoffed. "Like there wasn't anything behind what she did on the way over here."

Richard glanced at Cassie, and Cassie told him about the kiss that almost turned tragic.

Richard peered at Rodney's lip, the bruise, the discoloration. "She did that?"

"Yeah," Rodney said, rubbing it. "She got a little rough, you know . . . just as she was losing control."

"Well, *that's* interesting," Richard said, his brow arching.

"What's interesting?"

"Interesting. That's all."

"Oh, no, not just interesting." Rodney said, his eyes narrowing. "I saw what you did with your eyebrow."

"Excuse me?"

"When you arch your eyebrow, it means something."

Richard shrugged. "Well, it's just that biting is one way the curse is transferred."

Rodney's eyes flew open. "It . . . It was a nip!"

Richard gave him a mean smile. "Well, then I suppose you have nothing to worry about, do you?"

Cassie saw Rodney's panic. "Calm down," she said. "The werewolf has to be the wolf for the bite to do that. I think the *vampire* is just trying to scare you."

Rodney turned to her. "Well, maybe he knows something you don't!"

"Richard," Cassie said, "tell him."

"Tell him what?"

"The truth."

"What fun would that be?"

Cassie sighed. "How hungry are you?"

He scowled. "Oh, all right. It's true. She has to be the wolf before she can give anyone the curse."

Cassie nodded, satisfied. "The kitchen's this way."

Richard followed her and Rodney trailed behind, not at all sure about anything he just heard.

"What if they bite you when they're not the wolf?" Rodney asked Richard's back. "Does it mean you're just a *little* cursed?"

"Not possible," Cassie said, opening the refrigerator and handing Richard a pouch of blood. "You're either cursed or you're not . . . and you're not."

Rodney had planned on asking how she knew this, but the sight of Cassie handing Richard the bag stopped him. "Where . . . Where'd you get all this blood?"

"From the refrigerator," Cassie replied. "Weren't you paying attention?"

"No, I mean—where did you get it, *originally*? It's not like a commodity. You can't just run to the local blood bank and ask for a few pints to hold you over."

"Connections at the university," Cassie said. "Had a friend who owed me a favor."

When Rodney stepped closer, he saw bag after bag of blood. The refrigerator was full of it. "Must have been some favor. Where'd you put everything else?"

"There's a few things in the crisper, some things here in the door . . . the freezer. I sacrificed a little."

"Yeah, right, but what about everything else?" Agitated, he started moving bags of blood around to look.

"I told you," Cassie said, "I sacrificed."

"What do you mean, *sacrificed*?" Rodney said, standing to look her in the eye. "Where's my beer?"

She shrugged. "I had to make room."

"You got rid of my beer? I just brought a case two days ago!"

"It's just beer, Rodney. You can get more. But get a cooler for it. I need the room."

"I've had it," Rodney barked. "I'm out of here."

He went for an empty duffel bag sitting near the futon and began stuffing it with clothes, shoes, books. But then the door to Cassie's bedroom opened, and he stopped to look at Ceese.

"I *am* sorry I laughed at you," she said. "Please don't leave."

How did she know what he's planning? Cassie wondered. The walls of the apartment weren't thick, though. Perhaps she overheard.

"Not this time," Rodney told her, not looking at those sad eyes. "Cassie threw my beer out. I'm going."

"But you can't go. I don't have a good feeling about that."

Rodney, however, had already gone back to his packing.

"You should listen to her," Cassie told him. "My grandmother said werewolves can sense things when others can't."

"You want me to listen to someone who threw their friend in front of a car?" As Rodney spoke, he grabbed up more clothes, then his clock radio. The bag was getting full. "I don't plan on being her next victim, or Richard's next meal. Especially when I don't have any *beer* to help me cope."

"I wouldn't throw you in front of a car," Ceese told him. "You might not survive. I knew Richard would."

"What a nice thought," Rodney said as he zipped up his bag and turned. "Well, it's been real."

Ceese turned to Richard for help. "It wouldn't be good for us if he goes," she said. "It will be very bad for us. He could tell that man. That professor."

Richard responded, racing to block Rodney's exit. "As much as I hate to do this, I must encourage you not to leave."

Rodney glared at him. "So this is how you *encourage* people? Beating them to the door to block their only exit?"

"I would promise not to bite you but, I'm a man of my word, and it wouldn't be right to lie about such a thing."

"Great," Rodney moaned. "Now I'm a hostage."

Richard smiled. "Perhaps more of a bargaining tool. Just in case we need one."

"Okay, fine. Then I'm a prisoner."

Richard decided to give him that much. "Okay."

"If it's any consolation," Cassie said, "your beer's on the balcony. It's probably still cold."

"Great." Rodney let his bag fall hard, just missing Richard's foot. "Then I guess I'll be on the balcony."

The three of them watched him walk out, and Richard had to back away a couple of steps to avoid the sunlight now streaming in. It was six-forty-five in the morning. The sun was rising.

The instant Rodney pulled the door shut, Richard turned to Ceese. "Are you sure about this feeling you have?" Because I'd very much like to let him leave."

Ceese nodded. "His leaving wouldn't be good."

"Yes," Cassie threw in. "For once in his life, he actually knows enough to be dangerous." She hesitated, then added, "And maybe enough to be helpful."

Richard didn't look convinced. He turned to Ceese. "All I can say is you'd better be right about him. Because tolerating imbeciles is not something I'm good at."

Just then the door slid open again, and Richard threw up his arms for protection.

"Thought I'd read," Rodney said picking up the sports section of an old newspaper from the kitchen table. He then saw Richard, who was already suffering from the sunlight. "Oops, my bad. Not used to having a vampire around." He headed back out.

Having just fed, Richard recovered quickly. He whipped around to face Ceese. "I will ask you once more—"

"I'm certain, Richard," she said. "We need him—alive."

He sighed. "All right. If you insist."

CHAPTER 26

Rodney stayed out for at least an hour, having found two beers actually cold enough to be drinkable. He took his time with the second one, then headed back in.

Cassie was at her computer. To his question, she told him that Richard and Ceese were in her room, sleeping. She otherwise ignored him.

Five minutes of sitting on the futon in silence, and Rodney could stand it no more. "So how long are you not gonna talk to me?"

"I don't know what you mean," Cassie said, moving the computer's mouse around on its pad.

Rodney sighed and crossed his arms. "Would it matter if I said I was sorry?"

He had her attention. "Why did you do it, Rodney?" Cassie asked as she turned in her chair to face him. "Why did you double-cross me?"

"Do we really have to talk about it right now?"

Cassie sighed resentfully, went back to her typing.

"What are you doing anyway?" Rodney asked, coming to stand just behind her.

"What does it look like I'm doing? I'm typing."

"I know that, but *what* are you typing?"

After a moment, she said, "I thought I'd send Dr. Henderson an e-mail to let him know that I know what he's up—"

"No!" Rodney said, reaching over her shoulder to delete everything she'd just typed. "You can't tell him everything."

Cassie turned back around, eyes blazing. "And why can't I?"

"Look, we don't know what he's up to, just what he's told us. We have to be careful until we know his whole plan."

Her eyes turned to slits. "Maybe we *do* need to talk about why you double-crossed me."

Rodney took a deep breath. "He gave Josh a gun, Cassie. It was loaded . . . with silver bullets. I just thought he wanted to talk to Richard and Ceese. But now, I don't know about his intentions."

"But you were okay with his intentions before everything backfired."

He looked at the floor, then back at the computer screen. "Okay, you're right. But let's just think some more about what we want to say to him."

"*We?*" she replied. "I didn't think you wanted anything else to do with this. That's what you said at the hospital. If Richard hadn't stopped you from leaving a little while ago, you'd already be gone. You say you don't want to help, then all of a sudden, you do. But you really messed everything up, Rodney. And I just don't know if I can trust you."

"I know. But Dr. Henderson—something's not right about him. It seemed okay at first. I mean, he never said anything about hurting either of them. But then there was the gun. I guess what I'm trying to say is, I think Richard and Ceese, they deserve a chance to," he fumbled for words, "to do whatever it is they came to do. And the professor has no right to deny them the opportunity."

"That's a noble gesture—but you practically handed them over to him. And you lied to me and stole from me—"

"They were just e-mails, Cassie."

"Sent to *me!*"

"Okay, I *get* it! But you have to listen to me. I can help you now. I know things."

"Like what?"

Another deep breath. "Henderson's supplying Josh with coke."

She gasped. "Cocaine? Why?"

"Yes, cocaine. And because Josh used to be— Well, he's an addict."

"But why would Dr. Hen—"

"The way I figure it, he's trying to coerce Josh into cutting me and Kyle out of the deal. Initially he tried to cut me and Josh out with Kyle, but he couldn't seem to come up with a dollar figure Kyle could live with. I must have put a crimp in his finances."

Cassie nodded, and her face turned sad. "It's always about money, isn't it?"

"Yeah," he said. "He was going to pay each of us five hundred dollars to bring Richard and Ceese to him. I guess he decided it would be cheaper if he could convince one of us to cut the other two out. And, well, what better choice than Josh, who's a dopehead?"

Cassie gave a sad shake of her head. "I should have known you'd have a friend who's an addict."

It was a low blow he wasn't about to take. "Well, *you* have a friend who's a vampire, and another one who's a werewolf! Besides, Josh is harmless. And *he's* trying to clean up his act." Rodney's face turned sad. "At least, he was. But thanks to Dr. Henderson . . ."

Cassie looked back at the computer screen, thought about everything she'd shared with her boss since she met him. "And to think I trusted him," she whispered.

"Yeah," Rodney replied, leaning to type, "but you trust everyone. We'll just tell him you were expecting Richard and Ceese, but haven't heard from them yet. That they should have e-mailed you by now, but haven't. And you'll let him know more as soon as you know anything. That'll buy some time." He finished typing, then straightened.

"And why should I listen to you?" Cassie said.

"Because you trust me?"

"I'd be an idiot to trust you."

He shrugged. "Okay. Because I want to help Richard and Ceese, then."

"Why?"

Rodney rolled his eyes. "Because they are what they say they are, Cassie. I saw Richard change—I didn't see him in the rear-view mirror, just his clothes. I heard Ceese inside my head. Her touch, her eyes— I still don't know why they came here, but they need our help."

"*Our* help," Cassie repeated.

"Yes, *our* help."

She reached for the mouse. "Okay, then here goes nothing." She moved the cursor over the Send button and clicked. "We'll wait to see what Dr. Henderson's reply will be."

For the next few minutes they sat in near-darkness, in a room normally inundated with sunlight, in chairs usually unoccupied at this time of the morning. And as they sat, they listened to sounds they heard every Saturday morning, sounds that now seemed different in light of the circumstances. It wasn't just a typical day, and no day would ever be typical for them again. Things had changed for her, and she had to adjust. Now, a college professor she had grown to regard as a mentor seemed her enemy. Now, she had to protect her two new friends from him. And the only help she had was from a roommate who had a history of lying. Suddenly, she didn't know who to trust—except herself, and the words of a grandmother she'd barely known.

CHAPTER 27

Just like Cassie and Rodney, Clayton Henderson had been up all night too. And his patience was wearing thin. But he managed to stay calm, waiting and wondering if his gamble had been worth the risk. Josh was a human throwaway. That was clear. But he wanted to believe cutting Rodney and Kyle out had been a good idea.

He went through it all in his mind again. Rodney, the loafing student, ever-looking for the easy grade, had already helped him earn Cassie's trust. And he had never needed Kyle, except to humor Rodney and keep him in the web he'd woven. Yes, Josh had been the logical choice of the three. Josh might not be dependable, but Henderson was fairly certain he would be the easiest to work with.

But since Josh hadn't returned yet, he began to wonder if being fairly certain was good enough. Had he put too much stock in Josh? Could Josh actually bring the werewolf and vampire to him, as he'd promised he could? Would the prospect of more drugs be enough to persuade him to do exactly what Henderson had asked? Most of all, would the promise of drugs be enough to get him to betray his friends?

Henderson was still considering this when the knock came.

"Well," he said, answering the knock and staring out. "What have we here?" He looked past Josh's shoulder. "You're alone."

Josh shifted his weight. "Yeah, something happened. I need to talk to you." He needed more drugs, more of what Dr. Henderson had given him earlier, and he needed it bad.

But the professor didn't look accommodating. "So talk. Where are my guests?"

Josh was rubbing his arm, his eyes unfocused. "Let me in and I'll tell you."

"You went to the airport," Henderson prodded. "You rented a car—"

Josh just nodded.

"You got in the car with . . . my friends, and then forced Rodney and Kyle to leave with the gun I gave you—"

"Loaded gun," Josh muttered, still rattled from finding this out. "It—it was a loaded gun and I—I could've killed somebody." Hostility had crept into his voice.

Henderson gave a half-grin. "So you fired the gun."

"Yeah, like I said, it was loaded—I could've killed somebody."

"But you didn't."

"No."

"Did they get away?"

"Yes," Josh said, then noticed the door closing in his face. He jammed his foot in and spoke fast. "But I know where they are."

A satisfied grin slid across Henderson's face and he flung the door wide. "Well, why didn't you say so?"

He took Josh through the kitchen, then down some stairs to the house's basement. "Have a seat," he said, and motioned toward one of two couches facing each other. The rest of the room was a makeshift lab, everything he needed to pursue his work until the university came to its senses and granted him research privileges.

"I do so hope you aren't lying to me," he commented as he went for a syringe already loaded with the drug Josh was eagerly rolling up a sleeve for.

"I'm telling you straight," Josh said quickly, tying his left arm off with the long elastic cord he'd seen on the table before him.

Henderson moved toward Josh and waited, syringe in hand. "You won't disappoint me again, will you?"

"I won't," Josh replied, trying not to appear too eager. "I—I promise."

"Good. Because if you do, I won't be able to keep supplying you. Do you understand?"

Josh nodded but never took his eyes off the syringe. Finally, Henderson turned it over to him walked a short distance away.

Josh had already found the best vein, but hesitated before injecting. He thought of Rodney's efforts to help him stay clean. The time he'd spent in detox. Even now, it seemed like a lot to throw away. Perspiration formed on his upper lip and forehead.

Henderson noticed. "Having second thoughts?"

The words brought Josh back to the present. "Uhh . . . no, I'm good," he said, and deftly slipped the needle in.

"That's what I thought," Henderson replied. He wished he could continue trying to find out what happened. But Josh wouldn't have a coherent thought for at least a couple of hours now. Instead of grilling Josh, he went to check his e-mail.

His computer sat in a corner of the room, far enough away so he almost never heard the tone that reminded him he had new mail. This suited him fine. Most of his e-mails were from university administration, nothing he wanted to worry with anyway. But this time, the e-mail was from Cassie.

He clicked on it at once and read. His usual unfriendly look turned menacing, and he strode back to the sofa.

"Josh. Wake up. I need to ask you something."

Josh forced his eyes open. "Sure."

Henderson realized he could have asked him to drop a bowling ball on his own foot and his answer would have been the same. "I have a question about Cassie."

"Okay."

"Did she find out you and your friends were helping me? Was there ever any indication she might have known about that?"

"No, man."

"You're certain of this?"

"She didn't know. Clueless." He turned drowsy eyes to Henderson. "Why?"

"I'll ask the questions, if you don't mind."

"Sure, right—whatever."

"Do you have a cell phone?"

Josh gave a half-shrug. "Who doesn't?"

"Might I use it?"

Josh sat up a little, dug in his pocket and grinned stupidly. "What? Didn't pay your phone bill?"

Henderson's expression revealed nothing as he took the phone from Josh. "I told you, *I'll* ask the questions." He rose from the sofa and ambled away, dialing.

❧ ❧ ❧

Both of them jumped when Cassie's phone rang, and Rodney checked the Caller ID display. "It's Josh," he said, puzzled. He'd never given Josh Cassie's number.

"Hey, Josh, what's up?" he said, and then, "how did you get this number?"

"Well, I'm not Josh," Henderson said. "But then, I suppose it's understandable why you thought this was Josh calling."

Rodney tried not to sound to shaken. "Where's Josh?"

"None of your business, young man. What are *you* doing at Cassie's apartment? Where is she?"

"I live here, remember? And . . . uhhhh," he tried to think, didn't want to say too much, didn't want to tell the wrong lie. "She's not here right now."

Henderson noted Rodney's hesitation. "What about our deal? You were supposed to bring something to me."

"What about you trying to cut me and Kyle out? What was that about?"

Henderson's voice turned threatening. "You found them, didn't you? After they left the rental car . . . after Josh fired the gun, you went after them and found them."

Rodney's thoughts raced. Josh must have been running his mouth, but he usually did when he was high, and Rodney had no doubt Josh was presently high. Suddenly, the right answer came to him. "Josh doesn't know whether I found them or not. So what makes *you* think I did?"

"Why are you so defensive?"

"I'm not defensive."

"Then why are you lying?"

"I'm not lying."

"I know you're lying because you said Cassie was gone. If she were gone, how could she send me an e-mail?"

Rodney struggled again not to sound flustered. "I sent that e-mail," he blurted out. "I can do that, you know. I've been sending her e-mails to you all this time."

The silence that followed made Rodney very nervous.

"Yes, you have, haven't you? But it's the oddest thing. *This* e-mail, the one you supposedly just sent, was encrypted. If you aren't lying, then what is Cassie's digital ID? You would have to know it to send it. You see, it was added to my address book when I received her e-mail, so I'm looking at it. Do you know it, Mr. Kincaid?"

Rodney glanced at Cassie. If he truly knew her digital ID, had in fact sent the e-mail, he shouldn't have to hesitate.

"Why don't you just ask her?" Henderson said. "You know she's standing right there."

Without another word, Rodney hung up.

"What?" Cassie asked.

"You have a digital ID now, don't you— for your e-mails."

She nodded, embarrassed. "I made a new account because of what you said you did. I . . . thought it prudent to add the digital ID."

Rodney gave her a pained look. "Well, I guess I don't blame you. But because I didn't know about that, Henderson knows I didn't send that e-mail."

"Which means?"

"Which means he knows you're here. And if you're here and I'm here, and I'm talking to him about a vampire and a werewolf you're not supposed to know I know about— And then I get caught lying about sending an e-mail I couldn't possibly have sent because I don't know your digital ID . . ."

Cassie couldn't help smiling. "Oh what a tangled web we weave. You know, if you'd put nearly as much effort into telling the truth as you do lying, we might not be in this mess."

He shrugged. "Guess I deserved that."

"Well, you deserve a lot more, but we'll let it slide for now. What was he doing with Josh's cell phone? Is Josh there?"

"I'm sure he went there for more drugs, especially if Henderson's keeping him strung out." Rodney saw her look, knew he had to defend his friend. "I know what it sounds like, but Josh isn't a bad person, Cassie. He's just got a problem, and the professor's taking advantage of it."

Cassie nodded. "But what do we do now?"

There was a knock at the door. Startled, Cassie and Rodney looked at each other, thinking the same thing: What if it was Henderson? What if he'd been in the building when he made the call from Josh's phone?

Another knock brought Ceese out of the bedroom, and before they could stop her, she pulled the door open to reveal two bags: the suitcases Richard and Ceese had brought with them, but had to abandon in the rental car. Ceese picked them up and brought them in, kicking the door closed behind her.

"It was Kyle," Ceese said matter-of-factly to their stunned expressions. "I willed him to bring our luggage here."

"You knew he had your bags?" Rodney asked.

"I guessed that he did." She shrugged. "He helped return the rental car. Our bags were in the trunk."

Rodney shook his head, trying to understand. How did she know Kyle had returned the rental car? But something else she said made him more curious. "You *willed* him to bring them here?"

She nodded.

"So—So, where's Kyle now?"

"I willed him to leave." This she said just before disappearing back into the bedroom.

"Did you hear her?" Rodney said, his voice just above a whisper. "She *willed* him to bring the bags. What's she talking about?"

"I'm not exactly sure," Cassie admitted, causing Rodney to look like someone who just swallowed their gum.

"What do you mean, *not exactly sure*? You're supposed to be the expert here. If you don't know, then who does?"

"I don't know what makes you think I'm an expert. Everything I know is from books and legend, and from what my grandmother wrote. There's a lot I don't understand. That's why they call what I'm doing research, *Einstein*."

"Well, let me enlighten you," Rodney replied. "Richard drinks blood, lots of blood—and while he's not particular, he seems to prefer *human* blood. And Ceese," he sputtered, "can *will* people to do things."

Cassie nodded, her face somber. "I know, Rodney. And I have to admit it's a little frightening. But they're not going to hurt us. They know we're trying to help them."

He went to the futon, sat on it and leaned back. "Yes, well, I'm just a little fuzzy on this whole 'help them' thing. What exactly *is* it we're trying to help them with? What did they come here for?"

"They want to be mortal again. They want to be able to die on their own terms. They want a choice about where they end up—you know, after they're gone."

"Mortal," Rodney echoed. "Thus inferring they are presently immortal and unable to die, because of what they are, and . . ." His face contorted into a maze of lines. "And none of it makes any sense! There are no such things as vampires and werewolves or immortality."

"You didn't see Richard in the mirror," Cassie reminded him. "And how do you think Ceese can get into your head like she does—willing people to do things?"

"Well, I was kind of hoping *you* could tell me that." Rodney paused. "And since when could werewolves read minds anyway?"

"I don't believe she reads minds. I just think she senses things. In the same way people say animals sense things. Only I believe she's taken it to a whole new level."

Rodney stopped to take it all in, and couldn't. "What are we doing, Cassie? What are we supposed to be doing?"

She tried to explain. "Legend infers, and both Richard and Ceese can tell you, a vampire and a werewolf can be killed in several different ways. But if they die while they're still cursed, they don't get a choice about where they spend eternity. Grandmother said Richard's father was a minister, and from what she could gather—from what little Richard can remember—Richard wanted to become a minister like his father. Ceese and her family were missionaries, so her motive is similar.

"Neither Richard nor Ceese want to take the chance of dying cursed. At least, *Ceese* doesn't want to take the chance. I'm not sure what Richard's angle is. Grandmother said he wants to have the curse removed, but can't admit it. She said his curse is very strong. She tried until she passed away to help Richard."

"But this is all speculation, right? No one can come back from the dead to tell them this will really happen."

Cassie nodded. "But everything else of legend seems to be true. Richard can't tolerate garlic, or anything holy. Like crosses. Cemeteries are off-limits. Ceese is greatly affected by wolfsbane. And neither one can say or think holy thoughts without agonizing pain. . . . Their curse won't allow them to recognize the one thing certain to give them eternal life."

"You mean like John 3:16?"

Cassie's mouth gaped open, but Rodney spoke before she could say anything.

"I'm not *that* radical," he told her. "I did Sunday school— for a while."

She nodded, hid a smile. "Well, that's pretty much the heart of it. They want to be mortal. They want a choice about where they end up. Grandmother did a lot of research and sent it to me. A diary of sorts." Her face turned sad. "More about Richard, less about Ceese. But I could tell Grandmother put a lot of work into it."

"So you have some ideas on how to break their curse?"

Cassie nodded. "But I wouldn't feel right telling you before I told Richard and Ceese."

"I guess I can understand that," Rodney sighed, not realizing that he now accepted that vampires and werewolves existed. "But I still can't help but wonder what Dr. Henderson's angle is. I mean, I don't know a lot about the kind of research he's into, but . . . I don't think he wants to help them."

"I don't, either," Cassie agreed, realizing that, for good or bad, they were both on the same side.

Rodney looked at his watch. It was now early afternoon. "I guess they'll be getting up soon."

"Yes," Cassie said, and nodded. "Probably not long after the sun sets."

"We should get some rest, too." He looked at the futon he was sitting on, where he normally slept. Opened completely, it was the same size as a double bed. "Why don't you take my bed?"

"Why don't we both take your bed?" Cassie replied. "You can put your head at one end and I'll put mine at the other. Fully clothed, one on top of the covers, the other under them." She felt obligated to add, "We'll flip for preference." And she whipped out a coin.

Rodney had so many things he could have said, but didn't. He was just glad Cassie still considered him an ally. Richard, he didn't care much for. Ceese—it was different with her. He didn't know if he cared, but he knew he wanted to. She seemed so strong, so independent. But he couldn't help feeling she was vulnerable somehow. And though the realization surprised him, he wanted to protect her.

CHAPTER 28

It was somewhere around eight before Cassie knew it: seven forty-seven p.m., according to the blaring red numbers of Rodney's clock radio, which he had returned to the table from his duffle bag.

There was another light too, coming from the kitchen. Cassie craned her neck and saw Richard standing in front of the refrigerator, door open, the stark light making him seem paler than usual. His hair was down completely now, and she found it harder to ignore the odd attraction she had for him. Her grandmother had never said much in their conversations, or in her diary, about Richard's physical appearance. At least not about anything she herself found interesting: his lean physique, his stern jawline. Her grandmother always spoke of Richard in such glowing terms, though. Perhaps, in her own way, Grandmother felt the same way about the vampire as Cassie did right now.

Troubled by how worried he looked, she rolled off the futon and went into the kitchen.

"Ceese didn't rest well," he told her when she asked. "And I'm not certain why. She won't tell me. She hasn't said a word since we've been up."

Cassie looked to where Ceese was sitting at the kitchen table, her head buried in her arms.

"She's hungry," Rodney called from the futon. He got up and headed over to them, pushed past both Cassie and Richard and reached into the freezer. "She needs meat."

He took an aluminum-foil-wrapped package, identified it as hamburger. "I'll cook it for her."

Richard yanked the frozen block from Rodney's hands. "Do you want to kill her? Or make her sick?"

Rodney, startled and offended, spouted, "I can cook!"

Cassie stepped in. "It's not that, Rodney. It's just the meat has to be raw."

"Oh," Rodney said, and shrugged. "Well, I know how to defrost too." He took the block of meat back from Richard, readied it for the microwave.

It looked like dinner because it was evening, and they were at a table. But Ceese was eating raw hamburger meat, and Richard drank blood while Cassie ate sardines on crackers. Rodney was merely struggling not to hurl.

"You know," he said, "I was just thinking about those reality shows on TV now, where you can make big bucks by doing just what you're doing here. Only they eat pig entrails, cow bladders . . . you know. Then they chase it down with goat bile and sometimes blood." He looked at Richard when he said the latter. "You three should really consider participating. There's a lot of money in it."

"Ignore him," Cassie said, and brought another sardine-topped cracker to her mouth.

"Ignore who?" Richard replied.

Cassie gave him a grin, amazed at how easy it came to her.

Ceese was the only one who had nothing to add. She was too busy eating.

After everyone was finished and the table was cleared, Rodney got up to stretch and to hopefully secure the seat next to Ceese. He was quick to notice Richard's contemptuous stare.

"I believe I was sitting there," Richard said.

It was a challenge, and Cassie wondered, for a second, if Rodney would push the matter. But he didn't, just meandered away as though it meant nothing to him, really, and settled back where he was before.

It was unclear to Cassie why Richard cared whether Rodney sat next to Ceese; he seemed to care about so little. Perhaps she'd ask later. She added the question to her list, the one she knew would just get longer. That question went right after the one about why Richard had to constantly remind Ceese to fasten her pants.

"Okay," Cassie said, flipping through her notes, some computer-generated, some she'd scrawled on paper. She felt awkward, wondered how Richard and Ceese would take it when they learned she didn't have some miracle cure. What would they say or do when she told them her research hadn't turned up anything new. Would they leave? Would they forgive her for having said she could help when she was no longer sure she could? Grandmother had put so much faith in her, but at the moment, that didn't seem like enough.

She was delighted when Grandmother found her on the Internet, then asked for her help. Until then, she'd had no real family. She'd been adopted when she was an infant, began searching for her roots out of curiosity. But to actually find someone—someone so closely related, when she'd been told there was no one. And to learn that her grandmother was interested in the same things she was, she was thrilled. It had to be fate.

That was two years ago, and here she sat, staring at and talking to an actual vampire and werewolf, not the phonies she and Dr. Henderson had spoken with before.

The reality of it all hit her, had her feeling good again. But the moment lost some of its momentum when Richard blared. "We don't have all night!"

She really didn't know where or how to start. She looked at the back of another page, was drawn to a note added by Dr. Henderson, something about blood replacement or blood filtering. She shook her head, sighed. How far had he gone with his supposed research? What was he *really* planning? All she could do was wonder and hope she never had to find out.

At that, she straightened, took control of her uncertainty and realized she knew more than others did. And right now, her knowing was the only hope Richard and Ceese had. She couldn't let them down.

After a few more moments of her jumping from one page of notes to another, of her repeating things he'd already heard, Richard became uninterested, then agitated. "What do you mean, *one selfless act*?" he said, his words hard and direct as he pushed his chair away and stood, leaning heavily on his side of the table.

"Do you think we traveled all this way just to hear you regurgitate everything your grandmother said all these years? Don't you have anything new to add?"

Ceese spoke for the first time since dinner, or rather muttered: "Here goes the furniture."

"One selfless act?" Richard continued. "I can't tell you how sick I am of hearing that!"

"That's the vampire speaking," Ceese shared, just in case anyone had trouble understanding.

"Well, he's very *loud*," Rodney said in response, an observation that brought Richard very close to Rodney's neck.

"Don't speak of me as if I weren't in this room with you."

Rodney was quick to defend himself. "You didn't care when *she* did it."

"*She* isn't you," Richard pointed out, then turned on Cassie again. "Is that truly all the insight you have? That one selfless act will end this?"

Cassie leaned back in her chair, studying Richard. Why did men always feel they had the upper hand when it came to threats? But Grandmother hadn't been intimidated by him, and she wouldn't be either. "Well, there *is* one other theory Grandmother had. And I'll be glad to share it, *if* you'll calm down. But I'll tell you now, I've sort of ruled it out as a possibility, as I'm sure you will when you hear it."

"Then why tell him?" Rodney asked, his voice a plea.

Richard placed a decidedly cold hand over Rodney's mouth so Rodney couldn't speak.

Cassie looked at her grandmother's notes, then back up at Richard. "'Two wrongs do make a right,'" she read, then held up a hand when she saw Richard open his mouth. "I don't understand it myself, but Grandmother must have had some reason for telling me this."

"Balderdash!" Richard exclaimed, heading away from the table now.

The action had Rodney feeling a little better about his life, a little braver. "Balderdash?" he asked Ceese.

"Balderdash," Ceese replied. "It means Richard isn't happy."

"Would that be Richard the vampire or Richard the man?"

"I think it's safe to say they're both angry now."

Rodney's face showed his uncertainty. "Well, how good can *that* be?"

Cassie ignored the banter between Ceese and Rodney. She was more concerned with the way Richard was acting.

"I'm sorry," she said to his back. "But I trust Grandmother's work. She did a great deal of research and, as crazy as it sounds to you, it makes sense to me. She specifically states that one selfless act, carried out on one's own inclination against the curse, will be enough to rid one of the curse."

"Yes, I heard you," Richard snapped. "Either that, or two wrongs *do* make a right."

He stopped to take a breath, and in an instant, his look changed. As Cassie and the others watched, his cheekbones took on more definition, his eyes were now extremely hard to ignore, and his teeth were visible. He took two calculated steps back to the table, leaned very close to Rodney again. "Tell you what. How about I suck the blood out of this one, but spare you two? Is that selfless enough?"

"Vampire," Ceese offered once more, but it was clear the distinction was beginning to matter less and less. Vampire or not, Richard was getting personal.

Cassie rose from her chair. "I don't care who or what you are, but I won't be bullied."

Fangs appeared now. "You would be wise not to confront me."

"Then you would be wise to show more restraint," Cassie replied.

"I'm just gonna step outside and have a warm beer," Rodney said, darting by Richard and toward the door.

"I know it's hard for you to accept," Cassie continued, staring Richard down, "but I'm here to help you."

Richard looked more normal after a moment, but his words remained cold. "Then you had better try harder. Because right now, I don't have much faith in your theories." He reached into his shirt pocket, extracted a gold case and nimbly pulled a cigarette out of it.

228

"Not in here," Cassie said quickly. "I can't stand the smell. You can smoke on the balcony."

"But *he* is out there," Richard replied.

"Then I suppose you'll just have to tolerate him."

He glared at her, but she returned his look in equal measure. And so, out is where Richard reluctantly went.

"He doesn't mean to be that way," Ceese offered. "He can't help himself."

Cassie returned to her chair. She'd had so little conversation with Ceese, it seemed odd hearing her speak to just her. It was difficult for Cassie to know just what to say in return, too, and she wondered how Rodney did it. *Oh my God!* she thought. Did she actually envy something about him? She realized she did. She wanted so much for Ceese to feel as comfortable with her as she seemed to feel with Rodney.

"If he can't help himself," Cassie said of Richard, "then how can he help you?"

"I don't believe he can help me. But Penny said he could. And I believe her."

Cassie nodded. "I believed her, too. I mean, I still do. But Grandmother was adamant about your needing Richard's cooperation."

"What is *adamant*?" Ceese asked.

"It means she was very certain. Does that make sense?"

Ceese nodded, then grew silent. Cassie couldn't help but wonder what Ceese was thinking about as she stared down at the table. And then, all at once, she didn't have to wonder. Ceese's head came up and she looked at Cassie from behind those long bangs with those eyes. "She talks to me, Cassie." Her voice was mystical, as was her expression. "Her thoughts fill my head. Sometimes they're all I can hear."

Cassie shook her head. "They're just memories, Ceese. Grandmother is gone."

"She tells me things," Ceese continued. "The way she did before . . . when she led me to the castle."

"Tells you things? What kind of things?" Cassie asked, tried not to appear frightened.

Ceese lowered her voice to a whisper and leaned toward Cassie. "She tells me she is alive but—*shhhhh*," Ceese brought a stiff finger to her lips. "Don't tell Richard. He doesn't know."

"That's very interesting, Ceese," Cassie said opting to humor her.

"Oh, there's more. Father is alive as well."

"Your father?"

Ceese nodded. "He's with Penny. And she tells me he misses me."

Cassie was beginning to feel uneasy. "Grandmother tells you this—your father misses you?"

Ceese nodded and actually smiled. "Yes."

"Why doesn't your father just speak to you directly, like Grandmother does?"

She didn't mean to offend, but apparently she had.

"You don't believe me?" Ceese said as though pouting.

"No, Ceese, it's not that. I . . . I just want to understand. I'm just trying to make sense of it." She wished she could go get Rodney, ask his advice on how to talk to this strange individual.

Ceese brightened. "Penny is special, like you. She can project—at least I think that's what she calls it."

Cassie leaned back farther and fought a smile of relief. "Well, I'm sure I can't *project*."

"You can, you just don't know how to yet."

Cassie nodded slowly, wondered what she'd gotten herself into. "Ceese, I'm not sure how to say this but—"

"I'm frightening you," Ceese finished.

Now, Cassie could be honest. "Yes."

"It frightened Penny, too. But there will come a time when curiosity will take over."

Cassie looked away, then forced her eyes back to Ceese. "Well, until that time comes, could we not talk about this 'projecting' any more?"

"If you wish," Ceese said, and her expression changed. She cocked her head slightly, as though listening to someone else. And then, Cassie seemed to hear it as well.

"It-It can't be," Cassie said in wonder.

Ceese smiled knowingly. "You heard her."

Cassie's eyes bored into the odd-colored ones across from her, certain Ceese had caused something to happen. "You did that."

"I didn't. I can't. What did you sense? What did she tell you?"

Without knowing how she knew, she said, "Worried—" Cassie listened again. "Yes, Grandmother's worried."

Ceese nodded. "Penny's worried about me. And she worries about you. She *really* worries about Richard."

"Why would she worry more about him?"

"Because now she questions whether he can bring himself to admit he wants this—wants his curse lifted. And she worries what I might do to help him along."

Now, Cassie was worried. "And what might you do, Ceese? What might you do to help Richard along?"

"Whatever it takes." Ceese's look wasn't one to be reckoned with, and neither were her words.

"And why would you put so much on the line for him?" she said, curious.

"I don't want to talk about it anymore," was Ceese's answer. And she didn't.

CHAPTER 29

Rodney sipped his beer and did his best to ignore Richard, who was doing his best to ignore him. But after a while, it became too much for Rodney. "So how long do you plan on hanging around? You know, since Cassie doesn't really have anything to offer you."

Richard said nothing, just sent a trail of smoke out into the night.

"Because, you know," Rodney continued, "I don't think anyone would really care if you did leave."

"Do you think I want to be here?" Richard finally said, spitting out the words as if they needed to be spat, fixing Rodney with another contemptuous stare. "I only came here because—" He looked irritated about being drawn in, and turned away again. "Never mind."

"No," Rodney said, "finish it. You only came here because of what?"

"I'm sure I don't know what you're talking about."

Rodney, being qualified, knew Richard was lying. "You don't want to be here," he mused, "and yet you won't leave. You almost tell me why you're staying . . . but then you don't. Sounds to me like you're hiding something."

"Perhaps you should worry more about yourself," Richard offered, "instead of meddling."

"Oh, but I *like* meddling."

"So I've noticed." Another smoke-trail went out and up.

"What else do you like, Richard?" Rodney asked, baiting him.

"I'm sure I wouldn't tell you."

"Well, it's pretty clear you like Ceese," Rodney said, "since you try to keep me away from her at every turn. Is there something going on between the two of you?"

"I'm sure it wouldn't be safe," Richard said, "should it turn out to be possible, which it isn't."

"Oh, yeah," Rodney replied, remembered what Cassie had said. "The whole curse thing. It must be frustrating not to be able to . . . well, you know—do it."

"*Do it?*" Richard sneered. "Do you annoy on purpose, or is it just something you come by naturally?"

"Oh, come on, it's gotta bug you. You're a guy. Or at least a part of you is, right? I guess you'll at least have one thing to look forward to once the curse is lifted. Who knows? Maybe you and Ceese could, ah . . . get together then."

Richard was on him in an instant, pulling him off the ground and holding him by the collar of his shirt. "Do you think you're clever?" he hissed.

"I-I used to think I was," Rodney croaked, trying to touch the ground with his toes. "But I'm not so sure anymore."

"Well, for your future information, I don't want, nor can I *get together* with anyone, especially Ceese. And it isn't something I have any control over. Do you understand?"

"Yes," Rodney said, aware his neck was far too close to Richard's teeth. "I . . . was just making an observation."

Richard shifted his grip to allow Rodney more air . . . not much, but enough to keep him conscious a bit longer. Then he said, "Do you think she cares about *you*?

"You mean Ceese?"

"That's exactly who I mean."

In spite of his discomfort, Rodney smirked at him. "Well, she *did* kiss me."

"And you think it meant something?"

"You think it didn't?"

"She can't have those kinds of emotions, any more than I can."

"Well, she can obviously put a lot of effort into it," Rodney said, realizing a little too late he'd hit yet another nerve. Richard yanked his shirt collar again, making him gasp.

"Do you think you're brave enough to get close to her again?" Richard growled.

"I *told* you," Rodney babbled as he was pulled in closer to those fangs. "I didn't kiss her, she kissed me!"

"And you'll make sure it doesn't happen again."

"How can I make sure? She came—"

Rodney felt Richard's hot breath on his neck, the sharp points of those fangs. "Yes," he sputtered. "Yes, I promise. It'll never happen again!"

"And you'll stay away from her and not think of her in any inappropriate manner?"

"Right," Rodney agreed, "Right!"

"Because if you don't stay away from her," Richard said, "I'll suck the very life out of you. Do I make myself clear?"

"Yeah, yes— I-I got it. Just put me down, p-please."

So Richard did. He then turned back toward the balcony railing and gripped it with both hands.

"You could have just told me you like her," Rodney muttered, rubbing his neck. "It's not anything to be ashamed of."

"I *don't* like her," Richard sneered. "I can't!"

"Right," Rodney said quickly. "Sorry, I forgot."

Richard kept his hands on the railing but whipped his head toward Rodney. "You think that's all there is to it, don't you? You think all I have to do is convince myself I can feel things the way you and everyone else can. But it's not that simple. I can't feel things . . . I can't!"

Without another word, Richard hoisted himself up onto the railing and jumped.

Cassie stepped out at almost the same instant, to see if Richard had calmed, but she missed the actual plunge. She therefore didn't understand Rodney's look of utter disbelief as he stood, eyes wide, mouth open.

"Rodney, what's the matter?" she asked "And where's Richard?"

"He-He . . ." Rodney stammered but nothing else came out.

"He what?" Cassie prodded.

"He—uhh, sort of . . . jumped."

Cassie raced the few steps to the railing and looked over. "Are you drunk?" she asked. "The only thing down there is the sidewalk."

"I swear it," Rodney said, and came to stand beside her. "He jumped!"

"He levitated," Ceese offered, coming to stand behind them on the small balcony. "He just called out to me. He told me to tell you we're going hunting. And oh, to not wait up for us."

"Gee," Rodney said after Ceese left, "who knew?"

Cassie just looked bothered. "*Why* did he jump, Rodney?"

"Levitate," Rodney corrected, trying to buy time. He knew Cassie wouldn't be happy if she found out he'd upset Richard. And now, not having her upset at him was more important than it used to be. "I'm telling you, he levitated. And I'm not exactly sure why he did it."

"It wasn't something you said?"

"It, ah, might have been," he tried.

But when she squinted at him, he decided to hang it up. "Okay, it *was* something I said. I sort of inferred he and Ceese should get together and he . . . he lost it."

"You really are something," Cassie moaned, and placed her hand on the balcony's railing. "He can't have those kinds of emotions, Rodney. I thought you understood."

"You said *Ceese* couldn't have those kinds of emotions. You never said anything about Richard. And by the way, I still think you're wrong about—about Ceese."

But Cassie didn't seem to hear him. Instead, she asked, "You really think you upset him by bringing up his feelings for Ceese? By suggesting he and Ceese should have a . . . relationship?"

"Yeah, and here's the crazy part. Right after he told me he couldn't have feelings for Ceese, he threatened me. He held me off the ground and told me not to go near her. He said if I did, he would 'suck the very life out of me.'"

"So are you going to stay away from her?"

Rodney sighed. "I've never been close to her. Remember? She came to me."

"Well, what did Richard say when you explained? About her coming to you instead?"

Rodney thought a moment. "You know what? I don't think it matters to him. I think anyone who shows an interest in Ceese . . . or vice-versa . . . is fair game to be bitten." *Or held by their shirt collars until they agree with whatever it is he wants them to agree with.* He shook his head and muttered, "He really would benefit from some anger management courses."

He expected a snappish reply, but didn't get one. "Are you like, upset because he seems to care for Ceese?" he said gently. "Because you look upset."

"I . . . I guess I'm glad he's showing some signs of caring . . . for Ceese's sake."

But she had tacked that last part on a little too late for Rodney to ignore. "And maybe for your sake too?"

She glared at him. "Meaning?"

"Meaning you're attracted to him. You want him to care for you too."

She sighed. "Oh, yes, I've always wanted to date a vampire. Yeah, right, Rodney."

"It couldn't be any worse than the last guy you dragged in here. What was his name? Dennis? Daryl? Oooh wait, now I remember . . . Dumbass!"

"Very funny. But I'm not interested in Richard. Besides, he's cursed, remember?"

"But what if he weren't cursed?"

"Then he wouldn't be here, and we wouldn't be having this conversation. And besides, I haven't known him long enough to be emotional about him."

"I don't know," Rodney said. "I didn't think I could feel the way I do about Ceese—" He caught himself and spoke a little louder, just in case vampires had supersensitive hearing. "Not that I do."

"Right. Maybe we should just play things a little less personally."

"Well, *I* have to," Rodney pointed out, "or else I'll have the very life sucked out of me. Remember?" He drew quote marks in the air with his fingers.

With an exaggerated eye roll, Cassie whirled around and headed inside. Rodney drained his beer can and followed her.

CHAPTER 30

Unlike Richard and Ceese, Clayton Henderson didn't consider dying while cursed a problem, nor would he ever consider it a problem. He did understand from Cassie that Richard and Ceese were struggling with the idea, and he was determined to make this information work to his advantage.

The reason was simple. Dr. Clayton Henderson wanted to live forever, and if there was any truth to what he'd learned from Cassie about Richard and Ceese, he was well on his way to getting what he wanted. All he wanted was some of their blood: so he could test it and see what was different about them. And, of course, if it led to more testing, and the need for more blood, so be it.

He'd be the first to admit it sounded a little far-fetched to believe that vampires and werewolves existed. But Cassie's grandmother certainly believed, and she was very convincing; the diary she'd sent Cassie seemed irrefutable. Henderson had an electronic copy of her writings . . . as much as Cassie had typed in. Rodney had gotten it for him. The problem was, Cassie must not have finished typing it all in. Much was left hanging. Too much. And now, with Cassie onto him and Rodney no longer helping, he'd have a hard time getting the rest of it.

Sitting at his computer, he scanned through what he had of the diary, became more frustrated, and then began plotting. He had to know more about this werewolf and vampire. He had to . . .

When the plan came to him, he was sure it was divine intervention. Many would have written it off as just a happy coincidence. But he didn't. Not that he believed in divine anything.

It was just a grand idea, coming to him at a grand time. And it would work, he was sure of it. And when it did, all his years of research, of being called a fool, a charlatan and worse by the scientific community, would end.

❧ ❧ ❧

At that moment, Cassie was scrolling through her own electronic copy of the diary. It was early Sunday afternoon, and after being up most of the night waiting for Richard and Ceese to return, she wished she'd slept longer. But Rodney's tossing and turning put an end to any such wishing.

After a while, she finished reading what she had on her computer and reached to the desk drawer to read the words she hadn't yet transcribed—the words that were perhaps the most intriguing, and baffling.

She turned through the worn pages, considering what she didn't understand. *"Two wrongs make it right,"* Grandmother had written, and Cassie stared at that entry again. But nothing new came. She was tired, though. Much more than she should have been at twelve-thirty in the afternoon.

In hindsight, she wished she hadn't stayed up until Richard and Ceese came back from their hunt. But they were technically her guests, and she felt responsible.

Richard hadn't seemed appreciative of her concern, and had gone right out to smoke. Ceese, however, was eager to talk, and Cassie gladly accepted her invitation to sit at the kitchen table.

It hadn't been nearly as awkward as the first time they spoke, and Ceese went right into a story about Cassie's grandmother, back when Grandmother had been about the same age Cassie herself was now.

"You and she must have been very close," Cassie had said at one point.

The comment seemed to set Ceese back a bit, and she clutched the cross hanging around her neck before saying "Yes."

"Did she give you that?" Cassie asked, trying to lighten the mood that had turned dark so quickly.

Ceese nodded, tried to smile, and Cassie was startled to see the moisture in the werewolf's strange eyes.

Richard was just coming in from the balcony when Ceese passed him, on her way to their shared bedroom. When Cassie tried to explain, he harshly told her to let the dead lie, then stalked into the bedroom himself.

Cassie shook her head now as she looked back down at her grandmother's diary and thought about how confusing it all was. Knowing so little, how could she possibly help them break free of their curses?

But she knew she had to try. Perhaps tomorrow, though. Right now, she was too tired to think straight. She picked up the diary to close it, to put it back where she kept it, when the necklace her grandmother had sent along with the book fell out.

Cassie bent down to retrieve it, prepared to put it back, but stopped. Attached to the necklace was a cross, and while there was nothing at all significant about it, she couldn't stop looking at it. Something was familiar, very familiar, and suddenly Cassie realized what it was.

Cassie opened the diary again and reread the part where Grandmother wrote of two vampires, both wanting to be mortal again, both wanting to rid themselves of the curse. One evening and on their own accord, they had gone into a cemetery, to the small chapel there. Grandmother described each agonizing step as they walked, and then dropped to their knees from treading on the holy ground.

It was so real the way she described it, the way she wrote it all down. Amazing how well Grandmother depicted their struggle. Almost as if Grandmother were right there with them, feeling their pain, their anguish.

Cassie looked back at the cross. Grandmother never mentioned the names of the two vampires, and never indicated why she hadn't. And Cassie never had any ideas about who they might have been, or what the significance of the story was—until now.

⁂ ⁂ ⁂

Cassie placed the diary back in the drawer, but took the necklace with her. She eased opened the door to her room and looked inside. To her surprise, no one was there. And it was clear, from the covers not being disturbed, the bed hadn't been slept in recently. But she thought she heard movement under the bed.

Puzzled, she entered and looked beneath it. Richard and Ceese were there, sound asleep.

She went to the side where Richard was and called to him softly, hoping her voice wouldn't carry and wake Ceese. It didn't, and Richard's eyes opened. She dangled the cross in front of him, and he hissed.

Cassie moved back. "I need to talk to you."

"Fine." Richard slid out from under the bed and stood. "Just keep that bloody thing away from me."

He had on slacks but no shirt. Until then, Cassie hadn't really noticed. She pocketed the cross and stared, stunned by how affected she was.

He caught her looking and slid into the shirt he'd come out of earlier. In between buttons, he made a motion to the bed, reminding her Ceese was still under there, asleep. Cassie nodded, and they headed for the room's small bathroom and closed the door behind them.

There was a mirror over the vanity, and Cassie tried not to pay attention to how odd it was she didn't see Richard in it.

"What?" he quipped. "Never *not* seen a vampire before?"

She turned quickly, pulled the cross back out and held it for him to look at again. He threw his arms up to cover his face.

But this time, she wasn't going to back down. "This cross," she said. "It's yours, isn't it?"

"I don't know what you're talking about," he sputtered, "and I'll only tell you once more to put that thing away!"

Cassie had made her point and returned it to her pocket, her thoughts in high gear now. "Grandmother wrote of two vampires in her diary. Two vampires who tried to break the curse. She never mentioned their names, but I found this cross in her diary. Ceese is wearing another just like it. Last night she said Grandmother gave it to her."

She took a quick breath, then pushed ahead. "I'll ask again. This one— the one in my pocket. This one is yours, isn't it, Richard? You and Grandmother went to that cemetery to break the curse. It worked for her, and not for you. That's why you have no faith in her theories. That's why you can't let yourself believe she might have been onto something."

She looks so much like Penelope, Richard thought. *Before. When she was still cursed. Always so passionate about whatever cause she was following at the time.* "She could never prove what made it happen for her," he threw out.

Cassie fought a gasp. She didn't really think he would come clean that easily. And . . . what he'd just said. Her grandmother had been a vampire, too!

But she had to pull herself together and move on. "*One selfless act,*" she muttered. "Don't you understand? She was ready to *die* for you!"

"And you don't think I was ready to die for her? I still bear the marks."

He propped a leg on the edge of the bathtub, raised the pant leg to reveal an area around the ankle where the skin appeared to have been burned. The spot was still slightly pink, as though it had never healed completely or at least, properly.

He looked at her and said, "She was stronger than I. She had more control."

All at once, Cassie remembered something else Grandmother told her, in a phone call she made a few days before she died. "But Ceese can help you," she said, "with her mind!"

"No!" Richard fired back, pulling the pant leg back down and standing straight again. "My curse is more than I can fight. I won't do it again. I could never live with myself if—"

"If what, Richard?" Cassie pushed him. "What couldn't you live with?"

"It isn't your concern."

"It's Ceese, isn't it? You don't want her to go through what you went through, what Grandmother went through." *Was Rodney right?* she thought suddenly. *Does Richard have feelings for Ceese?*

242

"Don't you see?" Cassie implored, pushing the thought away. "You don't want Ceese hurt. You *care* about her!"

When he finally spoke, each word formed a sharp echo in the tiny bathroom. "I won't do it again. I cared, as much as I can care, about your grandmother. But it didn't matter!"

Cassie let that go for now. "Was it as painful as she described?" she asked, remembering the words she'd just read in the diary. "It was so vivid, the way she explained it all."

Richard shook his head. "Dying would have been less painful. I'm only happy she didn't suffer in vain."

Cassie opened her mouth to agree, but another thought stunned her. "Are *you* the reason she had to go through that in the first place?"

Richard's solemn face turned smug. "Are you suggesting I cursed her? Is that what you want to know?"

"Well, you *are* a vampire."

As though explaining to a child, he said, "I am someone who has a disturbing taste for blood, a taste I didn't acquire until I was bitten myself, by another, who most likely didn't understand their dilemma. *They* were cursed, and upon being bitten, *I* became cursed. It isn't something I understand, and it isn't something I'm proud of. It's just something I have to deal with. But I wouldn't knowingly transfer my curse to anyone, especially to your grandmother. She was already cursed when I met her. And besides, I'm sure she wrote how biting another makes the curse permanent. And why would I want to risk that?"

Cassie felt chagrined. She did remember seeing that, but it had slipped her mind. "I'm sorry," she said. "I guess I put too much stock in those old vampire movies."

"So it would seem. You just envision me running around the countryside ravaging whomever I come into contact with."

"I . . . I suppose I did have that thought."

He looked at her, and his eyes seemed to glow. "Do you think I'm that weak?"

They were in a small room. She had nowhere to go. "I hope you aren't."

"There are those who are," Richard said. "There are those who give in to the curse when it tries to control them. But most of them are gone now. And what of it? Is the world such a better place? There are mortals who do far worse things *without* a curse attached. They commit those atrocities by choice. I have never cursed another. What started with me, ends with me."

As he spoke, his eyes became more normal again, much to her relief. She wasn't sure she could have gotten the cross in her pocket out fast enough to stop him. But now, she was certain of one thing: he was capable of the one emotion she now believed was holding him back. "You don't consider *this* an act of love? Not biting others, even when you want to?"

He gave a harsh laugh. "*Love*? Perhaps by your standards, but not by mine. It's about saving myself. If I bite another, I will be forever cursed."

She looked at his profile. "I see. Well, I'm sure Rodney will be glad to hear that."

He turned his face to hers. "I would prefer you not tell him. And furthermore, if you do, I'll tell him you're lying."

This confused her. "Why?"

"Because it's the only leverage I have with him."

He reached out and put a hand on the doorknob. "If that's all, then I think we should—"

The sudden noise outside the door had him yanking it open.

Startled at seeing him with Cassie, Ceese bolted out of the bedroom. Richard raced after her, and Cassie after him. They came out in time to see Ceese drop to her knees just inside the kitchen, holding her head as though in great pain. Richard went to her at once and asked what was wrong. But she couldn't speak, and when Richard took a moment to look around, he saw why. There, very near the front door, was a large cluster of flowering wolfsbane.

The sudden appearance of the three of them in the kitchen had Rodney jumping up from the futon and staring, bleary-eyed. "What?— What?" he asked. And then again, "What?"

"There," Richard said, pointing toward the wolfsbane. "Get rid of it."

Rodney moved quickly, took up what Richard was pointing at and went to launch it off the side of the balcony. He returned and pointed, at once, to another plant, a malnourished fern hanging irritatingly over the futon. "How about that one? Can I get rid of it next?"

Their serious expressions made him reconsider what he'd just said. "I take it we're not randomly throwing plants out?"

Cassie groaned. "What Richard had you throw over the balcony was wolfsbane. Do I have to explain *everything* to you?"

"Okay, well— I didn't know. I'll make a note." He scribbled with an imaginary pen on the palm of his left hand. "Plants with little purple flowers—bad." Then, tearing out an imaginary page, he started another. "Pathetic, dehydrated fern that sheds on me every night— good." He then stopped, looked confused. "Who would bring something like wolfsbane in here anyway?"

"Kyle," Ceese said, her voice a whimper.

Rodney looked at Ceese, confused. "You willed Kyle to bring wolfsbane?"

"No," Ceese said, more composed. "He was just . . . here."

Richard turned to where Cassie was now, kneeling on the other side of Ceese. "Could he possibly be any stupider?"

"Hey," Rodney protested. "I know more than most do— about werewolves and things like that. And anyway, how could Kyle have been here? I would have known. I would have seen him."

"You were sleeping," Cassie reminded him. "How could you have seen anyone or heard anyone? The way you sleep, a garbage truck could've driven through and you wouldn't have heard it."

"Kyle was *here*," Ceese repeated. "He left the wolfsbane."

"How could he have gotten in?" Cassie said. "The door's locked."

It was Rodney who enlightened them, sounding puny as he spoke. "Uh . . . He has a key."

Cassie's head whipped around to him. "What do you mean, *he has a key*? No one's supposed to have a key but you and me. And *I* didn't give Kyle a key."

"Yeah, well, I lock myself out every now and then, and I feel better knowing I can get in when you're not here. So I gave Kyle a key."

"Great," Cassie muttered. "Who *else* have you given a key to?"

"Nobody," Rodney replied, sullen.

"Can we have this debate later?" Richard asked, and they all turned their attention back to Ceese.

"I'm sorry," Cassie replied, "but if Kyle hadn't had a key, none of this would have happened—and why would he leave wolfsbane?"

"Because he knew I would sense him," Ceese said. "He knew I would know he was here."

"Which would make one think he was up to something," Cassie replied. "But what?"

"He came for a book," Ceese said, looking off as she spoke. "And he got it."

Cassie thought for a moment, then turned pale. "Grandmother's diary." She sprang to her feet and raced to the desk. Its drawer was open and empty. "It's gone," she told them. "But what would he want with it?"

"He doesn't want it," Ceese replied. "Someone else does."

"Dr. Henderson," Rodney added, eyes wide.

"Fools!" Richard shouted. "Such idiocy! The two of you have put us both in danger! That diary talks about Ceese. About *me*. Why would someone like this professor want it unless they were up to no good?"

"They didn't know," Ceese said, trying to calm him.

"You're going to make excuses for them?" he bellowed, and stood to tower over her. "That was wolfsbane, and it could have killed you!"

She shied away from him, and Rodney called out, "Hey, you don't have to yell at her."

Richard jerked his head around to him. "I've heard just about enough out of you."

"Leave him alone," Ceese said unexpectedly, weary from dealing with the pain the wolfsbane had inflicted, made worse by his shouting. And then, to Richard's shocked look, "Just— Leave him alone."

"Fine," Richard said through clenched teeth, striding toward the bedroom and stopping just short of going in. "I'm going to make arrangements to leave. I'll give you five minutes to let me know if you'll be coming along."

"I don't need five minutes. I'm not coming."

"Then I'll give you five minutes to come to your senses."

When the door shut, Ceese stood, ambled after Richard, then stopped briefly in the doorway. Cassie sensed something in the look Ceese gave her, but didn't know what to make of it. The door closed behind Ceese before she had the chance to ask.

❧ ❧ ❧

Richard was already getting his things together, and wouldn't look at her when she came in. "Well, what will it be?" he asked.

"We can't give up, Richard. We can't leave. There's nothing to go back to. At least we have a chance here."

"A chance to die cursed because of their carelessness," Richard replied, his voice hard.

"It isn't Cassie's fault. She means well. And I believe Rodney means well, too."

Richard glared at her. "I'm not sure about Cassie, but one thing I'm sure of: you're blinded by how you feel about *him*." He looked away, then back to her. "You think it's some kind of great gift to have these emotions you say you can have. But you see all the good they've done you."

"I don't have feelings for Rodney. I can't. It's just— It's just I *want* to have them."

"I understand the part about wanting to have feelings," Richard replied. "But why would you want to have feelings for *him*?"

Ceese shrugged. "Because he's like me. Because, no matter how hard he tries, he messes up, too."

"I somehow have a hard time believing there's not more to it."

"I can't have the kind of feelings you're suggesting. But believe what you will."

"I would have to say you're an excellent actress, then."

"I can pull from what little I remember. It's enough to convince most. But I'm cursed, just like you. And no matter what you think, I can't rise above my curse. At least not to where I can have feelings for someone."

Ceese seemed almost angry now. *Will she turn into the wolf?* Richard thought. *What a fine ending that would be to all this mess!*

She fixed him with a stare. "I can't feel for Rodney the way you think I can. I can't feel for anyone like that. Why does it bother you so much anyway? Why do you always want to remind me of what I *can't* do?"

"I don't want to remind you of anything," Richard confessed. "And I'm quite certain it doesn't bother me." He wondered if she actually believed what he'd just said, especially since he couldn't be sure he did himself.

"Then stay," she insisted. "I want to end this, and I need you to help me do it. I know this because that's what Penny said."

"I honestly don't know what you think I can do." Richard meant his words to be the final thing he said. Then, he would finish packing and leave. But he placed the shirt he was holding on the bed, not in the suitcase. "However, if you feel you can trust those two—then I suppose I can."

※ ※ ※

Cassie and Rodney waited, but neither Ceese nor Richard came out. When they did, it was after sunset. Both were dressed appropriately for going out, and out is where they went, with Ceese stopping just long enough to say they would be back later. Richard looked at no one, just headed straight for the door.

CHAPTER 31

Looking for what they needed was simple in the unrefined English countryside, but a tricky matter on the streets of New York City. They'd found a nearby park on that first night, managed a rabbit here and there, a squirrel or two. But Ceese was beginning to look like she needed more, at least to Richard. And he was becoming frustrated. Was she angry with him for how he acted at the apartment, or was she just in such need nothing could satisfy her? But how could he know the answer? She had stopped talking, as though the debate about leaving had taken everything out of her.

He threw the last squirrel down after she refused it with a headshake, but made no move to bury it. What was the point? There wasn't enough meat on anything they'd found to curse anyone, unless someone went around and gathered it all up. And what were the chances of someone doing that?

※ ※ ※

Clayton Henderson knew what he was looking for, though. And after Richard and Ceese moved far enough along, he moved in, finding what Richard had cast aside, putting the drained carcasses in a bag, taking a moment to make sure he found the bite marks first, and then heading off.

In one section of Cassie's grandmother's diary, he'd read how vampires feed. The process required blood to be both taken and given. He supposed this was necessary to make room for the freshest blood. And thus, the curse was transferred.

Henderson decided to test this theory. What did he have to lose? Stem cell research had come a long way. So much was possible, with so little. Collecting stem cells from peripheral blood was now possible. The question was whether there were any stem cells worth working with in what he just collected. The mobilization process, which moves useful stem cells from bone marrow into the bloodstream, hadn't been done. But he had to try. Perhaps things were different with vampires. If there were useful stem cells in the blood he found—Richard's blood—it was a start. Anxious to get started, he sent Josh off to where he was certain he'd seen Richard throw something down, and picked up one last squirrel himself.

"How's this?" Josh said when he returned and showed Henderson what he'd found.

"Very nice," he replied, noting the fang marks. "There might be hope for you yet."

Henderson had the same hope for Josh and Rodney's friend, Kyle. Kyle had actually come through by delivering the diary. Yet then, just a little while ago, he declared he would do nothing else for him.

"I'll tell you when I don't need you anymore," Henderson had told him. "Until then, you will do exactly as I say."

"Or what?" Kyle sneered back.

Henderson showed Kyle the folder he'd had his cousin Phillip compile for him. There were similar files on Rodney and Josh. Kyle's name was on it, his academic records inside it—records Henderson threatened to have changed if he didn't cooperate fully.

Blackmail wasn't something Kyle was used to, so he wasn't sure how to react. But he tried. And then Henderson pulled out the other file he kept—one that showed Kyle's arrest for drug possession. "My cousin doesn't know about this file," Henderson said. "Yet. But all I have to do is show it to him, and your scholarship—and college career—will be over. Lying on a college application is highly frowned upon, you know."

Kyle didn't stand a chance, and he knew it. Henderson was a professor, he only a student. "What do you want?"

"It's not what I want, it's who. I want you to bring the werewolf to me."

"Now, *you're* mental," Kyle told him. "I can't make her do something she doesn't want to do."

"Then convince her." Henderson had then led him out and shut the door, knowing Kyle would fume and moan, but would do anything to keep his good record.

Josh walked up to Henderson holding a full burlap bag. "I think these are all of them."

Henderson nodded and gave a stingy smile. "Very well. Now, let's head back to the house and . . . your reward."

He strode out of the deserted park, Josh trotting eagerly behind.

⅍ ⅍ ⅍

Henderson's basement lab was a complete, if small-scale replica of the larger ones he was used to working in—without all the bureaucratic red tape. Furnishing it hadn't been easy. He'd taken everything he could get out of the lab he'd been thrown out of. The newest equipment had been donated to the new program, but he'd managed to have it delivered here instead. And now, he made one final adjustment to his microscope, and realized all the risk had been worth it.

Upon that realization, he laughed aloud. He couldn't believe it! The unique-looking cells were sparse, but enough. He began at once to separate the vampire's blood from the squirrels'.

His research was cutting-edge, but based on the work of others: to take ordinary white blood cells and turn them into stem cells, or at least make them perform like stem cells. He believed it was possible, and if he could do this, he could easily leap over the ethical hurdle of stem cell collection. He'd already had success with extracting stem cells from blood itself.

What did he hope to accomplish with his research? He wanted to go back to work at the research facilities, wanted to take advantage of their more sophisticated equipment, their funding. But now— He looked back into his microscope. If he could extract enough of the vampire's blood, he might possibly have what he'd been seeking all along.

251

As soon as he extracted the cells, he would infuse himself with them—to see if they would settle into his bone marrow and start producing. Get the ball rolling, so to speak. There was the matter of rejection, which he refused to think about now. Typically, stem cells extracted from one person could only be used on that person, unless the two subjects were closely related, like siblings. Yet he hoped this didn't apply to vampires, since their curse was surely transferred through the blood. Likely, their blood had anti-rejection properties.

For a second, as he kept working, Henderson almost believed in fate. Almost believed someone else might have had a hand in how things had turned out. A higher power of some kind.

But then he laughed. That was just a bunch of nonsense designed to make people feel good about the unknown. And if his ideas on immortality were right, he wouldn't *need* to believe the theories religion offered.

❧ ❧ ❧

Two nights ago, Rodney didn't believe in werewolves or vampires, didn't fear them or worry about them. Now, he couldn't deny experiencing both those feelings.

Yet it was the feelings he had for Ceese that truly disturbed him. Before the kiss, he'd thought she was interesting; after the kiss, he knew she was. He wanted to understand the mystery behind those eyes . . . the mystery behind *her*. But Richard's threat wasn't easy to disregard. The vampire threatened to suck the life out of him, and Rodney believed he would.

That's why he was more than a little upset when, after their hunt yielded too little food, Richard and Cassie made the decision to leave him alone with Ceese.

Cassie immediately made a few calls, found a friend who knew a man who owned a butcher shop, and arranged to meet with him. But Ceese was too exhausted to go with them. So he was left alone with the very person Richard's threat was supposed to protect. All alone.

Rodney settled on the futon, switched on the TV, and

considered what it might be like to have the life sucked out of you. Then Ceese walked out of the bedroom and into the kitchen, and the image became more real. Rodney sat like a stone to make sure he didn't say, think or feel anything a vampire might consider inappropriate, and he didn't relax until after Ceese went back into the bedroom.

The second time she came out, he was too suspicious to be nervous. He found her scavenging through the refrigerator, cupboards, the garbage. And then, just like before, she headed back to the bedroom. But this time, her arms were full.

Rodney waited a while, but then the urge to investigate won. Threat or no threat, something didn't add up. He knocked lightly, but didn't wait for Ceese to invite him in.

Empty food containers were everywhere, and Ceese sat in the middle of them, stuffing her face.

"I-I thought none of what we had here was good for you," Rodney sputtered. "I thought that's why they had to find that butcher sh—"

Ceese stopped chewing and looked at him. "Sometimes it *is* good for me," she said, speaking around a mouthful of potato chips.

"I think I'd feel better if you could explain—uh, *after* you swallow."

She gulped down what she had in her mouth, then said, "I don't think I can. Explain, I mean. I just wanted something salty." She reached for one of a dozen water bottles before her and drained it dry, then took another and drained it as well. "Richard wouldn't understand," she said, looked sad. "He would have tried to stop me."

"Why would he try to stop you? Seems to me he's going out of his way to *help* you."

"He doesn't want to help me become the wolf," she said, crammed another handful of chips in.

Rodney felt the hair stand up on his neck. "Well, I'm pretty sure none of us want to help you do that."

"But I must," she said, dropped the potato chip bag and stood. "I have to. And I need you to help me."

Rodney felt his blood pressure rise. "I don't think I like the way this is sounding."

"I need you to tell me where the professor lives."

"Okay," Rodney said, backing up, "now I'm *sure* I don't like the way it sounds. I—I'm not gonna tell you where he lives."

"I can make you tell me."

"He's dangerous, Ceese. He could hurt you and . . . well, I don't want to see you get hurt. And why do you want to go there anyway?"

"Richard needs me to. Richard needs help."

Rodney's face showed his confusion. "How is you going to see Hender— Uh, the professor going to help him?"

"I can't explain that, either. I need to get to the professor, and the wolf can help me get there. And if I accommodate it, it will help me in return." She looked at him with those odd green-gold eyes. "Now, tell me where the wolf needs to go."

"No, I—"

But then Rodney felt her in his head, and though he struggled to push her out, he couldn't. He thought of anything and everything else, but it didn't matter. Ceese knew exactly how to get what she was after.

"I'm sorry, Rodney," she said afterward. "But I have to go now." And she headed for the door.

"Wait a minute," Rodney said, rushed after her. "I didn't tell you anything!"

But as she exited, she spit it all back out to him, the number of traffic signals, how many turns, and just before the door leading to the stairwell closed behind her, she told him how many potholes.

"But you can't know," Rodney hollered. "There's no way you can know!"

A concerned neighbor stuck his head out the door. "You okay?"

"There's no way she can know," he said again. But she was gone.

Frustrated, he ignored the neighbor, went back into the apartment, slammed the door shut and raced to the kitchen. He found a pad and pencil, scribbled a note and then headed out. Maybe he couldn't stop her, but he had to try, for her sake and for his.

🐾 🐾 🐾

Cassie and Richard returned thirty minutes later, arms full of dripping packages wrapped in butcher paper. When neither could get a response from either Rodney or Ceese, Richard's face hardened. He dropped his parcel on the table and headed for the bedroom, returning seconds later, his face thunderous.

"She's not here," he told Cassie. "And she's been eating—a lot."

The note in his voice stilled Cassie. "I . . . I thought she couldn't eat the food we had here. That's why we went out tonight, right?"

"Apparently we've been misled," Richard said. He looked angry to Cassie. "How could I have been so blind? She's going to transform. She's going to become the wolf. Apparently, she's been planning this."

"But-But why?"

"I . . . don't know."

But then, his face turned neutral and his shoulders fell. "I suppose it really doesn't matter why she did it. She's gone now."

"Richard," Cassie said carefully. "We have to find her. We have to go after her."

"I won't play into her hand."

They both turned as the knocking started on the door they'd left ajar. It was Kyle, who'd done a lot of thinking.

"Is Rodney here?" he asked.

Richard strode up to Kyle, casually took him by the neck and forcefully slammed him against a nearby wall. "Where is she?"

Cassie was glad to see Richard charged up again for Ceese's sake, but frightened for Kyle. She took hold of the cross in her pocket and kept a hand on it.

"I-I don't know what you're talking about!" Kyle screeched. It was the truth, but it didn't seem to matter to Richard. "I just came to try and make things right. Dr. Henderson *did* send me

255

after— after your friend. Or whatever she is to you. But I wasn't gonna go through with it."

"What a convenient thing for you to say," Richard drawled, and produced fangs.

"He's telling the truth," Cassie said. She'd just found Rodney's note. "Ceese left on her own accord. Rodney says so right here. She's headed to Henderson's place."

Cassie wondered if Richard was going to lose steam again, waited for his response.

"You will take us there," he said, staring at Kyle hard.

Kyle nodded vigorously. "I'll take you. But you have to turn loose of me."

Richard did, but not before slamming Kyle against the wall once more, to make him think.

CHAPTER 32

A wolf didn't need clothes, Rodney soon learned when he found the ones Ceese had discarded near the Dumpster outside. But Ceese might need them later, so he gathered them up before setting out after her.

He thought it would be hard to follow, but apparently this was what Ceese wanted him to do; he didn't get winded or tired chasing after her. His newly acquired stamina had to be her work, he decided, because running wasn't something he could do well for very long. Following her was amazingly easy. Every once in a while the trail would go cold, but all he had to do was question just where it was he needed to head next, and the answer came.

He ran for blocks, then came to an alley where the trail once again grew cold. He waited, but no new direction came. The alley was dark, the circumstances all too familiar. And then there were voices.

Rodney groaned and turned to face the gang of five. "Go ahead," he said. "Hit me. I'm not gonna fight. Just watch the ribs. The last *rumble* I was in left 'em a little sore."

But the five didn't seem to be paying attention. They were all looking past him, frozen where they stood.

"Is that a dog or what?" one of them finally said, and Rodney heard a growl. A split second later, he sensed something coming up behind him, and then beside him. He swallowed hard and risked a glance. She still wore the cross he'd never seen her without.

Her response to the punk's question was a howl. The gang took off and never looked back.

She was huge, bigger than any dog he'd ever seen, and more

terrifying. Ceese might have been in there somewhere, but the wolf definitely had the advantage now.

Ceese circled him once, marked a nearby wall, then moved along.

The next few miles she stayed within range, and then they were at the cemetery just beyond Henderson's property. With her thoughts, Ceese ordered Rodney to leave the clothes he carried there, and go back to the apartment. When he hesitated, tried to protest, she snarled at him.

Rodney didn't believe she would harm him, but neither did he have proof she wouldn't. So he put the clothes down and moved along. But he wouldn't go back to the apartment, not unless she came with him. He didn't need Richard's threat to do this; he had to keep her safe.

He chose a less-direct route to Henderson's house, though, different from the one he knew Ceese had in her mind. He had no desire to meet up with the wolf again.

A row of bushes separated Henderson's property from the neighbor's, and he settled behind them. But when he peeked through them, he realized he couldn't cover every entrance to the house from there. He moved to the back of the house, but that vantage was worse. As soon as he returned to the front, he heard a door shut from behind the house. He ran back, but was too late.

"Damn it," he muttered, and tried to think. Thanks to the first gang, he no longer had a cell phone. But Richard and Cassie should've gotten his note by now. Maybe they were on the way. He hoped so. Until he had reinforcements, he'd be a fool to do anything but wait.

❧ ❧ ❧

Richard was angry, so angry he couldn't think straight. "I'll kill him," he said loud enough for Cassie and Kyle to hear.

Kyle was concerned for Rodney, but glad Richard's anger was no longer directed at him. The thought kept his mind distracted, though, and he almost forgot to give Cassie the next direction.

"Turn here," he said, pointing. She had to swing wide to navigate the entrance to the neighborhood without running up on the curb. "Could you be a little quicker with your directions?" she said, frustrated.

"Yeah, okay," he replied as she drove on. "I think there's a park or something down here. We can leave the car there."

"Are you sure you know where we're going?"

"Yeah," Kyle said. "Dr. Henderson's house is one street over."

Cassie put her foot on the brake, then turned in her seat. "Kyle, if his house is one street over, why are you directing us down *this* one?"

"He's got nosy neighbors. They'll call the police if they see a car they don't recognize. And if we come in this way, he won't see us either."

Richard, frustrated, opened his door and got out. Kyle and Cassie had to hurry to keep up with him.

❧ ❧ ❧

Because there was no sound of an approaching car, Rodney was caught completely off-guard when Richard tackled him in the bushes.

"Get off me!" he yelled, pushing for air.

"You were supposed to watch her," Richard growled. "Can you not even do *that* right?"

"I tried to stop her," Rodney snapped back, "but she got in my head. She *took* the directions."

"You're lying again! She knows this man—this professor—can't help her. She knows he's dangerous."

"She thinks coming here can help *you*!" Rodney threw out. "That's what she told me when I asked."

Richard loosened his grip on Rodney's neck. "Help me? How could her coming here help me?"

"I don't know. I asked her the same thing. All she said was she couldn't explain it."

Kyle chimed in before Cassie could stop him. "She came because she knew Dr. Henderson wanted her and—"

Richard whipped his head around, turned Rodney loose and stood. "And what?"

"—and you," Kyle said. "Dr. Henderson wants both of you."

Kyle looked quizzically at Cassie occasionally as he spoke, trying to figure out why she was swatting at the air. But it didn't stop him from talking. "Maybe it's like Rodney says . . . she thinks her going to Henderson will keep him from needing you."

Richard's face turned wary. "How do you know this—that this man needs me? Perhaps she came for some other reason."

Hearing this, Cassie was encouraged. Richard hadn't figured out that Ceese was possibly sacrificing herself for him. And if he didn't know, he might actually go in and save her— *one selfless act*! She decided to try to silence Kyle again before he possibly ruined everything. "What makes you think Kyle knows what he's talking about?" she said to Richard.

Kyle frowned at her. "Because she told me. The day I came after the diary, she asked me what the professor wanted." He looked at Richard. "I told her Henderson wanted some of your blood."

Rodney piped up. "I didn't hear anybody talking, and I was in the room when you came for the diary."

"You were sleeping," Kyle pointed out. "Besides, she didn't talk to me like we're talking now. It was freaky. She was in my head. Anyway, she asked me if the professor would settle for just her, and I told her I guessed so." Kyle then hesitated, and Cassie was hopeful. Maybe he would shut up now and let fate take over.

But much to Cassie's dismay, Rodney prodded him. "Why would you tell Ceese that?"

Kyle looked glum. "Because that's what I heard Henderson talking about."

Richard clasped his hands together. "Well, you've been so helpful. Now I know she's where she wants to be."

"What's that supposed to mean?" Rodney asked, coming up to stand in front of Richard.

"It means I'm not going after her." Richard said, and turned to leave.

"Wait," Rodney called after him. "You can't just walk!"

Richard shrugged, looked as arrogant as Rodney had ever seen him look. "You're right. I could levitate."

And for all they knew, Richard did just that, because once he got far enough away, they couldn't see him anymore.

The three were quiet for a moment, then Rodney spoke. "You're just gonna let him go?" he asked, dumbfounded. "You don't think we need his help?"

Cassie took offense. "Am I the only one here who can do any-thing? *You* could go after him!"

Rodney rubbed his neck. "Yeah, but he probably won't suck the life out of *you.*"

"He won't do it to you either. He told me—if he bites another, the curse is everlasting. They'll be no hope for him."

"There's no hope anyway if he can't rise above it to help some-body—to help Ceese."

Cassie was surprised by the comment, and sputtered, "Elo-quently put."

"So you'll go after him?"

Her frustration returned. "What am I supposed to do, Rodney? I can't make him care."

"He listens to you, Cassie. You know he does."

"He's not listening to anyone right now."

"Great," Rodney spat at her. "*Now* what kind of a chance does Ceese stand? The professor's good at tricking people, and he's probably got all kinds of drugs in there. Or maybe a gun. You know, like the one he gave Josh—with silver bullets!"

"Well," Kyle said, "maybe when he gets her blood— the stem cells he wants . . ."

Cassie looked at him. "What are you talking about?"

"You know he's all up into stem cell research," Kyle replied nonchalantly.

"Yes, we're all aware of that," Rodney said. "But what about wanting Ceese's stem cells?"

"Oh, well, I just heard him say something about it one day when I was over. He mutters a lot . . . still really pissed about his lab being shut down and all."

Rodney couldn't resist. "Well you two certainly have become *close*."

"I'm not proud of it," Kyle admitted. "Not anymore."

It was Cassie's turn to question. "So he told you he wanted some of Richard and Ceese's stem cells?"

Kyle nodded. "Yeah, something about needing their stem cells and the curse . . . yeah, something about the curse. I told you, he mutters a lot. I couldn't really make it out."

Cassie's expression went from horribly dazed to utter disbelief. "Oh, my God. . . . Oh, my God."

"What is it Cassie?" Rodney asked carefully. She suddenly looked so vulnerable, and she was their cornerstone. He looked into her stunned eyes with his questioning ones. "What do you know?"

"I'm not sure but . . . when Henderson and I were working together, he said he was hoping to find a cure for the curse. . . ."

Rodney looked puzzled. "Okay, but that's good, Cassie. That's not 'Oh my God' bad."

"He thinks the curse has something to do with their blood."

"Still—not bad," Rodney said, continuing to look at her.

"Rodney, if he gets their blood . . . enough of it . . . what if he knows of a way to . . ." she shook her head as she struggled with the implications. "Stem cells, Rodney . . . they're like a road map to who we are . . . *what* we are. Let's just say Dr. Frankenstein comes to mind."

"Okay, that's bad. So what do we do?"

But she didn't seem to be listening. "I can't believe I fell for his lies. I practically handed Richard and Ceese over to him." She turned to Rodney. "Did you know? When you started helping him— did you know any of this?"

"I didn't know, Cassie. I swear it. I was just like you. I thought all he was interested in was learning more about vampires and werewolves. And since I don't believe in that kind of stuff . . . well, *then* . . . I didn't see the harm." He looked at her, fear in his eyes. "What if Ceese doesn't cooperate? Do you think he'd . . .?" Rodney couldn't bring himself to finish the thought.

"I don't think I'd put anything past him, Rodney. Not now."

"Then we've got to get her out of there. Maybe we should call the police."

Cassie shook her head. "Too risky for Ceese. She might not be able to control the wolf."

All three grew silent and Kyle snapped his fingers. "I've got an idea."

Desperate to hear anything sounding remotely like a plan, Rodney and Cassie listened.

CHAPTER 33

There was little for the two men in the room to fear. Ceese was surrounded by wolfsbane and strapped down to a table. Josh looked at her, turned his head slightly as he listened to the soft, high-pitched whimpering.

"Is that her?" he asked. "She sounds just like an animal."

"Yes," Dr. Henderson said as he tapped the fluid in the syringe with his thumbnail. "Seems she still thinks she's the wolf."

"What's in the syringe?"

"A growth-factor," he replied. "To coax stem cells out into the bloodstream for collection. So I can study them. Stem cells are like a roadmap. They'll tell me more about her curse." He neglected to add how he planned to use them once he determined whose curse was more powerful—whose curse would have the better chance of taking hold when he did the infusion of the cells into his own body. But he wasn't one for wasting time.

Henderson injected Ceese with the drug. "This will all be over in a minute. Just need to make sure we have as many useful stem cells as we can get."

She barely flinched when the needle went in. But then, she was unable to move anyway. The restraints and wolfsbane were working well.

While he waited for the drug to work, Henderson went back to his microscope.

※ ※ ※

Now that he was standing over her and Henderson wasn't, Josh noticed her trying to look around, but the strap across her forehead made it impossible for her to see anywhere but up, right into the bright light positioned to point directly at her eyes.

She had come on her own, willingly, and this had surprised Josh. She didn't fight him, and she wasn't fighting now. He looked at her with sympathy; she looked so vulnerable compared to the woman who'd tackled him in the airport. He looked at her restraints, the way her wrists and ankles chafed at them. "Can't we loosen these?" he asked.

Henderson stopped working and looked at Josh, curious. "Is she directing you to speak?"

"Dude, you've got her gagged. How's she gonna *direct* me to do anything?"

"There are other ways for her to communicate," Henderson replied, wanting to add the word "fool."

"Well, I don't know about that," Josh confessed. "It's just her hands and feet are turning blue. I'm not sure . . . werewolves might be different. But I don't think that's a good thing."

Henderson considered the request. If by some stroke of luck she *did* manage to get free and transform, there was enough wolfsbane around to control the werewolf. He nodded, then went back to peering into his microscope.

Josh loosened each restraint slightly, but when he leaned over Ceese to loosen the final strap, his expression changed to one of confusion, and then astonishment, and then—more normal. "Now, why are we doing this again?" he said. "You know . . . taking her blood."

Henderson, absorbed in his work, answered, "I told you, I want some of her stem cells." After he spoke, he came back over and began drawing her blood.

To take full advantage of the mobilization process, to get the most stem cells, one usually had to undergo several sessions, with each session lasting a few hours. He didn't have that kind of time, and so he'd given the werewolf a healthy dose of the medication.

"That should do it," he said as he picked up the vial and headed back to the microscope. There, he loaded a Petri dish with what he'd just taken, examined it. "Damn it," he said. "There aren't nearly enough here. I found considerably more in the—"

He stopped, thought a moment, then turned and headed back to Josh. "You need to help me get the vampire. I need his blood, much more than what I have. I can help you, if you help me."

"Okay, yeah, sure," Josh said. But then his expression turned blank. "No, I-I can't"

Henderson stopped. "What did you say?"

"I . . . I don't know," Josh said, flustered. "I just don't think you should do what you're doing."

Henderson looked around at all the wolfsbane. It couldn't be what he thought; she had to be too weak. But still, Josh had never challenged him before. "Is she talking to you? Did she make you say that?"

"No—yes. I don't know. I thought I was just hallucinating or something."

Henderson studied Ceese now, removed the gag, pushed the light away and looked down. "You know," he said, "it would be so much easier if you would just bring the vampire to me. You can do this. I know you can."

"I will never do that," she said, weakly but also with vengeance.

"Then tell me why his blood responds so much more quickly than yours does."

"His curse is strong."

"Yes, it is, and because it's so strong," he undid her restraints, helped her to sit, "I need for you to will him to come here."

She slouched, looked disappointed, hurt. "I can't."

"Can't or won't."

"Can't *and* won't," she said glaring and breathing hard at the exertion. "I will never do what you ask. He— He's . . ." She looked toward Josh, who suddenly looked more than just a little stunned. And then she quit talking all together. Henderson caught Josh's subtle nod, though.

"Fine," he spat. "If you won't will him by choice, then I'll just make it easier for you."

He looked at Josh, appeared to be working hard to stay calm. He was sure the werewolf had talked to him, and he intended to find out what she'd said. But not now. He had other things on his mind.

The contraption he brought over looked like an electrical transformer on a pushcart: long wires with leads and small alligator-type clips attached to them.

"Shall we go for a little shock therapy?" he asked Ceese, and was encouraged by her frightened eyes.

Josh wasn't encouraged though, and though he'd been on-board before, it was clear he wasn't now. "What's that for?"

"Hopefully you won't have to find out," Henderson said, turning loose of the cart and settling atop the stool he'd brought over with him. He flipped a switch here, another there, then turned to face Ceese, who was struggling to remain in a sitting position. Her head hung heavy; she was having a time just keeping her eyes open.

Henderson put a hand under her chin, forced her to look at him. "Will him to come," he said. "Will the vampire to come here."

"I-I won't."

The hard slap across her face wasn't something she anticipated, and she might have fallen all the way back if Henderson hadn't grabbed her.

"I will get what I want," he said through gritted teeth. "And you will give it to me."

"Hey," Josh said, "you don't gotta be so rough! It ain't like she can do anything about it."

"Bring him," Henderson said, ignoring Josh, and raised his hand again.

But Josh was ready the second time, and caught Henderson's hand before he could strike. "I *said* you don't gotta be so rough."

Henderson jerked around, ducked when Josh swung and plunged his own fist in the young man's midsection. When Josh went down, Henderson turned back to his machine.

❧ ❧ ❧

Kyle's big idea amounted to storming the back door of the house and praying it was unlocked. Neither Rodney nor Cassie could come up with anything better, so they considered it. After all, Kyle had been inside Henderson's house often enough to have an idea of its layout.

"But what if the door *is* locked?" Cassie asked.

Kyle pointed to the windows on the door itself. "We can break them. But I don't think we'll need to. Henderson has deadbolts on the doors, but never uses them."

"How can you know for sure?" Rodney asked.

"He asked me to drop some things off for him once. Gave me his key, but told me not to worry about the deadbolts because he never locked them. Okay?"

Rodney still wasn't encouraged. If they had to break glass, the sound would certainly rouse those suspicious neighbors Kyle had mentioned.

"It's too bad Richard isn't here," Kyle thought aloud. "He could just tear the door off its hinges."

"Yeah, well, he's not here," Rodney said with resentment. "He deserted us, remember? And we have to get in there. So if nobody has anything better than breaking the windows out of the back door . . ."

All three took a second to consider this. Cassie glanced at the quiet house, then shrugged. "I wish Richard hadn't disappeared like that, but we've got to do something. If she's in there, and hasn't found a way out by now, she's in trouble. I just don't think we can wait any longer."

❧ ❧ ❧

Josh had no idea what his friends were planning outside, didn't even know they *were* outside. He just knew he had to do something for Ceese, and he had to do it fast. He got to his feet, barreled into the professor and took him down. But thanks to the drugs, his reflexes weren't what they should have been. Henderson threw Josh off, pulled him to his feet and slammed him into a nearby wall. Things went dark after that.

At some point he became aware again, and heard a voice, the one he'd heard before. "*Josh . . . Josh,*" it said, "*please, tell me you can hear me.*"

It was Ceese. She was in his head, like she was earlier. Josh opened his eyes and grimaced. When he stared up, he saw the professor's hand reaching for the machine's dials.

"No!" Josh said, scrambling to stand.

Henderson turned around. "Not you again. I guess your head's harder than I thought."

The insult had Josh rallying. He stood, took up the wooden stool Henderson had vacated and cracked it across the professor's back. As Henderson struggled to get up, Ceese managed to move off the table to pin him back to the floor.

"*Upstairs,*" she told Josh, "*upstair—*"

Henderson threw her off, and Josh ran.

※ ※ ※

When he heard the gunshots from inside, Rodney no longer cared about the sound of breaking glass; he charged the back door, found it unlocked and gained entry, Cassie and Kyle on his heels.

There was no one in the kitchen, but there was a light on, and one single drawer was open. Heart pounding, Rodney dispatched Kyle to a side room by pointing to an open doorway. He and Cassie explored a hallway with two doors on either side. He took one room, she the other. They met back up in the kitchen, disappointed. The house appeared to be empty.

The muffled footsteps from behind another closed door, one they'd missed because it looked more like a closet, made them all jump.

"Where does that lead?" Rodney whispered to Kyle.

Kyle shook his head. But before he could do more, the door opened and Josh emerged, carrying Ceese.

"He shot her," Josh sputtered. He took two more steps and handed her off to Rodney. "She wants you, dude. That's what she keeps telling me . . . you know, in my head."

Rodney took her, noticed the blood, wondered if the bullet had been silver.

"What about Henderson?" Kyle asked, glancing nervously at the door.

"I . . . I shot him." His voice was numb, his words too uncertain to be believable. "Ceese told me about a gun upstairs. I got it and shot him."

"Okay," Kyle said, "but did you kill him?"

"Yeah. . . . I think."

Kyle wasn't ready to stake his life on Josh's speculation. If Josh were wrong, Henderson could come racing up the stairs at any moment to finish them all off. He lunged toward an open drawer, extracted a knife from it, looked to Rodney, then Cassie. "I'm going to check."

Neither one said anything. It was clear they weren't going to stop him. Kyle headed off.

"She told me about where the gun was," Josh said after Kyle disappeared down the stairs. He nodded toward the open drawer. "Buh-But, she didn't actually speak. . . . Just sort of let me know—you know, in my head—"

"I know," Rodney said, maneuvering around so Cassie could check on Ceese. "She does that a lot."

"She has a pulse," Cassie said. "But she's still bleeding. And guys, what if the bullet was silver?"

Rodney nodded absently just as Kyle returned and announced, "Yep, he killed him, all right."

Cassie acknowledged him with a nod, but then noticed Rodney staring past her. "What is it Rodney? What's the matter?"

She whirled around to see Richard standing in the kitchen doorway.

Rodney brushed past Cassie and went to where he was standing. "She's dead," he muttered, and ignored Cassie and Kyle's stunned gasps. "Ceese is dead. Henderson shot her before Josh could shoot him—and she said the bullet was silver. Just before she—" Rodney took a deep breath. "Her last request was to be buried on holy ground, in a cemetery. A real cemetery."

Rodney kept his gaze on Richard, grief and anger mingling

on his face. "Do you think you could do that? After all, it's pretty much your fault she's— Well, I just think you owe her something. There's a cemetery behind Henderson's property. Take her there. It's the least you can do."

It wasn't clear if Richard had heard Rodney, but he picked Ceese up and left with her nonetheless, carrying her out the same way he'd come in.

"I can't believe it," Cassie muttered. "How can she be dead, I just checked—"

His expression didn't change. "You didn't lie to him, did you? I can't believe you just *lied* to him like that. Have you lost your mind?" And then, when his expression still didn't change, "you did lie, didn't you? She isn't really—"

Rodney turned, went to her and put an awkward hand on her shoulder, an action he would have never considered before to-night. But so much had changed. "It's all right," he forced himself to say. "You'll just have to trust me."

"Why would I trust you or believe you?" she said, batting his hand away. "Can't you see how much damage your lying's caused already? Is Ceese dead or not?"

He turned his back to her and she tried to regroup. "I'm sorry, Rodney, I just—I just need to know what to believe."

"She's not dead," he said blandly. Too blandly.

"So you were lying?"

"That's right," he said. "She's not dead." He turned back to Cassie, as if empowered by the truth. "I did lie but only because Ceese asked me to. She said that if anybody could make him believe it, I could. So . . . . yeah, I lied."

Cassie fought back an unbidden laugh. "You're not serious."

"Ceese asked me to," he repeated. "I wasn't about to let her down."

He had come so far, Cassie thought. Someone had to actually ask him to lie. "But why?" she said, wiping tears with a long shirt-sleeve. "Why would she want Richard to think she was dead?"

Josh spoke up, pulling from what he recalled being told in the basement. "Maybe she thought it would push him to remember who he was."

The other three looked at him. "And who would that be?" Cassie asked.

Josh shrugged. "Her brother."

"What?" Cassie and Rodney had spoken at once.

"It's something I remember her thinking when we were down in the lab," Josh said. "She seemed to be taking it pretty hard that her own brother couldn't remember who she was and come to help her."

"He's high," Kyle offered. "Old Henderson keeps him well supplied."

"Maybe I am," Josh said. "But that's what she was thinking."

And then, Cassie's eyes grew wide. "Yes!"

Rodney stared at her. "Okay," he said after a moment. "Would you mind sharing with the *rest* of us?"

And she did, her words tripping over each other. "Grand-mother called me about a week before she died. We talked about a lot of things, and at one point she said, 'If only Richard could remember.' I asked her what she meant, and she never would tell me. Just said it would make things so much easier if he knew."

Cassie thought harder, trying to remember. "Yes. Grand-mother wouldn't tell Richard who he was because, if for some reason he refused to believe her, then he would resent Ceese even more."

Josh spoke again, sounding anything but inspiring. "And Ceese isn't about to tell him."

Cassie looked at him, bewildered. "Why would you say that?"

"Because she wants him to remember on his own."

"But what if he can't?" Rodney said. "What will happen if he doesn't? Why's it such a big deal anyway?"

"I get it," Cassie said, and turned to Rodney. "Look at it this way. If you saw someone being attacked, wouldn't you be more likely to take an active role if the one under attack was your sister or brother? If Richard knows Ceese is his sister, then maybe he can bring himself to rise above whatever's holding him back. I can understand why my grandmother wanted him to remember by himself, but it's gone too far: We have to tell him, or force Ceese to do it."

Kyle looked unsettled. "You can't be suggesting we go wandering around a graveyard at night looking for a vampire and a werewolf. And what makes you think Richard will believe us? Suppose it just makes him mad—and hungry?" He rubbed his neck as though he felt fangs already.

Cassie started, then swung her head around the room. "Because, Grandmother just told me it's okay to tell him." And indeed, the voice was strong and clear. "Now, let's go before it's too late."

⁂

Kyle had checked on Henderson, had tried to find a pulse but couldn't, and headed back upstairs. But the stem cells Henderson had infused himself with the day before, the ones he'd filtered out of the squirrels' blood, had already begun to work, repairing and replacing his gunshot wound. In no time, he was able to crawl. Moments after that, he was standing. He moved to the bottom of the steps, listened to Cassie and the others talking.

Apparently, he'd been mistaken; he hadn't needed as much of the vampire's blood as he'd thought. But what if the werewolf came back for revenge? Or what if the vampire knew what he'd done, since they now shared the same blood cells? Either scenario was possible, and he couldn't risk it. They'd know how to kill him. He would kill them first, of course. But he had to hurry before the curse took a stronger hold. As it was, he could still see his reflection, and though it pained him a little, he could still hold the cross in his hand. If he waited too much longer, he might not be able to catch them in the cemetery. And besides, the sun would be an issue in another hour or two.

He marveled at how he knew all of this and how important it was to him now. Immortality. He had it! Now he had to make sure he kept it.

As soon as he heard their footsteps fade away, he took up his gun and followed.

CHAPTER 34

Placing his right foot onto the consecrated grounds of the cemetery was no easy matter. Deep down, he wanted to turn back. He had done this before. He hoped to never do it again. But here he was. For all the good it did. Ceese was gone. But Rodney had told him this was what she wanted.

Why do I care anyway? he wondered as he walked. He wasn't sure he did, but he couldn't convince himself to turn around and walk away. That's why he'd come back in the first place. He couldn't follow through with what he told Rodney he was going to do. He couldn't leave Ceese with the professor.

Both feet were officially on cemetery grounds now, and the feeling—a combination of loathing and fear—was agonizingly hard to ignore. He levitated for a short while, a few feet above the earth, but soon gave in to exhaustion and settled down to finish the journey on foot, pushing on despite the overwhelming desire not to, fighting the pain, the absolute pain working to overwhelm him.

He gripped Ceese's body tight and kept moving, feeling through his shoes the heat as each step took him further into the graveyard, all to make sure Ceese got a decent burial. *Yes, Rodney was right. It's the least I can do.*

As he stumbled on, he struggled to clear his head. But just like before, he began having difficulty distinguishing what was real and what wasn't. He thought he heard Mamá, then thought he saw her, standing in the parlor of the castle, near the intricate balancing piece dear Peter had toyed with the day he'd come to ask about his goats. The same piece Ceese had found so intriguing.

She was talking. Mamá was talking to him! *"You must let Ceese help you,"* she said. *"She can if you just let her."*

Richard wrestled with the words, the image. Ceese was dead. How could she help him? And then, oddly, he saw Zade, the werewolf who had confronted him in the woods, standing near Mamá. Zade was still wearing Peter the goatherder's trousers, still unfastened. He'd put on a shirt, but like the pants, it was too small and barely fit his form.

"Do care," Zade had said that night in the woods, and *"Do care"* was what Richard heard from him again, just now, his speech just as primal as before. But if the werewolf was making a plea for Ceese, it was too late.

The image faded after he spoke, and then there was someone else next to Mamá, a man whose hair was the palest blonde, his voice haunting and painfully familiar. *"No one expects you to do this alone, son—"*

"No," Richard said aloud, and forced the image away before the sentence could be finished, desperately trying to regain control. One voice said, *"Two become one,"* but as he'd done in the past, Richard immediately wrote the comment off. It just didn't make sense, and he couldn't bother with such nonsense now.

The chapel was up ahead now. He would place Ceese there, then leave. He would never think of this place again, or about anything that had gone through his mind while he was here.

The chapel steps were before him; he leaned forward and tried to strengthen his body to tackle them. But then, much like she'd done in the castle when he tried to put her on the bed, Ceese's once-dangling arms went to his neck and grabbed hold

"No. Do not place me there." Her voice was weaker, but just as desperate.

Richard straightened up, gasped. "You're not dead!"

"No, but I most assuredly will be if you place me there. I . . . I'm still cursed, and this is consecrated ground."

"I-I'm sorry, Ceese. Rodney said—"

Ceese nodded. "I know. I told him to."

"I . . . I don't understand." He was puzzled. "Why would you tell him to lie?"

She gazed into his eyes, as if looking for something. Then she quit looking and sighed. "It doesn't matter anymore. Nothing does anymore. Just take me from this place so I can die in peace."

"No!" he shouted. "You're just weak. I'll take you away from here, and you'll be fine."

The journey out of the cemetery was decidedly harder than the one into it, and Richard began to worry if he could stay the course. His feet were lead weights; he could barely pick them up. He pushed on anyway, desperate to give Ceese what she begged for, but not understanding why he cared.

❦ ❦ ❦

Henderson knew the cemetery well. He'd come here often trying to muster up the courage to rob a grave or two for his research. He cut around one section, went through another, and spotted Richard and Ceese. And when he saw them, he smiled.

"You could have just given me what I wanted," he said loud enough for his voice to carry. "It didn't have to be like this."

Richard turned toward the voice, saw the glint of metal. The man had a gun.

"That's right," Henderson said, "it's me. And in case you're wondering, the gun is loaded with silver bullets. You see, I had a change of heart. I don't need you anymore, or your werewolf."

"Richard, run—!" Ceese called out.

Henderson had anticipated this. Before Richard could move, he held the gun level and fired.

The first bullet was meant for Richard, but when Ceese threw an arm up to shield him, the bullet went through her and into Richard's left shoulder. Her blood combined with his when it entered his shoulder. The bullet exited, the wound healed in an instant. Richard never noticed.

When the next shot came, Ceese didn't have time to react. It caught Richard in his right calf and took him to his knees. Henderson got off another shot, but Ceese couldn't help Richard. She was too weak. He took it in the same shoulder that had healed a moment ago. But this time, none of Ceese's blood was there to heal him.

Henderson aimed for Richard's heart next.

🦋 🦋 🦋

The four had decided to split up. Kyle went with Cassie; Josh went with Rodney. They could cover more ground that way. Josh and Rodney had been closer to the sound of gunshots than Cassie and Kyle, and found Henderson after the gun went off the third time. Josh took him down, similar to the way he had done in the basement, but again Henderson threw him off.

"He's still got his gun," Josh yelled when he saw Rodney prepare to go after Henderson. But Rodney had one too: the one Kyle had brought up from the basement. Worried that Josh might get charged with the professor's murder, he took it, planned on ditching it later.

It didn't matter now though. Henderson was obviously alive. As he ran, Rodney retrieved the gun from his back waistband.

Henderson stopped running, took aim, and fired. Rodney dove out of the bullet's path and fired wild, and was relieved to see Henderson go down.

Josh and Rodney waited a few seconds, then walked to Henderson's still form. Rodney knelt to check for a pulse, and there was none. Of course, Kyle had said he was dead earlier. But maybe Kyle didn't really know how to find a pulse. Rodney did, though, and he was certain.

Cassie and Kyle heard the shots, and were on the scene a few seconds after that.

"He's definitely dead this time," Rodney confirmed when they approached.

"Josh thought he was dead too," Kyle pointed out.

"Hey," Josh snapped, "I was high, remember?"

Cassie held up her hand for quiet. "Why was he shooting in the first place?"

Rodney shook his head, stood to get his bearings. "He was aiming over that way."

Cassie gasped when she looked where he was pointing. Two figures were on the ground. One of the figures appeared to be holding the other one, and was attempting to stand.

She ran, half-stumbling on short, steep slopes; hurdled grave markers; and led the way while the others followed.

Richard was struggling to regain his footing, struggling hardest of all not to let Ceese touch the ground. He saw them approaching and gasped, "Take her from this place. *Now!*"

Rodney moved quickly to obey, while Josh and Kyle pulled Richard up, each taking an arm and placing it over their shoulders, not the least bit concerned that Richard, the vampire, was so close to their necks. Before long, they were out of the cemetery.

❧ ❧ ❧

Rodney eased Ceese down near a large tree, and Richard collapsed next to her.

"I'm sorry," Cassie said, looking at the two of them. "I am *so* sorry. None of this would have happened if I hadn't gotten involved with Henderson." And then, "Are . . . Are you going to be all right?"

Richard nodded. "But Ceese . . . I don't know how to help her. I mean— I'd take the bullet out, but I need her help to do that. It . . . It's too hard to explain, but I fear she's too weak to help me not transform completely. And there's so much blood. . . ."

His comment brought Rodney to life. "Would you try harder if you knew she was your sister?"

Richard looked at Rodney, confused, but said, "I . . . I suppose."

"Well, then get busy, because that's what she is."

Being hit by a train was the only time he'd felt more stunned. Richard turned to Cassie, studied her face, tried to draw something from her expression.

"He's right, Richard," Cassie said. "Grandmother didn't want to tell you who you were. Said she wanted you to figure it out for yourself. Maybe she was worried how you might take it. And apparently, Ceese had the same concerns."

Richard shook his head. "No. Ceese wouldn't keep such a thing from me."

Ceese stirred and opened her eyes. "I did keep it from you, Richard . . . I did." And her eyes closed again.

Will it be enough? Cassie wondered, keeping her eyes on Richard. *Will it be enough just to know?*

Richard wouldn't look at any of them, just said, "Leave us."

Josh and Kyle backed off at once, and Cassie prepared to follow. But Rodney wasn't moving. Gently, she nudged him. "Come on," she whispered. "He's the only one who can help her now."

Rodney stood for a moment, considering, then turned and followed the others.

🙶 🙶 🙶

Richard looked at Ceese. Her eyes were open again. But she still looked so weak, so fragile. Richard's frustration grew.

"Why didn't you tell me?" he asked.

"Because you wouldn't have believed me. I couldn't live knowing you knew the truth, but didn't believe any of it."

"How *can* I believe it?" he cried out. But then he tempered the harshness of his words. "How can I possibly be who you say I am?"

She held his eyes with her own, and began. "You were bitten by two. Your favorite color is purple. . . at least, until I told you it was *my* favorite color. Then you claimed yours was yellow. You used to love studying scripture. Even before you were cursed, you hated garlic. No . . . you were *allergic* to it. Broke out in hives just smelling it."

Richard tore his gaze away from hers. "How can I verify any of that? I don't remember it."

"You had a birthmark on your neck, where the vampires bit. When Penny saw mine, I sensed her thoughts about it. I have one in the same place. Mother had one too. Father used to tell me mine was from an angel's kiss. I often teased you, told you yours was most assuredly put there by—"

"—by some devil," Richard said catching a memory as it flew by.

Ceese nodded.

"You were an insufferable child—" Richard glared at Ceese. "And you should have been punished. But no one ever lifted a hand to correct you."

"You remember," Ceese said, sighing deeply. "I knew you could!"

More memories came back to him, wrenched from the depths of some sacred abyss. "You were there when I went into the woods," he whispered in astonishment. "You saved me from death. Why didn't you let me die?"

"I couldn't."

"You were holding me when I came around."

"Yes. And you produced fangs and tried to bite me."

"I carried you home," Richard said, "and I swore you to secrecy. I told you never to tell anyone . . . and specifically Father."

"And I never did."

"I used to call you Cee Cee."

"And I always hated it."

"Yes," Richard said, his gaze distant. "Because Father called you that, and you didn't feel anyone else had the right to use the name."

Ceese's eyes fluttered, as though she couldn't hold them all the way open anymore, and Richard's heart sank. "Why didn't you tell me sooner, Ceese? Why didn't you *tell* me?"

But she wasn't looking at him anymore. "Did you see her?" she asked. "When you were carrying me through the cemetery, did you see Penny?"

"I . . . I did."

"She said it again. 'Two become one.'"

"I heard her. But I still don't understand."

Ceese drew a ragged breath. "Do it, Richard. Make me like you."

What she was asking startled him. "How would that help matters?"

"It's the only way."

"Are you sure, Ceese? If I do this thing, I become cursed forever. And you'll most likely just trade curses . . . if you survive at all."

She looked at him with her odd eyes. "I have to at least try."

"Then why in the name of all that is—?" He searched for a way to say what he wanted to say without anguish. He remembered the technique Ceese had suggested once, in the parlor. "Why in the name of all that isn't unholy have we gone through all of this? Why couldn't you just live cursed?"

"Please, Richard, just do it. I don't have much time left." Her breath became more labored. "You have to. Don't let me die cursed. Please!" When he remained frozen in place, she added, "You forced yourself to forget. Now force yourself to remember!"

Now, he understood just why he'd forced himself to forget in the first place. He didn't want to live knowing he couldn't feel the kind of love he was once capable of, the kind of love that would have him sacrificing everything for another. And how was knowing supposed to help him anyway? It was only making things worse. Now he had to accept the fact that he could care—*did* care what happened to Ceese, and to himself. And caring was near killing him now.

"I can't," he told her, teeth clenched. "I just can't help you."

"Don't do it for me, then," Ceese said. "Do it for yourself."

"What good would that do? What possible good would that do?"

"The vampire wants this, Richard. Let it out."

"Don't you understand? I don't want to be cursed forever!"

"You'll understand, Richard. When it's done, you'll understand."

Richard fought the transformation, but there was so much blood to encourage it. He leaned in close, already had his eye on where to sink his fangs, but then pulled back. "Your cross," he hissed, and she pulled it off and threw it as far as she could.

With it out of the way, there was nothing to stop the vampire. Richard tried anyway, fought with it. But at his strongest moment, Ceese bloodied one of her hands and put it on his face, his lips.

The indescribable, euphoric feeling overwhelmed a part of Richard, and it pushed the vampire on, had him sinking his teeth into Ceese's neck. Another part of him couldn't condone what was happening, was devastated by what was taking place. He didn't want to live like this, cursed forever— And then to hurt Ceese. But there was little he could do about it now. Long ago, the two vampires had won.

CHAPTER 35

The room was dim, but Richard could make out someone resting in a chair nearby. He called out.

Cassie roused, straightened, and moved forward to take his hand. "You're awake. Good."

"Where am I?"

"In a hospital."

"What happened?"

Cassie looked puzzled. "You don't remember?"

"No," he said frustrated, and then, "Yes. I guess I remember . . . the cemetery."

"You wanted to be alone with Ceese," she prodded, "after Dr. Henderson—"

"Yes," he said, recalling it all, then looked at Cassie in shock. "I bit Ceese. She asked me to, and I did. But where is she? Is she—?"

"She's in ICU—the Intensive Care Unit. They're . . . working with her."

He looked around. "Should she really be in a hospital? Should *I* be in one?"

"It's all right, Richard. They haven't questioned anything yet. I was hoping you'd come around before they did. In fact, I'd have to say I'm a little amazed. They claim you have a heartbeat and breath. And unless Ceese had a hand in that this time—"

"It was incredible," Richard said, relaxing. "I've never felt anything like it. And yet it sickened me to think of what I was doing to her. I've cursed her again, and myself forever."

Tears formed in his eyes. The tears broke free and ran down his cheeks, and he touched his face in wonder. "I-I haven't had these since—"

Cassie smiled. "Before you were cursed?"

"Your cross," Richard said quickly, "you have it?"

She removed it from her pocket. Richard took it, put it to his lips and hesitantly kissed it. There was no burning, no heat. He then held it to his forehead, his chest. "Sweet Mother of God," he whispered, ignoring Cassie, who was fumbling in a nearby drawer. She came back seconds later with a small mirror, which she handed to him.

He stared in disbelief, sat up and pushed himself to the edge of the bed.

"Bigger. Get me a bigger one."

She helped him to his feet and walked with him over to the mirror above the vanity.

"Ceese was right," he muttered. "I . . . I'm no longer cursed."

Cassie smiled and nodded. "Then I guess it isn't Ceese helping you this time."

"I have to see her, Cassie. I have to see my— my sister."

He grabbed the sink, and Cassie grasped his arm to support him.

"You were in surgery for a couple of hours," she said. "To remove the bullets."

He gave a weak chuckle. "Guess I'll have to adjust to not healing as quickly."

"I'll get a wheelchair," Cassie offered, and found one outside the door.

Richard settled in and winced as he leaned back. The scratches were still there, the ones from when Ceese was the wolf. They'd stopped bothering him for the most part, had healed a little more, but now they were throbbing. At his request, Cassie lifted the bandages to look.

"Oww, that looks like it hurts," she said. "Want me to get the nurse?"

"No!" he said, wincing. Right now, he had more on his mind than some scratches. He wanted to believe what had happened, yet something didn't seem right. He didn't have time to worry about it now, though. He had to see his sister.

✷ ✷ ✷

Cassie pushed Richard into the ICU waiting room, then toward the doors of the patient area. Rodney stood at once and walked their way, glaring at Richard. "What're *you* doing here?"

Cassie tried to ease the tension. "Richard's no longer cursed, Rodney. And he wants to see Ceese."

Rodney ignored her. "Yeah, well, that's great. Really warms my heart. But Ceese isn't exactly doing as well as he is. And the last time I saw him, he was passed out from *feeding* on her. That's what you call it, isn't it, Richard—*feeding?*"

Richard looked regretful, but couldn't defend himself; that's exactly what he'd done. And Rodney had seen it all. When they returned to the cemetery, Richard was beside Ceese, his face bloodied, his mouth . . . her neck. They'd cleaned them both up before calling 9-1-1 but Rodney wouldn't forget. Not for a long time.

"She's your sister," Rodney said now, "and you nearly killed her!"

"Rodney," Cassie said, lowering her voice, "whether you like it or not, you can't keep Richard from seeing her."

"Yeah?" Rodney replied. "Not very long ago he was a vampire, and he bit her, and probably would have killed her if we hadn't gone back when we did."

"I told you, it wasn't like that," Richard said. "She asked me to do it."

Rodney glowered at him. "What a convenient thing to say, since Ceese can't possibly prove you wrong in her present condition." His glare turned mean. "You know, I could tell them the truth. Ask them to compare the blood collected from the puncture wounds on Ceese's neck with yours. I'm pretty sure they wouldn't let you go back then."

Cassie placed a sympathetic hand on Rodney's shoulder. "I think if you asked Ceese, she'd want to see Richard."

Rodney gave a scoffing laugh. "Well, then I guess it's lucky she can't talk right now."

A nurse appeared from the other side of the automatic doors.

"Your friend is awake," she said, looking at all three of them. "And she'd very much like to see someone named Richard?"

Richard's relief was obvious. "I am he."

The nurse nodded. "She's just down the hall, second door on the right, one person in at a time." She glanced at Richard's wheelchair, then looked from Rodney to Cassie. "One of you can take him back, but only one person goes in with him at a time."

The nurse left them.

"You heard her," Cassie said to Rodney. "Ceese wants to see him."

Rodney took a step back, still staring at Richard. "You do one thing to hurt her, one thing and I'll—"

"I would never hurt her, Rodney. I would never hurt Ceese."

His sincerity had no effect. "You better hope you don't."

❦ ❦ ❦

Cassie held the door open so he could wheel himself in. He was barely able to make out Ceese's still form in the midst of all the equipment around her: tubes going in, IV's dripping. There was an occasional beep, then a rhythmic humming. Richard could feel now, and he felt horrible. How could he have done this to her?

Richard wheeled over and took the one hand that didn't have a tube coming out of it. Ceese opened her eyes.

"No," Richard moaned when he saw their color. When she was younger, her eyes were a soft green, not the odd color they were now. Though they had changed, become less golden, they still weren't as he remembered. "I don't understand. Are you still cursed?"

She reached up with her free hand and removed the oxygen mask from her mouth, gave him a smile. "You're still cursed, too."

"But-But I can pray." In fact, he'd done so on the way in. "I can see my reflection."

"The scratches on your back are worse."

286

Richard's brow furrowed, wondering how she could know this.

Her eyes turned sad. "Soon the wolf will reclaim what the vampires abandoned."

She seemed so certain. "What manner of madness is this?"

"It's all part of what has to happen. Now, we must finish it."

Suddenly Richard became the skeptic. "Where are you getting your information?"

"Penny told me."

He threw his head back. "Ah, yes. Conversing with the dead. You seem to have a knack."

"I told you, Richard, she isn't dead."

"No, I don't suppose she is. And neither is Father. In fact, I saw him as we were walking through the graveyard." His chuckle was bitter.

Ceese either didn't note the sarcasm in his voice, or chose to ignore it. "Yes, he's alive. And he misses you. With your hair dyed," she added, "you look just like him."

And he did. He realized this after seeing his reflection in the mirror. In all his efforts to look so different from him, he had actually come full circle.

"Yet you colored it so you wouldn't look like him, didn't you?"

He looked away, but suddenly, it seemed important to answer truthfully. "Perhaps. All right, I did."

She seemed pleased at the long-awaited response. But then, still stinging from the confession, he asked her, "And now you must tell my why I always have to remind you to fasten your pants. Remember? You promised to tell me that night I took you flying—if I but answered your question."

She looked dismal. "You'll laugh. And you won't understand."

"But you promised."

"Oh, all right. Sometimes I have to scratch."

To his puzzled look, she added, "I told you you wouldn't understand."

"So explain it to me."

"It's harder to get one's foot behind one's ear when constricted around the waist."

"You mean to scratch like a wolf?"

She nodded.

"Well, then. I'm glad to know. And please take note, I didn't laugh."

"You wanted to," Ceese said. "And why does talking about Father bother you so?"

"I can't explain it. And please don't ask me to." It was the truth; he couldn't explain that, or why he'd worked so hard to forget him.

"All right, I won't ask. But I would like you to help me with a memory. One about Father."

Richard nodded. "I'll try. But I can't promise you anything."

"There was a time," she started, "when I was very young, perhaps four or five. I had come out of the dress Mother had made for me—"

"Because it itched you so," Richard recalled.

"Yes," Ceese said. "Father tried to make me understand the importance of being clothed. I had made him late for something . . . what, I can't remember. I just remember feeling horrible about it afterward."

Richard leaned back in his chair, wincing at the memory. "You were six. Not four, not five. And Father had arranged an ordination ceremony for me. But he spent so much time looking for you, worried some horrible fate had befallen you—we had to put the ceremony off. . . . I was cursed that night. That's the last real memory I have of Father or you."

Ceese's eyes filled with tears "You must have hated me."

Richard squeezed her hand. "How could I ever hate you? You saved me."

"But— the night the vampire came for you— I saw his fangs. I wanted to tell you before you left but I was too frightened."

Richard nodded. "Understandable. But if I'm not mistaken, you're the reason I didn't die at the hands of those vampires. And if I understood you correctly, you know how to save us now." He leaned in closer. "What do we do, Ceese? How do we end this? I . . . before I thought it possible, I didn't want to. Now, I do."

She took a deep breath. "From the way I understand it, I've retained some of the good the vampires had to offer."

"There was nothing good about either one of them," Richard said quickly.

"There's a little good in everyone," Ceese told him. "Father said this often."

"Yes," Richard said. "But what do we do with this, *good* you've retained? How can it help us?"

"We share it," Ceese said. "Only—" She looked uncertain now. "Penny says it's risky, and one of us— perhaps both of us could die. And if we die, there's no guarantee we won't die cursed."

"One selfless act," Richard whispered. "Has it come back to that?"

Ceese nodded. "The other part—what Penny wrote about two becoming one—"

"The cemetery," Richard concluded, "when the vampire—"

"Yes," Ceese said, seeing how much it pained him to think of what he had done. Then she smiled. "Now, we regain control of our souls, Brother. The way it was before. But we must move quickly, before our new curses have a chance to take hold. The seed's been planted, but it's not too late."

"But how? I don't understand."

"Faith, Richard. Have you forgotten everything? Prayer."

The actual process of praying, it had been so long, memories buried so deep . . . so deep. Rusted wheels would have been easier to move, easier to turn.

"According to your faith, so be it unto thee," Ceese prodded, the words seeming to come out of nowhere. "You must remember how, Richard. Father used to say you prayed more than you talked."

He laid his heavy head in his free hand. "I'm trying, God knows I'm trying. . . . I just can't remember . . ."

Ceese closed her eyes, and Richard heard her start humming. Then she added words. She half-said, half-sang, "When you open up your heart. . ."

Richard's head jerked up and he stared at her, wondering. Where had he heard that before?

Then she repeated herself, sounding exactly the way she had the first time.

This time, Richard remembered. When, as children, the concept seemed too difficult to grasp, Father would have them sing their prayers.

Richard hesitated too long in his acknowledgement. Ceese assumed he didn't remember, and uttered the hymn-like chant once more, patiently waiting, so patient.

"When you open up your heart. . ."

". . . and let the Spirit move," Richard replied. And then, together, "You can ask and it will be done."

Ceese sighed deeply. "Yes, Richard, you're doing it. Now let's finish it."

Richard's hand tightened around hers. "Yes, Sister, let's."

❧ ❧ ❧

Before the ambulance arrived at the cemetery, Cassie and Kyle slipped away. There were some things back at Dr. Henderson's house it was better for the police not to know about, and Cassie wanted to get to them first. Henderson had the latest computer, and with Kyle's help, she copied Henderson's computer files onto a DVD. While it was copying, she searched his file cabinets and found what she had really wanted. But when she picked up her grandmother's diary, she saw the files Henderson kept on all of them—Kyle, Rodney, Josh, and her. Now, she sat in a corner seat of the ICU waiting room and flipped through the file with her name on it, astounded. He had everything she'd ever given him in the file, and more. And in that file were all his last-minute notes about what he'd been doing down in the lab—notes he hadn't yet had the chance to transcribe into his computer.

She flipped through what she recognized, and paused to look at what was new to her. Her eyes fell on a yellow Post-it attached to one report that read: "Vampire's Blood Sample."

She went to the first page, read where he described how he'd drawn samples of Richard's blood from the animals Richard had fed on. He'd found stem cells. "Useful" stem cells, he'd termed them.

She then saw another Post-it hastily stuck to the last page. "Werewolf's blood not productive, even after mobilization." Scrawled beneath that: "Must have vampire!"

Cassie closed the folder, and her eyes. "And you almost had him," she said, shaking her head.

When she returned to the folder, she caught something else: an envelope. She opened it, read the letter inside. The letter was to a Dr. Savine. Henderson wanted all the information Savine had on how to coax stem cells to become sperm. He assured Savine that if he helped him do this, he would share the credit for creating the first vampire-human hybrid in history. And he assured Savine that he already had the woman picked out who would carry the child to term.

Cassie's mouth fell open, her eyes grew huge, then her attention was drawn away as the lights in the room dimmed for a split second. She heard both Ceese and Richard cry out, and raced to Ceese's room.

꿎 꿎 꿎

Three words into his prayer, Richard felt a surge of energy shoot through him, which intensified with each word he uttered. He kept praying despite this; Ceese told him they both must keep praying. At one point he was pulled to his feet, muscles tensed, his back arched as though he'd been hit by lightning. In the brief second when he could think at all, he thought about letting go of Ceese's hand. *She won't be able to survive this,* his mind screamed. *She's not strong enough!* And he did try, but he couldn't turn loose. They would both die, right here, right now.

꿎 꿎 꿎

The second he heard them cry out, Rodney rushed through the automatic doors, ran down the hall and straight to Ceese's room.

He ignored anyone who tried to tell him to stop, focusing only on the cries before him, concerned only for Ceese, caring little for Richard.

But Richard was the first person he saw, standing next to Ceese. The tortured look on Ceese's face had him racing again, anger consuming him. He charged, pulled Richard back and slung him into the nearest wall. Richard gasped, then sank down.

"I told you," Rodney said, his eyes wild, "I won't let you hurt her!" He placed himself between where Richard slumped and Ceese lay. "I told you!" he repeated.

An orderly moved in, tried to get him to calm, tried to escort him out. He backed off, however, when Rodney turned on him.

As soon as Richard could speak, he did. "I didn't . . . I don't know—I don't know what happened."

Cassie came into the room, followed by more medical personnel. "I heard the yelling, and—"

She stopped, looked at Richard pressed against the wall, gasping, then looked at those now swarming around Ceese's unconscious form.

"What in the world—?"

"Why don't you ask Richard?" Rodney bellowed.

"I didn't hurt her, Cassie," Richard said, looking physically drained, mentally crushed. "I would *never* hurt Ceese."

Cassie wanted to believe him, but wasn't sure she could. Not after the cemetery. Not after seeing what she and the others had seen. Had he lied to her? Was he still cursed? Was he feeding on his own sister? It didn't make sense. But then, neither did anything Henderson had done, or was planning to do in the letter she'd just read.

Another machine was brought in, but abandoned when the heart monitor's alarm sounded. Over the noise, Cassie heard an order to charge the paddles. She stood horrified as the inconceivable scenario played out before her. Could it end like this? Could it really?

Then, the heart monitor started up again. Silence prevailed as everyone waited to see if Ceese's heart would hold out.

It did.

Richard steadied himself against the wall, whispered a reverent thank-you to the One he knew was responsible. Rodney, however, was beyond thanking anyone. He stood, glaring at Richard, as though waiting for him to make just one wrong move.

And then, Ceese pushed herself up and looked around, scattering the amazed medical staff, much the way Cassie imagined Moses had parted the Red Sea.

"I . . . I do believe I'm better," she said to the stunned group. Then she turned her attention to address an equally astonished Richard. "How do you feel, Brother?"

"I— I don't know," he said. But then, he began gingerly moving each part of his body, testing them. He looked at Ceese, wonder in his eyes. "My back—the scratches," he said. "I-I think they're gone."

Cassie remembered the scratches, and went to him at once to help him look.

"They *are* gone," she said, amazed. "Completely healed."

"I told you, Richard," Ceese said, satisfied, and Richard smiled. Now, her eyes were as he remembered them being, before she was cursed—a soft emerald green. And as he watched, those eyes filled with tears.

Richard pushed his way past a still-stunned Rodney, moved through those standing around the bed until he was directly in front of Ceese. Carefully avoiding the shunts and tubes, they embraced each other.

"I told you, Brother," Ceese said. "I told you."

"Yes, you did," he said. "By our faith we've been freed, and by your love."

"And Father's love too. And Penny's."

"And Zade's, too, I suppose," he remarked. "I saw him, too."

"Tighter," came her breathless plea. "Hold me tighter, Richard. I never want to forget."

This they did, until Richard remembered the others in the room, and that they were being watched.

He loosened his hold on her and stood back. As he did, Ceese gasped.

"Richard," she breathed. "Your birthmark—it's back!"

He touched his neck, couldn't feel anything, of course, but trusted her reaction.

"I want to go home, Richard. I want to leave this place."

But those standing around, while taken by Ceese's miraculous return from death, weren't ready to let either one of them go just yet. Coincidence or faith, they wanted to run some tests.

Hearing this upset Ceese. "I don't want that," she said quickly, shrinking away from anyone who tried to touch her.

Cassie took a few tentative steps forward and spoke to the doctors and nurses around the bed. "She's not used to hospitals. But I think I can help." Then, to Ceese, "They just want to make sure everything's all right."

"But it *is* all right," Ceese insisted. "And I want to leave this place."

"Yeah," Rodney piped up. "They can't keep her here if she doesn't want to stay."

"She needs to let them do this, Rodney," Cassie told him. "It won't take long, and it'll be better if she can leave here with a clean bill of health."

Ceese looked to Richard for help. "I don't want to stay."

"I'll stay with you," he offered.

There was a commotion, and before anyone knew it, Rodney had Richard's arm twisted behind his back, and another around his neck. "I don't think so," he said. "Not this time. I won't let you hurt her again."

Ceese called out, "Please, Rodney. I need Richard. I need my brother."

With reluctance, Rodney turned Richard loose. "Sure, whatever."

Cassie hadn't seen anyone look more hurt or crushed, and a part of her felt for Rodney: the part of her not still angry with him for everything he'd done—the lying, stealing her e-mails, working against her in the beginning.

Rodney was suddenly a man without a cause. "Okay," he said, let Richard go, and turned to head for the door.

"I didn't mean I wanted you to leave!" Ceese cried. "I need you too. Please!"

Yet the nurses wouldn't allow this. They would let Richard stay, but not Rodney, too. When they said one visitor, they meant it. Ceese was near tears as they continued to insist.

Cassie stepped in again. "Look, technically, Richard is a patient as well, which would make Rodney the one visitor. And I'll wait in the waiting room."

Everyone seemed satisfied with that, so Cassie turned to leave the room, secretly happy for Rodney but disillusioned for herself. She couldn't put a name to the feeling she was having, except that it was almost the same way she'd felt when she broke up with her boyfriend the year before—not exactly heartbroken, but drained and out of sorts.

"Allow me," Richard said, moving past her to push open the door for her.

Cassie couldn't hold back her smile, or her absolute and unexplainable delight. "Really, it's not necessary."

But he already had. "It's the least I can do," he said, pushing the door wider and then following her out. Cassie was encouraged by his closeness, by the way he leaned down a bit when they stepped into the cluttered hall, where standing close wasn't only a desire, but a necessity. *Does he feel it too?* Cassie wondered. Hoped.

Suddenly, his face was very close to hers, his hair falling down and around his shoulders. His eyes were wide, but no longer held the hardness they had when he was cursed. And for the first time since she'd known him, he seemed . . . uncertain.

"I . . . just couldn't let you leave without thanking you," he said, his words hesitant. "I'm not certain I can . . ."

But she could no longer follow his words, because her heart was nearly beating out of her chest. Could this be the same drawing feeling she had for Richard ever since they met . . . and that it *wasn't* just because he was a vampire? Was she really attracted to him, and he to her?

And then their lips touched, and she no longer had to ask. Instead, her mind flew around the question, *Could it possibly get any better than this moment?*

"Here," the voice came, startling them.

"I'm, ah, excuse me?" Cassie managed.

The large woman held out a sheaf of papers to Richard. "You'll need to start filling this out if either you or your *independent* sister wants to go anywhere anytime today."

Richard didn't reply, so Cassie stepped toward the woman and snatched the papers from her. "Certainly," she said, "he'll take care of them right away."

The woman stalked off and Cassie turned back to find Richard gone.

Panicked, she glanced inside Ceese's room, and saw him standing at her bedside again.

Cassie thought of a line from a movie, one she used to watch often when she was younger. As she headed down the hall, she muttered that line: "Could be worse. . . . Could be raining."

She looked overhead, as if half-expecting a cloudburst.

EPILOGUE

The man stood in front of the long sofa table, which still held the intricate balancing piece, and sighed. "I can't believe he's had it all this time. I had no idea where it had gotten off to."

Penelope walked easily over to stand next to the table. Thanks to Ceese, her body had continued its transformation. Her hair was no longer gray, and her face now held a soft, youthful glow. She reached out, touched the balancing piece lightly. "He never would tell me where he got it, or why it meant so much to him."

The man glanced up at her. "I can't believe he forgot about me. I've never forgotten him. It hurts to think that after what I went through to find him—"

"I know you must be hurt, Meri, but you have to understand," Penelope said, and sighed. "Richard hasn't been particularly . . . easy to deal with. But I believe he pushed you from his memory because he loved you so much. And the rest of his family, too, for sanity's sake. He hated what the vampires made him. In all the years I've known him, I've never seen anyone despise anything more." She gave Meri a reassuring smile. "But, he remembers you now. And because of your love for Richard and Ceese, they'll be coming home to us soon."

"And Cee Cee?" he said, concerned. "She's all right? No harm came to her during the breaking of the curse? You're certain of that?"

She recalled telling him how weak Ceese seemed at one point during the ordeal. "None, Meri. She told me this herself." She shook her head. "It's funny, isn't it? I sent them to New York because I thought Cassie might hold the key to curing them. And the ability was inside them all along."

He gave her a strained smile. "I have a new respect for that ability of yours. What did you call it? Projecting, wasn't it?"

"Don't you worry what I call it," she said lightly. "Just know your Richard and your Ceese are fine." *My Richard, too.*

Marissa entered from the hall, stopped briefly to be recognized before speaking. "I have prepared your dinner, Miss Penelope."

Penelope turned to her and smiled. "Fine, dear. I'll be there shortly."

The maid curtsied and left.

"How do you think they'll take my . . . condition?" Merideth asked. "When they find out?"

"Your being cursed?" Penelope said, thinking it odd how he couldn't bring himself to say it, considered her answer carefully. "I think they will wonder. Be prepared to answer many questions."

He nodded. "I'm just glad Brendan came to me when he did."

Her serious look evaporated. "Yes, and a sneaky one your second oldest must have been. Ceese has no idea he followed her the night the vampire came after Richard. She thought herself clever to have gotten out of the house without anyone knowing."

She looked at Merideth, sympathy in her eyes. "But why did Brendan wait so long to tell you? What was it, twelve years after Richard was cursed?"

Merideth nodded. "After Richard left I . . . well, I just didn't cope well. Cee Cee needed someone and Brendan took over. They became quite close and when Cee Cee started revisiting the site where Richard was cursed, twelve years later . . . he became concerned. When he couldn't stop her from going . . . he knew he had to have my help."

She knew Merideth couldn't feel emotions the way humans could. But it was clear that his rage at the memory of what nearly happened to Brendan was growing. Best to head it off before the vampire wanted out. "Back to your question," she said quickly. "I think they'll understand why you did what you did. Especially since they're no longer cursed themselves. And now they can help *you*." She looked at her hands clasped at her waist. "I just hope they can forgive me for lying to them. Especially Richard. I never meant to hurt—"

"You're just as responsible for helping them as I am," Merideth said. "I could never have led Cee Cee here the way you did."

Penelope looked up, gave him a small nod. "But what of this Zade? When he first came here, you welcomed him in, and then ran him out."

"I had no idea who he was at first," Meri said, frustrated. "I should have, though."

She said nothing, just looked at him with a question in her eyes.

"He was the one responsible for my Julia being—" Merideth stopped, looked away. When he looked back, there was hatred in his eyes. "Julia was attacked by another man. My beloved was forced to carry his child. All at the direction of that—that monster!"

"I'm so sorry. No wonder you were so upset when you realized this. Whatever became of the child?"

He stared at her, glassy-eyed. "Julia was my life. Anything belonging to her was mine. I promised her . . ."

Penelope looked at him for a long moment before understanding came. "Ceese?"

He nodded. "Yes. And this Zade . . . after Julia went through . . . what she went through, he scratched her. To prove to me what he was. Cee Cee was . . . affected."

She reached out and squeezed his shoulder. "Ceese only told me her mother was attacked by a wolf—"

"She doesn't know. Neither does Richard, although he suspected at the time. We told no one. Julia was already so devastated. We planned to tell Cee Cee when she was old enough to understand, but . . . we never got the chance." He shook his head, willing old memories away.

"So, what does this Zade want now?" Penelope asked. "Why was he here? Will Richard and Ceese be in danger when they return?" She seemed certain they would come back.

Seeing his face, she stopped speaking. Merideth's stare was

harder now, and he'd pulled his hands away from the balancing piece and curled them into fists.

"He wants what he will *never* get!" he shouted. "Something he thinks belongs to him. He wants Cee Cee. And if I must stay cursed forever, he will never have her!"

ॐ ॐ ॐ

Josh sat near the body, pulled his arms around his shoulders and tried not to think about being in a cemetery, in the dark, with an unburied corpse. They'd gotten their stories straight, the authorities had been notified, and Kyle had gone back to the main road to lead them in. So Josh was presently alone, and things were starting to get to him.

He thought he heard a sound, thought it came from behind him. But when he turned to look, nothing was there—literally nothing. Henderson's body was gone.

That was the last thing he noticed before he felt the supernaturally strong hand grip his shoulder and the fangs slice into his neck.

§

The sequel

Forever Richard

The saga of redemption and spiritual triumph readers enjoyed in *Never Ceese* continues in **Forever Richard . . .**

Cassie Felts, graduate student and reluctant believer of such things as vampires and werewolves, couldn't be happier for Richard and Ceese Porter. Their curses lifted and after hundreds of years apart, they can now celebrate being brother and sister once more. Even Rodney, Cassie's college roommate and former nemesis, shares her relief. But will the faith that saved Richard and Ceese be enough to defeat the new evil that threatens them all?

Cassie learns that Dr. Clayton Henderson, the corrupt stem-cell researcher she once looked up to, has acquired the vampire's curse. Even worse, he managed to transfer his curse to Rodney's troubled, drug-addicted buddy Josh. Addict or vampire, Cassie can see Josh isn't handling his new cravings for blood any better than he did his old habit. Their best hope seems to be taking Josh to Richard's isolated country estate in England. There, Josh can learn to temper his desire to curse another while they try to figure out how to deal with the impossible-to-kill Dr. Henderson.

Their mission becomes more complicated when they find a new vampire inhabiting Richard's castle, a malevolent werewolf stalking Ceese, and a long-lost relative who shows up carrying a sawed-off shotgun and an ancient knife he claims has supernatural powers. Will the faith that redeemed two lost souls before be enough to overcome the wicked forces that now threaten to destroy them all?